A DETECTIVE'S DILEMMA

By Peter J Charles

Glossary

This glossary includes terms, acronyms, and slang commonly used in UK policing, as well as bits of rhyming slang and street language that appear throughout the story. While many are part of everyday law enforcement vocabulary, others reflect the culture and nuance of the world these characters inhabit.

These are terms I've heard, used, or come across during my time in the job, and some that have crept into everyday conversation in ways you might not expect.

If you're ever unsure what someone means by "you're having a giraffe", this section should help.

Term	Meaning
Early doors	First thing (probably in the morning)
My gaff	My house
The nick	The police station
The factory	The police station
To nick	To arrest someone
Back to the factory	Back to station (sometimes the office)
My manor	Your ground – area which you control
Lump the motor	Install electronic tracker on the vehicle
Boshing	Cutting of drugs to increase quantity
Whacking	The same as Boshing
Get a tug	To get stopped by the police
Interference	Drive vehicle to attract police attention
Bubble them up	To inform on them
Snout or Source	An informant
Colombian	Cocaine

marching powder	
To ring a motor	To change a stolen vehicle's identity
A ringer	Vehicle that has been rung (see above)
R/A	A roundabout – In the USA a 'circle'
Keep it in your bin	Keep it quiet
Forty winks	A quick sleep
Jury nobbling	To influence a jury during a trial
In his shell-like	In his ear
He's bang to rights	The evidence is overwhelming
Pelican crossing	Pedestrian-activated crosswalk
Having a giraffe	Having a laugh – cockney rhyming slang
Gone Pete Tong	Gone wrong - cockney rhyming slang
SOCA	Serious Organised Crime Agency
OP	Observation Post (a house or similar)
Recip	Reciprocal - about turn and go back
CID	Criminal Investigation Department
A line (on a phone)	A phone intercept
CROP	Covert Rural Observation Post
RCS	Regional Crime Squad
FOB	Forward Operating Base (Military)
Pegged it	Died

Chapter One

January 2010

Detective Constable Tom Kessler sat in the back of Courtroom 3, arms folded tight across his chest, jaw clenched so hard his molars ached. The air was thick with the scent of old varnish and institutional fatigue. A fly buzzed near the strip lights overhead, tracing lazy loops above the judge's bench. There was an indistinct murmur as the anticipation built.

The jury had returned after only three hours of deliberation. Tom couldn't decide whether that was a good or bad omen. He cast his eyes across the jury, trying to read their expressions. Nothing. Not a glance in his direction. That was not a good sign. You often got a clue if one juror caught your eye and gave you a smile.

"Court rise," said the clerk. Everyone stood as the judge waltzed in, full of self-importance.

"Here we go," muttered Tom.

"Have you reached a verdict with which you all agree?" the clerk asked the foreman.

"We have," he said.

"And do you find the defendant guilty or not guilty?"

"Not guilty."

Even the judge had a stunned expression. Silence hung like smoke, and then the public gallery erupted as the news sank in to the friends and relatives of the defendant.

"Mr Falstead, the jury has found you not guilty, and you are free to go," he said.

Tom didn't move. Didn't blink. He just stared at the foreman, willing the words to change. They didn't.

"You are fucking kidding," he muttered, voice low and hoarse.

His head dropped, eyes fixed on the floor while he took in this disaster. He jerked his head up and tried to catch the eye of the jurors, but they could not, or would not, meet his stare. If they had, they would have seen the utter despair on his face, which he failed to conceal. He could sense they knew this result devastated him.

John Falstead didn't flinch. He turned, nodded to his solicitor with the ease of a man collecting a pub quiz trophy, not dodging a Class A conviction that should've buried him. His shoes clicked with casual precision on the courtroom tiles. That wide, smug grin made Tom want to break something. Preferably Falstead's neck.

Falstead passed close, close enough for Tom to smell his expensive aftershave. He winked.

"Better luck next time, Tom," he said with a grin.

Tom didn't respond. He couldn't. His fists curled in his lap, nails biting into his palms. He watched

Falstead walk out, shoulders loose, swagger intact. The door swung shut behind him with a soft thud. Surely the jury had been nobbled for this to be the result. He was bang to rights. The evidence the jury had seen did not get better than this.

Outside, the world carried on. Inside Tom, something didn't. He would now make it his life's work to nail this arrogant shit.

Tom had nicked Falstead twice. The first time, it was a warehouse stacked with nine bars of resin. Eighteen months he got then, just a slap on the wrist. He'd done twelve months on remand, so walked from court. That was the achievement of a full surveillance team working for three weeks, sixteen hours a day. Falstead came out leaner, meaner, and better connected. Prison hadn't broken him; it had promoted him.

And now Falstead had walked out of this one. What the hell were the jury thinking? Had they even considered the evidence?

He thought back to when they had caught him on this latest little caper. Tom had got a tip-off from a very good snout who put Falstead up as travelling to Brighton to pick up five kilos of coke sometime over the next few days. Falstead's home was in a lovely area of Woking with houses a fair distance apart. It meant it was impossible to get an OP on it so the surveillance team could pick him up from his home, and they didn't have time to get the authorisations signed to get a camera in place. Tom arranged for the source to meet with Falstead prior to the run to Brighton so they could pick him up at that meet and take him from there. He said he had seen a bag on the front seat of Falstead's motor, which he assumed was a bag of cash. All good so far.

He did loads of anti on the way: twice round roundabouts, slowing down on dual carriageways, that sort of stuff the spooks call dry cleaning. That just reinforced their thoughts that this was the day. This type of surveillance was bread and butter for the team most of the time, but they lost him twice and only just pulled it back, which, Tom thought, was pretty lucky. No one likes a loss, but a show is so much worse.

Falstead settled down and thought he was clean. All went well, and they took him all the way to Brighton. A foot man picked up the address in Brighton that he went to, but they weren't quick enough and didn't see if Falstead was carrying the bag in, which put them on the back foot. However, he came out of the house with a similar bag. Now it was decision time. Do they strike and find a bag of money because the supplier didn't have the gear ready? Did he have to go somewhere else to pick up the gear, and was the bag empty?

Tom decided they would just play it by ear for the time being and see what panned out. Back up the A23 and M23 they went. Tom tried calling the snout to see if he could get an update, but he didn't answer.

Bugger. I told him to be available, thought Tom.

Then it all went wrong. The target left the A23 at a slip road, and the following vehicle went with him. That was OK, but they should have handed it over at the roundabout at the top as they now had no cover. If the back-up wasn't in position, then so be it; call the bike through. He would pick it up in no time. But they went with it and risked a potential show. They should never have done that and would get ripped to pieces in the debrief.

All the team were too good and too professional to make this sort of cock-up, as it can be devastating. Falstead suspected he had a tail and started looking again. Tom called a stand-down so as not to blow the job. They were lucky to pull it back the first time, and he didn't want to blow the thing. The DI would not be happy, though. The daily cost of a full team is huge, and the big bosses were always trying to save money by cutting the squad numbers and overtime allocation.

He hated these people. They couldn't catch a bloody cold, let alone a decent villain. All they were interested in was the next rank up so they got a better pension when they retired. Nepotism was rife, as they only promoted clones of themselves.

Tom loved a good debrief and, depending on your point of view, this was a fierce one. Army life had drilled it into him. AARs, After-Action Reports, broke down the op and flagged what worked and what didn't. No blame, no ego. Just cold analysis to sharpen the next job and keep people breathing. It wasn't quite the same as a debrief, but they could get very heated.

Surveillance wasn't life-or-death, not usually. But the principle held: review the day's surveillance, discuss what went wrong, and make sure it doesn't happen again. Learn from your mistakes. The mistake that day was just not acceptable and, by the skin of their teeth, they had got away with it. It must not happen again. Ever.

After the debrief, Tom got back to his snout. He wasn't happy either, having just missed out on a big payday. Tom needed to know where Falstead's safe house was if he was going to progress this, and he tasked his source with finding out.

The entire team was in the office the following day to tidy up any outstanding paperwork when Tom got a call. The source had found the location of Falstead's stash, and Tom knew the area well.

"We're on, boys," said Tom. "The source has come good, and we know where Falstead's holding the gear. Everybody head for Goldsworth Park in Woking."

The professional thing to do was to keep calm, but it was difficult to hide the excitement in his voice.

The team scrambled from the office, but this was seat-of-the-pants stuff now. This was not normal. They planned operations before they took on a target, but this was different. Tom briefed the team over the air as they rushed to the area.

His partner, Sharon Girton, was driving so Tom could concentrate on putting a plan together. She was a fantastic crewmate. a brilliant driver, safe but fast. Never panicked and fabulous at surveillance. She was invisible sometimes and frequently got closer to the target than should ever have been possible. Villains just ignored women most of the time, and she took full advantage of that.

Tom's phone buzzed. His missus. Of course it was. For God's sake, her timing was uncanny.

"Fuck," muttered Tom, looking at Sharon as she glanced across at him. She didn't need to ask; his face said it all. Like all surveillance team partners, they knew each other so well they could read each other's minds.

"Take it, Tom," she said. "You'll be in trouble again if you don't."

"It's alright for you. You don't have these problems."

Sharon's partner, Claire, was on SOCA. She got it. She understood the hours, the unpredictability, the emotional fallout. Sue never had, and he doubted she ever would.

Tom sighed and answered anyway. He knew he'd be in the shit if he didn't.

"Sue, sweetie, everything alright?" he said, trying to inject some sparkle into his voice.

"Don't 'sweetie' me, you bastard. No, it's not all right. That bloody washing machine's flooded the kitchen again. There's water everywhere. I thought you said you'd fixed it at the weekend, Tom?"

"I did," Tom replied with a grimace. "The bloody hose on the pump must've come off again."

He screwed his eyes shut, pinching the bridge of his nose.

God, I don't need this now, he thought.

The phone buzzed again. He glanced at the screen. An incoming call from the source. Of course it was. What was it with these bloody people? Their timing was amazing. He put the phone back to his ear and turned back to the domestic mess he'd just walked into.

"Look, I'm sorry, love, I'm on a rush job and I've got to take this incoming call. I don't know when I'll be home, but I promise I'll fix it this weekend. If it acts up again, we'll just get a new one."

He hung up before she could respond.

It was the same dilemma every copper faced. The job consumed you. It didn't care about flooded kitchens or loose hoses on pumps. It didn't pause for domestic rows or missed dinners. Here he was, chasing down a scumbag supplier with a decent-sized stash of charlie, and Sue was mopping the floor like it was the crisis of the day. So what? Of course, to her, it was. To him, it was background noise. And that was the problem. She'd never understand. Not really.

"Give me some good news, mate. I need it," said Tom when he answered his mobile.

"He's on his way to pick up some gear, mate. Is that news good enough for you?"

"Yes, it is, pal. I won't ask you how you know, but I've told you before, you do not buy gear from him just to get me info. Promise me you didn't do that."

"I wouldn't do a thing like that, Tom. What do you take me for?"

Tom could sense the smile on the face at the other end of the line, but he would have to deal with that later.

Tom put the news over the radio. The job was on.

Tom and Sharon were first on the plot. There was nowhere decent to watch the safe house from and no time to get an OP sorted on the hoof, so they parked a little way away, angled just enough to catch the front door of the safe house in the wing mirror. The estate wasn't the usual collage of peeling paint and rusting kids' bikes, at least not on the surface. But estates had layers. And as the minutes ticked by, the familiar itch crept in.

Surveillance was a real skill. Some had it, and some didn't. It was no good being six-foot-five and built like a brick shithouse, you'd stick out like a sore thumb. The best were just medium everything: build, height, hair length. Everything. Changing clothes, wearing a cap or glasses, and walking differently can transform you. You learned to sit still for hours on end without becoming impatient and just let the world forget you existed. You could fall asleep and, in an instant, be wide awake again, ready for anything. And Tom loved it. Every single day.

A kid cycled past, glanced at them, then moved on. Tom exhaled. He didn't like this. He knew the bad guys used kids on bikes to cycle around and report back anything that didn't look right. Five minutes was pushing it. Ten was reckless. They'd need to move soon.

Sue would never be told this, but he and Sharon had, more than once, stretched their time on a difficult plot by pretending to be necking. It wasn't glamorous, but it worked. Civilians imagined a couple having a moment, not a surveillance team. When they did it, they always tried not to laugh. It was a serious job, but it had its funny moments. They were close, very close, but it was like trying to snog your sister. Awkward, ridiculous, and by chance, or maybe not, Falstead turned up in a shitty old Mercedes, driven by his father. He got out and walked towards the safe house. He was on edge, constantly looking about. He walked past the premises, and Tom's heart sank.

Had he identified the wrong place?

[Comms] "Standby, standby, standby. Four-four has the eyeball. The target has arrived on the plot as a passenger in a black, old-style Mercedes saloon. This will now be the target vehicle. No registration number at this stage. He's towards the target premises. Past the target premises, looking all around, and it's a loss of eyeball."

"Calm down, Tom," said Sharon. "He's just doing a bit of cleaning."

She was right again, which, He also loved having a female partner. You appeared so much more natural. A man and a woman in a car bought you time; people make assumptions, lovers, exes, just a couple chatting. Two blokes? That got you noticed. And not in a good way.

Tom shifted in his seat, eyes flicking between the mirror and the windscreen. Sharon didn't move. She had a stillness he envied, like she could switch off her pulse at will.

"You know," he said, voice low with a smile on his face, "we'd look more convincing if you'd just hold my hand or we had a nice cuddle."

Tom giggled, knowing what was coming. She snorted.

"Sod off, Tom. You're not my type. You know which side I bat for."

It was an old line, worn smooth between them. No edge, no offence. Just the black humour that kept you sane when you'd read every paper from cover to cover, had had a kip, your arse was numb, your bladder was full, and you'd been waiting for movement for twelve hours.

No one else on the team could say it like that. With anyone else, it would've been a line crossed. But between them, it was just part of the rhythm.

just plain wrong.

in a friendly sort of way, pissed him off a bit.

You could feel the tension.

[Comms] "Four-four, do you want me to put a footman down?"

It was Karen, who had just arrived.

[Comms] "No, no, let him run. He'll be back. We've got the front door and the vehicle. For information, he's being driven by his father, Craig Falstead, previous for manslaughter, so be aware if we hit them. Karen, can you run a log?"

[Comms] "Yes, yes."

Excellent Karen. No arguments, just got on with it. Which is what you need when the pressure's on.

Of course, Tom wasn't certain Falstead would be back. He didn't need this day to end like yesterday, having scrambled the team from the office, so he kept his fingers crossed.

Fifteen minutes. They knew they'd been in situ far too long when Falstead came back into view.

Thank fuck for that, Tom thought, with a sigh of relief.

"You need to calm down, Tom, or you're going to have a heart attack. You're not normally like this, mate," said Sharon.

"After yesterday's cock-up, I need this to work," said Tom.

"Eyeball regained as the target is on a recip towards the target premises. He's looking all around. He's now at the door of the premises and in, in, in, and it's a loss of eyeball. The target vehicle remains in situ. For information, we are going to hit this if he comes back to the target vehicle.

[Comms] "Can someone put a foot man down and get the reg of the vehicle? Just keep it to yourself for now in case we need it."

[Comms] "Four-three foot is out."

And they waited. And waited. No matter how many times you did this, every second felt like a minute.

It was times like this he reflected on how little needed to be said to do surveillance properly. So few words over the radio, but they were in total control.

Long may it continue, he thought.

Tom wasn't aware that old man Falstead was still around. The snout had said he was back on the scene helping his boy out with a bit of driving. When he first joined CID as a learner, a Temporary Detective

Constable, the squad seconded him to a murder investigation. Craig Falstead had stabbed a bloke in a local pub in town. Tom remembered it well. It was Christmas Eve, and it buggered up the entire holiday period. Another chip taken out of his relationship with Sue.

The CPS reduced the charge against the old man from murder to manslaughter. Six years. Out in three. This was the first time he'd seen him since he went down.

Seeing the elder Falstead again stirred something in Tom he hadn't expected, resentment, maybe, or just the bitter taste of being screwed by the system. From what he could see of him in the vehicle, he appeared smaller now and greyer. Tom remembered the blood on the pub floor, the chaos, the way Sue had barely spoken to him for two days after he missed Christmas dinner. It wasn't just the disappointments of the job that had taken pieces out of him; it was men like Falstead, walking out after three years while Tom was still trying to pick up the fragments of his marriage.

How the fuck he got away with manslaughter still baffles me, he thought. You don't stab a bloke in the guts if you don't want him to die.

Falstead junior was out of the house.

[Comms] "Standby, standby, standby. The target is out of the target premises and heading back towards the target vehicle. Move in and wait for the call."

[Comms] "Strike, strike, strike."

The team was sharp. Cars boxed in the Mercedes with precision. Personnel from the vehicles. Falstead and his old man dragged out and forced face-down onto the grass. No messing about, nicked and cuffed.

It was so quick they didn't know what hit them. However, this was only part of the job.

Now came the tricky bit. They didn't know who was in the safe house, and if anyone inside had clocked the commotion, they could wash a load of charlie down the sink. Tom ran towards the house, adrenaline surging, trying to stay calm.

No warrant was needed, as Falstead had just come out of the house before being nicked. Tom kicked the door hard, but it didn't budge. He slammed his boot again. Wood splintered a bit but held.

Fuck, get in, you bastard.

Was that a shout from inside? Or just his pulse hammering in his ears?

For goodness sake, this was turning into a bit of a Fred Carno's Circus.

Next to the front door was a window. Tom punched through it with his fist, hoping to climb in and open the door from the inside. The glass shattered. Blood bloomed across his knuckles like ink in water.

"Bugger," he said. "I should've thought that through."

Sharon just stared at him and shook her head.

At first, as he cleared the broken glass from the frame, he barely registered the naked man staring back at him, mouth agape. But when he saw the fear and confusion in the man's eyes, he knew this guy had nothing to do with the safe house.

Oh dear. Flats made up the entire block. The downstairs unit was accessed through the window. The safe house was upstairs, and on the other side of the door they were trying to access, there were stairs. This was the problem with doing things on the hoof. If they'd had time to plan this, they would have known the layout. Sometimes, though, you had no choice, you just had to run with it and hope it all worked out.

He'd just smashed the window of the wrong premises.

The team would dine out on this one for weeks. It'd cost him a few beers, minimum.

"Fuck," he said again. "Sorry, mate. We're the Drug Squad. I promise we'll fix it later."

By now, one of the others had brought over the "key", a great lump of metal with two handles. With a couple of swipes and the door was down. Tom wrapped a handkerchief around his bleeding hand and ran upstairs. To his relief, the flat was empty.

Time to slow down and take a breath.

While Falstead and his old man were taken to the local nick, searched, and booked in, Tom, Sharon, and a couple of others searched the flat. It didn't take long to find the best part of eight kilos of charlie under the sink. To be fair to Falstead, the place was tidy, clean and organised, except for the scales and bags on the kitchen table, plus containers of baking soda and caffeine. Obviously cutting agents. Cutting and weighing the gear was potentially why the target was on the premises for so long.

Then came the message from the nick: Falstead had about five ounces of charlie stuffed down his underpants. They had him bang to rights. The lab would later confirm it was part of the same batch found at the flat.

They debriefed back at the local nick, wrote up their statements, handed everything over to the CID office at Woking as usual, and all went down the pub.

You'd think it would be easy from there. But Falstead pleaded not guilty.

His defence? A debt owed to the original supplier of the cannabis resin they had nicked him for the first time. Because he owed money, he received death threats, forcing him to deal drugs to repay the debt.

And the jury bought it.

How the hell had that happened?

Outside the courtroom, Tom stood with shaking hands. He watched Falstead disappear into the rear of a waiting vehicle, a very nice Range Rover Autobiography with tinted windows. That said it all. To add insult to injury, Falstead smiled and waved at him before slamming the door.

The system had failed. Again.

***

Another member of the team led an operation that kept them busy over the next few days. It was uneventful, just routine surveillance, nothing to write home about. But Sharon was aware Tom wasn't quite himself. He was quieter, more withdrawn. Their friendship, because that's what it was, not just a working partnership, had always allowed them to give each other space when needed. No questions, no pressure. But this time, after several days of this, she believed the silence had gone on long enough.

"You OK?" said Sharon.

A minute passed, silence except for the noise of the rain.

"You ever been somewhere," he said, "where the rules didn't mean shit?"

Sharon glanced at him. "You mean like CID?"

He gave a dry smile, but it didn't reach his eyes.

"No. I mean, like when I was in Bosnia. It was the winter of '04. I had little time left to serve. We were supposed to be peacekeepers. They called it a 'Stabilisation Force', whatever that was supposed to mean, but there was no peace to keep."

She didn't speak. Just waited. That was one thing he liked about her; she didn't fill silence with noise. Like every good detective, she knew when to keep her mouth shut.

"We came across a village that was completely burned out. There were bodies in the street. Kids. Old people. No soldiers. Just civilians. We got there too late. Way too late. There's just me and my eight guys, good guys, experienced soldiers. Three Land Rovers. Armed to the teeth."

He paused, fingers drumming on the steering wheel.

"One lad found a local guy hiding in a cellar who said he knew who did it. He gave us the name of the leader of this group, for what that was worth, but said they were holed up in the mountains a few clicks east. They called him 'Mesar', which means 'The Butcher'. And that is what he was. You know, on a previous tour, one of my guys got hit by a sniper. He died in my arms, with me covered in his blood. But this was much worse. The devastation, the smell of burning bodies, it will never, ever leave me. And it haunts me to this day."

Sharon shifted, feeling uncomfortable. She let the silence play out, then said, "And?"

"And we went after them. No orders. No backup. Just absolute rage. Just me and my eight guys."

He glanced at her then, eyes darker than usual. Not angry, but haunted. His eyes were wet, and she'd never seen him like this before. She never thought she'd feel this way about a man, but her heart ached for him. She could feel his torment.

“We didn’t arrest them. We didn’t radio it in. We just... dealt with it. Justice, we called it.”

Sharon didn’t flinch. Didn’t ask for details. She knew what he meant. But her voice was quieter now.

“Did it help?”

Tom turned his head, stared out of the side window and let out a sigh.

“Not really. You always think it will. But at least it stopped them from doing it again. That’s all I’ll say.”

The rain picked up, drumming harder on the roof. Sharon took another sip of coffee, nodded as she took in the enormity of what Tom had just said, then offered him the flask. He shook his head.

“You’re the only person I’ve ever told that to,” he said.

She nodded. “I won’t tell anyone.”

“I know.”

They sat in silence for a while, the kind that only comes when something real has been shared.

Then Sharon broke it.

“You know what that tells me?”

“What?”

“That you still care. Even after all of it.”

Tom didn’t answer, but his fingers stopped drumming. His eyes were wet, and something inside him shifted. He didn’t know what it was, but he felt it coming, a turning point. Something he couldn’t name yet, but it was circling. Waiting.

Chapter Two

Tom joined the force late, at thirty. Army discipline and a genuine sense of duty had already shaped his mind. He'd served for twelve years in the Army, ending as a sergeant in 2 Para, commanding eight men he would have died for. He cared for all of his men, and they cared back.

Two tours in Bosnia. One in Kosovo. Peacekeeping, they called it. But there was nothing peaceful about it. The things he'd seen and the things he'd done, things you couldn't unsee and things you couldn't undo, had left marks deeper than anyone could imagine.

Some kids he worked with now didn't have a bloody clue. Most of them fresh out of training, full of theory and optimism. Because of their immaturity, he just wanted to grab them by the lapels, smack them around the face, and tell them to grow up. They hadn't watched villages burn. They hadn't seen what people do to each other when the rules fall away.

Tom wasn't a copper who eased into the job. He started strong, and from day one, made a difference.

Married with three girls, a mortgage and a Labrador named Deefer, he loved the job. Not just the chase or the collar, but the structure he needed after coming from a disciplined environment. The sense that he was part of something that mattered.

His wife, Sue, did not want him to join the police. Twelve years as an army wife was enough for any woman and, when he left the Army, she'd been hoping for something more nine-to-five so they could repair the damage his long tours away from home had caused, not only to their marriage but to his mind as well. They had married very young, both seventeen, after finding she was pregnant with twins. A year after they were born, she had another girl. Tom joined the Army just after they married, as they needed a steady income to support the family.

She knew he was an absolute natural and that he flourished in that environment. The problem all the wives had with their other halves was the heavy drinking. When they came back from a deployment, they all drank for England. They were "men" and did not share their feelings like their wives; they bottled it all up inside and drank themselves into oblivion.

Anyway, try as she might, she could not dissuade him from joining the police.

Two years and four commendations later, he made temporary detective, jumping the queue and ruffling the feathers of many who had been waiting years for the opportunity to do their "learner". But he didn't care; that was their problem, not his. He played by the rules, made the tea when asked, earned the respect of the more seasoned detectives and absorbed their knowledge. Of course, at first, he got all the shitty jobs no one else wanted, but he took it all in his stride.

He also had the respect of a lot of the villains out there. They knew they could rely on his word if he said he would look after them if they coughed a job. They also knew that if they put up a fight when they were nicked and lumped him, they got double back. He was an absolute natural at recruiting informants. His communication skills were exceptional, and he built up a good bunch of sources. He always played by the rules too, and would never let a snout set up a straightforward job for him.

Having passed his "learner" with flying colours, for the next year or so he stayed on CID, standing in for those away on their detective courses. He'd heard horror stories of the goings-on when guys were away for the four months, drunken nights and stupid pranks by kids who had never been away from home before. When he was in the Army, he got kicked out of more clubs and bars around the world than those guys had had hot dinners. But he'd grown up now.

Most blokes had to save up for years to afford all this bollocks on their courses. As soon as they passed their learner, they opened up bank accounts their wives were unaware of and put their weekly expenses in order to save up. Fortunately, the accounts department paid all the expenses in cash; otherwise, no one could have got away with it. If only the wives knew what went on.

He'd even heard a story of one guy who had to sell his car to afford all this. Apparently, he told his wife he had crashed it and had forgotten to renew the insurance. The naivety was astounding. Sue would never have bought that one. Tom didn't want any of that nonsense when it was his turn, albeit he had a bank account Sue did not know of, just in case he had difficulty avoiding the expense. The cash card sat in the top drawer of his desk, bottle of Scotch in the bottom one for when the DI called him in for his "weekly chat".

Tom's DI at this time, Frank Hardman, was a great guy. Old-school detective, ex-rugby-playing Yorkshireman who just wanted bad people locked up, and wanted his detectives to put themselves about the pubs just to show the local villains their manor was not out of bounds to the tecs in the CID office. It was amazing what you could pick up when doing the rounds, who's mixing with whom, who's got out of nick early, etc. If you messed up, he would tear into you, but if you had meant well and just made a mistake, he would back you every inch of the way. Just don't make the same mistake again.

Tom remembered one occasion when the DI walked into the main office one Monday morning with a stack of expenses forms. He stared straight at Tom and said, "Kessler, where's your expenses form?"

"I didn't have any, guv," Tom said.

"Why not?"

"I didn't get time to do the rounds on Thursday when I was on lates," said Tom.

"Well, I expect you to make time. I want you out there this evening doing the rounds. I'm assuming you won't be claiming the overtime, but that's always your option, of course." Frank then strode back to his office. Point made. Tom would not be claiming the overtime, as he knew that would be the end of his Temporary Detective role. No way could he tell Sue that, though.

Tom knew the DI had done all this in front of a packed CID office just to make his point. The other DCs were looking down at some paperwork, pens in their hands, smiling from ear to ear. Most had been through this with Frank and, whilst they would take the piss later, they sympathised with him. Even the three DSs, in their little side office, were grinning. They had all been Temporary DCs once.

Once a month, Frank would lead a posse of his detectives on a pub crawl. In he would walk, hands in pockets, with a bunch of big, hairy-arsed detectives following him and covering his back. He would stop, look around, and dare any of the locals to kick off. It was like a gunslinger walking into a Wild West saloon. We loved him for it and would have followed him anywhere. The deathly silence that came across the room was almost tangible. Every single punter in there would look straight at him.

He would stand stock still, survey the room, nod his head in greeting and say, "Evening all," pretending to be the 'Dixon of Dock Green'. Then he would walk to the bar and order best bitter for everyone. No lager, glasses of wine or G&Ts. Frank was a Yorkshireman, and you only drank bitter in his presence. It was pure theatre.

Tom thought back to a particular time.

One evening on the pub crawl, we went into a rough pub on the edge of a grim estate. It had been a while since we'd set foot in this place, and Frank was ready to make a statement. The entire office turned out, and we warned the duty sergeant where we were going in case it kicked off and we couldn't handle it on our own, and we needed uniform backup.

In we went, Frank leading the way and playing his usual role of town sheriff. You could feel the atmosphere, and we were sure it would end up in a scrap. I wished I'd worn an old suit, but hey ho. I couldn't stop myself from grinning as we piled in.

As Frank walked up to the bar, the way ahead parted, allowing him access so he could give his order.

"Fifteen pints of your finest best bitter, please, landlord," said Frank in a broad Yorkshire accent.

"I'm not sure this is a good idea," said the landlord.

Frank leaned on the bar with his elbows, moved his head forward and, staring the landlord straight in the eyes, said in a soft Yorkshire accent, still loud enough for the rest of the pub to hear, "I'll tell you what would be a fantastic idea, matey. Pull fifteen pints of bitter now or, in five minutes, I'll have uniform coppers swarming all over this place to shut this shithole down. Do you understand me?"

Brilliant. The purpose of the exercise was to show who was boss in this place, and it was them.

A few people had left the pub when we arrived, not wanting to be party to any potential goings-on. Just after a little scroat left, they heard a dull thud. Frank sent two guys out to see what it was. Someone had kicked in a side panel of one of the job cars. They ran after the guy, caught him and dragged him back to the pub car park. One of the seasoned DCs took off one of the guy's trainers and smashed it against the middle of the panel to make sure there was a nice, legible footmark on it. Then they nicked him, arranged for a couple of uniforms to come and transport him back to the nick, and lock him up until they got back.

This was the first time Tom knew such things went on, but, even though the guy said the damage to the vehicle was nothing to do with him, he pleaded guilty at court.

The Drug Squad came three years later. Surveillance, undercover work, and the best informants he could take with him. Tom thrived in the environment. He could sit in a freezing car for twelve hours waiting for movement and still call it a good day. Then down the pub with the rest of the guys for a swift couple of beers before home.

But the job outshone the marriage. His wife said he was married to the job and, to be fair, he was. He would have died for his mates on the squad, and they were the same. The professionalism he witnessed every day from solid detectives was a pleasure to be a part of. They were not all mates and socialised little outside the job, but everyone cared, every day. Luckily, she didn't know he had never claimed all the overtime he worked.

Tom was the bloke you wanted beside you when things went sideways. Ex-military, hard as nails, and not someone with a degree in media studies who last experienced a bit of pain when Mummy smacked their bottom.

Until Falstead walked free.

Chapter Three

February 2010

Woking nick buzzed with the usual late-shift static, phones ringing, boots thudding, the low hum of tired officers nursing coffee as they tidied up some paperwork. This being his nearest nick to home, Tom had dropped in, as he often did, to see what the locals were doing and to pick their brains about what they were seeing on the streets. It was always good to put yourself about. In reality, he was no better than any of these guys, just at a different stage of his career. He always hated the idea that the young PCs could see him as unapproachable. Yes, some of them were immature and needed a slap, but they would grow up. The job needed these lads to ask questions, put up suspects, and just be able to communicate with guys on the squad.

As he was walking past the locker room, he became aware of a voice.

"...Johnson's getting his door kicked in tomorrow. Six sharp," PC Jim Stratford muttered to his crewmate, oblivious to Tom's presence outside the door. "Shot another scumbag in the knee over a debt. I've had a snout tell me the silly sod still has the gun stashed under his kitchen cabinets. Bloody bloke thinks he's invincible."

"That's because he normally is, pal," said his crewmate. "They say he never touches the gear and is very smart. He seems to be one of the untouchables."

"Agreed, mate, but his time has come and he's got too big for his boots," said Jim.

Tom's pulse ticked up. Peter Johnson. The one that always slipped through the net. Tom had spent two years trying to nick and turn him. He was smart, slippery, and well-connected, and they were right; he never touched the gear. He'd always known that if he could turn him, he'd have a great source.

Tom had a lot of respect for Jim Stratford. He would make detective one day and probably get on one of the squads, but how could he use this bit of info?

Tom had bent the rules in Bosnia but promised himself when he joined the police he would play it straight down the line. He'd always believed, or at least had convinced himself, there was no point in doing this job if you didn't. He'd thought that from day one, but the poor results at court were wearing him down. Juries that hadn't got a clue and, even if you got a guilty, judges that believed the sob stories given by the defence briefs about a bad childhood, 'Your Honour, my client has turned his life around since being arrested', and all that bollocks. He just wasn't sure that playing by the rules got the results the public deserved. But could he ever cross the line and do it differently?

Tom sat in his car for a full thirty minutes, going through things in his head. Surely, he should just crack on and do his best, draw his salary, and not worry about it? But he cared. He wanted to lock these bad guys up. It was the system that was wrong, wasn't it?

Decision made.

He drove about five miles out of town to a phone box in a small village where he knew there was no CCTV, nothing that could catch him out on a reverse billing of Johnson's landline should anyone other than the Drug Squad be looking at him.

"Yeah?" Johnson's voice, wary.

"They're coming for you, Pete. Six in the morning. That shooter you've got in the kitchen, get rid of it."

Silence. Then, "Who is this?"

"You'll find out, and you owe me."

Tom hung up. He had crossed the line. He had left one world, entered another, and there was no going back.

Tom sat in the driver's seat, engine off, rain streaking the windscreen in slow, deliberate lines. The phone box was behind him now, just a shadow in the rearview mirror. He hadn't moved since hanging up and getting back into his vehicle. His hands rested on the wheel, steady but cold. He didn't smoke anymore, hadn't for years, but right now he missed the ritual, the flick of the lighter, the distraction, something to do with his hands while his head spun. He'd crossed the line. Just a quiet tip-off to a man who'd spent his life dodging the law. A man Tom had spent years trying to nick and then cultivate.

All for the greater good.

He thought about Sharon. Her face when he told her about Bosnia. The way she'd listened, really listened. No judgement. Just understanding. Would she understand this? Not a chance. She played it straight and always had. She'd bend the rules for the job slightly, maybe, but this wasn't bending. This was breaking.

Tom leaned back and stared at the roof of the car. The silence was heavy and pressing down on him. It wasn't for Johnson. He convinced himself that it was for the job. For the result. Because maybe, just maybe, this would lead somewhere. Even so, he'd tipped off a villain. Protected him. And left a gun on the streets.

He closed his eyes and whispered, "What the fuck have I done?"

Tom had been aware of Peter Johnson since he'd joined the job. At thirteen years of age, he was dealing puff outside the school gates and never stopped making a living that way. He was one of those villains who, had they been legit, would have made a fortune. But he'd made a fortune anyway, just on the wrong side of the law. He was smart. Very smart. Tom wasn't sure how he did it, but never touching the gear made it very difficult to nick him.

So now he needed a plan.

Chapter Four

Monday 8th February 2010

Tom built a target package on Johnson and took it to the DI. Jamie Capstick backed him and knew his competence. Everyone knew Johnson and agreed he was a solid target. The team moved him up the list and set a week's focus starting Monday morning.

Tom had already set up an OP opposite Johnson's home address. This nonsense you endured on the telly, when they sit in a car outside someone's home as if they were invisible for hours on end, just doesn't happen, and always made him laugh when he viewed it on TV. They'd got away with murder on the Falstead plot when they scrambled from the office, but that was pure luck. Entry to the OP was through the back gate, so they were never in view of the target or his HA.

Tom walked into the briefing at the main squad office well before 06:00 on the Monday morning with Sharon. Most of the team were already there, nattering about what they had done over the weekend and suchlike. You were never late for the briefing. The rest of the team arrived, and Tom kicked off bang on 06:00.

Tom was Operational Commander even though he was a DC and there was a DS on the plot. That was the way it was; your target, you ran it. A DS rarely overruled the OC, and if this happened, they would do it with a phone call or a meet, never over the air.

"OK," said Tom, "here we go. The target is Peter Johnson. You've all got the map with his HA in Woking and details of the target vehicle, which is his usual BMW M3. Sharon did a drive-by this morning and the target vehicle was in situ, facing out towards the road.

"You don't need a description as he's well known to all of you. We've got all week with him if needed. He has been nicked twice with no luck by the locals, who executed a search warrant on him a week or so ago.

"The dust has settled on that now, so we should be OK. Up in town, he shot some low-life druggie in the knee over a debt. Our local plod executed a warrant at his HA the following morning after one of Jim Stratford's snouts told him Johnson still had the gun stashed under his kitchen cabinets.

"The Met seemed unconcerned; they thought the man who got shot deserved it. I doubt he still had the shooter, to be honest. I can't imagine he would be that stupid. But we all know Jim; he's one of the good guys, so be careful."

"What resulted from the warrant?" said Samantha.

He was sitting up in bed with his dressing gown on and a cup of tea in his hand when they went in at 06:00. Someone had left the door on the latch, and he knew they were coming because Martina, his missus, was at her mother's. Jim is ticking like a nine-bob watch and can't work out how he knew, as the circle of trust was tiny. So, a blowout."

"Blimey," said Jack. "I assume no one other than us knows what we are doing this week, then?"

"No, they don't, and we stay away from Woking nick. The leak could have come from the Met, but it's possible it came from someone local, so no one goes there this week. We either debrief here in our office or at a nick well away from the plot. I considered telling Jim so we could get some updates from his source, but decided against it. The risk is too great.

"Moving on unless there are questions at this stage?" Tom scanned the room. There was a general shaking of heads.

"OK. Sharon and I are in four-four.

"Dick and Craig in four-five, you've got the OP and are coming out to join the convoy. If we get movement away and then back to the HA, it's easy for a footman to hold it until the OP are back in situ. Obviously, run your own log.

"Jack and Samantha in four-one, you take the nearside from the HA and do our log."

"Oh, come on, Tom," said Jack, "we had the log all last week."

"That's because you're so good at it, mate," said Tom, smiling.

"Charlotte and Karen in four-three, you've got the offside." Karen was the DS and super-good at the job.

"This is a pretty simple plot, guys, but Jamie, on the four-two, can you plot up with four-three, as that end is where it could get tricky if he does the offside and we hit the one-way system, so we may need your bike there.

"Four-six, Alex and Joe, you plot where you like but favour the nearside.

"I don't want to teach you to suck eggs, guys, but as you are all aware, the target is sharp as a razor and, as always, I would rather a loss than a show. We can always return to fight another day, but if the target waves at anyone, we'll be finished for weeks, and the crew that shows out will buy the beers for a month. We could have done with another crew out there, but Lisa and Mo in four-zero have a court commitment. With a bit of luck, they will get released early and can join us later, but don't bank on it.

"OK. On plot for 07:00, please."

The convoy dispersed after the briefing, each crew heading to its designated position. Tom and Sharon climbed into four-four, the familiar hum of the engine breaking the morning stillness.

"I'll drive," said Sharon.

Tom just stared at her and hesitated. It was his turn to drive that day, but he got into the passenger seat.

Sharon adjusted the rearview mirror and glanced at Tom. "You OK? You look tired, Tom."

Tom shrugged. "I'm fine."

Changing the subject, Tom said, "This one's smart. He's always two steps ahead. Like he's playing chess while we're still setting up the board."

Sharon smiled. "That's why we're here. To flip the board."

They drove in silence for a while, the streets still quiet, the early-shift traffic thinning out. They picked up a copy of the Telegraph from a local newsagent and settled down to wait. Throughout the day, the cars would meet up and exchange papers and, if there was no movement, every crew would read every word in every daily paper. Tom was always trying to master the cryptic crossword in the Telegraph, and it always defeated him.

"Did you sleep last night?" Sharon asked, not looking at him.

"A couple of hours, I guess. Scotch helped."

She didn't comment. Just nodded.

"Karen's watching you," she said after a beat.

Tom turned to her. "Watching me? Why?"

"She's worried. Thinks you're drinking too much. Thinks you're carrying too much."

Tom exhaled. "She's not wrong. Is that why you wanted to drive again?"

Sharon didn't answer immediately. "Just don't let it get in the way, Tom. You're too good at this, mate. One of the best, and I'd hate to see you take a fall."

Tom nodded, eyes fixed ahead. "Let's just get through today."

With the OP already in place, each unit called in to say they were on the plot. Radios crackled softly. The plot was live, and it was well before seven.

Tom woke with a start. He'd been asleep for goodness knows how long. When the radio blared at him, the shift from sound asleep to awake was instantaneous.

[Comms]: "Standby, standby, standby. Target from the HA to the target vehicle and in, in, in. Wearing blue jeans, a white T-shirt and white trainers. Confirming the target vehicle is facing the main road. Four-four?"

[Comms]: "Four-four, yes, yes," said Tom.

[Comms]: "Engine started and to the main road."

[Comms]: "And it's an off, off, off, left, left, left. Towards you, four-one?"

[Comms]: "Four-one, yes, yes."

[Comms]: "And loss of eyeball by the OP. Four-one?"

[Comms]: "Four-one, yes, yes."

[Comms]: "Four-one has the eyeball. Two for cover as we approach the junction with Maybury Hill. Lane one of two preparing for the nearside with a nearside indicator and left, left, left."

They stayed with the target all day and evening, and everything ran smoothly. The same the next day, and the next. It's so easy to question your tactics when it goes like this, but you have to stick to the plan.

It was on the Thursday of that week that it got interesting. The target vehicle stopped in Chestnut Grove, a cul-de-sac close to a known dealer's house. Johnson parked his vehicle and walked through an alleyway towards the football club. A foot man followed, only for Johnson to be sitting on a fence at the end of the alleyway watching who came through. The foot man didn't miss a step and just kept going. He did not look back.

[Comms]: "Stop, stop, stop at the end of the alleyway near where the old Sea Scouts building used to be. All units hold back. The target is sitting on a fence, watching who comes out, and I am burned.

[Comms]: "OK, let him run and just plot the vehicle."

It was obvious Johnson was doing this for a reason, and Tom didn't want to blow the entire job now.

[Comms]: "Four-three, can you see if you can get an OP on the vehicle?"

[Comms]: "Four-three, yes, yes. Four-three foot is out."

[Comms]: "All units. There is no eyeball," said Tom over the radio. They did not want to lose him now.

Karen could find a single female pensioner anywhere on the planet when they were on the move and sweet-talk her way into their front room for as long as it took to give movement. Within five minutes, Karen had it.

[Comms]: "Four-three foot has a visual on the target vehicle, which is unoccupied."

[Comms]: "Yes, yes," said Tom. "Eyeball is with you, four-three foot. Permission to plot?"

[Comms]: "Yes, yes."

[Comms]: "Vehicle for the nearside onto Westfield Avenue."

[Comms]: "Four-one."

[Comms]: "Four-one, yes, yes. Vehicle for the offside."

[Comms]: "Four-five."

[Comms]: "Four-five, yes, yes. Vehicles plotted eyeball."

[Comms]: "Four-three, yes, yes. No change."

Tom called Karen on her mobile. The job didn't supply the team with one each, and only the DS had a job-issue phone. It showed how short-sighted the bosses were, but most people had their own and didn't mind using them. Unlimited-minutes contracts had come in about three years ago, making it much cheaper to justify work use of a personal mobile. Before that, the bills were tough to get past the missus, as the job didn't allow you to claim phone bills on your expenses.

“We only have today and tomorrow, Karen, and I’m conscious of the expense of this,” said Tom, playing the game and showing he was aware of the politics.

“Agreed, Tom, and the DI has already been on the phone to ask how we’re doing, and pointing out we will all be on overtime soon,” said Karen, aware of the pressure she was putting him under. “I suggest we see how the next phase of this goes. He’s doing this anti for a reason, and we could take the risk of striking if we take him away from known premises.”

“I’ve got a better idea,” said Tom. “I’ll get hold of the Traffic guys and see if they’ve got anyone on with more than half a brain cell to do a routine stop. That way we don’t blow the surveillance if it’s a dud.”

“Fine, Tom,” said Karen. “You sort that out with Traffic.”

“OK. I’ll leave you to tell the guys I’m leaving the plot to organise this if I can. Call me or text if you get movement.”

Karen was a good DS and had known what Tom was thinking. She didn’t need to push him in the direction they were now going to resolve this operation.

She also knew he was going through a bad time at the moment and was getting a lot of grief from his missus. How many marriages had she seen go south in this bloody job? She was married to another copper familiar with squad work, yet they still had difficulties. She knew she had to monitor Tom as he was drinking too much. They all liked a drink after work, but early starts might catch him out if he kept going when he got home, and she didn’t need him on the plot still pissed up from the night before or, at best, stinking of booze.

She lodged a thought in the back of her mind to speak with him when there was a suitable moment.

She liked Tom. He was popular with the other guys on the squad, and she didn't want to lose him. She'd already mentioned it to Sharon, knowing they were close, so perhaps she could rein him in.

"Traffic Centre, Sergeant Crawford speaking."

Tom breathed a sigh of relief. "Hello Frank, Tom Kessler here. How are you, mate? Long time no speak."

Tom had known Frank Crawford when he was the uniform sergeant on his rota before he went upstairs on his learner. This was a bit of a result. Frank was another one of the good guys, and Tom was sure he would help if he could. Why on earth he had moved on to Traffic, goodness only knows.

"Hello, Tommy, my old son. How are you? How's the squad treating you? I was told a funny story about you the other day that's doing the rounds. Something about a radio not working?" Frank chuckled, and Tom could feel his blood pressure rising, even though that was a long way in the past.

"Well, that's a story for another time over a pint, Frank. Right now I need your help with something that could be urgent in short order. Have you got any of your minions with more than half a brain cell in the Woking area that could give a vehicle a tug for us?"

"I've got Jonny Wilkes crewed up with a probationer PC on an attachment in Maybury at the moment. Will they do?"

"Yes, mate. Jonny will do. Get him to call me, and I'll arrange a meet ASAP to get him briefed and give him one of our portables. You've still got my mobile, haven't you, Frank?"

"Yes, matey, I have, and let's catch up for that beer. I want to hear the full story."

Tom could sense Frank chuckling to himself as he hung up the phone.

These bloody people. They always took the piss but didn't know how tough it was to follow someone without showing out. Done well, it's an art form, and satisfying. To follow someone all day, especially if they were looking for you, is tough. To a man and woman, the squad were hard on each other, and woe betide anyone who tried to come up with an excuse if they cocked up. The only way was to throw your hands up, cough the mistake, and move on. Even if you thought you hadn't messed up, if the rest of the team thought you had, then you had. Take it on the chin, apologise, and move on.

Five minutes later, Tom's mobile vibrated. "Tom Kessler," he said.

"Hi Tom. It's Jonny Wilkes in Tango 57. I understand you need a hand with something."

"Yes, mate, thanks."

They arranged a place to meet. Tom briefed Jonny and his probationer PC and gave them a handheld radio.

Jesus, that PC only looks about twelve, and was about eight stone wringing wet.

Just then his mobile vibrated again. It was Karen.

"We've got movement, Tom. The target went to that address we suspected he would. He was only in there a couple of minutes, and when he left, he put something in his pocket, but I couldn't be sure what it was. What do you want to do?"

Tom didn't hesitate. "We call the traffic guys through and let them do a routine stop. It will be Jonny Wilkes with a young probationer. Jonny's a good guy, so he should be OK. I've briefed him; he has a handheld, and he knows what to do. This probationer PC looks like a schoolboy, but the target doesn't have a history of kicking off if he gets stopped. Any sign of anything and the target gets nicked or, at worst, detained for a drug search. Then we hope for the best."

Tom raced back to the general area of the convoy's current position with the traffic car in tow. When he got near and into radio range.

[Comms]: "Four-two has the eyeball."

[Comms]: "Four-three is with you now, four-two, has one for cover and can take it."

[Comms]: "Yes, yes, four-three over to you."

Once it had settled down, Tom came over the radio.

[Comms]: "Four-four permission?"

[Comms]: "Yes, yes, four-four."

[Comms]: "All units, we have Tango 57 in the convoy who is going to come through and do a routine stop on the target vehicle. Four-three, can you talk him through?"

[Comms]: "Four-three, yes, yes. Tango 57, how are you receiving?"

[Comms]: "You are R5 to Tango 57."

[Comms]: "Yes, yes, Tango 57. You are R5 to four-three. Talking you through now."

Sweet as a nut, four-three talked Tango 57 through the convoy until they were behind the target.

[Comms]: "Thank you, Tango 57. Turn off the handheld now so, if you nick or detain him, he doesn't hear it, and hide it until we can pick it up later."

The squad plotted the target vehicle in case something went wrong and waited. Tom hoped he'd made the right call.

Four-four kept eyeball on the stop check and watched as Jonny searched the target. He'd found something as he grabbed him, turned him round and cuffed him. Then Jonny, with the help of the young schoolboy, put the target in the back of the traffic car. Jonny moved away from his vehicle and pulled his mobile out of his pocket.

Tom's mobile vibrated. "Tom? It's Jonny. A bit of personal, I think, matey. He's not saying anything, but he's got a couple of grams of white powder. I've nicked him and will get him to Woking nick. I've got another traffic car meeting me here to get the car in. Nice motor, by the way. He's making a few quid."

"Well done, Jonny. Appreciate your help, mate. We'll see you at the factory. We'll stay out of the way. You book him in and, when he's banged up, we'll see you in the CID office. Do an arrest statement, please, mate, and don't bugger off with our handheld. The last time we did this, Pete Carson took it with him, and we didn't see it for a month."

Tom called Karen. "Hi Karen. He's got a bit of personal on him, which is something. Nothing much, but enough to get him across the table from me so I can try to turn him. All to Woking now, and we meet in the CID office. We don't have to stay away from there now that he's nicked. We'll meet Jonny, get our radio back before he slides off with it, and then I'll find a quiet room to debrief in and we can decide a way forward. I'll let you organise the troops if that's OK?"

"No probs, Tom. Leave that to me, and we'll see you there."

They all met up at the CID office at Woking, except for Tom, who went off to find a quiet room for the debrief.

One of the local CID lads interviewed and bailed Peter Johnson. A couple of grams of powder wasn't CID territory, but Tom wanted it kept simple: interview, bail back to Woking, lab analysis, and then deal with it himself. Familiar turf. The locals knew the score, went along with it, and didn't kick it back downstairs to uniform.

Chapter Five

Friday 26th February 2010

It was 14:00. Tom and Sharon were chewing the fat in the CID office, having bailed out of the day's op so they could handle Johnson's surrender. Few people in Woking CID knew Sharon. She was sharp and a good-looking woman, and the young bucks had taken a real shine to her. Tom chuckled to himself. They didn't know what he knew. Let them chase shadows, he thought.

He was half-listening to a story about a botched burglary in Knaphill when the phone rang on Bill Pearson's desk.

"Is Tom Kessler in there, Bill?"

"Yes, he is," said Bill, finger jammed in his ear to hear over the din.

"Tell him Peter Johnson's at the front counter. Reporting on bail."

"Will do." Bill replaced the receiver. "Tom, your bloke's here. Front desk."

Tom's stomach tightened. He gave Bill a thumbs-up and nodded. He hadn't expected it to hit like this. The room kept moving, phones ringing, banter flying, but it was all distant. Muffled. Like he'd stepped outside the moment. This was it. The genuine point of no return.

He could play it straight. Keep the tip-off buried. Let Johnson walk in and out like any other punter and pretend to himself the call never happened. Or he could face it head-on. Tell Johnson the truth. That he'd crossed a line. They were both standing at the edge now. He could intimate that it was him. Not admit it. Just let it hang.

Until now, he'd kept his options buried in a box in his mind with the lid sealed. Now the box was open, and all the fears poured out and had to be dealt with. But there was a world of difference between denying it, not denying it, and saying it out loud.

"I want to do this one on my own, Sharon. You OK with that?"

"If you say so," she said, puzzled. "This informant stuff's more your bag than mine. If you think that's the best way forward, then off you go."

Tom stood, walked out of CID, and went off to the locker room. He could feel Sharon's eyes boring into the back of his head. He didn't go straight to the front desk. Not yet.

He needed a minute.

He pushed into the toilet block, chose the far cubicle, and sat. The seat was cold. The walls had tiles of that institutional grey and never gave the impression of being clean. He leaned forward, elbows on knees, face in hands. His heart was racing. Breath shallow. This was serious.

He could go to prison for this. And no matter how tough you are, prison's not a good place for ex-coppers. He remembered Sharon's warning about his drinking. He was aware of the slope beneath him, slippery, steep. If he was going to do this, he'd have to trust someone who made their living as a criminal. He wasn't a control freak, but he needed control now. He'd never done this before and was flying blind.

Informants, yes. But not like this. Not someone he'd bent the rules for, broken the law for. He breathed in through his nose. Slow. Deliberate. Like before an op. Back in the army. Back when fear was a tool, not a weakness. He could still pull out. Say nothing. Let it ride. But Johnson wasn't just another name on a bail sheet. He was a chance. A risk. A potential asset. And once Tom walked out of that cubicle, the decision he made could change everything.

He went downstairs to the front counter.

"Hello Pete. Come on through." He gestured towards the corridor.

"Mr Kessler. How are you?" said Johnson in a cocky tone.

"I'm fine." Tom kept walking. He needed to take control of this. Keep control of the narrative. "Save the chat for downstairs, mate. Plenty of time for that."

The custody suite was buzzing.

"Afternoon, Jim," said Tom to the Custody Officer, trying to keep his heart from exploding. "I've got Peter Johnson reporting on bail. I've had the lab report back, but I need to talk with him."

They booked Johnson in. He knew two grams of charlie was nothing and was likely to go nowhere. He had the confidence of someone who'd been nicked a few times and never charged. Once booked in, they headed to an interview room.

Outside the door, Tom turned to him, making Johnson stop.

"These rooms are wired for sound and vision. I would know if someone was watching, but they could be listening without my knowledge. You say nothing in there about the phone call you got. You understand me?"

Johnson's head moved back. Eyebrows raised. He couldn't hide his surprise.

He hadn't suspected the call came from Tom, albeit he thought he may have recognised the voice at the front counter, but he hadn't expected a brazen admission. What the hell did this mean? Where was it going? A few bent cops' names floated around his circle, but Tom Kessler's wasn't one of them. He'd expected a meet. A shake-down. Maybe a few quid for the tip-off.

Not this.

He stared at Tom in amazement and said, "OK."

Tom had done this plenty of times, though usually with more than a couple of grams of powder to bargain with. Sometimes it worked, sometimes it didn't, but it always began the same way: give them a reason.

People agreed to become a source for a handful of motives:

Money, never as much as they imagined.

Ego, it made them feel important.

Clearing the field, the most common. Removing the opposition meant expanding their patch and, with luck, pushing up the price of their product.

And above all, they had to believe you wouldn't burn them.

"Right. We both know this is a poxy bit of charlie. Normally you'd get a warning, possession of a bit of personal. I've got the power to charge you, but you've got no previous, and I'm sure you don't want a conviction on your record. No taking the kids to Disneyland in the US in the future could piss Martina off big-style. I also have the power to make this go away. No warning. No paperwork. That's what I'm proposing. But I want something in return."

Now you wait. Pitch made. Don't break the silence. Let it fester. Let them take all this in. They speak next.

Johnson leaned back, rocking on the rear legs of his chair, slow, deliberate, the way he always did when he was thinking. Not just about the pitch he'd expected to hear, predictable as ever, but about the shooter tip-off from Tom Kessler. That changed things.

He'd walked in ready to prop up a rival dealer, to set up some poor bastard sniffing around his manor who needed reminding whose turf it was. But with the shooter intel in play, the swap didn't feel right. This wasn't just about territory anymore. The plan he'd half-formed before stepping through the door was no longer a fair trade.

Still, he didn't prevaricate.

"Deal."

"Good," said Tom.

Shit. That was too easy.

He wished there'd been at least a bit of pushback, a bit of jockeying for position. But of course he knew why.

"This is all off the record, isn't it? This conversation we're having now?"

"My partner, Sharon, and our DI will know what was said, but if you're worried about that, it won't be evidential."

"OK. You know that couple of grams of charlie wasn't for me."

"Really?"

"It's true, and I need you to know this. I was just doing a favour for a mate. I don't do two-gram bags, Tom, so couldn't help him out. As you probably know, I go nowhere near the gear, so have nothing round me. Never have I ever used anything. Not even a toke of a spliff in my life. Never even smoked ordinary cigarettes.

"When I started on this road I'm on, outside the school gates all those years ago, I swore to myself I would have nothing to do with taking gear myself. Even at that age, I had seen people go down a slippery slope. I wanted to do it differently. I never planned to do it forever, but it's a hard place to get out of once you're in it. The money is just nuts. But... one day.

"My Martina wouldn't stand for it, anyway. She comes from a lovely family who have no idea what I do for a living. They think I'm in import-export, which, in a funny way, I suppose I am.

"Anyway, I needed you to know that."

"OK. I hear you and have absolutely no reason to doubt you."

They considered each other for a few seconds, taking each other in. Then Tom said, "What have you got in mind for the future, then?"

Johnson paused, looking up at the ceiling. Then rocked forward, forearms on the table.

"Considering *all* the circumstances," he said, locking eyes with Tom. Eyebrows raised. Head tilted. The look said it all. The tip-off, and the knowledge of where it had come from, had changed the game. "I propose you give me a few days to come up with something that fits the gravity of this situation.

"I promise I won't let you down. I'm not blowing smoke up your arse, Tom. The chat on the street is you're a man of your word. I can work with that. I give you my word, and I'll make sure this whole thing happens."

"OK," said Tom. "Let's get out of here. I'll call you on Monday."

"Make it Wednesday," said Johnson, trying to control the clock.

"Monday," said Tom, holding firm. "I'm running this, not the other way around. I make the rules. Got it?"

"Yes, understood," said Johnson, smiling.

After a quiet word with the custody sergeant, they released Johnson without charge.

Let's hope he keeps his word.

Sharon watched from the corridor leading to the front door of the nick, half-shadowed by the door frame.

Johnson turned around just before he got to the front door.

"Before I go, I understand that John Falstead's bought a nightclub in Guildford, the one that was up for sale a couple of months ago opposite the main shopping centre car park."

"Really? How did he get the licence?"

"He hasn't. He's got someone fronting it for him. It's obvious any gear sold in there will be his."

"OK, I'll call you," said Tom, as Johnson turned and walked out the front door.

Sharon waited until the door clicked shut behind Johnson.

"You trust him?" she asked, retreating from the shadows.

Tom didn't answer right away, not looking at Sharon and still watching the door.

"Trust is not the right word. I wouldn't trust him as far as I could kick him with a broken leg, but I do think he'll come good," he said. "He is a smart fella, Sharon. He's not your average snout, that's for sure. And on Monday, we should find out just how smart."

Chapter Six

Saturday 27th February 2010

Tom had just got back from the gym. He'd risen early, determined to carve out time without disrupting the day too much. The house smelled of toast and wet dog. It was comforting, familiar, and chaotic. Sue was in the kitchen, sleeves rolled up, folding laundry she'd brought back from the launderette, her movements brisk and methodical.

Tom dropped his keys into the bowl by the door, poured himself a coffee, and kissed her cheek. She didn't flinch, but she didn't lean in either.

The girls hadn't even noticed when he walked in. He sighed, feeling like a guest in his own home. Even the bloody dog was female, he thought, not without irony.

"You could try talking to them," Sue said, her voice neutral and sensing his thoughts. "They're not aliens."

"They kind of are," Tom replied, half-joking. "They're your daughters."

Sue paused, turned her head just enough to shoot him a look, scowled for a beat, then returned to folding.

"Ouch," she said.

"Sorry. That didn't come out the way I meant it," Tom said, already regretting the line.

"You said you'd take them swimming," she reminded him, still focused on the laundry.

"I will. I just need ten minutes to cool down."

"You always need ten minutes. Then it's a call. Then it's a job. Then it's next weekend. And you also said you'd fix this bloody washing machine," she added.

Tom didn't respond straightaway. He didn't want a row, not now, not over this. He'd had this before, and while she wasn't wrong, she wasn't right either. Rarely did he work weekends, and when he was home, he tried. But the job didn't care about calendars or family plans.

"Give me a break, Sue. Let's not start this now," he said, keeping his tone measured. "I'll do both," he added, his voice low and more careful now. "You just tell me the order you want me to do them."

The twins, Maya and Lily, were in full teenage mode. Phones out, music blaring, locked in a low-grade argument over outfits for a party next weekend. They all had the newish iPhone 3GS, even better than the one Tom had. The youngest, Evie, hovered between childhood and adolescence, trying to keep pace with her sisters while still clinging to Dad when no one was looking.

Evie, being the youngest and not one of the twins, sometimes felt like an outsider. The twins moved through the world like a matched pair, speaking in glances and finishing each other's sentences. Tom sometimes joked they shared a brain. Evie didn't. She had her own orbit, and more often than not, it circled her dad. Maybe it was the age gap, maybe the quiet way he listened, but she saw him in a way the twins didn't. Sometimes, when the house was loud with twin laughter or twin fights, Evie was like an only child. And in those moments, Tom was the one who reached for her first.

Tom glanced over at them. He was trained to read rooms, decode threats, anticipate violence. But teenage girls? Total mystery.

"Morning, girls," he offered.

"Mm," Maya replied, eyes glued to her screen.

"Can you not wear that hoodie?" Lily said to Evie. "It's embarrassing."

"It's comfy," Evie mumbled.

"It's Dad's," Lily snapped.

"Yeah. Whatever," said Evie.

Tom eyed them, amused at the exchange, unsure whether to step in or step back. He poured more coffee, listened to the pop song thumping from someone's phone, and assumed he'd wandered into a foreign country.

Someone had to make a move. He walked over to Sue, slid his arms around her from behind, and gave her a gentle squeeze. She'd kept herself in great shape, he thought. Not just physically, but emotionally, too. Three kids, him missing in action during the week, and she still carried herself with strength. She'd put up with so much when he was in the army, away for months at a time, never knowing if he'd come home. Some didn't. Everyone knew someone who hadn't. But there was a support network then, wives who were all in the same boat, watching the news with clenched jaws and shared silence. That network didn't exist within the police. No one swapped casseroles or sat together through the worst nights. It was just her holding the line.

She stopped folding, paused for a moment, appeared to stare into the distance, and seemed to come to a decision. She turned within his grasp, leaned into him, looked him in the eyes, paused for a couple of seconds, and sighed.

"OK," she said. "Truce. We'll do something as a family today. But you have to promise me something."

"Anything," he said.

"Turn that bloody phone off. And leave it off until Monday morning."

Tom hesitated.

What if a snout calls?

"OK," he said.

"Great. Maybe look at the washing machine first, then we'll all go swimming. Perhaps hit Pizza Express on the way back?"

"OK," he said, nodding. "Let's get cracking."

Tom jumped straight into fixing the washing machine. He did not want the expense of a new one at the moment. They had a fixed-rate mortgage ending soon, and he was unsure how they were going to cope. It was going to be more expensive than they had at the moment and, great copper that he was, he was not a financial wizard, so he wanted to play it safe.

Later that day, after a swimming session at the local leisure centre in Guildford, they had lunch at Pizza Express in Woking. He thought he spied Prince Andrew with his two daughters sitting in the corner, but he couldn't be sure.

Tom had kept his word about the phone, but without it, he felt exposed. It was one of the best days they'd had in a long time, and all was well. Tom and Sue sat at one table; the girls at another, just beside them.

They sat with their own thoughts for a while, relaxing in the moment, when Sue blurted, "Tom. Can I ask you something?"

"Of course," said Tom.

She paused, thinking of the right words.

"We've had a great day today, the best I can remember for months." There was another pause before she continued, knowing this was not likely to go down well but realising there was never a right time for this question.

"Would you consider coming out of the police and doing something else so we could do this more often?"

Shit. Where's this come from? The last thing I need now is a conversation like this.

"I know nothing else, Sue."

"You're good at lots of things, Tom. Everything you turn your hand to, you make a success of. It could be something nine-to-five so we can be like a normal family. The girls are growing up now, and I could do with you around more."

Tom slowly breathed, allowing his eyes to drift across the next table where the girls were still engrossed in their own world. Maya and Lily were in an animated debate about a playlist, while Evie, ever the quiet observer, sketched something on the back of a napkin with a stubby crayon. He turned back to Sue, who was watching him with that familiar mix of patience and quiet determination.

"I understand why you're asking," he said, keeping his voice low and steady, not wanting to disturb the fragile peace they'd built over the course of the day. "And I know it's not coming from nowhere.

"You've been carrying a lot, and I haven't always made that easier."

He paused, letting the words settle between them, then continued. His voice was steady, but quieter now, as if speaking more to memory than to the present. His eyes appeared to be looking into the distance, as if he were viewing something far away.

"There were things I saw and did on those peacekeeping tours that I've never really talked about with you. Not because I'm trying to cut you out, but because I don't know how to explain them without sounding like I'm still stuck there. And trust me, if you weren't there, it's impossible to understand what it was like. Some of it was just... relentless. Not the violence you see in films, but the slow, grinding kind, the kind that wears people down over months, not minutes."

He glanced at the girls, still laughing at Evie's drawing, then turned back at Sue.

"I've stood in places where the air felt heavy with grief, where that grief was almost tangible, where the ground was still warm from what had happened the night before. I've watched families search for loved ones in the rubble, knowing they wouldn't find them alive. I've seen so many dead bodies I've lost count. So much blood on the ground you wonder how much can come out of one body. I've guarded convoys carrying aid to people who'd lost everything, and I've had to keep my weapon ready while children smiled at me like I was some kind of saviour, knowing that a sniper could have me in his sights at that very moment."

He rubbed his hands together, not out of nerves, but as if trying to scrub off something invisible.

"It changes you. Not all at once, but bit by bit. You stop sleeping. You stop trusting quiet moments and learn to read every twitch, every glance, every shift in tone, because sometimes that's the only warning you get. And when I came home, I couldn't just switch that off. I still can't. It changed me forever, and there is no going back to the old Tom."

Sue didn't interrupt, but her gaze didn't waver. She was giving him space to speak, but he could feel the weight of her hopes pressing against his words.

"I know it's hard for you to understand why I hold on to this job," he said. "But it's the only place where that part of me still fits. Where the instincts I've built over years aren't a problem, they're a strength. I'm not saying it's healthy, and I'm not saying it's right or fair to you or the girls. But it's the truth. I wouldn't know how to be anything else or do anything else.

"It's just... this job isn't something I can walk away from," he continued, choosing each phrase with care. "It's not just about the work itself; it's about the part of me that feels useful, that feels like I'm doing something that matters. I know that sounds dramatic, maybe even selfish, but it's the truth. I've spent years learning how to do this well, and I don't know who I'd be without it."

Sue nodded slowly, her fingers tracing the rim of her wineglass, not in frustration, but in thought.

"I've tried to imagine a different life," Tom said, glancing again at the girls, then back to her. "One where I'm home more, where I'm not checking my phone every five minutes or missing Christmas because something's kicked off. And I want that too. I want more of this, more of today. But I also know that if I left the job, I'd be bringing home a version of myself that's half-alive. I'd be present, sure, but I'd be restless, distracted, and unbearable."

Sue gave a small smile at that, not because it was funny, but because she knew it was true.

“I’m not saying things can’t change,” Tom added. “I can do better and try harder to keep carving out time like today. I can be more deliberate about protecting weekends, about saying no when I need to. But I can’t promise you a nine-to-five life. That’s not who I am, Sue, and I don’t think it ever will be.”

There was a long pause, not uncomfortable, just full of everything unsaid. The girls were laughing now. Evie had drawn a cartoon of Lily with wild hair and exaggerated eyebrows, and even Maya was chuckling.

Sue said nothing, letting the silence sit between them whilst they looked into each other’s eyes in a way only those who have been married for years can. She reached across the table and placed her hand over his, her touch light but grounding.

“Alright,” she mumbled. “I just needed to ask. I needed to know where the line was.”

Tom nodded, grateful for the moment, for her understanding, relieved that the day hadn’t unravelled. But deep inside, he knew this wasn’t the end of the conversation.

“And hopefully,” she added, her voice lifting just slightly, bringing the tension to an end, “someone will fix the washing machine so I don’t have to take the laundry to the bloody launderette again.”

Tom laughed, the tension easing.

Tom kept his word, as difficult as it was, and his phone remained switched off all weekend. He knew Sharon had his home phone number, albeit the only time it ever rang was when someone cold-called, so if there was a shout, she could get hold of him.

Sue knew this, of course, but was grateful to Tom for keeping his word.

Tom had a theory about “brownie points” men earned from their wives. The best you ever got was zero, and most of the time they were negative. If you did something fantastic, you got zero points, so you were always in the shit; it was just the depth that varied.

It had been a rare, good weekend, and he was clinging to it like a man on leave who knows the call could come any minute. It was also a chance to recharge his batteries, something he needed every now and again.

He didn't believe in karma, but if there was such a thing, this was him trying to earn it; one load of laundry, one switched-off phone at a time.

Sue watched him from across the table as he folded a napkin, not neatly, but with effort. He was trying. She knew that. And the weekend had been good. Better than most.

But something had settled in her chest since that conversation. A quiet ache. Not anger, not disappointment, just the slow realisation that this was as far as he could go. He'd given her his truth, and she respected that. But it wasn't the answer she'd hoped for.

She smiled when he glanced up, and he smiled back. But behind hers was the knowledge that nothing had changed. Not really.

She'd asked. He'd answered. And now she knew. This could not go on.

Even good weekends had shadows.

Chapter Seven

Monday 1st March 2010

Monday morning came, and Tom's mind switched back to work. Sharon picked him up from home as she'd kept the car for the weekend. They went to the office for a planning meeting since the planned job had failed. Nothing to do with them, another crew's target had got himself nicked on Sunday evening and was still in custody in Reigate. So, op postponed: do your own thing and develop other targets.

In silence, he considered how to play it with Peter Johnson this morning. He wanted to do everything at this stage with Sharon present. He would play this by the book, knowing the time would come later when it needed to be just him and Johnson together.

"Good weekend?" Sharon asked with a smile.

"Great," said Tom. "Best in years, if I'm honest. You?"

"Yeah, superb. Claire and I went over to her mum and dad's for Sunday lunch. It was nice."

Tom caught something in her voice and turned to her.

"How were they with you?" he asked. "I remember you saying they were old school about you and Claire."

She glanced at him, smiled, and shook her head, realising he'd picked up on the tone in her voice. Too sharp for his own good sometimes.

"Not too bad, to be honest. I think they're getting used to the idea. But yeah, they're old school. And with Claire being an only child, they think grandchildren are off the table."

"Modern tech can work wonders."

"We've thought about it. Maybe one day. Not for a while."

"Well, if you're looking for a sperm donor, you know I've got strong genes," he said with a big grin.

She snorted and then laughed. "Tom! Jesus Christ. It's a bit early in the morning for that, mate."

Sharon's laughter lingered for a moment, then faded as they arrived at the office and dropped into work mode. Tom glanced at his watch. The Johnson call was minutes away.

They parked and went into the office. Several people had already arrived and were discussing their weekends.

"Morning, team. Anyone catch the Aussie game on Saturday?" said Tom over the hum of the office.

"I was there," said Jack with a big grin. "Great game, Tom. You'd have loved it. The atmosphere was amazing. We were sitting with a bunch of Aussie ex-pats in front of us. Great fun."

"Did you go into Kneller Hall, like we did last year?" said Tom.

"We did. That intro of yours to your mate, Harry, was amazing. I take it you watched it on telly?"

"No. Domestic duties for me all weekend, I'm afraid."

Tom was a big rugby fan and, last year, had taken Jack to the England versus Argentina match at Twickenham. It turned out to be a smart pick as it was England's only win during that autumn series. An old army mate, Harry Mercer, based at Kneller Hall, the Army School of Music just down the road, had sorted access to the Sergeants' Mess before and after the game, where the beer was still at 1940s prices. Army caterers laid on a hot meal beforehand, and pizzas turned up later once the match was done. It was always a great day out. Tom would run into a few familiar faces, trade stories, and catch up over a couple of pints.

"Well, I'm glad Harry came good for you. Did he drag up a sandbag and give you a few of the old war stories?"

"He did. Got serious at one stage, but we dragged him out of that with a couple of large whiskies."

"Great stuff," said Tom, as he and Sharon headed into the DI's office.

"Morning, guvnor," said Tom to the DI. "We're just about to call Peter Johnson to see what he's come up with."

"Morning, guys. No problem. You can use my office. I'm just off to a budget meeting, so fill your boots and let me know how you get on."

"Thanks, guv. Good luck with that. I don't know how you deal with all that bullshit."

"Someone's got to bat for the team, Tom. If the bosses had their way, there wouldn't even be a drug squad. They just see it as an enormous expense that doesn't give them crime stats to feed the press. I won't bore you with the details, but I've just spent the weekend in this office working out how much overtime you lot didn't claim last month."

"How many?" said Sharon.

"Believe it or not, it works out at fifteen hours per man, and that was not a typical month. It's usually more than that, and that's totally unreasonable. I haven't had time to work out the unclaimed expenses, but that'll be huge too. She doesn't know it yet, but I'm taking Karen with me to back up the operational need for the time. You know this already, but we could run two full teams and still be occupied every day."

"Bloody hell," said Tom. "Don't tell my missus about the overtime and expenses."

"Anyway, I'm off. See you later," said Jamie.

"Karen. You're with me," Jamie said as he strode into the main office.

Tom and Sharon turned to each other and smiled. "OK. Snout head on," said Tom, and sat behind the DI's desk.

Tom put his mobile on loudspeaker and rang Johnson's mobile, which was answered after a couple of rings.

"Morning, Tom," said Johnson. His tone was businesslike, and Tom sensed he was taking this seriously.

"Morning, Pete. I'm here on loudspeaker with my partner, Sharon. How's it looking?"

"It's looking very good, Tom. I've got something special for you, but I can't do it over the phone. We need to meet, and it needs to be a long way from my gaff."

"Of course, no problem. I'll message you with the location and procedure. I didn't ask last time, but I assume you use WhatsApp?"

"Of course. I'll wait to hear from you." The phone went dead.

"Well, that was very short, sweet, and very businesslike," Tom said. "No banter. Just get to the point. I like that. I don't want us to be his best mates; I want this straight down the line."

"Good," said Sharon, watching him. It appeared he was playing this how she wanted.

"Just make sure you're not freezing him out too hard. We still need him warm enough to talk."

"I know how to handle him, Sharon. Don't forget, this stuff's right up my street."

Tom's expression shifted. "I suggest the pub in Horsham we've considered before but not utilised. It's also one we have never used, and will never use, after a debrief. We can keep that as our meeting place for now. It's way off his manor, but the usual rules will apply. If you're OK with that, I'll message him with the rules and procedure?"

She nodded. Tom ran through the message in his head as he typed:

The meet will be at The Black Swan in Horsham. You arrive bang on 14.00. You look around first to make sure there's no one in there you know. If there is, you buy a pint of beer and talk with, meet with, or whatever you need to do with them to make it all look very natural. If not, and you are 100% sure you are clean, you buy a small soft drink. You wait at the bar. We will arrive at the bar at 14.10. If you have a soft drink, we know you are clean. Either way, we get a drink, find a table and sit down. You join us if safe. If you have a pint of beer, we ignore you, go our separate ways, and later rearrange the meet for tomorrow by message. We will park our car well away from the pub and walk in. You act as normal and park in the car park. Just send me a thumbs-up if you've got this and understand and then delete this message.

Sharon was reading over his shoulder. "Wow," she muttered.

Within seconds, Johnson had sent a thumbs-up.

"What?" said Tom, turning to look up at her.

"I've never run a source with you before, Tom. That's very professional."

"This is agent handling, Sharon. Not informant handling. It's on a different level. In the army, I did a stint with the Intelligence Corps and took a course with MI5. Back then, we didn't have mobile phones. We'd set a meet like this using a dead letter drop or a phone box. If the source called it off by having a pint in front of him, we always had a fallback meet twenty-four hours later at a different venue. Same rules applied.

"If that went wrong, we'd go back to the drop and rearrange. We would instruct the source to leave their house at an exact time and have a full team behind them from the moment they left, just to make sure there wasn't another team on the plot. The bad guys run surveillance too. They had to have a cover story in their heads for why they were in a particular place at that time. We'd give directions for them to park in a specific place, walk a set route to the meet through a pinch point, something like a footbridge over a river or road, so we could see if they had a foot man behind them. We didn't want them doing any anti-surveillance themselves; that would look suspicious. If they had a tail, or we even suspected they did, we wouldn't show and would rely on the fallback. If we went to the fallback, we did the same thing the following day, and the source knew all the details in advance.

"We also had a team behind us leaving the venue to make sure we were clean. It was a different level, personnel-intensive, but we were talking national security. It warranted the expense."

There was a pause. Sharon nodded slowly, a serious look on her face. "Understood, Tom."

"Let's go and recce the pub now, then grab a coffee nearby. We'll leave our phones, warrant cards, wallets, etc., in a Faraday bag by the spare tyre in the boot so we go in clean as we want nothing on us whatsoever that can identify us. We have cover names too, same first name, and a last name starting with the same first letter. Pick yours."

"Garfield. Sharon Garfield."

"I'm Tom Kirkland.

"We'll have a cover story for the meet too, in case we get interrupted by someone who knows him. He can choose suppliers or customers; it's up to him as he needs the cover story to fit his place in the hierarchy of his world. It also makes him feel as though he has some input into the meet. You got that?"

"Yes, impressive," Sharon said. "I'm going to enjoy this. You're taking me on a journey I've never been on before."

Tom smiled at her, enjoying the admiration, and said, "OK. Vamos."

Sharon looked at him.

"Vamos?"

"It's Spanish for 'let's go,'" he said, grinning.

"Every day's a school day," said Sharon, shaking her head as they walked out to the car.

Tom retrieved a small leather Faraday bag from the boot, into which they put their phones, warrant cards, credit cards and anything else they each had on them that could identify them. He then put that under the spare tyre in the boot for safety. They were getting towards the sharp end of this now and needed to stay focused.

Chapter Eight

Monday 1st March 2010

Sharon drove whilst Tom concentrated on planning where they would park, go for a coffee and still be in striking distance of the meet. They parked in the Marks & Spencer car park in Swan Walk, checked the pub was open, then headed to Costa Coffee. Tom insisted on holding Sharon's hand. They were just another couple out shopping. She knew who was running the show and went along with it.

There was no tail, but paranoia never got you compromised. They paused often, using shop windows as rearview mirrors. Occasionally they stopped and turned, playing it off like a change of plan, watching for hesitation or diverted glances. If nothing else, it was good anti-surveillance practice. The secret was carrying out anti-surveillance without looking like you were carrying out anti-surveillance.

They had a coffee at Costa, picking a table as far back as they could so they could monitor the door. A few people came in, and they fixed the descriptions in their minds. Tom had told Sharon to clock the men customers who came in after them, and he would clock the women. On leaving for the meet, they stopped as though they were discussing something. They were facing each other, with Tom looking at the door of Costa over Sharon's shoulder, checking for someone coming out behind them.

If they were running this op themselves, they'd never follow someone straight out of a place like Costa. Another foot man would cover the exit, and the inside operative, if they had put one in to cover the chance of a meet, would leave much later when the target was well away. A third would join on foot to complete the outside team. Once exposed, the inside man would return to the vehicle, burned for that day at least.

This proper tradecraft was far superior to anything Sharon had done before, which impressed her.

They walked into the bar of The Black Swan at bang on 14.10. Johnson was standing at the bar with a small glass of orange juice, so all was good in the world. Sharon found a table in the corner and sat with a view of the door. Tom got a couple of drinks from the bar and joined her. After a couple of minutes, Johnson came over and sat down.

"I need to say I appreciate the way you two have set up this meet. It gives me a great deal of confidence in the future," said Johnson with a serious look on his face.

"I can assure you we will never put you at risk, Pete. With that in mind, let's get the cover story in place. If, by chance, someone known to you interrupts us and trust me, no matter how far you're off your manor, it happens, we need to have a reason for this meeting. Be assured that whenever we meet up, we will carry nothing on us that could identify us if it all goes Pete Tong, and we are not even carrying our phones.

“Do you want us to be your suppliers or customers? You choose, as you know where a meet such as this might fit in with what you do.”

Johnson thought for a few seconds.

“I think you should be potential buyers of a product, albeit in the unlikely event of us being compromised on this or any other meet, I wouldn’t declare that straight away to someone who just came up to me. It would be nothing at all to do with them, but I get the point. There’s no harm at all in having that in our back pockets should it be necessary.”

“Good,” said Tom. “We also have pseudonyms. I am Tom Kirkland, and she is Sharon Garfield. Our first names are the same. Got that?”

Pete repeated the names twice to fix them in his head.

“Right. Let’s get down to business then. However, before we do, I have to set a few ground rules so we all know where we stand. One, and this is important, Pete, you may not act as an agent provocateur. You cannot set up a job just for us to catch someone. There are certain things you may do as what is termed a participating informant.

“You could drive an associate to pick up a load of charlie. You could drive the getaway car on an armed robbery, if that’s all you’re doing. But under no circumstances do you take a more active role, and your participating in the crime must not be essential for it to take place. Without you, it’s still happening, but with you, we know what’s going on, and without your participation, we would not know.

“You would have to tell me in advance, and I would get written authorisation from one of the bosses for you to take part to that degree and that degree only. The bottom line is you tell me exactly what it is you have to do to make it work. Go outside of that remit and you will be right royally screwed and get no support from us. Is that clear?"

"Yes, clear and understood," said Johnson.

"The other thing to note is this. We have to register you in the system for your own protection. I, Sharon, and our boss will be the only ones who can access the information you give us, and we will never reveal your identity. We have a duty of care towards you, and I promise you, if we cannot get a result on a job without revealing who you are, we won't do it.

"As an example of confidentiality, if we were on a job and another person on our team asked where the information had come from, they would be told to sod off. In all honesty, no one would ever ask, but just so you know.

"We would rather lose the job than blow you out. But you always tell us what you know and, between us, we will try to find a way. If we can't, as I say, we will not progress it. Please remember that, because we can often think of ways to make something work that you may not think of. All understood?"

"Yes," said Johnson.

"OK, what have you got then, Pete?"

"How would you fancy fifty keys of charlie in the boot of a car in north London?"

"I'd prefer it to be fifty keys of charlie in the boot of a car in Surrey, but beggars can't be choosers, Pete," said Tom, unfazed by the quantity mentioned.

"This is coming in from Amsterdam. I will know where it will be parked awaiting collection in north London, but I don't know which ferry it's coming across on. It will just be some stooge driving the car across for a wage and another stooge driving it from the car park to the buyer, the name of which I don't know."

"And how do you know this?" said Sharon, wanting to get involved. Tom didn't mind. He wanted her involved in the clean stuff. The shady bits? He'd handle those himself when the time came.

"I know a mate of the guy driving it across who is party to all the information except the details of the car and actual ferry it will be on. The driver himself probably doesn't know that yet either. The suppliers keep that bit back for security reasons. It's what I would do if I were in their shoes. I'm pretty comfortable that I'll know the details of the vehicle once it's parked up in the car park though. Once the driver who brought it across has parked it up, that's him done. He goes off into the sunset, picks up his dosh, and disappears without asking questions.

"I would add," said Johnson, "that the run from the car park is likely to be carried out in the morning rush hour. There's less chance of a random tug then because of the weight of traffic. I don't know this for sure, and I won't be able to find that out, but I'm just telling you how I would do it."

"OK," said Tom. "We will think about how to deal with this when we get back to the office but, to be sure, if we sat on this vehicle and just took the gear off the street rather than make it too complicated by following it to the buyer, would that cause you a problem?"

"No," said Johnson.

"OK. Leave it with us for now and we'll get back to you with a plan and anything else we need. There will be more questions we'll need to ask. Give Sharon your phone, and she'll plumb in her number so you have it in case you can't get me at any time. We'll leave now. You give it ten minutes before you leave."

Sharon put her number in his phone, and they left.

They walked along in silence, hand in hand, with individual thoughts spinning around their heads. Sharon knew she was a great surveillance operative and had taught Tom plenty. She could now see what a good source handler Tom was and how much she could learn from him. He won't be a detective forever, she thought. One day, the security services will snap him up.

After another bit of dry cleaning on the way back to the car, they retrieved their personal stuff from the boot and drove back to the office, Sharon at the wheel again.

"What are your thoughts operation-wise, Sharon? Let's brainstorm this for a while. How do you think we should play it? What are our options?"

Sharon nodded, eyes on the road.

"OK. First, how close is the source, and how do we make sure we never expose him?

"Second, do we sit on this ourselves and take it out, or do we try to follow it to the buyer? It'd be nice to know who it's going to, but it's risky. That's a lot of gear, mate, and we can't afford to lose it.

"Third, if we knew the details of the vehicle, we could hand it over to the SOCA so they could involve the Dutch and take it to the pickup point. But we don't yet.

"Also, North London is not on our manor. Protocol says we hand it to the locals. If the buyer were in Surrey, and we knew that for sure, then maybe we could justify keeping it in-house, but that's a big if. This would be an expensive operation with lots of overtime for a lump of gear that could even go north and nowhere near our own ground.

"This wouldn't even be Jamie's call. And you know as well as I do, if the Superintendent gets wind of it, which he will have to at some stage, he'll want it dealt with by anyone else but us and out of our hands tout suite before any cock-up gets anywhere near him.

"We could lump a tracker on the motor, but we both know the potential issues there. How many times have we done that because the target was surveillance-conscious, and when the foot man got to the stop, all we had was an empty vehicle and no sign of the target?

"You can't even risk an OP on the hoof. There would be every chance of your picking the premises with the target inside and blowing the whole thing.

"We could get the TSU guys to screw the motor to make sure the gear's in the boot, but we do not know if they have put any devices in, on, or near the car to check if the old bill were all over it like one of your cheap suits. It would be ideal if we knew the gear was in the boot but, I guess, we just have to trust the info.

"I'm rambling a bit here, Tom, but I'm guessing you're having similar thoughts?"

"Yes, I am. Let's sort out the registration, paperwork, and all that bollocks, and then run it all past Jamie."

They sat in thought for the rest of the journey, both content with the silence except for the engine and road noise. The tyres hissed over damp tarmac, worn-out windscreen wipers squeaking intermittently as the drizzle came and went. The low hum from the engine filled the cabin, steady and unobtrusive.

Tom leaned his head against the window, watching the hedgerows blur into grey-green smears. His mind wasn't idle; he was already running scenarios, weighing risks, mentally drafting the version of events Jamie would accept without raising an eyebrow. Sharon drove with one hand on the wheel, the other resting on her thigh, fingers twitching now and then as if scrolling through invisible files. She didn't speak, didn't need to.

Tom already knew how he wanted to play this. He thought he could steer Jamie towards tasking the source to determine the destination of the gear. If the source confirmed Surrey as the end point, they'd have a legitimate reason to keep the job in-house and avoid handing it to anyone else. The tasking just needed to look like Jamie's idea. Johnson, once Tom had him alone and briefed him, would repeat whatever he was told to.

Of course, the gear likely headed for Surrey. Otherwise, why would Johnson know about it? Time would tell.

He would push to keep it in-house once he sorted that bit. To reduce the risk of losing the gear or exposing the source, they'd strike when the vehicle moved in the car park. Clean, fast, no noise. Fifty keys in the bin. Thank you. Good night. And down to The Ship at the bottom of Sandy Lane in Guildford to celebrate, stone-baked pizza, decent Guinness, and no one asking them to sing.

After that, if they confirmed Surrey, they could task the source again to discover the buyer's identity and separately target him if they could do so. Wouldn't it be lovely if it were Falstead? That would simplify things. Or complicate them beautifully. If he were fifty keys down and out of pocket, he'd be in deep shit.

Tom smiled to himself and chuckled. He was in a world of his own.

Sharon smiled too, and thought, What are you scheming, you sly bugger?

When they were on the M25, Tom phoned the DI.

"It's Tom. Are you still in the office, guvnor?" he said when it answered.

"Yes, Tom, but I was about to go home to my darling wife. Supper is in the oven, and there's a lovely bottle of Sancerre, the crisp whisper of the Loire Valley in a glass, in the fridge."

"Do you mind hanging on for a bit? Sharon and I have just had a meeting, and we've got a big job we need to put to you."

"How long will you be? Please don't tell me it's a call-out for the team, Tom. After the day I've had at this bloody budget meeting, I could do without that."

Tom looked at Sharon. She mouthed, "Thirty minutes."

"Half an hour. And no, it isn't."

"OK, thank God for that. I'll hang on. See you when you get here."

Tom hung up and muttered, "Those bosses would be happy if we kicked a door in every morning, recovered two ounces of puff, and didn't incur a penny in overtime or expenses. It makes my blood boil."

Sharon just sat in silence. When he started ranting, it was best to let him get on with it.

They got back to the office and went to see Jamie.

"Come in, guys. What have you got?" said Jamie.

They ran the whole thing past him and let him absorb it.

Jamie sat there for a good couple of minutes before saying, "If I go to Superintendent Blake with this as is, you know what he's going to say, don't you?"

"Yes," said Tom. "Hand it over to the locals or even SOCA."

"Exactly," said Jamie. "What are the chances of the source finding out where the gear's going?"

"I don't know," said Tom, "but we could task him with finding out."

"OK, Sharon, you get him registered. Tom, you call the source and task him. We'll see where that gets us by tomorrow evening. With a bit of luck, I can go to Blake with something that lets us keep this job in-house, and he won't make us pass it on. I'll call Karen and tell her you two aren't on the plot tomorrow and are doing something else. For now, unless I say otherwise, you're both running this job full-time.

"Assuming we keep it, I'm leaning towards hitting it static, not taking it mobile. We wait until the driver gets there so there's a body with the job, even though he will know nothing. We cannot afford to lose that amount of charlie. But we'll make a final decision once we've got all the info. If we take it mobile, we'll lump the motor as backup and run it conventionally. We'll throw as many crews at it as we can find, and I'll come out to play too. We could get seven or eight cars out there if we single-crew a couple. If it looks like it's going squirrelly, we'll just take it out. Anyway, I'm thinking aloud, and that decision's for another day."

Sharon left the office to sort out the admin.

Jamie glanced over Tom's shoulder, checked Sharon was out of earshot, and then looked Tom square in the eyes. He sat forward, lowered his voice and said, "We need the source to tell you it's coming to Surrey. You get me, Tom? Let me add that that's as far as I'm prepared to go, Tom. Everything else gets played straight down the line."

Tom thought, you're a step ahead of me, you smart arse. You earned the title of DI, and for good reason.

"I understand, guv," said Tom with just a hint of a smile. He turned and walked out of the office.

Tom walked out to the car on the pretext of retrieving something. He called Johnson when he was well out of earshot of the office.

"Tom," said Johnson.

"Pete, I'm by myself at the moment since Sharon is taking care of the administrative work regarding you, so we can talk freely."

"I understand, Tom, and assume that's so you can keep hold of this job and not pass it on. I know I would have no say in this, but I would prefer that to happen anyway. By the way, am I looking at a lump of cash for this? What's the payout on this kind of job these days? Fifty keys of charlie has got to be worth a big lump. I want more than a pat on the back and a Sainsbury's voucher, Tom."

Tom gave a half-smile, the kind that reached his eyes. He'd wondered when Pete would raise this.

"It's still discretionary, Pete, and still a bloody mystery until the job's jobbed. But if it lands clean and we keep it in-house, you might see ten grand, maybe even fifteen. We've got our DI right behind this, and he's one of the good guys."

"That's OK. I can live with that. Can I assume you want a piece of it?"

"Abso-bloody-lutely not, Pete. I can assure you one hundred percent I want nothing from you like that in the future, and you are never to raise such a thing again. Am I clear?"

"For sure. Don't get offended, just thought I'd ask. You know that some of your colleagues are taking 'halvos' when they're dishing out the dosh?"

"I do, but all in good time, matey. We can deal with those sorts of people at some stage in the future maybe, but for now, let's concentrate on getting this first one done and then we'll see where we go next.

And remember, nothing other than straight as a die if Sharon is in the conversation. That's important."

"OK, Tom. Understood. I can see this blossoming into a solid long-term relationship."

"Me too," said Tom. "But softly, softly catchy monkey though, Pete." He hung up.

Tom walked back into the office where Sharon was on her laptop registering the source.

"Bloke just offered me half the reward. Cheeky bugger."

"Surely not," said Sharon, glancing at him with a slack jaw.

"He did. Anyway, I put him straight. You need to know the offer was made and, obviously, in the strongest terms possible, it was rejected. We won't put it in a contact sheet though, or they'll make us ditch him."

They tidied up a couple of loose ends and called it a day.

Chapter Nine

Tuesday 2nd March 2010

Sharon picked up Tom at nine-thirty the next day, and they drove to the office. At bang on nine-forty-five, Tom's mobile vibrated. It was Johnson, on time as instructed.

"Morning," said Tom as he turned on the loudspeaker so Sharon could hear.

"Morning, Tom. The gear is coming south to Surrey. I don't yet know who it's destined for, but at some stage, maybe I can find that out. I would need to wait until the car is parked up and the driver's nominated before that bit is possible. And it might not be until after you've got it and word gets around.

"If it were me, I'd have the stooge park it in Guildford. A side road near flats, close to the station. Somewhere commuters leave their cars during the day. Nothing flashy, nothing clapped-out, just a standard family motor.

"I would want to keep a view on it for a day or so before the next move into a lock-up. I'm just giving you what I can from this side of the fence, so to speak, so you can look at it from all angles. Even though I think you'll take it out in the car park.

"I also think I'll be able to give you a day, or even a couple of days' notice on the plans for the run south, as they will want it sat there for a while to let the dust settle before moving it."

"OK," said Tom, looking at Sharon. "If you think of anything else, call me. By the way, if I ever call and you don't answer, I'll assume you can't talk; just call me back as soon as you can. If I don't answer, call me back later, or if it's urgent, call Sharon. OK?"

"Understood," said Johnson, and he hung up.

"Well," said Tom. "That's sorted that bit out. We'll tell Jamie when we get to the office."

"Are you thinking the same as me, Tom? It's too clean. Like someone laid it out for us."

"I'm with you. This is all a bit too good to be true. No vehicle details yet. He won't get them until it's parked. Plenty of notice for the run south."

He was nodding his head, looking at Sharon.

"This could be a 'who's running who' situation here. But fifty keys of charlie is not to be sniffed at. As long as we keep that in the back of our minds, and I'm sure Jamie's clocked it too, even if he won't say it out loud, unless we are told otherwise, we just run with it and see where it takes us. Pete must be closer to this than he's saying, but not close enough to cause him an issue if the gear's seized."

"What if the driver fingers Johnson as the supplier?"

"That won't happen, Sharon. Pete's not that stupid. If he has set this whole thing up, whoever is due to be driving that gear south will not know Pete's name."

Tom felt the familiar itch at the base of his neck, the one that came when things lined up too neatly. Fifty keys. Enough to make reputations, or bury them if it all went tits-up.

The main office was empty when they got there, so they went to Jamie and updated him on the new information.

"OK," said Jamie, "Sharon, you update the contact sheets. I'll read them so I've got everything and then see Blake. What's his pseudonym?"

"Spaceman."

"OK. Tom, you stay here as I want to discuss another matter. Close the door on the way out, Sharon."

He waited for Sharon to leave and said, "Off the record, Tom, what are your real thoughts?"

Tom thought for a few seconds. The silence hung in the air between them. Jamie was far too smart to fill that void and waited for Tom to speak.

"Well," he said, "we have here a 'who's running who' situation. He's a very smart cookie. He followed the meet rules to the letter and, during the meet, said that he appreciated our security and how we'd set it up. I think Johnson is much closer to this than he's saying. He thinks he's running the show and pulling the wool over our eyes."

"I'm glad you think that," said Jamie, "because, from the outside, that's what it is. However, that does not stop us from running with it and taking this gear off the streets. You're good at this, Tom. I just needed to know you see it clearly and aren't blinkered.

"Fortunately, and this is between us, Blake is too stupid to notice. However, if the evidence leads us down the path of Johnson's deeper involvement, then he just gets nicked."

"I see it for what it is, guvnor, and can assure you, if he needs nicking at any stage, then I'll be first through the door. Having said that, I believe he is, long term, going to be a great source. I just need to keep a good handle on him, keep him under control and keep him boxed in. Also, as I said to him last night, softly, softly, catchy monkey. One job at a time.

"On another note, guv, he's going to be due a decent lump of cash for this if it comes off. Ten or fifteen grand seems about right for fifty keys. What do you think?"

"I'm with you on that," said Jamie. "That's the one pot that still has a chunk in it and, try as he might, Blake can't get his hands on it and divert it elsewhere."

"We have to get the job home first, but I wanted to flag it early so you know he's got it in his mind."

"No problem. You will have my full support.

"Another thing, Tom." Jamie contemplated his words, then said, "I am a very practical copper, Tom, and understand how difficult this area of policing can be. It's not always possible to follow the rules to the letter, and a certain amount of, shall we say, sometimes, flexibility is required.

"Sometimes you need to be a bit deaf when a source says something they shouldn't, or admits something that could land you both in it. But I need to know how much flexibility has been exercised at all stages to cover your back if it goes tits-up. You already know this, but very often, the better the snout, the more slippery they can be."

"Also, Sharon is less experienced in this area and, as far as I can judge, would not be as flexible as you or I would be. I flag this up because I suggest certain things may well be best shared between you and me that Sharon would struggle with. I'm not saying for a second that you cut her out of this, but she doesn't need to know everything that goes on."

"Understood, guv." He hesitated for a second and then said, "In the interests of full disclosure then, he offered me harvos last night. Just dropped it in, casual as fuck."

"Oh, for God's sake," said Jamie.

"I told him to sod off and never raise it again."

"You didn't put that on a contact sheet, did you?" Jamie's voice carried a flicker of panic.

"No, not a chance, but I told Sharon."

"That's OK. She knows it goes on anyway."

"I don't think she does. Johnson does, and can tell us who wants it from their snouts, but I've told him that's all in good time."

"OK, we'll keep that in our back pockets for now then and keep our eyes on the prize in front of us. Good job, Tom. By the way, call me after hours if you need to. Day, night, weekends, whatever. It doesn't matter."

"Understood, guv," said Tom, standing up to leave.

"One last thing. Does anyone else on the squad know you've turned him?"

"No, Sharon, but no one else, not even Karen."

"OK, keep it that way."

"Understood," said Tom.

He walked into the main office, waved at Sharon and said, "I'm going over to the canteen for a coffee. You coming?"

"I'll just finish this contact sheet and be over in a tick," she said without looking up, typing with her two index fingers.

Tom stepped out, the door clicking shut behind him, thoughts still circling. Jamie was sharp, razor-sharp. A solid copper with the job stitched into his bones. Practical, no-nonsense, and comfortable operating in that grey area many coppers won't tread. That bit about flexibility hadn't just been reassurance; it was cover. If Tom ever had to meet Pete one-on-one, and he was bound to, and got spotted, unlikely but not impossible, he could lean on that line. Tell Jamie the source wanted to raise something Sharon might not stomach. That gave him room. Not carte blanche, but enough to manoeuvre. A quiet nod from Jamie, tucked away for later. One of those little nuggets you don't spend straight away, you keep it in your back pocket until it's needed.

Of course, Jamie could always deny the conversation. They'd been alone, but he had said it. All of it. Which meant he trusted Tom. That was another bonus.

There's bent, and then there's bent. What he was now doing, he could justify to himself. 'Common cause corruption' it was called. Tom didn't like that term. It was for 'the greater good' in his mind now. But a one-way street, info flowing from the team to the bad guys? That was proper bent. No grey area there. He told himself that wasn't what he was doing.

Tom walked into the canteen and spotted Stevie Coates from TSU sitting alone.

"Billy No Mates today, Stevie?" he said, grinning as he strolled over.

"Hello, Tommy," Steve replied, brushing off the banter. "Haven't seen you in ages. I thought you'd retired."

"I've been too busy to sit around drinking coffee all day like you, mate. Fancy another one?" Tom said, pointing at Stevie's cup.

"No, I'm good. I'm only halfway through this one."

"You couldn't fit another in, you've had so much," said Tom, chuckling.

Tom grabbed a coffee and dropped into the seat opposite. "So, what do you know then, Stevie?"

"You know me, Tom; I know everything. But if I told you, I'd have to kill you."

Just then, Sharon walked in and joined them. As she sat down, Stevie stood up.

"Nothing personal, Sharon," said Stevie as he got up from the table, "but I've got to see a man about a dog. Catch you two another time."

"See you," they said in unison.

Sharon turned to Tom, her face like thunder.

"What was that all about?"

"What?" said Tom, eyebrows raised in mock confusion. He knew what she meant; he just fancied winding her up.

"Don't 'what' me, Tom. You know what," she snapped, jaw clenched.

"Jamie just wanted to make sure we were running the source, not the other way around. That's all," said Tom, arms out, palms upwards.

"What, for twenty bloody minutes? Don't you dare cut me out of this, Tom Kessler. I won't stand for it."

"Easy, tiger. Slow down. Wrong time of the month or something?"

Sharon's eyes flared. "Don't you dare go there, you shithouse. That is bang out of order."

She shot up so fast her chair skidded backwards and clattered to the floor. The canteen froze. Then, as she stormed out, the background hum resumed, lower, warier.

Oops. Crossed a line there.

He grabbed another coffee and let things cool off before heading back into the tiger's den. He got up, picked up the chair and went to the queue.

As he queued, a voice behind him piped up: "What was that little hissy fit all about, Tom? Thought I'd walked into bloody EastEnders."

A few chuckles rippled through the canteen. Tom forced a smile, but the knot in his stomach tightened. He knew he'd gone too far.

"Just squad dynamics, mate. You know how it is," he muttered, slinking back to his seat.

Tom drained his coffee and trudged back to the office. Empty.

He glanced out the window. The car was gone.

Bollocks. She's gone off without me.

He pulled out his phone and rang Sharon. No answer.

Fuck. I deserve this.

Five minutes later, he tried again.

She picked up. "What."

"I'm sorry," said Tom. "That was out of order."

"Oh?" Her voice dripped with irony. "You don't have to live with this shit every bloody month. And what's that got to do with the price of bread, anyway?"

"I'll say it again. I'm sorry. Will you come and get me?"

"No. Sod off. Walk home, you shit."

"Sharon, I can't walk home. And a taxi's forty quid I don't have."

"Get a train then. Bus to the station. Train to Woking. Walk from there. What's your problem?"

"For God's sake, Sharon. Just pick me up, will you? I've said sorry."

"Fifteen minutes. Be ready. I'm not hanging about." She hung up.

Thank fuck for that.

He was outside and waiting when Sharon pulled up. All four wheels locked up as she braked and skidded to a halt.

Tom got in and said, "I'm sorry."

She turned to him and said in a stern voice, "Alright, don't go on about it."

Fuck me. It's like having two wives.

"I'm going to have a day off tomorrow. I'll message Karen and tell her."

"Whatever."

He needed a break from the emotional crossfire that came with working shoulder to shoulder, day after day. From the closeness that masqueraded as comfort.

Until it didn't.

Chapter Ten

Wednesday 3rd March 2010

Tom stirred as Sue got out of bed to sort the children and get them ready for school. Aware he was awake, she said, "What time are you going in?"

Tom rolled onto his back, smiled, and said, "I'm not."

"What are you doing then?" She asked with a puzzled look, pulling on her dressing gown.

"I thought we could have a day together, so I've taken the day off."

"Blimey. What's got into you?" she said.

"No need for that, love. I said I'd try, and I am."

"Sorry. I'm just surprised, that's all."

"How do you fancy seeing the kids off and coming back to bed?"

She paused for a second, then smiled. “It’s been so long I’ve forgotten how to do it, Tom.”

“Well, you get the girls off, then come back to bed and I’ll remind you.”

Sue went downstairs into the kitchen, where the girls were eating breakfast. She didn’t trust the softness in Tom yet, although she wanted to.

Maybe we’ve turned a corner.

“What are you smiling about, Mum?” said Lily.

“Nothing, Lily. Come on, hurry. I want you three of you out of here. I’ve got things to do this morning.”

Once they’d gone, Sue climbed the stairs with a spring in her step. The sound of the shower met her halfway. Don’t get your hopes up, she thought. And don’t expect too much too soon. It’s all probably an act.

Later that morning, as they lay in each other’s arms, Tom said, “What do you fancy doing for the rest of the day? Shall we go out for lunch at The Anchor down by Pyrford Lock? It’s a nice day, and we could sit outside.”

“Great idea,” she said, slipping out of bed with a lightness he hadn’t seen in weeks.

They had lunch together for the first time in ages. He didn’t turn off his phone, and she didn’t ask him to. But it didn’t ring. Not once.

The sun beat down, warm and insistent, and Sue said, “Do you fancy a walk along the canal?”

“Let’s do that. If we time it right, we can drive home, then walk to meet the girls from school. They’ll be surprised to see us.”

As they walked hand in hand along the canal, Sue thought, This can’t be happening. We haven’t done this in years. Her skin tingled in the heat of the sun.

Birds flitted through the hedgerows, their songs threading the silence. Ripples danced across the water, painting shifting reflections of the sky. She hadn't felt like this in a long time. Not just content, but happy.

Nothing needed to be said as they drove home in silence. Lost in their own thoughts, each wished the day could stretch on forever. Tom had needed this. Maybe it showed. Maybe it meant something. He couldn't believe how easily the noise had faded. No mental checklists, no operational puzzles demanding attention. For once, he'd pushed it all aside, just long enough to give Sue the attention she deserved.

They parked the car at home and sauntered to the school gates. The girls were surprised to see them, even though they were less enthusiastic than Tom had hoped. He expected too much. Teenage girls wrapped up in their own existence, selfish, but not in a bad way. That's just the way they are at that age.

They were walking back towards home, Tom and Sue hand in hand, the girls trailing behind, phones out, messaging friends they'd only just left, when Tom became aware of the crunch of tyres on gravel. A black Range Rover with tinted windows pulled up alongside them, and the hairs on the back of Tom's neck stood up.

He moved fast. He pushed Sue behind him, instinct kicking in before thought.

"Get behind your mother, girls," Tom said in a commanding voice, without looking back.

They did as they were told, sensing this was not the time to ask why.

John Falstead stepped out of the rear seat, calm as ever, with a sickly smile on his face. One minder climbed out of the driver's side and took position on his left. The other circled round from the passenger side, flanking Falstead's right. Both had their hands clasped in front of them like a couple of nightclub bouncers, which is what they were now he'd bought the nightclub in Guildford. They could have been twins. No words. Just a well-practised formation.

All three wore dark suits and sunglasses. The minders had black shirts; Falstead's was white, a subtle show of who was in charge. Tom checked up and down the road for other people, in case he needed witnesses. He did not fancy their being the only ones on the road and vulnerable to this man's presence.

"Hello, Tom," said Falstead, removing his sunglasses. "This is your dear lady wife, Sue, and your beautiful girls. Maya, Lily, and Evie, isn't it?"

He said it in a sarcastic, questioning tone, but it was rhetorical. He'd done his background checks.

"What do you want?" said Tom, in a tone neither Sue nor the girls had heard him use before.

"I was just passing, saw you, and thought it would be nice to stop and say hello, Tom," said Falstead, arms out, palms up in a faux show of friendliness.

Tom was well into work mode now. "Well, I don't want to talk to you, so get back in your motor and fuck off."

He didn't see them, but the language their father used shocked the girls. The odd mutter under his breath, yes, but never like this. Sue and the girls had never seen Tom this aggressive either, and it scared them. It was as if someone had flicked a switch and his personality had changed. He was standing with his legs set wider than normal, arms by his sides, fists clenched, a man primed and ready to protect his family if the need arose.

"Oh dear, oh dear. Language, Tom, please. Not in front of the family. What must they be thinking?" Falstead's tone dripped with sarcasm.

Falstead stepped forward. The heavies didn't budge. They were now in an arrow formation. Tom didn't move an inch.

Falstead stared him straight in the eye with a vicious glint. "Our little..." he paused for a couple of seconds "...interaction over the last few months has been a bit of a distraction for me, Tom. I feel the need to explain to you, in no uncertain terms, that a bit of breathing space would be in the best interest of both our families. Am I making myself clear?"

He looked past Tom, locking eyes with Sue and the girls.

Tom was furious, though he masked it well. "Let me make one thing clear to you, you piece of shit. If you, or anyone connected to you, or anyone who lives in the same fucking postcode as you, comes anywhere near my family, I will make it my life's work to fuck up the lives of you and your goons forever. Am I making myself clear? Now, get back in your motor and fuck off."

Falstead stepped in, too close. Tom shoved him back. The minders tensed, but Falstead raised a hand, smirking. "Easy, tiger. Just a friendly chat."

He didn't flinch. He adjusted his cuff as if Tom's shove were a gust of wind. "Still so reactive, Tom. That's what makes you predictable."

As he took a pace backwards, Falstead made a point of looking up and down the road, then back at Tom. "It's a pity there are so many people around, Tom. It would have been nice to continue our conversation but, hey-ho. There's always another time, eh?"

He turned back to the Range Rover. One minder opened the rear door for him; the other got into the driver's seat. Tom and his family stood watching as the door closed. A split second later, the rear window rolled down to reveal Falstead's smiling face.

"Bye for now, Tom. See you soon."

Falstead turned his head forward as his sunglasses rose towards his face and the smile vanished. The window rolled up, and the vehicle drove away to the sound of crunching gravel fading into the distance.

Tom turned. They were all looking at him with frightened eyes.

"Right. Home. Now. As fast as we can."

They walked in total silence.

Fuck, I did not need that. I didn't see them, and that confrontation was no coincidence. They must have been following us for God knows how long, and I didn't spot them. My guard was down, and my failure to keep alert has put my family at risk. I cannot and will not let that happen again.

When they got home, Tom ushered them into the sitting room like a shepherd corralling his flock from a storm. No one spoke. The air was thick with shock, the kind that makes even familiar rooms feel foreign. They had just crossed a threshold into his world.

"I'm sorry you had to witness that," Tom said, his voice low, almost hoarse.

Lily sat on the edge of the sofa, her knuckles white around her phone. "Who was that, Dad?" she asked, above a whisper.

"His name is John Falstead," Tom said. "He's not a very nice person. My team arrested him a while back. He walked free, dodgy defence, slick lawyers. He's held a grudge ever since. Today was his way of reminding me."

"I'm frightened, Dad," Evie said, her voice cracking. Something tore inside him.

“I know, sweetheart. I’m so, so sorry,” he said, crouching in front of her. His eyes were glassy, fists clenched. Rage and guilt churned inside him like acid. But he couldn’t afford to unravel. Not now.

“There’s no need to be frightened, Evie. Or any of you,” he said, forcing calm into his voice. “I’ll sort this. I promise. Now, girls, upstairs. I need to speak to Mum. And listen to me: no messages, no gossip, no telling friends. This stays in this house. Do I make myself clear?”

“Yes, Dad,” they said in unison, voices hollow. They climbed the stairs like shadows, and one by one, bedroom doors clicked shut. Silence fell.

Sue turned to him, her face pale and tight.

“What the actual fuck, Tom?” she said, her voice trembling. “What just happened? I’ve never seen you like that. You scared me.”

“I didn’t see it coming,” Tom said. “I let my guard down. That’s on me.”

“Who is he? He looked like something out of a gangster film. Range Rover, goons, the whole bloody package.”

“He’s the one who walked free. Falstead. And now he’s made it personal. He’s crossed a line.”

Sue’s eyes flared. “Then you don’t make it personal. Tell him to stay away. Tell him we’re not part of this.”

Tom shook his head. “It doesn’t work like that. If he had wanted to hurt us, he wouldn’t have stopped to chat. He’d have done it. The ones who talk are the ones who want you to know they’re watching. It’s the quiet ones you never see coming.”

Sue stared at him, her voice quiet. “So what now? We just wait for the next time?”

“No,” Tom said, pulling out his phone. “Now I call Jamie. And then I make sure there isn’t a next time.”

“This is the first time this has entered the lives of me and the girls, Tom, and I’m not prepared to put up with it. I have never seen you like that, and I didn’t like it. It was like you changed into another person I didn’t know existed.

“I’m not prepared to deal with this sort of thing, so get it sorted.”

“I will. I promise.”

Sue didn’t reply. She turned and walked upstairs, her footsteps slow and heavy. Tom stood alone in the sitting room, the weight of two worlds pressing down on his shoulders.

“Guvnor, it’s Tom. I need to tell you something that just happened whilst Sue and I were walking the girls back from school,” Tom relayed the incident to Jamie.

Jamie took it all in and said he needed some time to process it and would call him back.

Fifteen minutes later, Tom’s mobile vibrated.

“Right. Stevie’s on his way to your gaff now, Tom. He’ll put in a panic alarm and install some outside security cameras. I’ve contacted the local Superintendent at Woking to tell him what’s going on, and he’ll make sure that, for the foreseeable future, patrols bear in mind your HA and the school at kicking-out time. I’ve told him a panic alarm is being installed and that if it goes off, they need to get there fast. There’s a uniform car on its way to you now to sit outside until Stevie’s done his magic.

“I’ve told Blake, and he’s in total agreement that, if at any time you need to stay with the family instead of coming into work, then that’s what you do. It doesn’t matter if they are one light on a plot; they will cope, and Sharon can run solo. I have to say, he was supportive of you and suggested we target this bloke and put him away for as long as we can. He surprised me with that one. I didn't think he had it in him. Let's make this go away by banging the guy up. He's attacked the police family, Tom, and has pissed off the wrong people.

"With that in mind, can I assume your current source is aware of this guy and we could task him if necessary?"

"Thanks for all of this, Jamie. That's a lot to achieve in fifteen minutes, and I appreciate it. I'll never forgive myself for letting my guard down and putting the family in danger. And yes, I'm sure the source will know Falstead. How close he's likely to be I don't know, but I'll find out."

"Tom, you can't have your guard up all the time, mate. You'd burn out in no time. What's happened is unacceptable, and we will sort it out as a team. The guys had a result on their job today, so I'll make sure everyone's in the office tomorrow morning for a briefing on this. If we can get this North London job out of the way ASAP, then we can all concentrate on Falstead.

"I think, under the circumstances, it would be fortuitous if, by chance, you bumped into the snout at some stage when you're on your own. Don't you?"

"Understood. I'm on it. Before you go, guvnor, could you do me a favour and call Sharon and tell her what's going on? I've got a lot on my plate here, and I don't want to go through this again with her this evening. If you ask her to pick me up at about eight-thirty, as long as it's OK with you, we'll give the girls a ride to school on the way to the office."

"Not a problem, Tom," and Jamie hung up.

Upstairs, the house was quiet. Too quiet.

He climbed the stairs slowly, pausing outside the bedroom he shared with Sue. The door was ajar. She was sitting on the edge of the bed, her back to him, shoulders hunched, hands clasped in her lap.

"I spoke to Jamie," Tom said. "They're on it."

Sue didn't turn around. "Good."

He stepped inside, unsure whether to sit or stand. "I meant what I said. I'll sort this."

She nodded, but her voice was flat. "I know you will. That's not the point."

Tom waited.

Sue looked up, her eyes tired. "You keep saying you'll protect us. And I believe you. But what I saw today, that version of you, I don't know how to live with that. I don't want the girls growing up thinking that's normal."

"It's not," Tom said. "It's not who I am day to day."

"But it is who you are when the line gets crossed," she replied. "And that line seems to follow you everywhere."

Tom didn't respond. There was nothing to say that wouldn't sound like justification.

Sue stood, brushing past him. "I'm not leaving. Not yet. But I need you to understand something, Tom. I won't live in fear. And I won't let the girls grow up in it either."

She walked out, leaving him alone in the room.

Tom sat down on the edge of the bed, elbows on knees, head in hands.

Falstead hadn't just crossed a line.

He'd drawn one right through the middle of Tom's family.

Tom sat in contemplation for a few minutes whilst he got his head around it all, leaning forward with his elbows on his knees and his hands over his face.

Chapter Eleven

Wednesday 3rd March 2010 – evening

"Tom. How are you?" said Pete.

"Not good, Pete. I need to see you urgently. Could you be in the St George's Hill Golf Club car park in exactly one hour? Far left-hand corner." Tom glanced at his watch. "Say six-fifteen? Don't ask me what it's about. I'll tell you face to face. Our lot are definitely not behind you, mate, but have a look to be sure no one's on your tail before we meet up. Any issues, then call or message me and we'll rearrange. This is urgent, but we still have to do the important things to make sure we're clean."

"OK. No problem," he said, and hung up.

What a pleasure to deal with a snout that does as he's told. This one's worth hanging on to.

Twenty minutes later, the doorbell rang. It was Stevie with a pile of kit.

"Thanks for this, mate, come in," said Tom. "What a shit-show."

"No problem, Tom. You know I drop everything when it's one of our own," said Stevie with a serious look on his face. No canteen banter this time.

He introduced Stevie to Sue and told her to let him do whatever he needed to do.

He took Sue to one side and said, out of earshot of Stevie, "Stevie's one of the good guys, love. Let him do everything he needs to do. I have to go out for a bit but will probably be back before he's finished. If I'm not back in time, he'll show you how all this works before he leaves. The local nick have put a marked car outside until Stevie's finished."

"I'm frightened, Tom," said Sue, her expression tight with worry.

"I know, love, and I'm sorry the job has encroached on our lives like this, but it will all be OK. You'll see."

Tom gave her a big hug, then held her by the tops of her arms and pulled her close for a kiss.

He let her go and said, "I'll be back as soon as I can."

"Where are you going?" she asked.

"Best you don't know. I promise. I'll be back as soon as I can."

Tom drove to the golf club. He was calm enough now to do his own dry cleaning and was 100% sure he was clean before he drove into the car park at ten minutes past six. He parked in the bottom left-hand side and got a view of the entrance.

It was silent in this corner of the car park, miles from the main road. He could hear the gentle twitter of a few birds, and that was it. The golf club was right in the middle of the vast area of high-end properties on the St George's Hill estate, just outside Weybridge, and not frequented by many non-members.

The only copper likely to show up here was the Chief Constable, and even then, only if he fancied a freebie round of golf. Tom wasn't sure he'd recognise him, anyway. Then again, he wouldn't recognise a villain either.

He didn't see Pete driving his BMW, but he was aware of a nice, silver SL500 Mercedes that pulled in at six-fifteen.

That's him.

The car parked next to him, and Pete got out. Tom stepped out of his own vehicle, and they walked away towards a shaded area. They just appeared to a casual observer to be a couple of guys who'd finished a round of golf and were chatting before leaving.

"We'll be doing a lot more of these solo meets, Pete, even though we are supposed to be doubled up. Your story can be that I'm your pet copper. Your cover is the most important one here. But if ever any old bill, the rubber heel squad or such like, ever try to speak to you about us talking, you just tell them you don't know what they're talking about. Clear?"

"Clear," said Pete in his usual precise manner.

"Why the Merc, by the way?" said Tom, nodding at it.

"I got a mate to park this at the end of that alleyway opposite the football club, down that new road by where the old Sea Scouts hut used to be, it's houses now, and put the keys under the visor. I parked my Beemer at the other end, in Chestnut Grove, ran through, jumped in this, and drove off. Even your lot couldn't cope with that, Tom."

Tom smiled. "You're right; we'd struggle. But don't get too cocky, and don't pull the same stunt too often. If you build a pattern, you'll get overconfident and mess it up."

"Got it," said Pete.

Tom then went through the afternoon's events. Pete took it all in with a serious expression and the occasional shake of the head.

"That is bang out of order, Tom. Families are well off-limits."

"I know, mate, and I am ticking like a nine-bob watch. He's crossed the line, and I want him sorted, Pete. I don't care how we do it, but we fit the guy up big-style. Tuck him up like a kipper and put him away for an endless stretch. The rules have changed. Now, there are no rules. You get me?"

"I get you."

"If we could have got hold of those fifty keys of charlie in North London without anyone knowing and put them in his house, I would have done. That's how much I want this bloke banged up. To a fair degree, we have the support of my DI for this. He wouldn't support putting fifty kilos of charlie in the bloke's gaff, mind, but he will allow us to bend the rules a little. If it really goes tits-up, expect everyone to do a bomb burst and leave us on our own.

"And don't forget, Sharon must know nothing iffy at all. We'll work out a good time and way to do this but, to keep her onside and so she doesn't feel as though she's being pushed out, we manufacture you not being able to get hold of me with something urgent. Probably, off the top of my head, the knowledge that this vehicle with the fifty keys of charlie is in place. I'll be honest with you, Pete. I feel very guilty about how we'll likely treat her with this stuff, but she would never see that what we're doing is for the greater good."

"That's the way you see it, is it?" said Pete, looking Tom in the eyes.

"I do. Don't start making me doubt myself now, matey."

"OK, Tom. In line with your thoughts on this then, I should have more on that North London caper tomorrow or the next day. In the meantime, I'll get my head around all of this and put my thinking cap on. No promises here, but straight off the bat, what if I set him up with two hundred and fifty thousand MDMA from the INLA in Northern Ireland?"

"You are a crafty bugger, Pete. Happy pills from the Irish National Liberation Army. How long have you been dealing with them?"

"Don't ask too many questions now, Tom," said Pete with a serious look on his face. "There's a time and a place for the answer to that one. Suffice to say, the INLA is as much a criminal organisation today as it is a paramilitary. Whilst they started off robbing banks and dealing drugs to fund the aims of the organisation, as the violence reduced and the Good Friday Agreement kicked in, they now mainly do it all to line their own pockets."

Tom paused for a few seconds whilst he took in what Pete had said.

"You're a dark horse, Pete, and an intelligent guy. Why have you never gone into legitimate business? You'd have made a fortune."

"Where's the fun in that, Tom? And I've made a fortune anyway," said Pete, with a huge grin on his face.

"OK. Hopefully, you will find out about this job the day after tomorrow so I can have a day's breathing space to sort out this other balls-up," said Tom, looking up to the sky with a thoughtful look on his face.

“Thinking about it, it’s probably going to be tomorrow afternoon or evening that I find out,” said Pete.

Tom turned to him and said, “Look, Pete, I know you’re closer to this than you’re letting on. I don’t want to go into that now, but please don’t take us for a bunch of mugs, mate, because we aren’t. I want this to work, and I can assure you I have never made a call like I made to you to anyone before. This is unfamiliar territory for me, and it comes at a high personal cost.

“You, on the surface, come across as an OK guy but, and I mean this, I can be a good friend to you, but you do not want me, under any circumstances, as an enemy,” Tom paused. “As Falstead is going to find out to his cost. I don’t want this to come across as massively aggressive, Pete, but I need you to understand. OK?”

With his usual brevity, Pete said, “I understand.”

“Tomorrow morning I’m going to be dropping my girls off at school and then going to the office. I’ll be leaving there in time to pick them up too. Sharon will probably drive, so when I’m home, around three-thirty to four, she’ll be alone. I will message you to ask if you have anything for us.

“Wait about half an hour and call me. I won’t answer, so then call Sharon and give her the info. The vehicle with the gear in will be in the car park. You don’t know exactly where, but you know which one. A partial registration number and make of the car may be all you have. You, hopefully, will know when the trip south is happening.

Hopefully, you understand what I mean: enough information to find the vehicle and its movement but not sufficient to take it to Holland, or we must give it to another agency.

“Clear. But understand this situation is fluid. I can only get the information to you once it’s come to me. I can give you an estimate of when I will know, but that’s all it is, an estimate. But be assured, when I know, you will know.”

“Right, OK, got that. Just give her some bullshit if you can’t give her anything solid, just something to make her feel that she’s part of the team. You go first, and I’ll follow in a few minutes.”

Pete gave a double thumbs-up, walked back to the Merc, got in the driver’s seat and drove off without looking back.

Tom sat and pondered the day. It seemed ages ago that he and Sue had been lying in each other’s arms. The warmth of that morning had faded, replaced by the cold mechanics of his working life. Why did that twat Falstead do that? He’s spoilt a lovely day.

He watched the empty road for a moment longer, then stretched. The weight of everything settled back onto his shoulders. Whatever this was, it would not be clean. He’d danced close to the edge before but never fallen off.

And Pete, for all his charm, was a man who smiled while setting fires.

He was careful and would not let his desire to see Falstead sorted lead him into a false sense of security. He repeated to himself that he was in unfamiliar territory and must be extra careful, or he would get locked up, and Falstead would laugh his head off.

That would be unforgivable, as he wouldn’t be able to look after his family.

I think the Scotch bottle may get a bashing this evening.

He drove off, his head still full of different scenarios and knowing this was bound to get messy at some stage.

By the time he got home, Stevie Coates had left, but Sue was sharp and had the panic alarm mapped out in her head with no trouble.

Stevie, though, had gone full bunker-mode with the CCTV cameras everywhere. He'd rigged it so the feed ran through the wi-fi to the sitting room TV, and also to his office at Police Headquarters in Guildford, where every camera recorded twenty-four-seven onto a massive hard drive and to "the cloud". "The cloud" was a new concept to Tom, but Stevie was a top man with technology and had explained that this was off-site storage which the force arranged with Microsoft. Above his pay grade at the moment, but, Stevie said, one day, everyone will use it.

Well, if Headquarters burned down, which wouldn't be a bad thing, he thought, at least any evidence would be safe.

The Scotch bottle got a bit of a bashing that evening, but at least it made Tom sleep.

Chapter Twelve

Thursday 4th March 2010

"I don't want to go," Evie said, still in her pyjamas, arms folded tight across her chest.

Tom looked up from his coffee. "School's not optional, Evie."

"It should be today," Maya muttered, slouched at the kitchen table, phone untouched beside her, a rare thing.

Lily hadn't spoken yet. She was staring out the window, spoon suspended mid-air, cereal untouched.

Sue stepped in, towel over her shoulder, hair damp from the shower. "They're shaken, Tom. You saw their faces last night."

Tom nodded, but didn't reply and replayed every second of the encounter, every angle he'd missed.

"How come he knew our names?" Evie whispered. "He stared right at me."

"He's not coming back," Tom said, more firmly than he felt. "I've made sure of that."

"But you didn't see him coming the first time," Lily said, turning from the window. She spoke softly, but her message landed hard.

Trust me, that won't happen again.

"If we show we're frightened of this man, then he's won," said Tom, trying to stay calm.

"Then he has won, because I am bloody frightened," said Lily.

"Don't swear, Lily, please," said Sue. She was standing with her head in her hands, unable to deal with the situation. She hadn't slept, and it showed.

Tom was heartbroken. He had failed to do what every man on the planet should want to do, protect his family, and he hadn't just failed; he'd failed miserably. He would never forgive himself, and he would never forgive Falstead.

"Sharon and I will take you to school and pick you up. How about that?"

The girls turned to each other and understood this was a battle they couldn't win. It was quiet as they trooped upstairs to get ready.

He turned to Sue. The fury on her face was almost tangible. He put his arms out to comfort her, and she flinched. It was like someone had stabbed him in the heart, physical pain.

"Don't. Just don't," she said and walked out.

Sharon and he took them to school in the job car. Sue was going to call the school later to tell them there had been an "issue" with Tom's job. They knew he was a police detective and no one would press. She instructed them that nobody but she or Tom could take the girls from school, even with a warrant card. If someone tried, they should dial nine-nine-nine. She explained to the girls that they must wait by the school office each day to be picked up, and they must never leave with anyone else. Even if it was a police officer in uniform.

On the way to school, Tom instructed the girls that, until further notice, they should wait to be picked up each day by the school office and never split up. He tried to stay calm and impart these instructions, but they could sense the tension in his voice.

Tom took the girls right into school, scanning for threats. He expected none, but after what happened yesterday, he wouldn't be surprised again. He did it surreptitiously so as not to worry the girls. They appeared to be fine now that they were on perceived safe territory.

Now to deal with Sharon.

As he got into the vehicle, he could see Sharon's knuckles were white as she gripped the steering wheel. She drove in silence and then after a couple of minutes said, "What the actual fuck, Tom."

"Funnily enough, that's, to the word, what Sue said."

"I'm not surprised. What on earth happened?"

Tom went through it all. Sharon said nothing, just drove in silence and took it all in. She shook her head now and then, disbelief etched across her face. This wasn't normal, nowhere near normal, even in their world. When Tom had finished, the silence hung in the air.

"The girls must have been terrified. Weren't they?" said Sharon, with understatement.

"They were, and I'll never forgive myself for switching off for the day. I took the day off because I wanted to show Sue I could at least meet her halfway with things. You know she would jump with glee if I packed the job in, and I understand why. This has done me no good whatsoever in that regard. I was making so much progress, and now this happens.

"So you are aware, both Jamie and Blake have said we will use the source to get into Falstead if he is, or can get, close. We box off this North London job and then see where we are. I am hoping this gear is Falstead's, as he will be in deep shit if it is and it gets seized. I can only assume that once the gear is in the boot of that car in Holland, the responsibility for it is his. If it gets seized, he will have to take some colossal risks to make enough money to pay for it, and that gives us an advantage.

"Let's put the Falstead incident to one side for a while, please, Sharon. I'm done with thinking about it for now and need a sideways step for a while to lower my blood pressure. Every time I recall it, my blood boils.

"I've been thinking about the value of this charlie. I've been doing some research and spoke to my mate Barry Stewardson at SOCA. It would appear the wholesale price has soared over the last year as agencies around the world have made some pretty big seizures. It's wholesaling at just under forty grand a kilo at the moment, so that parcel must have cost about two mil. Then there's whether they'll cut it. Barry said they are just kicking off an op to track large imports of cutting agents like benzocaine, lidocaine and phenacetin. It never occurred to me before that getting hold of the cutting agents in bulk would raise a red flag, but it's obvious when you think about it.

"Anyway, he said, it's early days but, because of that, the distributors are selling more of the gear uncut now, and an uncut individual kilo is going for sixty grand. Assuming it's staying uncut at street level, at eighty quid a gram, that gives our fifty keys a street value of about four mil. Of course, it's always difficult to give an exact street value as, if it's heavily cut, it could be as low as fifty quid a gram."

Tom had been staring straight ahead out of the windscreen, watching the wipers swing back and forth as he reeled off the numbers. He then turned to Sharon and said, "Did you know that, if they can cut a kilo of charlie one-to-one with benzocaine, a key of benzocaine being about three hundred quid, they can get ninety grand a kilo? That's nuts."

Sharon had been absorbing all these numbers; it was always good to know.

"Ninety grand? That's bonkers."

They sat in silence again until they reached the office, each of them analysing the numbers involved in a seizure of this size and the potential implications for the buyer after it had been seized.

The usual hum of the office faded as they walked in. Eyes turned. Conversations stalled.

Jack stood up from his desk. "Are you OK, Tom? Are Sue and the kids alright?"

Karen said, "What happened?"

Questions came from every direction. Tom held up both hands in front of him, palms out, and said, "Wow, wow. Slow down, for God's sake."

It went quiet, and he said, "I can't keep going through it, guys. I imagine Jamie's given you a rundown of what happened, and I don't want to go through it again; it's just too distressing to think of what it put Sue and the girls through. Suffice to say, John Falstead pulled up beside me, Sue and the children whilst we were walking back from school and there was an altercation. Stevie Coates has put a panic alarm in the house and installed more CCTV cameras than are around Fort Knox, so that's covered.

"My understanding is we are going to get this other job done and out of the way and then, hopefully, we can work on Falstead. He's a legitimate target. We can do a bit on him whilst we wait for the other one to kick off."

"Why don't we just kick his door down and show him who's boss? Bastard," said Jack.

"That's not the way to do it, Jack. Do you remember the story about the old bull and the young bull at the top of the field? The young bull says to the old bull, 'Why don't we run down there and fuck one of those cows?' The old bull says, 'Why don't we walk down and fuck them all?' And that's how we need to deal with this little shit."

Just then the DI walked in from the rain and, with a gesture of his hand, said, "Tom, Sharon, my office."

The office door was closed, and they all sat down. Jamie leaned forward, put his forearms on his desk and clasped his hands. "Right," he said with a thoughtful expression on his face. He had a lot to say.

"At his request, I've just been to see the Chief Constable. He, I am pleased to say, is just as concerned about this as we are. However, he wanted me to give him a good reason we didn't hand Falstead over to SOCA for them to deal with."

"For Christ's sake, guvnor. Why is it that all these people, when they get a bit of rank behind them, just want to push problems onto someone else in case it goes tits-up and they catch a bit of the fallout?" said Sharon.

"In this case," he said, looking at Sharon, "I don't think that's the reason. To his credit, and you know my general view on this matter, albeit I don't want it broadcast to all and sundry, I think he has the integrity of the squad, and Tom and his family in particular, at heart here. If we target Falstead and get a result, then the altercation with Tom has to come out. You can predict that the defence will say we fitted him up because Tom has a grudge against him."

He turned to look at Tom and said, "I take it this is all written up in your pocket book, Tom?"

"It is," said Tom.

"Thinking ahead now," said Jamie, leaning back in his chair and clasping his hands behind his head, "I'll get one of the local DCs to pop round to see Sue and get a statement from her whilst all this is still fresh in her mind. I know she will not forget it in a hurry, but from a court point of view, the sooner we get her account in writing, the better. I don't want it to be one of our guys for obvious reasons. Tom, when we've finished here, can you call her to square that off, and are you OK giving me her mobile to pass on to the locals so they can deal with her directly?"

"Yes, to both, guv." He picked up a pad of Post-it notes off the desk and wrote Sue's number.

This will not go down very well.

His hand hesitated over the last digit.

"Taking a sideways step for a minute, do you think we could get a line on Falstead's phones?" said Tom.

"I asked the Chief that," said Jamie, sitting forward again. "He pointed out that, were we to apply for one, SOCA would find out and want to know what we wanted it for, and, if we thought our job was big enough to warrant it, why hadn't we given it to them. By the way, before I went to see him, I ran Falstead through the system, and he isn't flagged to anyone, which is good. I've had one of the analysts flag him to me now. I don't want him flagged to either of you as it would look too personal.

"OK, moving on. Believe it or not, the Chief gave me a special budget on this one, and it's considerable.

We can't take the piss, but we claim every hour we spend on it. I've spoken with Karen, and she's organising the troops to get OPs sorted. She's tasked Lisa and Mo to do his HA and run it until further notice. It appears it's a pleasant area where he lives, which you would expect, of course, with someone at this level. Stevie Coates is also aware and will be available at a moment's notice with all the kit he can muster.

"Whatever we want, we get, and he may suggest things we don't even know about. And if he hasn't got it, he'll borrow it from his mates up in the Met. He also says he'll square off all the paperwork on everything too. Depending on what Lisa and Mo get, we may stick a camera in the OP so we get it twenty-four-seven."

Tom was shaking his head. "You won't get an OP. The houses are too far apart. We'll need a camera."

Just then, there was a knock on the door. It opened, and Karen leaned in, still holding the doorknob with one hand and the doorjamb with the other. "Mo's just called. No chance of an OP on the HA. The houses are just too big and too far apart. We'll need a camera up a telegraph pole opposite."

"No problem," said Jamie. "Call Stevie and he'll get it done. He'll do all the authorisations too."

"Blimey."

She closed the door.

"We'll let Karen deal with all this stuff now, and you both knock off. I'm sure Sue would appreciate you being home this afternoon, Tom, and, Sharon, your phone will be on if you're needed for anything."

Jamie glanced at his watch and said, "Would that work for picking the girls up?"

"Yes, it would, and thanks, guvnor. I appreciate the support from everyone."

Tom had dark rings under his eyes, and his exhaustion showed. As soon as they were in the car, he called Sue to warn her she would get a call from the local CID office about a statement, and to say he would pick up the girls from school. He laid his head back and closed his eyes for a few seconds.

The girls' pick-up was uneventful, and they got out of the vehicle with a quick, "Thanks, Sharon," before disappearing into the house. They hadn't said a word all the way home, and their faces were pale with fear.

Tom was halfway out of the passenger side of the vehicle. "I'm turning my phone off this afternoon, Sharon. I need a break and to concentrate on Sue and the girls for a bit. Having thought about it, I can't see anything happening around the school gates, so Sue can do the run in the morning. I'll see you at about eight-thirty if that works for you?"

Sharon gave him a thumbs-up and, when the door closed, drove off into the distance.

Right. Time to message Pete. Just two words, I'm home.

And he turned off his phone.

Tom went indoors expecting to be met by a very pissed-off Sue. And he was right.

"Did you get a call from the local CID?" said Tom.

"I did, a chap called John Bondey. He's been and gone."

"Crikey, that was quick. I know John. Nice guy. OK, I'm going to have a shower and throw some trackies on. Perhaps after dinner we could watch a film or something? And my phone is off until the morning."

“It won’t work,” said Sharon. Arms folded across her chest and a tough look on her face.

“What won’t work?”

“Trying to be all nice,” said Sue. “Mr bloody nice guy trying to pretend nothing’s happened. It’s too late, Tom. I’m just not sure there’s a way back from this.”

“Do you not think this is a bit of an overreaction, Sue?” said Pete.

“A bit of an overreaction,” she said, looking at the stairs and lowering her voice so the children wouldn’t hear. The steam was coming out of her ears. Her feet stayed planted, but her body leaned towards him so her words would sting more.

“A fucking overreaction. Are you serious? I am fucking terrified. This is not my world you’ve brought us all into. Right now, I don’t know whether I will ever be able to get over this. You said it was an unusual thing to happen. Well, think how we fucking feel.”

She walked off and stomped up the stairs, leaving him dumbstruck. In all their years, he had never seen her so angry. How on earth was he going to pull this back?

Tom stood in the hallway, still holding his keys, the front door closed behind him. Upstairs, Sue’s footsteps echoed, sharp, deliberate, final.

He didn’t move. Didn’t speak. Just listened to the silence that followed.

Then, from the living room:

“Dad?” Maya’s voice. Quiet. Hesitant.

He stepped in. All three girls were there, Evie curled into the corner of the sofa, Lily cross-legged on the rug, Maya perched on the armrest like she didn’t want to settle.

“Is Mum OK?” Lily asked.

Tom nodded, but it was a lie. "She's just tired. It's been a lot."

"We're tired too," Evie said, not looking up. "I didn't sleep. I kept thinking he'd come back."

Tom sat down, elbows on knees. "He won't. I promise you that."

"You can't promise that," Maya said. "You didn't see him coming the first time."

It hit harder than she knew. Out of the mouths of babes, brutal in its truth, and it stung him. Tom didn't argue; he couldn't.

"I don't want to go to school tomorrow," Lily said. "None of us do."

Tom looked at them, really looked. The fear wasn't dramatic. It was quiet. Lived-in.

"We'll discuss it in the morning."

***

"Hi Sharon, it's Pete. I just tried Tom, but there was no answer."

"He's switched off for the night. He needs a break, and he's with Sue and the girls."

"Fair enough. Just wanted to pass on the update. We've got movement on the Dutch end, but I'm struggling with more than that for now. I assure you I am on it though. I'm ninety-nine percent certain it's coming back on Sunday night and will be parked in a car park near Alexandra Palace in north London."

She listened, grateful to be looped in. It kept her steady. Kept her close and made her feel part of it all. As planned.

She hung up and exhaled. Tomorrow would be busy.

"Hi Sharon."

"Afternoon, guvnor. In from the source, the vehicle is in Holland now, but he doesn't know the make or reg number yet. He is ninety-nine percent certain it's coming back on Sunday night though and will be parked in a car park near Alexandra Palace. There's more than one car park there, but he should be able to tell us the make and model and at least a part reg so we can find it."

"Excellent. Ally Pally, eh? Long time since I've been there. Leave Tom for this evening then. If it's coming back on Sunday, we've got plenty of time to box this off tomorrow. Just make some notes for now and do the contact sheet in the morning."

"OK, guv. See you tomorrow."

Chapter Thirteen

Friday 5th March 2010

Sharon picked Tom up at the normal time and, with a massive amount of patience, had persuaded the girls to go to school. Same routine, walk them in and keep your eyes peeled.

"Mum will pick you up this afternoon, but remember what we said about staying by the office and, under no circumstances, do you go off with anyone else. Even if they are dressed as a police officer. OK?"

"OK, Dad," they all said and walked off to their classrooms.

All this stress at home and the job to deal with too. He was struggling now but just had to crack on.

They needed to get everything sorted for Monday, early doors. She updated Tom on the latest from the source and confirmed she'd spoken to Jamie late yesterday afternoon.

"This is all coming together," he said, his mind spinning. "We need to head north then. There's no point in going to the office, we have to check out the plot today. I used to live near there, you know? My mum and dad owned an estate agents in Wood Green. My mum used to run that, and my dad ran a service station in Enfield. I was born up there too."

"Well I never," she said, looking sideways at him. As close as they were, she realised she knew so little of his background. She made a mental note to delve deeper into that one when they were plotted up on a long job.

"Shall we go into Wood Green nick to set up a place for the briefing on Monday morning?"

"No. I think we should stay well away and just pitch up about five-thirty in the morning. You never know if anyone inside the nick has connections outside that could filter out to someone that we're in town. It wouldn't take too much to work out that the Surrey Drug Squad is here for a Surrey target.

"The early turn won't be in when we pitch up Monday morning, and we should have no problem finding an empty room. It's on the corner of Nightingale Road and the High Road. Tiny car park there, mind, we won't all fit in. No matter, people can park nearby."

He was not in a great place this morning, not surprising when you considered what he and the family had been through only a couple of days ago.

"How's Sue coping?"

"I have a wife, three girls, a female dog and a female partner. In all honesty, all that does is confuse me. Just when you think you've got it cracked, something makes you realise you know nothing about women, and never will.

"I've never seen Sue so angry. She swore like never before and said that she's not sure there's a way back from this. The girls don't want to go to school, and I am way out of my depth."

Sharon turned her head towards him. He was lounging in his seat, head back, eyes closed.

"Ally Pally, here we come. I have to bury myself in work for the time being," he said, and settled down for a kip.

"Fair enough," she said.

They recce'd the entire area around Ally Pally for a good hour and a half on foot.

"We need to know where this car is going to be parked as soon as possible. There are so many places they could put it where we couldn't get an OP," said Tom.

"Absolute cow of a plot at the moment," said Sharon. "We could need a CROP in. There are loads of places it could park up where we'd need a CROP. You know I'm CROP-trained?"

"I do, but we need as many on the plot as we can get. What about that ex-RCS bloke at Godalming, Shaun something?"

"Shaun Lawday. It was years ago he was on the Regional, Tom, they turned into the National Crime Agency in, what, '88, '89?"

"Yes, but once you're used to sitting in a hole in the ground for hours on end and shitting in a bag, I can't imagine you lose it. Oh, my God. I've just had this horrible picture in my mind of you doing that."

"For God's sake, Tom," she said, with a screwed-up face.

"I tell you what, you call Jamie and get him to get a CROP on standby. You can mention Shaun, I guess, and I'll call Pete."

Sharon gave him a thumbs-up and got out her phone.

Tom got out of the vehicle and called the source.

"Tom, how are you doing? All OK after that altercation the other day?"

"Let's just put all that to one side for now, Pete, and concentrate on this current thing. We are up at Ally Pally at the moment looking round to see how it might pan out. The bottom line is we need the details of the vehicle as soon as possible, mate. It's a bastard of a place to plot up."

"OK. Well, I won't get what you need today. It's probably going to be late afternoon or early evening on Sunday, even midnight. There's nothing I can do until it's back in the country."

"OK, mate, I appreciate that. The phone's now on twenty-four-seven. Speak soon."

He hung up and went back to the vehicle and got in.

"Jamie's going to call Deano, the DI at Guildford, and square up putting Shaun Lawday on standby."

Tom closed his eyes in thought. "Good. It could be as late as midnight on Sunday that we get vehicle details from Pete."

"Bugger."

"I know. Do you know what, the only thing we can do here is to assume the worst-case scenario and plan for that. Let's say we get the details at midnight, we come up, find the target vehicle in situ in a really awkward place and need a CROP in. There will be little time to call Shaun out from Surrey to get up here and get him in place.

"I think you and I need to split up. You and the DI crew up and get Shaun on board to prepare for needing a CROP in place. He won't mind if he's being paid. We will need to be up here ready and waiting for the call and, assuming we need him in place, having found the target vehicle in a tough spot, we have plenty of time to do it in the middle of the night. Once he's in, you and Jamie stay as back-up for him, and I'll do the briefing on Monday morning at Wood Green nick. Even if the CROP is in by two in the morning, there's no point going home if we're briefing at five-thirty.

"We'll be up all night Sunday but so be it. We can grab some kip in the car as and when we can. That's it for the day, I think. Shall we see if we can get the team down to The Ship for a swifty at 16:00? We can break the news that we are briefing at five-thirty Monday morning at Wood Green nick."

And they did.

***

Pete rolled in at 19:00, smelling of beer and, probably, over the drinking and driving limit.

"And where have you been?" said Sue, as he walked through the front door.

Tom breathed out a sigh before answering but never got the chance.

"I can smell it now. You've been down the pub with your mates," said Sue, arms folded across her chest again.

Tom decided this was her angry position.

"It's been a tough week, Sue. I just needed a beer with the guys to unwind just a little. It's been a tough week for all of us, and I am included in the 'us'."

He had yet to tell her he was going to be out on Sunday at some stage. That wouldn't go down well either.

"Well, I've had a mare of a day too. I was picking the girls up and thought I saw a Range Rover with your mate in it."

"He's not my mate, Sue. For goodness sake, give me a break. I'm as cut up about this as you are, but I still have to go to work. It wasn't Falstead, I take it?"

"No, one of the mums has got a new car, but it scared the life out of me. I didn't know what to do."

Tom stayed silent. He didn't know what to say.

"Do you know," she said, and then paused as if thinking whether to continue. "I was happy as an army wife. You went off to these, God awful places and always came back. I was frightened whilst you were away, for sure, but somehow I always thought you'd come back. Not all of you did, of course, but all of us wives were in the same boat, and we helped each other every day just to get through it until you all came home.

"There's nothing like that with the police. You don't even socialise with these guys outside of the pub after work, and there's no social network to help me in times like this."

She paused.

"I miss the army."

"So do I, Sue. But I can't go backward now. We have to deal with what's in front of us."

Sue didn't respond. She just stared at him, not with anger now, but with something colder. Something that made Tom feel like he wasn't standing in his own hallway anymore.

"You say we have to deal with what's in front of us," she said, voice low. "But you're never here to deal with it. You drop in, you patch over, and then you vanish again, into work, into ops, into whatever the hell this life is."

Tom opened his mouth, but she cut him off.

"I was scared today, Tom. Properly scared. And I looked around for someone to talk to, someone who understood. There was no one. Just me, trying to hold it together for the girls while my stomach was in knots."

She stepped closer, arms still folded, but her voice was shaking now.

"You think a beer with the lads fixes that? You think switching your phone off for a few hours makes it better?"

Tom's jaw tightened. "I needed space."

"So did I," she snapped. "But I didn't get any. I got fear. I got flashbacks. I've got three daughters asking if they're safe and me not knowing what to say."

His head dropped, then came back up. "I'm trying, Sue."

She nodded slowly. "Try harder."

Then she walked past him, not touching, not looking back. Just gone.

And Tom stood there, still smelling of beer, still over the limit, wondering how far gone things were.

Chapter Fourteen

Monday 8th March 2010

Wood Green nick. 05:28. The briefing room smelled of dirty socks and burned coffee. It had been a tough night, but after getting details of the target vehicle just after midnight, tracing it, and then Sharon and Jamie getting the CROP in place, Tom had grabbed a couple of hours' sleep.

"Morning, everyone. Sorry for the early start, but I'm pretty sure you'll like this one if it goes as planned."

"Where are Sharon and the guvnor, Tom?"

"I'll come to that."

"Right, off we go. The target vehicle is a dark blue Ford Mondeo, 2.2 TDCi, registration number 08-D-28564. We have not, for security reasons, run any checks in Dublin on the vehicle. We've avoided any checks so we don't trigger alerts in Ireland.

“It is parked in the East Car Park of Alexandra Palace, near here. We have information that there is a fifty-kilo parcel of cocaine in the vehicle’s boot.”

That raised some eyebrows.

“It is due to be moved from its current location to Guildford sometime between the hours of 07:30 and 08:30 this morning. That time frame is because the driver wants this run to be in the rush hour, during which he believes, because of the weight of traffic, he is less likely to get a tug.

“As per your map, the exact position of the vehicle is at the very end of a side car park area called the East Car Park and is furthest from the eastern entrance to Ally Pally itself. If you were to exit that eastern entrance and keep walking in a straight line down the footpath, you would walk past the vehicle with it to your offside. We couldn’t get an OP on this spot or get a camera installed in time, so during the night we got a CROP in place in bushes nearby. If any of you know him, it’s Shaun Lawday from Godalming.”

There was general nodding of heads.

“He’s ex-RCS, some years ago, to be fair, but knows his stuff. Sharon could’ve done it, but we didn’t want to reduce our team on the ground if we didn’t have to. That’s the reason Sharon and the DI aren’t here now. They are his back-up on the plot whilst we brief. They are briefed and have everything you have. The CROP is in the bushes between the vehicle and the Rose Garden on the map.

“Now, some of you would expect us to take this all the way to Guildford to see who it belongs to. However, after discussions with the DI and people at a higher level than us, we are going to hit it as soon as it moves. We want at least one person arrested with the vehicle rather than just hitting it cold now, so we have at least a small chance of getting some information from them, albeit we believe the driver will know very little, is just doing a driving job for a wage, and doesn't even know the quantity of the gear in the boot. Also, we cannot risk losing the vehicle. We have to take the gear off the street.

"We do not know if the driver is going to be dropped off at the target vehicle or if he is walking in. That is why your first positions are so far away from the target vehicle. Whatever happens, we concentrate on the target vehicle only. If our driver is dropped off and the person driving the drop-off vehicle gets away, then so be it. If possible, just get details of the drop-off vehicle, description of the driver, etc., as it gives us a bit more intel. The gear is the prize.

"Questions so far?"

There was general head-shaking.

"OK, crews are:
Four-zero, Lisa and Mo.
Four-one, Jack and Samantha.
Four-two, Jamie Carmichael.
Four-three, Charlotte and Karen.
Four-four, Sharon and the DI.
Four-five, Dick and Craig.
Four-six, Alex and Joe.
Four-seven, me solo.

I will relay the OP, who will give us two clicks every fifteen minutes for a no-change and a series of clicks for a standby.

"We have recce'd this plot and have marked everyone's position on your maps. You have a holding position and a forward position to which you will move when I relay the standby. This will be a quick call. Hold in the forward position until I call the strike. I will not do that until the target vehicle moves. The driver sitting in the vehicle isn't enough; it has to be moving. You may not get to your holding positions before the strike's called. If so, just carry on and box it in. Also, remember that the driver might be armed.

"When you get on the plot, do not radio in that you are. I'll make sure I'm the last out of here and get permission from the OP to do a radio check and do it in sequence once I'm on the plot.

"Questions?"

He surveyed the room as people stood up, gathered their belongings, and prepared for the day.

"No? Good. On the plot straight away, please."

Karen came over to him as he put his briefing notes into his bag.

"Great briefing, Tom. Do you know who this parcel was destined for?"

"Thanks. And no, not exactly, but we know it's due to go to the Surrey area, hence our not having to pass it on to the locals or anyone else for that matter. We suspect it's Falstead's. Not enough to play this differently, but enough to hope it is and hope it puts him in a tough position with whoever he bought it from. That will push him into making a mistake and make it easier for us longer term to nab the bastard. There's a lot of hope going on here.

"This lot must have cost about two mil, and I would imagine they have at least half of it allocated to decent kilo-minimum dealers in the south already so they can gather in the dosh and get it paid off as soon as. When they can't do that, the shit will fly."

She nodded. "How's Sue and the girls?"

"Not good, I'm afraid. I think it's affected them much more than I'd hoped. The girls have just retreated into their shells, and Sue has just gone into meltdown."

“Oh dear. I’m so sorry, mate.”

She smiled at him, squeezed his biceps, and said, “See you at the strike,” before walking off.

Tom watched her go. See you at the strike. He smiled at the thought. That was surveillance-team talk, something only insiders said to each other. It showed the unspoken bond they shared, the belief that they would be one.

Thank you, Karen. I needed that.

Riding solo, Tom was last out of the small parking area behind the nick. It was only thanks to the late hour that they’d all squeezed into the cramped lot at all. As he pulled away, the familiar streets tugged at something deep within him. He’d grown up less than a hundred yards from here, close enough to hear the sirens at night and the engines of the double-deckers when they stopped at the bus stop outside his bedroom window.

Back then, it was rough, sure, but it had a pulse. A kind of scrappy pride. Now? It was a shadow of itself. A shithole, if he was honest, the kind of place where hope had packed up and moved on.

He went to the school just on the side of Woodside Park, a short walk that was a trek some mornings, especially in the rain. This job, this bloody job, was stirring up memories he hadn’t invited. Some good, some bad. But that was life, wasn’t it? A patchwork of moments stitched together by time and regret.

He passed the church his sister had got married in. He didn’t slow down, but he felt it all, the weight of the past pressing against the windscreen as he drove on.

Back to the day job.

He was last on the plot as planned and did a radio check with the team.

[Comms]: "OP, permission for four-seven to do a radio check?"

The OP gave two clicks.

Tom called everyone, and all responded that they were on plot.

Here we go. We are off and running. Let's hope this goes as planned.

[Comms]: "All units on plot, OP back to you."

[Comms]: Click, click.

[Comms]: "Two clicks, no change, no change. Four-four?"

[Comms]: "Four-four, yes, yes."

Tom checked his watch. 06:40 in the morning, sod all sleep to speak of and starving hungry. He'd managed a dodgy kebab last night and had forced himself to eat it. It wasn't his favourite, but needs must when the devil drives. You take what you can get when you can get it. He had binned many a Chinese takeaway over the years when they were on plot and sudden movement kicked off. Movement waits for no chicken chow mein.

He cast his mind to what he knew of the INLA. Pete's involvement with them was a surprise. Maybe Pete was higher up the food chain than he'd thought. Back in his CID days at Woking, Tom had had some involvement with them, and he delved into his memory.

Mid-70s split from the Official IRA. Seamus Costello, a Marxist, didn't buy the ceasefire. Wanted a socialist republic, the entire island - aligned with the PLO. Operated mostly in the North. Small outfit, maybe a hundred strong, but lethal. Airey Neave was killed with a car bomb, London, late '70s, their headline hit.

[Comms]: Click, click.

[Comms]: "No change, no change, four-zero?"

[Comms]: "Four-zero, yes, yes."

It was times like this he felt guilty about crossing the line with the call to Pete. It concerned him now how he was justifying it to himself. He remembered he wasn't just bending the rules; he was breaking the law. But they wouldn't be here, taking fifty kilos of charlie off the street, if he weren't doing what he was doing. He was justifying it now, and that was the problem. The moment you explain it to yourself, you've already crossed the line.

He checked his watch again. 06:52. Hunger gnawed, but the real ache was deeper.

Not long now.

[Comms]: "Four-five, permission."

[Comms]: Click, click.

[Comms]: "Yes, yes, four-five."

[Comms]: "There's a black VW Passat travelling up the hill towards Ally Pally. Two up and they are looking all about.

[Comms]: "That vehicle is now held, and the passenger is out of the vehicle. He's looking all about.

[Comms]: "He's now back in the vehicle.

[Comms]: "That vehicle is now away slowly toward the target vehicle.

[Comms]: "For your information, four-seven, and back to you, OP."

[Comms]: Click, click.

[Comms]: "Two clicks, yes, yes."

Here we go. We're on.

The OP was whispering quietly and he relayed it to the team.

[Comms]: "The OP has sight of that vehicle. It's held about fifty yards from the target vehicle. Both remain in the vehicle."

Tom could imagine the adrenaline pumping through everyone's veins now. Getting ready for the strike. They all knew this was it.

[Comms]: "The passenger is from that vehicle, which is now reversing and is away from my view."

Shit. I hope that doesn't impede the strike.

[Comms]: "The passenger is male, white, early 40s, medium build. Wearing blue jeans, a black top and a black leather jacket. He is standing at the edge of the car park looking all about.

[Comms]: "Now walking slowly towards the target vehicle, looking all about. And he's in, in, in.

[Comms]: "Standby, standby, standby."

Tom knew that on the standby, all cars would move to their forward positions.

[Comms]: "Engine started. Vehicle forward.

"Strike, strike, strike."

All hell broke loose. As Tom drove as fast as he could towards the car park, he could see others converging on the target vehicle. As he approached, it was obvious the driver had seen what was happening. The target vehicle turned and drove at speed from halfway down the car park, through a gap in the trees, over the grass, towards the road that led down away from Ally Pally.

Fuck. He's going to get away if we're not careful.

He would not let this guy escape. As it came out of the trees, Tom drove into the right-hand side of it, smashing it against a tree. The airbag deployed, flinging him forward, and he hit it with tremendous force. He bounced sideways, his head slamming into the window, which disintegrated into a million pieces.

Light vanished.

And it went dark.

Chapter Fifteen

The three Land Rovers snaked through the valley, tyres crunching gravel, engines low. The hills pressed in, green and silent. Tom sat forward, scanning the tree line. He hated this road, too quiet, too easy to ambush. They had left their FOB at 06:00 and expected to be out at least twelve hours, or more.

He had good men with him, and he needed them. His Land Rover led. Corporal Andy Summers, the tech guy, was in Two, 'Annie' to everyone who'd ever served with him, thanks to the unfortunate overlap with a certain lingerie shop, the kind of bloke who could wire a toaster to a drone and make it fly. Corporal John "Simmo" Simmonds was in Three. He and Simmo were best mates, friends since school in Ipswich, Suffolk.

Tom held up his arm, and the convoy came to a halt. They were four hours from base now and in what they called bandit country.

"I don't like this, guys. I can smell trouble," Tom said, scanning the road ahead.

Smoke curled up from the village, a mile out. Not good. They had no choice; they had to investigate. The village sat among a group of hills surrounded by trees, bushes and scrubland. The roads, if you could call them that, were tracks for donkeys and carts. This was one track in and one track out.

Tom reached for the radio. "Eyes up. We're going in." No one spoke. They all knew the drill. But this felt different, the quiet that came before something broke.

He looked back at Annie and Simmo in the other vehicles. The corporals gave slow nods. Tom indicated with his raised right hand, forward, let's go. They were ready. Or as ready as anyone ever was.

They had been here before. Not this village, but ones like it. Same smoke. Same silence.

Tom checked the map. They were approaching Brdovac. Protocol said he should call it in, but what would that change? HQ was hours away, and the smoke was fresh. He let his hand drop. There was no time and no point.

The wagons' tyres crunched gravel as they crept along the winding track towards the village. Deathly silence. No voices. No children playing. No birds singing. Just smoke curling upwards. The smell was awful, the smell of death.

Then Tom spotted the first body. He raised his arm, and the convoy halted, then, on his signal, moved inched forward. Ready for anything. What he'd thought was a pile of rags in the corner of the town square was another body, so broken it was barely recognisable.

As more of the square came into view, more bodies came into view. Mangled beyond recognition. *My God, there are dozens of them.* Some were so small they had to be children. No matter how many times he came across scenes like this, he still wondered at the cruelty it took to do such things to another human being. Just to add insult to injury, whoever did this had set fire to the buildings as well as destroying the entire population. He'd seen this before, Kandahar. Places where the dead weren't just killed. They had been erased. Smoke hung low, clinging to the rubble like shame.

The convoy halted. The men dismounted and spread out. There was no point in checking for signs of life; there were none. His anger was almost palpable. Tom swirled his arm above his head to indicate a search of the surrounding buildings.

Whoever had done this was long gone.

Tom took in the surrounding buildings. Poor quality, but clean and tidy, in a country ravaged by years of civil war. He scanned the rooftops. No movement. No glint of glass from the windows. The buildings weren't just burned; they were gutted. Roofs collapsed inward like punched lungs.

"Sarge!" A shout from one of his men.

Tom turned sharply, ready for action, raising his sidearm. One of the guys was marching a young, scrawny man of about eighteen towards him, holding him by the scruff of the neck.

"Where did you find him?" said Tom.

"He was hiding in one of the cellars beneath a house over there, sarge."

"What's your name?"

"My name is Rasim, sir."

"Well, Rasim, who did this?"

"I don't know, sir; I know nothing."

"Did you do it?"

"No, sir, of course not, sir. Please, please, I know nothing."

"OK, shoot him," said Tom, turning to walk away. He didn't mean it, but he didn't have time to mess around; he needed to scare the truth out of him.

"No, no, sir, please. OK, OK, I tell you."

"Don't mess me around, Rasim. I haven't got time."

"No, sir, of course not, sir. I'm sorry, sir," he said with his hands together as if in prayer.

"Well, go on then."

"There were about ten or twelve of them. I was hiding in the basement of the building over there in a wooden box, but I heard the men searching call their boss man, Dragan. He is the Bosnian Serb they call 'Mesar'."

Tom was aware of the whispers. A band of ex-Bosnian Serb paramilitaries, known as The Scorpions, terrorising the area. "Mesar" translates to "The Butcher."

"Why would they do this?" Tom swept a hand over the devastation in the square and beyond.

"For food and supplies." Rasim shrugged.

Tom turned to walk away.

"I know where they are, sir," Rasim blurted.

Tom stopped, turned back, and stared at him. Rasim was shaking, terrified.

"Where?"

Silence.

"Where?" Tom barked, stepping towards him.

"Up in the mountains, sir. They're about an hour from here, towards that big mountain." He pointed. "There, where the ridge dips. You see it?"

"How do you know this?"

"I heard them talking, sir. I've lived here all my life, I know all of it, and that's where they've gone."

"OK. Get out of here."

The soldier released him, and Rasim ran like a man possessed towards the outskirts of the village.

Tom watched him go, jaw tight with anger he just contained. He believed the youth, and that made it worse. Because now this wasn't over. Not by a long shot.

Tom gathered the men at the square's corner.

"This isn't over, boys. That little fella that just tore out of the village like a bat out of hell says the scumbags that did this are holed up in the mountains. There." He pointed to the dip in the ridge. "About an hour's march, not so long in our wagons. We're due home soon, but I say we leave them a parting gift. You with me?"

To a man, they nodded. That was enough. They remounted and drove away from the carnage, towards the mountain, towards the people who had done this, towards revenge for the dead.

Around midday they parked up, dismounted, and continued on foot; an hour's yomp to their destination. Deathly silent as they crept forward. They had trained for this many times, and Tom knew all his men were competent, seasoned veterans. Tom, being Tom, led the way.

Suddenly, the sound of a cracking twig.

He raised his arm, and the entire platoon froze. Tom strained to listen. One sound, then nothing. Could've been a footstep. Could've been a bird. But his gut said otherwise.

He raised his arm, palm flat. One sharp sweep downward. No words. No hesitation. The men dropped slowly, in total silence, rifles close. Low to the ground, scanning the tree line. Fingers on triggers. Eyes darting.

Not a sound. Just readiness.

He didn't believe in sixth senses, but something was off. The kind of off that made your spine itch and your heart slow down.

Tom turned to Annie. He didn't speak. Just tapped two fingers to his eyes, then pointed through the trees. The corporal nodded once, low and tight. He was gone a moment later, crouched, silent, already part of the terrain.

Total silence. Not a murmur, cough, scratch of the nose. Nothing. Not even birdsong. The men had melted into the trees and were invisible.

Annie had been gone for twenty minutes. When he came back, he didn't speak. Just caught Tom's eye, tapped his chest, and pointed to his mouth. Tom nodded as Annie approached and crouched beside him, breath tight.

Whispering, "Fifty yards. Ten men outside around a fire drinking. One on the roof of a small barn as lookout. AKs. No movement inside but possibly more in the barn. One Toyota pick-up the other side of the camp."

Tom didn't answer. Just looked past him and nodded, calculating.

Whispering into Annie's ear, Tom said, "We take them all out from just inside the tree line. You take out the guy on the roof. That's our signal."

Annie formed a circle with thumb and forefinger. All received and understood.

The fire crackled in the distance. Laughter drifted through the trees. None of them knew what was coming.

They passed the whispered instructions down the line. For a brief second it reminded Tom of the old story when the message was supposed to be *send reinforcements, we're going to advance*, which, when sent down the line, changes to *send three and fourpence, we're going to a dance*. Amazing what goes through your head sometimes.

They crept through the undergrowth into position. Simmo on the extreme left of the line, Annie on the right, nearest the barn. Simmo crept to the right, quiet as a mouse, and tapped the shoulder of each man, getting thumbs-up in return without them turning round. When he reached Tom, he gave the circle signal.

Tom took in the scene in the clearing, the lookout on the roof, the men around the fire drinking and eating, throwing chewed bones into the flames. Their potential exit routes when it kicked off. The Toyota pickup parked forty yards away, not close enough for them to get in and make an escape before they were face-down in the dirt with bullets in them. He'd led ops like this before. The trick wasn't speed. It was silence. Kill the lookout, then the rest. No warning. No mercy.

And they were ready. He nodded to Annie.

Later, when dissecting this operation in his mind, Tom would remember how quickly it was all over.

Annie took out the guy on the roof and, a split second later, a barrage of fire took out the rest of the men around the fire. No one came out of the barn. Five seconds. Eleven men gone. They remained in place without moving for a full five minutes to make sure there were no survivors. There weren't. On the signal, they slipped back through the trees as silent as when they'd arrived and back to the wagons.

In total silence, they drove back through the village, the way they had come. That was for you, poor souls, he thought. They all considered the carnage without saying a word. They knew what it was. Revenge. Nothing noble. They had just dealt out the necessary justice.

Tom woke with a start.

God, have I been dreaming?

He blinked at the ceiling tiles. Not Bosnia. Not the village. Not the FOB. Just white light and antiseptic. But the smell of smoke was still in his nose. And the silence. God, the silence. But also an overwhelming feeling that justice had been served.

"My fucking head," he said, coming to but not realising where he was. He tried to sit up but failed.

"Mind your language, Mr Kessler," the nurse said, amused. "Glad you're back with us. Would you like some water?"

"Where the f..." He stopped. "Where am I?"

"You're in the Royal London Hospital in Whitechapel. You've been in a car crash and were unconscious when they brought you in," said the nurse, holding a beaker with a straw to Tom's mouth.

"Jesus, my f... my head's killing me," he said, screwing his eyes shut tight.

"You have a severe concussion. That's very normal. You're bound to have a headache."

He remembered what had happened.

Oh fuck. I'm going to be in deep shit for this.

He lay back on the pillow, closed his eyes and tried to piece it all together, the surveillance, the drop-off vehicle, the movement of the target vehicle, the dash through the tree line, him driving into the target vehicle to stop it getting away. Then it hit him. He opened his eyes and regretted it. The pain in his head was almost unbearable.

The gear. I hope the gear was in the car.

"Was the gear in the car?" he said to the nurse.

"I'm afraid I don't know what you mean."

His mouth was dry. His thoughts were slower than usual, like wading through fog. And then he was sick. He hadn't seen her put it there, but the nurse was expecting this and had placed a bowl in front of him. She didn't flinch, just held the bowl steady, eyes calm. She'd seen worse.

He was struggling to get his thoughts together and was very confused. Everything was scrambled.

God, what an angel. How do they do this job?

A doctor appeared.

Where did he come from? I didn't see him come in.

"Ah, Mr Kessler. I'm glad you're back with us. You have been unconscious for over four hours. We have carried out a brain scan and, whilst you have a severe concussion, there will be no lasting damage if you do as your consultant tells you to.

"Your wife has only just gone down to the canteen to get something to eat but should be back soon, I would imagine."

"Thank you," said Tom, not understanding what was going on.

"Did they get the gear?"

"Pardon?" said the doctor, confused.

"Did they get the gear? For f... God's sake, someone tell me."

"I'm afraid I do not know what you are talking about, Mr Kessler, but I suggest you take it easy for now and the questions you have will be answered in good time."

He must have fallen asleep again and woke up to Sue talking to him.

"How are you feeling?"

"Awful. Water, please," Tom croaked.

She held the beaker up to his dry lips, and he sucked on the straw.

"Did they get the gear?"

"Yes. Sharon took the children home for me so I could sit with you, but she said you were bound to ask and to tell you it was an excellent result. As expected."

"Thank Christ for that. At least I didn't crash the car for nothing," he said, closing his eyes and laying his head back on the pillow again.

She watched him, jaw slack, breath shallow. Her grip on his hand didn't loosen.

Sue said, "That's a matter of opinion."

He couldn't keep his eyes open, but now he knew they'd seized the charlie, he could rest awhile.

I need to go back to sleep.

So he did.

Chapter Sixteen

Tuesday 9th March 2010

Sharon came in with Jamie in tow.

"Christ, Tom. You look like shit," said Sharon.

Tom looked up at them in surprise as they entered the room, her words dragging him from a gentle slumber.

"Oh,? I wonder why."

"Well, you did a cracking job on four-seven, Tom," said Jamie with a smile as they walked in. "I've been trying to replace that motor for months, so writing it off was a cracking result."

"Every cloud, eh? What about the driver of the target vehicle? Is he OK?"

"He's fine. Ran like a hare from the vehicle until Jack rugby-tackled him down the hill. We had him checked out, just a few bruises, and a sprained ankle, nothing serious, thank goodness.

"It looks like you got a concussion when your head smashed through the driver's door window, Tom. And I have to say, you scared the shit out of the team, mate. You were out cold, and no one could wake you up. We all thought you'd pegged it. Fortunately, there's an ambulance station in Wood Green, and they got there in double-quick time. You know Air Ambulance brought you in here?"

"I didn't know that. Jesus." Tom took that in, then said, "What about the rest of it?"

"All you need to know at this stage is we got the fifty keys of charlie in the boot. Before we touched it, we got a SOCO from Wood Green to dust it for prints. They lifted some partials but nothing evidential. We spun the driver's address, Frederick Sharp, by the way. Nothing there. We have his phone, and an analyst is working on it now.

"It's as we suspected. He was just driving for a wage. He admitted in the interview that he knew there was gear in the boot but not how much. Out of the interview, he said, if he'd known what was in there, he'd have buggered off with it."

"That makes sense," said Tom.

"We traced the drop-off vehicle." We nicked that driver too, but nothing there either, just doing his mate a favour.

"Apart from you pissing off the Chief with a car crash, it's a cracking result. The locals have taken the job on as it was on their manor and, by the end of next week, we'll have everything boxed off except your statement and you signing up the log. That can wait until you're back."

"Well, I just want out of here. The food is bloody awful, and I'm bored out of my mind."

"Yes, Sue said you were being grumpy. All in good time though, Tom. You're not coming back to work until the doc signs you back. Understand how serious an injury you've sustained. You could have been killed, mate."

Tom was in the hospital for five days in total. He'd tried to discharge himself more than once, but Sue was having none of it. The headache lasted until the Friday and hadn't gone when he was released.

He spent another week at home, getting under Sue's feet and moaning all day. Then, on the Friday of that week, he conned the Police Doctor into believing he was fit, who then signed him off as ready to return the following Monday, a full two weeks after the seizure of the charlie.

Sue had spoken little since the crash. Not about the car, not about the concussion, not about the fact that she'd spent five days pacing hospital corridors with three frightened daughters and no answers.

But now he was going back to work.

She stood in the doorway, arms folded, watching him pack his kit bag as if it were just another Monday.

"So that's it, then?" she said.

Tom' head jerked up.

"I'm cleared. I've got to get back."

Sue nodded slowly. "Right. Because if the doc says you're fit, then everything's fine. Never mind the fact that you were close to death. Never mind the girls waking up screaming. Never mind me sitting in A&E wondering if I'd have to tell them you weren't coming home."

Tom opened his mouth, but she kept going.

"You didn't even mention the crash. Not once. Like it was just another job gone sideways. Like it didn't matter."

He sat down, the bag half-zipped. “I didn’t want to worry you.”

“Too late for that,” she said. “You worried me the moment they called and said you were unconscious in the back of an ambulance, you moron.”

She stepped into the room, voice low but steady.

“If you’re ready to go back to work, Tom, then you’re ready to hear this: I’m not OK. The girls aren’t OK. And if you think we’re all just going to bounce back because you’ve ticked the ‘fit for duty’ box, then you’re not as sharp as you used to be.”

Tom didn’t respond. He couldn’t. Not yet.

Sue turned and walked out, leaving the silence behind her like a dropped file.

Jesus, I’m desperate to get out of here and back to work.

But first, he had to meet up with Pete and plan the off-the-books stuff with Falstead, so he pulled his phone from his bag.

“Hi, Tom. You’re still alive then?”

“Only just, it would appear. I was unconscious for over four hours, apparently, and had, or still have, a serious concussion. The brain scan was OK, so I think all will be all right in the end. And, as they said in the film, if it’s not all right, it’s not the end yet.”

“Well, I’m glad you’re OK, Tom. An excellent result, I understand?”

“It was a cracker, mate. The fifty keys you said it would be. Any more on who it belonged to?”

“Yes, it was Falstead’s, and he’s in deep shit now.”

“Outstanding, Pete. We’ll come back to that. What about the driver, this Fred whatever-his-name-is? What’s his connection to Falstead?”

“Just a stooge, mate. On a wage and didn’t know what was there. If he had known, I imagine he’d have buggered off with it.”

“Yeah, he said that.

“OK, moving on. We need a proper meeting to see what we’re going to do with Falstead going forward. Just you and me. How are you fixed for Sunday afternoon? That same pub in Horsham?”

“Yeah, that’s fine.”

“OK. Same procedure as before then. Same timings if you like? 14:00 and 14:10? Don’t forget to look behind you.”

“OK. See you there.”

Saturday came and went with Tom brighter and moaning less. Sue put it down to recovery, but it was down to the meet planned for the following day.

Late Sunday morning, Tom told Sue he wanted some fresh air and was going for a drive and a walk. Not untrue, he told himself.

He did all the necessary cleaning as he drove to Horsham, parked on a side road, then walked into the pub, completing anti-surveillance on foot.

He walked in, glanced across as Pete drank a small orange juice, so, once again, all was good.

When he’d been on attachment with the Intelligence Corps years ago, he’d been compromised on a meet with a source. The cover story had stood muster, but it had shown Tom the need to follow procedures. They were there for a reason.

He sat down, and Pete joined him. “You look like shit,” said Pete.

“Thanks, mate. You’re not the first to think that, unfortunately. I don’t feel as bad as I look, to be fair, albeit I’m not on top form yet and my memory is shot to pieces at the moment. With that in mind, I am going to call you to go through this stuff again at some stage so I can write it down. It will need to be tomorrow mid-morning if that works for you? I'm back at work tomorrow, but I'll get Sharon to pick me up late morning so I can ease myself in. I've found out how to encrypt a file on my iPhone using an app, and I'll use that for any of our off the books stuff.

"And before I forget to tell you, we have a camera twenty-four seven on Falstead's home, so stay away from there as we progress this. I'm sure you'll have no problem convincing him you don't want to see him there?"

"That won't be a problem at all, but if you are behind him, for Christ's sake let me know."

"I will mate. I do not want you seen with him by the team. It wouldn't be a complete cock-up, but it's best that doesn't happen. Anyway, what are you thinking regarding the INLA and the 250,000 of MDMA? Still think that's an option?"

"I'll cover that in a minute. You now know, after my giving you the details of the vehicle doing the charlie run, although I notice you have said nothing about it yet, that the vehicle was Irish. Dublin, I believe. Well, that charlie was from the INLA, via Holland but not for me, thank Christ."

"I'd like to think that fifty keys of charlie is too big for you, Pete. Correct?"

"It is."

"Before we cover the Falstead situation, I think this is a good time to cast in stone the relationship I see between us. First, and I have to make this one hundred percent clear, Pete, I am not a bent copper looking to keep you out of the shit for a payday."

Pete opened his mouth, but Tom raised a flat hand. "Wait."

"I'm here because the system failed me. Falstead walked on a job that should've buried him. I couldn't stomach that one, and it's not the first time it's happened.

"I joined the police to lock up bad people. Simple as that. I did twelve years in the army before this, and I've seen things you couldn't imagine. Not in films. Not in books. Real things. I've held dying lads in my arms and been covered in their blood. I've stepped over bodies that didn't look human anymore. And I've done things, things I don't talk about. Not to Sue. Not to Sharon. Not to anyone, but justice has always been at the forefront of my mind.

"So when I say I want this arrangement to work, I mean it has to work for the right reasons. You feed me intel. I act on it. We take bad people off the street who deserve it. But this isn't a licence for you to expand your business. You don't get to build an empire off the back of my help. It has to be a game that works in my favour.

"If I get wind that you're using this to climb the ladder, to push more gear, to bring in heavier hitters, I'll burn you. And I won't lose any sleep over it.

"I like you, Pete. That's the truth. You've got charm, you're smart, and in another life, maybe we'd have had a pint and talked about the rugby instead of surveillance protocols. But this isn't that life. You're a drug dealer and I'm a copper. And this," Tom waved his hand back and forth between the two of them, "this is a transaction.

"You give me Falstead. You give me the next one and maybe some more after that. But you don't get richer from it. You don't get safe. You just get tolerated.

"So if you're in, be in. But if you're thinking of playing me, or hedging your bets, walk away now with no hard feelings. Once we start, there's no halfway. You're either useful, or you're gone.

"I hope, one day, you've made enough money to go straight and buy, or start a legitimate business which makes you a decent amount of money, you can live a good life, provide for your family and you add to society. You do your intelligence a disservice. You owe yourself and your family better.

"Martina is going to want children soon. What would say to them if you were in prison? That you were clever? That you had connections? That you were a superb drug dealer. Until you weren't?"

They sat in silence for a minute or so. Before it was Pete's turn.

"OK. First, I thank you for your frankness and, in all honesty, I'm not sure how to respond. I don't, for a second, see you as a bent copper, Tom, and understand the need for this to be something that works in your favour. It's not even a zero-sum game. It has to work for your end more than mine. I promise you I will not use this as an opportunity to raise my stakes and will treat it for what it is."

There was a pause. Tom didn't fill the gap. He let the silence stretch.

"I know I'm not clean. I know what I've done, and I know what I'm still doing. But I'm not stupid. I've seen lads go down for a long time for less than I do. And I've seen what it does to the people left behind. I do not want this life long term."

He leaned forward. "So yeah, I want out. Not tomorrow. Not next week. But soon. I want to walk into a room and not wonder who's watching. I want Martina to look at me and not worry I'll be gone by Christmas. And I want my children to be proud of me."

Tom nodded once.

"You give me Falstead," Tom said. "And we'll see what kind of future you earn. I'll get another couple of drinks, then we'll discuss how we're going to sort the guy out."

"OK," said Tom, when he returned from the bar, "back to Falstead. How are we going to get him with 250,000 tabs of MDMA?

We're not," said Pete, smiling. "We're going to get him with fifty keys of charlie."

Well, fuck me, that's caught me by surprise.

"He owes the Irish roughly two mil. I don't know the exact number yet. They are bound to be ticking when they find out. They may not know yet. But when they do and get over the initial anger, they will realise there's no point in taking the guy out. That just leaves them around two mil out of pocket. If Falstead can come up with a credible plan to carry on working with or for them, they will let him do that. But they will want to know the ins and outs of a cat's arse before agreeing to give him another parcel of that size, though.

"That's where I come in. I will act as a go-between them and him. I need to convince him I can get him a deal that will keep him alive and convince the Irish that he can deliver. And whilst convincing the Irish, I need to keep myself out of the firing line so, when you get this parcel too, I don't take responsibility. It's going to be a tough ask, but I think I can do it. But I'm putting my life on the line here. These are very nasty people, and if they smell a rat, I'm a dead man."

Tom sipped his drink whilst thinking of the implications of all this. He didn't like the idea of Pete's blood on his conscience if this went tits up but now, this very moment, was not the time to pull the plug. They were yet to get to the point of no return, so he could let this all run for the time being and see how things panned out.

“So, what’s the next move?”

“I’m going to Dublin on Wednesday.”

“OK. I’ll call you Monday, as arranged. Also, I’m going to do all the paperwork for your dosh Monday afternoon. I’ll get that sorted on the hurry up and get you paid out Tuesday with a bit of luck. As stupid as this is, because of the amount involved, you need to come up to headquarters to get paid out by the Assistant Chief Constable. I’ll set it up to be in the sports pavilion as we need to be as far away from the main buildings as possible.”

“OK. How much?”

“I’m putting in for fifteen, but it will get knocked back to something between ten and twelve and a half. Twats that they are, they will want to be seen to be in control.”

“OK. I’ll make myself available all day, and you just tell me where and when.”

“I’ll slide now then, Pete. You wait ten minutes.”

Tom drove home with this all revolving around his aching head. He could do without this concussion clouding his brain at a time he had so many things swirling around in it. But he just had to crack on.

The drive back was steady, deliberate. He kept the window cracked, letting the cool air cut through the fug in his head. The concussion was still there, a fog that dulled the edges of his thoughts, but the plan, or at least the shape of one, was forming.

Falstead. The Irish. Fifty keys. Pete playing middleman. It was a dangerous cocktail, and Tom knew full well that once it was mixed, there’d be no pouring it back into the bottle.

At home, Sue was in the kitchen, radio on low and the smell of coffee in the air. She glanced up as he came in, reading his face in that way she had.

"You've been out a while," she said.

"Needed to clear my head," Tom replied, hanging up his jacket.

She didn't press. She never did when he had that look, the one that said the job was still running in the background, even if he was standing in their kitchen.

Upstairs, he sat on the edge of the bed, rubbing his temples. Dublin on Wednesday. A payout on Tuesday. And somewhere in between, the quiet understanding that he was now committed to a course that could end careers, or lives.

He lay back, staring at the ceiling. The headache pulsed in time with his heartbeat.

Crack on, he told himself. Just crack on.

Chapter Seventeen

Monday 22nd March 2010

Tom discussed everything from the Sunday meeting with Pete during a call, wrote it up on his phone, and encrypted the file.

At 11.00 Sharon picked him up from home. Sue walked out to the car with Tom and said with a smile on her face, "Thank God for this. I'm sick to death of him getting under my feet, Sharon. He's done nothing but moan, moan, bloody moan, all week."

She said it in jest, but it held an element of truth.

"Don't worry, Sue, I'll keep him out of your hair. I know what he needs," said Sharon as they drove off.

It is a pleasure to be back.

"Well, Tommy boy, how are you feeling? You look better, mate."

"In all honesty, Sharon, I don't feel one hundred percent, but, by Christ, I needed to get back to work. There's stuff to tell you too, as I called Pete this morning for an update."

He got out his phone and navigated to the notes within the encrypted section.

“I’ve set up this encrypted file on my phone for me to keep notes in. We don’t need to be using pieces of paper anymore if the technology is available to us. And my memory is shot to pieces at the moment, so I need to write everything down. I’ll show you how I did it later if you want me to. Anyway, this is the good stuff.”

He gave her the gist of it all.

“The best bit is the gear was Falstead’s, and he now owes the INLA around two mil.”

“Wow,” Sharon exclaimed. “That’s outstanding. He’s in deep shit now, I take it?”

“Not ‘arf guvnor,” said Tom with a grin from ear to ear.

“He now has to convince the Irish to let him deal himself out of the shit. Pete is going to get close enough to find out what the hell is going on. It will not be easy, though, and will take some time. In the meantime, we can get the analyst to do a load of phone stuff, and we can monitor the comings and goings of the camera on his house. Do loads of background and intelligence work, maybe the odd day of surveillance on him and just wait for the source to tell us what’s going on.”

“Sweet.”

“And when we get in, I’ll get the reward paperwork done, so that’s boxed off and out of the way. I would like to get him weighed off tomorrow if possible. Jamie should be able to push it through.”

“Jamie’s already done it, Tom. He’s got the whole fifteen grand. All you have to do is go over and see the ACC to sort out a time and a place.”

"Well, I'm buggered. I'm redundant. I'm not needed anymore."

When they got to the office, he went over to see the ACC. He didn't like it here. It smelled of shoe polish and freshly ironed uniforms and was full of lightweights. He was out of his comfort zone.

"Morning, Janet," he said to the ACCs PA. "Is the boss in?"

"Hi Tom. How are you feeling?"

"I'm fine, Janet, thank you. Just a minor bump on the head. These things happen."

"Not quite how I understood it, but whatever you say. He's expecting you. Just knock and go in."

Tom nodded, knocked on the door and went in.

No wonder there's no money for overtime; that desk must have cost five grand.

"Morning sir,"

The ACC was sitting at his desk. His eyes rose over his glasses at Tom.

"DC Kessler. Good to see you. How are you after the accident? I say 'accident' but we both know what it was."

That made Tom's hackles rise, and he'd only been in here ten seconds.

"I'm fine, thank you, sir, and, to be honest, getting fed up with people asking.

"No, it wasn't an 'accident', but, in the moment, in that split second I had to decide, I thought it was the only way to stop the vehicle escaping. If it had been allowed to get away onto the more open public roads, it would have put the public in serious danger."

"I can see you've thought that answer through in advance, Constable."

Tom said nothing at first and paused for a few seconds to calm himself. What is it with these fuckers? If he'd been on the plot, the gear would have been on the streets by now.

"Not really, sir. I hadn't thought about it until you mentioned it. It's the truth. When you are on an operation, you have to make decisions on the hoof. Sometimes, in a split second. Sometimes you get it right and sometimes you get it wrong, but if you make those decisions in good faith, you can sleep at night knowing you did your best. Hindsight is a wonderful thing. Don't you agree?"

I will not take any shit from this twat!!

The ACC just stared at him in silence over his glasses. He was not expecting pushback from a DC but, under the circumstances, he let it ride.

"You're here about the reward payment for your informant?"

"Yes, sir. I understand the DI has sorted it out in my absence, so I would like to arrange for it to be paid as soon as possible. This is a reliable source, and I want to keep him onside."

"Is it really worth fifteen thousand pounds? That's an awful lot of money."

Speechless.

Tom stood there with his mouth open, in shock.

"Well, my understanding is, it's already authorised, so everyone in that chain of authorisation must have thought so. Fifty kilos of cocaine has a street value of four million pounds, so, in my mind, I think it should be at least double, but hey ho, that's just my opinion and fifteen thousand is what's been authorised."

"Yes, quiet. Well, I'm away at a conference starting on Wednesday. We'll need to sort something out for next week."

What the fuck.

Tom paused, took a breath and stopped himself just in time.

"Erm. This source has other information we need to work on, sir. Would it be at all possible to arrange it for tomorrow so it's before you go to your conference? At a time of your choosing, of course. I can get hold of the keys to the sports pavilion, so it wouldn't take that much time out of your day. It's only a short walk down there from here."

"That's inconvenient."

"Perhaps so, sir, but it is important."

He was still looking at him over the top of his glasses.

Why don't you take the fucking things off, you knobhead. You look like a fucking librarian.

"If it's that important...."

"It is, sir."

"....then get him to the pavilion at 17:30 tomorrow afternoon and we'll get it done."

"Thank you. Can I assume you will pick the money up from accounts?"

He sat down and, not looking at Tom, said, "Janet will arrange that. Thank you, DC Kessler, I will see you tomorrow."

Tom turned and walked out. Seething.

Twat.

As he walked past Janet, he said, "Do you enjoy your job, Janet?"

"Yes, Tom," said Janet with a confused expression.

Tom didn't look at her but, as he walked out, shaking his head, he muttered, "Amazing."

He stepped outside; the air was cooler than he expected. Back to the real world. Back to the work that mattered.

At the office, Sharon wasn't around. He stuck his head in Jamie's doorway.

"Have you seen Sharon, guvnor?"

"She's over at the canteen."

"Oh, good. Have you got a minute?"

"Of course. Come in. How are you feeling?"

"Please don't, guv. I'm fed up with answering the question."

Jamie held up both palms. "Sorry, Tom. I have your welfare at heart."

"I know, but I'm fine, and we need to move on. Anyway, I've squared up the ACC to pay off the source tomorrow afternoon. I won't bore you with the details of that conversation, but... what is it with these people, guv? They're on a different planet from us."

"I know, but we have to live with them. If you want to get promoted, and I hope you do, you'll have to learn how to play the game."

"Sod that. Not interested. Maybe DS one day, but not your job, that's for sure. I can't do politics. It wasn't like this in the army. Most of the hooray henrys were alright. I didn't realise until I met this shower how all right they were. Mind you, they had blokes' lives at stake, so they couldn't make many cock-ups. If they did, when we were out on a live job, they'd stay at the back in case one of the lads they'd pissed off put a bullet in them.

"Anyway, I'm not sure if Sharon told you, but the gear we seized was Falstead's."

"Outstanding," Jamie said, nodding.

"Exactly. He's now in deep, deep shit with the INLA. I don't know whether to tell Sharon this, but on Wednesday the source is going to Dublin to meet with the Irish to get a handle on it all."

"You can tell Sharon. He's allowed to do that."

Jamie leaned back, rubbing his chin. "If this was Falstead's gear we seized, the vehicle it was in was Irish, and the source is going to Dublin to see them... what involvement did the source have in the gear's supply?"

"You know what it's like, guv. If you don't like the potential answer, don't ask in the first place, so I don't know."

He did of course, but this was a step too far for Jamie right now.

"How long is he going to be out there?"

"He didn't say."

"OK. On another note, I want you to take it easy for a couple of weeks. I know you, you lied through your teeth to the doc to get signed fit. Late starts, early finishes. Sharon can crew up with someone else or ride solo. She can keep four-four, and you can have the new four-seven. I know Sue's sick of the sight of you, but try to build some bridges. This will have affected her too, mate. She suffered as well."

She had. He'd seen it in the way she didn't ask if he was OK, but watched him from the corner of her eye.

"And whatever you do, don't balls it up and crash four-seven, eh, Tom?"

At least he was smiling.

"I'll try not to."

He skipped the canteen, couldn't face another round of, 'Hi Tom, you OK, mate?', and instead pulled up the live feed on Falstead's gaff. Still quiet.

I wonder how you think you're going to get out of this mess and stay alive, you fucker. At least this will keep you off my case.

When Sharon came back, they went over the plans for the next few days. Tom was exhausted but fought it. He told her he'd have a lazy day tomorrow, not realising how much this one had already taken out of him.

"Loads of people asked after you, Tom."

"That's why I didn't go over there," he said with a short laugh.

They'd arranged to meet at the sports pavilion at 17:15 for the payout to Pete. Just a quick message and he'd be off:

Sports pavilion, police HQ, 17:15. Don't drive your Beemer. Use another one. The Merc will do if you want. Dry cleaning. Thumbs up if good for you and you know the location. Sharon knows about your going to Dublin. Delete this message after reading.

Back came the thumbs-up. Another day was over.

***

As usual, everyone was bang on time at the meet.

"You don't have to show you'll be eternally grateful when this bloke pays you out, Pete, but don't be a twat and make any silly comments, no matter what he says. OK? In fact, the less you say, the better."

"Noted."

Sharon added, "And when you sign for the dosh, don't sign it Mickey Mouse. But don't use your actual signature either, just a squiggle that looks like something real."

"Again, noted."

"And don't tell him anything about anything. He might try to play the detective and squeeze you just to show you how important he thinks he is, but don't engage. Just tell him the information is for another day. OK?"

"All received."

"He's here," said Sharon.

"Afternoon, sir."

"DC Kessler, DC Girton. Good afternoon." The ACC turned to Pete with a cross between a smirk and a smile. "And good afternoon to you."

That look shows everyone here you've never run a source in your entire career, you dick.

"I have to say we are grateful for your continued help with all the things you are talking to my officers about, and long may it continue."

"No problem."

"If you would sign here, please."

The ACC indicated the line on the receipt form. Pete signed with a squiggle.

"Thank you. Here we are. Would you like to count it?"

"Yes please. You hear so many stories, so you never know."

Tom and Sharon fought to keep straight faces as the ACC's head jerked up.

Pete counted the money fast, in a way that showed he was used to handling such sums, not that the ACC would ever notice such a thing.

"Spot on. Thank you."

The ACC nodded, turned, and walked out.

Tom held a finger to his lips and whispered, "Shush. Wait until he's gone before saying anything."

They stayed quiet until they were sure the coast was clear.

"That was bloody funny, Pete," Tom said, and they all burst out laughing, just within earshot of the ACC.

Chapter Eighteen

Wednesday 24th March 2010 – morning

Peter Johnson was thirty years old, and there was Italian blood somewhere in his past. His six-foot-three frame accentuated a slim, wiry, athletic build. A sharp jaw, olive skin, and eyes that flickered between charm and calculation. His hair was dark, clipped neat, always looking like he'd just stepped out of a cold shower and into a tailored mess.

He moved as if he were casing the room, even when he wasn't. His voice was low and deliberate, and when he spoke, people listened. He smiled when he shouldn't have. Didn't when he should. There was something about him that made people talk, and sometimes regret it later.

He'd been a drug dealer at thirteen but never touched the stuff himself. From the very first day outside the school gates, selling puff to older kids, he'd made a promise to himself, no drugs, no cigarettes, little alcohol.

He wasn't a big drinker, but, like Martina, he loved a glass of Masseto Toscana IGT, followed by a pour of Macallan 25-Year-Old Sherry Oak scotch. Expensive? Yes. But he could afford it.

If he were honest with himself, he'd been in the game too long. He'd made a fortune. He and Martina lived in a beautiful apartment surrounded by beautiful things. A new M3 BMW every year. Life was comfortable, yet a lingering feeling persisted. It could all come crashing down at any time.

Pete sat in his walnut and black leather Eames Lounge Chair with his feet on the ottoman and thought of where he could take this relationship with Tom Kessler. He accepted that Tom wasn't a bent cop. His reaction to the harvos suggestion was proof of that. It appeared, at least on the surface, that the motivation for his turning to the dark side was based around a real desire to lock nasty people away and, because of the 'system' letting him down so often, he believed this was the way to do it. One thing front and centre of his mind was he did not want to be one of the 'nasty people'.

Tom did not know where Pete sat in the food chain. He was higher than Tom believed, and he wanted to keep it that way. Paying others, often through cut-outs, to move gear around was expensive, but greed was the downfall of many a dealer. Better never to have hands-on and make less money than to put all this at risk.

He surveyed the apartment and took it all in. The sculpture sat low on its plinth, half-shadowed by the bay window. The Kiss, Rodin's embrace frozen in bronze, caught the last of the light like a secret. Tom had paid £105,000 for it, a posthumous cast, authorised by the Musée Rodin. Not for show. Not even for Martina. Just something he needed to look at when he wanted to disappear into his own space.

The paintings on the wall, all legitimate purchases. Pride of place was his Katherine McNeill. A not-widely-known Canadian artist from Vancouver. He just loved the colours. It was always summer when he looked at it. This had cost him £150,000 at auction.

When they raided his house a while ago, none of the police even gave these pieces a second glance. It was like it was his secret. He smiled at the thought.

His mind flicked back to him shooting that idiot in the knee up in town. What was he thinking bringing the gun back here, into the apartment? He and Martina had known each other from the age of twelve and loved each other dearly, but he had put her and their future at risk. He had got too big for his boots, thought he was untouchable, and would be eternally grateful to Tom for the call. That had not only brought him down to earth with a bang but allowed him a bit of protection in the future. If he played this right, there was a glimmer of light at the end of the tunnel with where his life was going.

One thing was certain; he needed to play this very, very carefully. The Irish were very tough and very smart. They were difficult people to deal with. One wrong move and he would be toast.

But first, he needed to convince John Falstead that he could get him out of the situation he was in.

Pete didn't have any numbers for Falstead. Tom did, using some special tech their analysts had, but it wasn't wise to touch that. Falstead might've only handed it out to a select few, and Pete wasn't about to tip his hand.

There was only one way to do this, so he drove to Guildford, parked in the open-air car park by the law courts. The irony didn't pass him by. He locked the car, crossed the street, and walked towards the nightclub.

He walked around the building in which the club sat and got a feel for the place. There was a Range Rover Autobiography parked at the rear, which he assumed was Falstead's. He walked back to the front and through the main door of the club.

What a bleak place!

Then again, places like this always seemed worse under the unforgiving glare of daylight.

A big bouncer-type walked towards him and said, "What do you want?"

"Is John in?" said Pete.

"Who's asking?"

"I'm Pete Johnson."

"Never heard of you."

"Good. John has, and will want to see me."

"He's not here."

"Yes, he is. His car's around the back."

"He doesn't want to see you."

"How do you know when you haven't asked him, you tosser?"

The goon walked towards him but, just in time, Falstead said, "It's all right, Pinky. I know him."

Pete smiled and turned as John Falstead walked towards him from a dingy, distant corner of the room. He said in a questioning tone, "Pinky?"

"Yes," said Falstead. "Pinky and Perky. My little joke." But he wasn't laughing. "What do you want?"

"I understand you have a bit of a problem, and I think I can help you solve it."

Falstead stared at him for a full fifteen seconds with an expressionless face. Pete stared back, motionless.

This is the moment. He either tells me to fuck off or I'm in.

Falstead broke the silence. "Do you now. Then you'd better come through to the office."

He turned, walked towards the shadows whence he had come, and Pete followed him.

Without looking back, Falstead said, "Pinky. Now I am not in for anyone."

They went through a barely lit corridor, past some toilets that smelt like a sewer, round a corner and through a door marked Private. It was like stepping into a Tardis, from narrow corridors into a large, well-appointed office.

Looking round, Pete could see a fine roll-top desk with a captain's chair behind it. The carpet was plush and appeared brand new, as was the Chesterfield settee sitting under Andy Warhol's S&H Green Stamps.

"I know the original is in New York. Which version is that?" said Pete, pointing at it.

"You know something about art?"

"A bit."

"That's a 1965 offset lithograph. Signed too."

"Very nice. Well, if you're ever looking to sell it, it's worth what, six to eight grand?"

"I'm not." He paused. "Coffee?"

"Black. No sugar."

As Pete settled onto the sofa, Falstead pressed a button on the grey box on the right-hand side of the desk. "Perky. Coffee, black, no sugar. And my usual."

"Yes, boss," came the reply.

"Right. What do you know then?"

"I know you're in the shit. You had a parcel get seized and are into some very dangerous people for a tidy sum," said Pete, looking straight into Falstead's eyes.

He had to be respectful but show no fear or weakness.

"How do you know?"

"It was common knowledge among several mid-level players around the south, the people I deal with too, that you had a parcel being shipped in. They were all waiting for it to be dished out. Cash only. Decent price with a minimum of one key. Nothing on the tick. The supposition was that you needed to gather in the cash to pay for the parcel.

"Suddenly no gear, and people sensed panic in the ranks. My guys kept receiving calls because your people had been let down and had smaller buyers of their own to service. They had the cash ready. I had nothing available and couldn't help them. I wish I could've done it, but I couldn't. It didn't take long for the word to get around that you had a serious problem."

He paused.

"Go on," said Falstead.

"I didn't know for sure who had supplied you the gear, or the size of it, but because of the number of people calling my guys, I worked out it was between thirty and sixty keys. Now, that's a serious amount of gear, and only a certain number of people can do that.

"I asked around a few people I know, and then it hit me." He paused. "If I say two names, you can see if I'm right." He paused again, then said, "Patrick and Shaun."

"OK, smart arse. How do you know them?"

"I've been dealing with Patrick and Shaun for years. Mainly happy pills but charlie too. It had to be them."

"Just for the..."

Perky arrived with the coffee on a lovely silver tray. It was ridiculous in his enormous hands, and Pete couldn't help but smile at him. He put it on the desk and walked back out of the office.

"Just for the sake of argument, let's say you're right. How can you help me?"

"Well, you are into them for a serious lump which, after buying this place, I suggest you can't cover. That means there's only one way you can get out of this, and that's getting another parcel to shift on the hurry-up. The problem is, everyone knows, except Patrick and Shaun, as they are on the other side of the Irish Sea, and won't give you any gear."

"How do you know they don't know?"

"If they did, this place would be burnt to the ground by now with you, Pinky, and Perky in the middle of it, with bullets in the back of your heads."

The look on Falstead's face showed he agreed with him. Pete could sense Falstead's swallow.

"And you can help how?"

"I have a solid, long-term, longer than you, relationship with the Irish. I can vouch for you and potentially get you another parcel. That would allow you to deal your way out of trouble."

"And what's in it for you? Why would you do it?"

"I want half your profit left over after you've paid what you owe. How big was the parcel?"

Falstead paused, appeared to be thinking what to say, then said, "Fifty."

"Ouch," said Tom. "How much?"

"One point seven."

"OK. That wasn't a terrible deal. Let's do the numbers then. You get another hundred keys and then owe five point one. I have tucked away for a rainy day, and it appears to be pissing down at the moment, twenty keys of benzocaine."

"Do you now?" said Falstead, sitting up in his chair and taking a lot more notice.

"In the interests of this... partnership... I'll throw that in the pot. Whacked fifty-fifty, that's forty keys at ninety a key. That's three point six mil. That leaves eighty left. We'll cut those heavy, not that it matters. I've got enough cutting agents for that too. Say we stretch it to a hundred and twenty keys at forty a pop. That's another four point eight. Total, eight point four mil. Five point one to the Irish. We split the rest.

"The conditions are, I go nowhere near the gear at any stage. You know that's my MO. I never do. I also take no responsibility for it at all, and we both make that clear to Patrick and Shaun. This is your gig, not mine. I'm just brokering the deal."

"You could just get a big parcel yourself and make a killing. You could let the Irish know; they'd come over here, sort me and the boys out, and leave you with a bigger manor. It would do you no harm at all to get me out of the way."

"I don't want to get that big, John. If I were, I'd be putting my head above the parapet, which is where I don't want to be. All that does is bring people in like SOCA, and I don't need that. I want out of the game altogether. I've had enough. With what I've got stashed away, another chunk on top with no risk will set me up to walk away. You can have it all. For a price, but that conversation's for another day."

Total silence. Falstead leaned back in his chair, clasped his hands behind his head, his eyes looking at the ceiling.

"If I said yes, what's the next move?"

"If you say yes, then you have to mean it. There's no going back. The first thing I do is get on a plane at 20:00 tonight from Southampton to Dublin and speak to Patrick and Shaun. This is all face-to-face, mate. No phones involved unless they are one-call-only burners."

Falstead considered it all for another couple of minutes, seemed to decide and said, "OK, let's do it."

"Right. I have a bag in the car with five burner phones in it. Each one has a number on the back. Plumb your mobile number in here."

Pete gave him his mobile.

"If I need to speak to you, I will message you on WhatsApp the number of the phone I am going to call you on. Note the number and delete the message straightaway. My message will designate the number of the phone you switch on, and I am going to call you on it. We work through them. As soon as the call has happened, you remove the SIM and destroy it and the phone, and we move on to the next phone.

"Each time I message, I will state the number of the phone we are going to use. I will start the message with the year written backwards with four digits. So, that's 0102. If there is no date backwards in the text, or I write it forwards, you know there's a problem and I'm making the call under duress. If you can, you run like hell because the Irish are coming for you."

Pete went to get the bag from his boot, came back, and handed it to Falstead just inside the doors to the club.

They shook hands.

“Let’s get you out of this mess and make some money,” said Pete, looking Falstead straight in the eyes.

Falstead just nodded.

“Any chance you could get Pinky or Perky to run me down to Southampton?”

“No problem,” he said. He went to walk away, stopped, turned and added, “Why have we not teamed up before? You know what you’re doing, don’t you?”

“That’s in the past, John. Let’s worry about the future.”

Falstead paused, nodded, then turned away. “Pinky!” he shouted without looking round, “Get the keys to the motor. I’ve got a job for you.”

Chapter Nineteen

Wednesday 24th March 2010 – afternoon

Pinky and Pete remained silent on the journey to Southampton Airport. The gulf in intellect here was vast. Pete doubted a debate about the pros and cons of EU withdrawal was on the cards, so he just sat back, closed his eyes, and slept.

Plane on time. That's a result.

Pete passed through security without incident, no questions, no second glances from anyone. The burners were in his carry-on, the SIMs still untouched. He grabbed a coffee he didn't drink and sat near the gate, watching the other passengers. A hen party, two suits, a priest. No one who mattered.

Boarding was slow. He kept his head down, nodded at the flight attendant, and took a window seat near the rear. No one beside him. Good.

As the plane taxied, he checked the time. He hoped Patrick and Shaun would be in Dublin when he arrived. He couldn't ring ahead under any circumstances but knew how to contact them when he was there, and that's what mattered. If they weren't around, he'd improvise. Again.

He closed his eyes. No point in rehearsing it now. Either they'd listen, or they'd bury him. And if they buried him, they'd be burying Falstead and his goons too.

Pete opened his eyes. The descent had begun. Dublin below, and two men who could end his life with a nod. No point worrying now.

"Ladies and gentlemen, we are now making our descent into Dublin, so please fasten your seat belts, raise the trays in front of you, and make sure your seats are in the upright position. We would like to thank you..."

Pete stepped out into the grey Dublin drizzle, the kind that soaked you without ever quite becoming rain. He flagged a taxi. Black, battered, the driver leaning across to pop the boot.

"Where to, boss?"

"The Central Hotel, please, mate."

"That's grand, so it is. You're only a stone's throw from the cathedral there. Bit of culture, eh?"

Pete didn't answer. The driver glanced at him in the mirror. "Yous alright there? You look like you've seen a ghost."

"Sorry, mate. I'm just tired. It's been a long day."

"Ah, sure we're all wrecked. This weather'd put manners on a greyhound."

They pulled out onto the motorway. The driver kept talking.

"Flight in from England, was it?"

"Yeah."

"Southampton this time of night, isn't it? You're better off in Dublin, so long as you don't mind the price of a pint. Jaysus, it's gone mad altogether, so it has."

Pete watched the city roll in. Low buildings, red brick, the odd burst of colour. The driver pointed out a pub.

"Now there's a spot. McGowan's. Bit lively, mind. You wouldn't be tekin' your granny there."

Pete gave a half-smile. "Noted."

"Sayin' nuttin', but you've the look of a man wi' business. You're not here for the craic, are ya?"

Pete met his eyes in the mirror. "Not exactly."

"Fair play, fella. Just keep your head down and don't be mekin' a show of yourself. Dublin's small, and word gets around."

"Noted again."

Pete booked into the hotel, dropped his bag in his room, and went straight out. He walked into a particular bar on Fleet Street, not the loud one with trad music and stag parties, but the quieter one, two doors down. The kind of place where the regulars smile little, and the barman knows who's local and who's not.

"A pint of the black stuff, please, fella," said Pete, and waited.

As the barman put the pint of Guinness in front of him, Pete gave him a ten-pound note and said, "Keep the change."

"Thanks," said the barman, looking at Pete.

"No problem. I'm asking after Shaun. I'm at The Central, Room 127. He'll know who I am."

"I've no knowledge of anyone called Shaun that may want to be chattin' to the likes of yous."

"I know," said Pete, and he walked away from the bar.

The barman looked at him for several seconds whilst polishing a glass, then disappeared into the back room behind the bar.

Pete finished his pint. Not doing so would draw attention, and he left. As he stepped out, he clocked the pub across the street. Different crowd. Different flags. Fleet Street might be tourist ground now, but old loyalties don't die. They just stopped advertising.

Back to the hotel he went. He was tired, but there was still a way to go with this before he could settle down for some sleep.

Back in his room, he lay on the bed and waited. This procedure was how it had to be. He knew that Patrick and Shaun, if they were in town and available, would now check out who had come to the bar and left the message. They would soon work out it was him, but they would still check lots more things before they made contact.

He woke with a start. He had fallen asleep while still dressed. It was the hotel phone that was ringing. He answered it.

"Hello."

"Leave the hotel by the main entrance, turn left, then first right onto South Great George's Street. Keep walking down that road on the left-hand side." Then the phone went dead.

Pete rinsed his face to refresh himself and did as he was told.

He'd been strolling down South Great George's Street for a minute when the van pulled up. A dark Transit-type with no markings. The side door slammed open with a bang. Two men in balaclavas jumped out, grabbed him hard, and hauled him inside. Another bang as the door slammed shut. The van peeled off. It was over in seconds.

He muttered, “What the fuck,” as someone placed a hood over his head.

The hood was coarse and clung to his face. It smelled of mildew and old sweat, as if someone had used it before, perhaps more than once. The fabric scratched at his cheek, and every breath pulled in the sour tang of nylon and stale breath. The fabric muffled and distorted the sound.

“Take all your clothes off. Leave your pants and socks on though.”

It wasn’t a request. He stripped without protest. They’d be checking for wires, transmitters, or anything tucked into a pocket that could send a conversation back to someone.

“Now put these on.”

They gave him a pair of tracksuit bottoms, an Irish rugby top, and a pair of trainers.

He dressed, sat, and waited. They must have driven for thirty, maybe forty minutes. Not fast enough to draw attention to themselves, but not so slow as to stand out either. Just normal. Just a normal day for guys driving around Dublin with balaclavas on their heads.

The van slowed and turned onto what appeared to be a rough track. Then it stopped. The side door opened, and Pete could hear what appeared to be barn doors opening. The van then started forward again and stopped for a second time.

They hauled Pete out of the van, and he waited. It was deathly silent, and he hoped against hope that there wasn’t a gun pointing at the back of his head.

Boots on gravel. A door creaked open. The wind, low and constant, like a distant engine. He couldn't see, but he could feel the shift in temperature. It was colder now, heavier. The kind of cold that meant stone or timber, not open air.

Hands gripped his arms, firm but not brutal. They steered him, not dragged him. The ground changed underfoot, from gravel to dirt, then to something softer. Straw? Mud? He couldn't tell. But the smell changed too. Diesel. Wet wood. Animal. And something metallic, faint but sharp, like rust or blood.

Someone pulled off the hood, and to his relief, Patrick and Shaun stood in front of him grinning.

"Jesus Christ, guys," said Pete, voice thick with relief.

"Hows yous doin' there, big fella?" said Shaun.

"You know how to put the shits up someone, Shaun."

"A necessary step, pal. We haven't seen yous for a wee while."

"To be fair, guys, I can't call you up on a Saturday for a chat when I'm at a loose end," Pete said with a smile.

"To be sure, ya can't, Pete. But you're here now, so what can we's do for yous?"

"Can we sit down and chat? This one's delicate."

"I'm not too sure I like the sound of that," said Patrick. "Let's sit over here."

They walked over to a table with a few chairs around it and sat down. On it were a bottle of Jameson and three glasses. Patrick lifted the bottle, gestured with it towards Pete, and raised his eyebrows.

Pete shook his head.

“Right then, big fella,” said Shaun. “Off yous go.”

“Recently, you sent over a parcel of fifty keys to John Falstead.”

Patrick stopped, mid pour.

“And how the fek do yous know that?”

“Because the old bill have seized it. The major players in the south know it, and I’m one of them.”

“Jaysus,” said Patrick and Shaun in unison as they turned to look at each other, then turned back at Pete.

“How the fek did that happen?”

“I do not know and don’t know anyone who does, but I think I may have a solution.”

“And what would that be, other than us sending someone to blow his feckin’ brains out?”

“But then you’d be one point seven mil down.”

“How do yous know the number?”

“Because I’ve spoken to Falstead, and he told me.”

Patrick and Shaun’s heads swivelled again, back to each other, then to Pete. It was like a choreographed comedy sketch. And even though the room was tight with tension, maybe because of it, Pete nearly burst out laughing.

Patrick was still holding the bottle aloft, and it was irritating Pete immensely.

“I’ll have one of those now, please, Patrick,” said Pete, nodding at the bottle.

Patrick poured him a measure and stood the bottle on the table. Pete took a sip.

He didn’t want to drink too much. He needed a bit of Dutch courage but had to stay sharp.

“OK, yous carry on. What do you expect us to do?”

"Give him another parcel. A hundred kilos."

"Are you feckin' joking, big fella?" said Shaun, amazement in his voice.

"No. I have enough benzocaine and other cutting agents to turn that hundred key into eight point four million quid. I have a deal with him to weigh you off the five point one of that, and we split the rest fifty-fifty."

"Why don't we just shoot the feckin' eejit and be done with it, and deal with yous in the future?"

"Because you'd still be out of pocket for ages. I can't deal with a parcel of that size myself. You know I never get hands-on, and I don't want to put my head above the parapet."

"You know how to put the cat among the pigeons, don't you, boyo? Sit in the van. We need to discuss this between ourselves."

Pete got up, walked over to the van, and sat in the passenger seat.

He watched as Patrick and Shaun got up, both put their hands in their pockets, and walked back and forth in the barn, well out of earshot. At one stage, Patrick made a phone call. He'd never expected that he was meeting the high-ups in this organisation and guessed that was to whom the call was being made.

At one stage during the call, Patrick stood stock still, facing the van. That made Pete think his days were numbered. Not even days, maybe minutes.

What the fuck have I got myself into?

After some twenty minutes, Patrick and Shaun walked over to the van.

"Right. Get Falstead over here tomorrow. Without fail."

"So you can top him?" said Pete.

"First, big fella, that's got feckin' nuttin to do with yous. Secondly? If we wanted to do it, we'd have done it by now, and done it in his feckin' house. Just get him here tomorrow."

And they both walked away.

The guys that 'kidnapped' him off the street came back with a bin bag full of his clothes and passed them to him.

"Get changed."

He stripped off and dressed in his normal attire.

"Nothing in there then," said Pete with a grin.

"If there had been, yous would be dead by now, Sonny Jim," said one of them. Not one of them smiled, and Pete's disappeared quickly.

"Here. Take this," said one of them, handing him a burner phone.

He got back to the hotel at four in the morning, pulled out his phone, and sent a message to Falstead.

0102 1

He waited five minutes, then called burner number one.

"Do you know what time it is?"

"Really? Do you know where I am?"

"Well, yes."

"Right. Well, shut up and listen. Get yourself out to Dublin on the first flight tomorrow."

"Are you kidding? They'll just waste me."

"Trust me. If they'd wanted to do that, they would have done it by now, and you wouldn't be answering this phone."

It went silent.

"Are you still there?" said Pete.

"Yes, I am. Let me think. You've just woken me up in the middle of the night, for fuck's sake. Let me think."

"There's no thinking to do, John. Get yourself over here on the 9:40 from Southampton. I'll meet you at the airport. If you're not on it, you're a dead man walking. And remember the instructions with the phones."

He hung up.

Chapter Twenty

Thursday 25th March 2010

The Southampton to Dublin flight landed at 11:30. Pete was standing in Arrivals and, to his absolute amazement, Falstead had Pinky and Perky in tow.

Are you having a laugh?

As Falstead and his goons walked out, Pete stepped up to them.

"Tell those two to walk over to the coffee place and sit down. You and I need to talk."

Falstead did as he was told, and Pete, holding Falstead's bicep, ushered him over to a corner.

"Are you mad? Are you trying to get us all killed?"

"What?" said Falstead, his tone questioning.

"Pinky and Perky cannot be here. What on earth were you thinking?"

"I needed a bit of muscle."

"Muscle? The British Army couldn't sort this shit out, John! What chance do you think those two fuckwits have got?" said Pete. He didn't move. Just stared with his arms extended and palms up.

"OK. What shall I do then?"

"Send them back on the next flight. They stay here at the airport until then, and we do what we need to do. You sort that with them now, and I'll see you over here when you've done."

How on earth has this man stayed out of prison or not got himself killed?

Falstead sorted out Pinky and Perky and came back to where Pete was standing.

"Sorted?"

"Sorted."

Pete said, "OK. Let's get a cab back to the hotel, and I'll fill you in." They started walking to the cab rank.

"They'll have been watching me, so will know you're in town. You are not out of the shit yet, but from what I've seen so far I think you're in with a chance of getting away with this."

"OK," said Falstead. "What will happen next then?"

"We sit in the hotel and wait. They will call me and give me the instructions for the meet. If it goes like last night, they'll pick us up in a van and take us to a barn in the middle of nowhere."

"I can't say I'm looking forward to this."

"Me neither. Because if you cock this up, they'll shoot both of us."

They got in the cab at the front of the queue and sat in silence all the way to the hotel.

"You check in and I'll get us a couple of coffees. I'll see you in the bar over there," Pete said, pointing at the bar on the other side of the foyer. "What do you want?"

"A latte with an extra shot and five sugars."

"Five?"

"Yeah, what's wrong with that?"

"Nothing," said Pete, shaking his head and walking to the bar.

Falstead checked in, walked over to Pete, and sat down.

"All done. How far have you got with it then?"

"Well, they are considering it, or they wouldn't have got you over here. They made it very clear that if they'd wanted you topped, they'd have done it in your house by now."

"Jesus."

"Look, you're the one who's got yourself in this situation. You must have a leak in your organisation, mate. If you think about it, that could be a bit of a sticking point in all this. They won't want to give you another hundred keys if they think it's just going to get seized again. Whatever plan we come up with, it has to be watertight. Convince them you can pull this off."

"I can do that. I've been putting some feelers out up north too, without going into too much detail. I think I can offload shedloads of that fifty-fifty mix of charlie and benzo."

"Good. Well, keep your powder dry for now, and we'll see how this pans out."

Just then, the burner provided by the Irish vibrated. Pete quickly picked up his phone lying on the table and answered.

"Hello."

"Get yourselves to where you were picked up earlier. Stand there and wait. Can you remember where it was?"

"How could I forget?" Pete said, and hung up.

"OK. Let's go."

They walked to the designated spot and waited. The van pulled up beside them as expected, and someone ushered them into the back less forcefully than before. This time, no one put bags over their heads, but were still made to change into tracksuit bottoms, sweatshirts, and trainers. They placed their clothes in bin bags and threw them to the back of the van.

When they got to the barn, Patrick and Shaun greeted them. There were no smiles on their faces this time, though.

"Well," said Shaun to Falstead, "it looks like yous have fecked this up, wee fella."

"Yes, I'm sorry this happened. I just don't know how it could have leaked out."

"Are yous sure the big fella here didn't know?" Shaun pointed at Pete, and Pete gulped.

"He couldn't have done it. Although I knew of him, I'd not even met him before yesterday."

"Good," said Shaun. "In which case he remains breathing." He was looking straight into Pete's eyes, searching for signs of weakness.

The earlier meeting had ended up tense, but this was on a different level. If they didn't get this right, they wouldn't be walking away from it.

"Give us a good reason, wee fella, for us to be so feckin' stupid that we'd give yous a hundred-key parcel and not just blow your brains out?"

"Well, I've already put feelers out around the country and, with the help of Pete here, I can make up enough product to pay you back for the lot. If you get rid of me now, then you end up out of pocket."

"And why do you think it won't go wrong again?"

"Because the only people who would know would be you, me, my two guys, and Pete here."

"I don't want to know anything once you've got this up and running, guys. That way, if it goes tits up, you know it's nothing to do with me."

Patrick and Shaun's faces swivelled to look at each other.

Don't start that again, boys. Please.

"Well, with that in mind, let's just discuss basic details here without giving too much away, shall we? The way we see it is this. We use a stolen Range Rover, just like the wee fellas here, which we source from the mainland, and we clone your plates. We bring it here, load it up, place it on the mainland somewhere in Holyhead for you to pick up. With me so far?"

"Yeah," Pete and Falstead said in unison.

"We vet the driver. And no one except the one we vet, or yous wee fella," said Shaun, tapping Falstead's chest, "can drive that gear away from Holyhead. Is that understood?"

"Yeah."

"Who do yous want to be the driver?"

"What about both Pinky and Perky?"

"Why both of them?"

"As insurance, in case one of them is ill or something."

"Then yous drive."

"I'd rather one of them did."

“I bet yous would,” Shaun said, looking at Patrick, who nodded.

“OK. I want their full names, addresses in the UK, phone numbers, everything. Even their inside leg measurement. You get me, wee fella, because if we find anything we don’t like, then the deal’s off.”

“I get you. And thank you.”

“Don’t thank me yet, wee fella. There’s a long ways to go before yous off the hook.”

Shaun put his hand in his pocket and pulled out three electronic fobs for the Range Rover.

“I’ve had an extra fob made and have t’ree of these. One for me for delivery of the vehicle. One for yous, wee fella,” he said, giving one to Falstead, “and the last one for yous, big fella.”

“What do I need that for? I’m going nowhere near it, Shaun,” said Pete, backing off with his forearms raised, trying not to take it.

“Yous take it. You’re the insurance, just in case yous needed. Or don’t we need yous anymore?”

Pete didn’t like the look on Shaun’s face, so he took the fob. The temperature in the barn seemed to have dropped a few degrees.

“Now then, yous two get back to the mainland and wait for instructions. We’ll source a suitable Range Rover, but yous two need to come here whilst we load it up so you know what we’re doing. We’ll be in touch.”

After changing clothes and being given a lift back to the centre of Dublin, they walked back to the hotel in silence, each taking in the events so far.

Pete had made it clear he didn’t want to know where the stolen Range Rover containing the gear was going to be parked whilst awaiting collection. But if his plan was going to work, he did really.

Whilst they were at the airport awaiting the last flight out of Dublin for Southampton, knowing what the answer to this question was going to be, Pete said, "Do you trust either Pinky or Perky to drive fifty keys of charlie back from Holyhead to Guildford without being tempted to drive off into the sunset?"

"Do I fuck," said Falstead.

"In which case, we watch the handover from a distance and keep a close eye all the way back."

"Good idea," said Falstead, smiling.

They returned to the mainland, and Pinky dropped Pete off in Woking. As soon as he was in his own car, he called Tom.

"Hi Tom. I have pretty good news."

"OK, fire away."

"The Irish have agreed to give Falstead another fifty keys to deal his way out of trouble. Both the first lot and the second lot are priced at one point seven."

"Crikey. That's not a bad price. They must be sat on a lot to sell it at that."

"Agreed. But they didn't, obviously, say how much, but it must be a chunk for them to go with this deal too. Anyway, the finer details are being sorted at the moment. It will be a similar plan to last time, but the vehicle with the gear in will be parked up in Holyhead whilst awaiting collection. I have told them I don't want to know where it is being parked, but don't panic.

"They have insisted on vetting the potential drivers, and only those will be allowed to drive the vehicle away. Falstead has propped up Pinky and Perky, his pair of goons. He doesn't want to drive it himself, but we can force his hand. The Irish will insist on a specific time for the handover. That morning, you nick both Pinky and Perky having kicked their doors in."

"How do we know they'll have gear on the premises?"

"They will."

"I understand. Where do they live?"

"They share a flat in Guildford. I'll need you to get the address through your means for me. I could get it through someone I know, but it's best I don't in case that request comes out after the dust settles."

"OK. Leave that with me."

"That leaves only one person available to take the handover and drive it back, Falstead. He will need driving to Holyhead, which I will have to do as he can't trust anyone else to be aware of what's going on. That tells me where the vehicle is, and I tell you. You take it from there. I'll follow the vehicle back to Surrey, running interference in case it looks like it's getting a tug, so you will always know where it is. Even once the gear has been seized, I will be out of the frame because I only knew where it was at the handover.

"You need to give it some thought now, Tom, but because I'll give you the location of the vehicle at all times, I suggest you could let it run into Surrey before you hit it. Your call, of course, but the further away from Holyhead it is, the better it is for me."

"OK, Pete. Leave the thought process to me for now. What's the next move on your end then?"

"They want me and Falstead back over to Dublin to load up the vehicle. I'm not sure why they can't do that without us, but that may become apparent in time. They will message or call me, and we'll need to get over there on the hurry-up."

"OK, mate. Great job so far. Let's hope it all pans out."

"As I've said, I've told them I don't want to know where the vehicle is. It's way safer that way, but I've been thinking… if I were clever, I'd track it. Just in case."

"How?" said Tom.

"Do you know anyone who can rig up something discreet? Tech guy, off-grid stuff."

"No mate, not my bag but… hang on, someone in the office was talking the other day about a tech guy. Let me make a couple of calls and call you back."

"OK, mate. Speak in a bit."

Tom sent a message to Sharon telling her he'd had an update but would fill her in the next day, as there was nothing urgent that needed doing immediately, and to pick him up at the usual time. Then he made another call.

"Hi sarge. How are you doing? It's been a long time," said Andy Summers.

"Hi Annie. How are you, mate? How's civilian life treating you?"

"Not bad. Simmo and me have got a little business running up here in Lavenham doing electronics stuff. Day-to-day repairs of things and also a bit of tech work for some private investigators. All legal, of course."

"Of course, mate. I wouldn't expect anything else. Listen, I've got a bit of a proposition for you that requires a lot of trust and the feelings of loyalty that go back to our previous lives."

"Go on," said Annie, intrigued.

"I want to give your name to a bloke who will track you down through his own contacts and will require your specific skill set regarding tracking equipment. I don't want to give him all your details or make the introduction direct because I don't want him to know you know me. That's important."

"This sounds interesting."

"All will become clear. When you get a call from this guy called Pete, who will have been introduced to you through someone else who knows you he's tracked down, just get him whatever he wants and needs. He will pay top dollar for it too, so you'll make a few quid."

"OK."

"I then want you to track his movements. Possibly with Simmo, as he's working with you, and this Pete guy will have seen your face, making your tailing him difficult."

"OK, I'm not being funny, mate, but how will we get paid for doing this?" said Annie.

"I'll work that out, but you'll get a chunk of cash from this Pete guy. Trust me, I won't let you down. We go back too far, Annie."

"And I just keep reporting back to you with everything?"

"Absolutely."

"OK. I'll wait to hear from him then," said Annie, who then hung up.

Tom then called Pete back.

"Pete, all I can get is that there's a guy called Andy Summers who lives in Suffolk who's a wizard with tech stuff. One of the girls in the office said she has a mate who's a private investigator, and that person mentioned him as someone they're aware of. Sorry, mate, that's all I can get for you."

"OK, Tom. Not much to go on, but I'll do some digging. See you."

Seed planted. Fingers crossed.

Pete spent the next hour making calls to anyone he could think of who would have need, at any time, for a tech expert.

Finally, he got there with a shady PI he knew.

"Yeah, I know Andy. Have done for years and use him all the time. He's a real wizard on the tech front and doesn't mind crossing the line. Keeps himself to himself. I'll make the intro if you want me to?"

"Yes, mate, I do."

"OK. Expect a call."

Thirty minutes later, Pete's phone vibrated. An unknown number.

"Hello," said Pete.

"Hi. Is that Pete?" said Annie.

"It is. Is that Andy Summers?"

"It is. I understand you may need the services of a tech guy who knows his stuff?"

"I do, and you come well recommended, mate. Look, we'll skip the pleasantries. I need your advice. I'm looking for the smallest tracker you can lay your hands on. Ideally, one I can turn on and off remotely. It needs to fit snugly in my underpants and stay hidden. That's just for transport before placement. It's locating a vehicle's location. I will have a rough idea but need to pinpoint it. It'll be stationary, not mobile."

"The remote turn-on's tricky. Can you fix an antenna wherever you're putting it?"

"No, definitely not."

"Then remote activation's out."

"Fine. Tell me about the signals these things put out. Can it be found if someone scans the vehicle?"

"Commercial ones, very likely. So if that's a problem, you'll need military-grade. Commercial units use GSM or SMS, which are easy to detect. Military ones transmit encrypted, low-RF bursts. They're smaller too, maybe three to four centimetres. Commercial ones are bulkier, maybe five to ten."

"How long can these things transmit for?"

"Depends on how often they ping a signal. If that's every five minutes, then the battery will last one to three days."

"That's no good. How do I get the best battery life?"

"Just set it to ping once a day. You'll get three or four weeks."

"OK. That's the way to do it then. And it has to be military-grade. How would I see it on a screen in my car?"

"You're stepping into a high-tech world now, mate. This is expensive kit. You'll need a full setup, receiver, software, mapping overlay. This isn't something you can see on your phone."

"And how far can these things transmit? I think I need up to a couple of miles."

"That's fine if you've got line of sight."

"OK, I've got that. What if the tracker's inside something like a suitcase, packed in the boot of a vehicle with loads of stuff around it? Would that reduce the distance it could be detected from?"

"Not enough to cause you a problem if you're only a couple of miles away and have a line of sight."

"How much?"

"When do you need it?"

"Yesterday."

"Blimey."

"If I can source it, and I'll make a call after this, it's ten grand for the lot."

"If you can get it ready for tomorrow morning, I'll give you fifteen. Call me back on this number when it's confirmed."

It was over an hour before Andy called back.

"I can source everything. See you in the morning. I'll message you the address?"

"I'll be with you first thing."

Suffolk, here I come.

Chapter Twenty One

Friday 26th March 2010

Pete turned off his phone, removed the SIM card, and put the lot in a Faraday pouch. No point in leaving it traceable through cell site data if things go sideways later. He had a few burners with him, and Martina knew the number of one of them to reach him if she needed to.

Pete drove the Merc, lent by his friend again, to Suffolk, leaving at 18:00. He didn't do any dry cleaning straightaway. He had a plan. When he joined the M25 at Junction 11, he wrote a WhatsApp to someone he knew who worked at Cobham Services.

Barrier code?

And waited for the reply.

270953

That was all he needed. After parking near the entrance, he noted the registrations of the next ten vehicles after driving in. He then drove to the rear exit of the services, used only by the staff who worked there. He punched in the code at the gates, exited after they opened, and drove away. No one could follow him down here. He then stopped at the end of the lane and watched. A single vehicle came past, a solo female driver. He checked the registration number against his list. Clear. Dry cleaning. Done.

He arrived in Lavenham just after nine and went to Andy's workshop on a farm on the outskirts of this beautiful village.

This is lovely. Maybe here's a place we could settle after all this is over?

Andy was expecting him. Back to business. They shook hands and walked into the workshop, which was tucked behind a hedgerow and shielded by rusted corrugated panels. It smelled of diesel, solder, and damp straw. Pete stepped inside. The kit lay out with military precision on a spotless workbench. It appeared Andy didn't do clutter, and Pete appreciated the professionalism.

"OK, Pete. Good to meet you, mate. I know you'll want to crack on, so we'll get straight down to it. We have:

"A military-grade GPS tracker with a compact, hardened casing. Three centimetres long. Preconfigured for an encrypted burst every day at one minute past midnight. Battery sealed. No external antenna. It will work for at least two weeks, maybe four.

"A Faraday pouch for transport in the leg of these boxer shorts I've had made up for you. Blocks all signals until deployment, just in case there's an odd chance someone is looking at one minute past midnight. Black nylon, stitched tight. It sits on the inside of your thigh. Very hard to detect unless someone grabs your nuts or you have to take them off.

"This is the receiver rig.

"An SDR, Software Defined Radio, HackRF One, tuned to the tracker's frequency.

"A directional antenna. This is a foldable Yagi antenna, mounted on a magnetic base for car roof or boot lid. It will work if it's fitted on the inside of your boot lid, but I suggest you put it on the outside because of the distance involved.

"A signal booster. This is optional and for fringe reception zones. You should take it just in case."

Pete said, "Does the signal booster sit with the tracker or the receiver?"

"With the receiver rig."

Pete nodded.

"A burner laptop. This is a hardened Linux build with SDR decoding software installed, with GPS mapping overlay. No Wi-Fi, no Bluetooth, USB-only.

"The mapping interface, custom GIS script. When the tracker pings, you see a red dot on a grey-scale map. Timestamped. No cloud sync. Local only.

"Power kit: lithium battery packs, car inverter, backup USB charger. All tested."

Andy took Pete through each bit of kit piece by piece over the next hour.

"Run it past me again. How far away from the tracker can I be to receive the signal?"

"That depends on what's in the way."

"I'll be about 160 to 180 metres above sea level with almost line of sight to the centre of where I expect the tracker to be, about a mile away, maybe two at most."

"Two miles would just about be fine, but I would use the signal booster. Any more than that would push it. The battery is a high-capacity lithium pack, which is enough to run the booster and SDR for several hours.

"You should plug the laptop into the cigarette lighter socket, just in case." You don't need the engine running.

"There's also the backup USB charger for redundancy. If the main pack fails, you have a fallback for the signal booster or the SDR receiver.

"You're only going to be waiting for the one-minute-past-midnight signal, so you don't have to have everything switched on much before that. I suggest you're in place about fifteen minutes beforehand. No doubt you'll do dry runs setting the kit up so you're familiar with everything. Also, because you're a fair distance away, I stress the antenna has to have a clear line of sight. So, placed on top of your boot lid, or inside with the boot lid open."

"Now, let's get everything set up in your car and test it all. I've got another tracker here I can use can force a signal burst."

They spent the next hour setting up and testing everything. All was perfect.

"Thanks, Andy. Good doing business, mate," said Pete, and handed him a thick envelope.

The plan is coming together.

As soon as Pete had left, Annie called Tom.

"Hi Tom. This Pete guy has picked up all his stuff. It looks like he's doing a onetime track for a vehicle parked in a large area. He's got himself an OP on high ground and will park up. The kit has been set up to ping once every day at one minute past midnight. This is military-grade kit and, the way it's set up, even someone using a scanner will never find it. What he's asked for is clever, Tom. This guy is smart."

“But not smart enough to know I’ve put a tracker in the laptop he’s got, which is easy for Simmo to follow. Simmo is behind him now on the way south. I’ll update you when we know where he’s going.”

“OK, Annie. Well done, mate. How much did he give you?”

“Fifteen grand.”

“That’s good. That’ll tide you over for a bit. Pete doesn’t know this, but you’ll get all your kit back.”

The trip to Holyhead from Suffolk took six hours. The ‘friend’ who worked for Pete had already packed the boot with the benzocaine and other cutting agents. Boxed and taped whilst wearing nitrile gloves, just as Pete insisted.

A steady drive. No rushing. Just above the speed limit. Nothing to draw attention.

Once in Holyhead, Pete headed straight to a self-storage facility he’d researched. Not on his own laptop or phone, obviously. He’d used the local library. The place offered 24/7 access via a security code at the outer gate, then individual unit entry by keypad. Insulated and hermetically sealed.

“Morning,” he said to the receptionist. “I’d like to hire a unit, please.”

The entrance door opened behind him. Pete turned around to see someone standing there.

“Sorry, mate. I’m just hiring a unit. I’ll try not to be too long,” said Pete over his shoulder.

“No problem. I’m going to be doing the same. Take your time.”

“What do you want to store in the unit, sir?” said the receptionist. “I just want to point out that we can’t allow certain items on this list here.”

The receptionist was indicating a list pinned on the wall behind her desk of items that could not be stored.

"No, nothing like that. This is ideal for my collection of rare books. Irish titles mostly. I like to pick them up after tours around the island, hence the need for a facility in Holyhead. This is perfect.

"Just remind me of the CCTV you have here?"

"We have CCTV on the main entrance, but not on the individual units."

"OK. Thanks," said Pete.

Perfect.

He registered under a false name. That sort of paperwork was standard kit. Paid cash for a deal they were running, three months at half price if you paid up front. Natural. Nothing to raise eyebrows. Great cover.

Having done all the paperwork, Pete left the reception and the other customer to do his stuff. He moved the boxes from the boot into the unit. Job done.

As Simmo filled out the paperwork at reception, the CCTV monitor caught his eye. Pete was hauling boxes from his vehicle through the main entrance and into his unit. Job done.

Before heading home, Pete drove up Holyhead Mountain. He needed to recce a place from which he had an uninterrupted line of sight over the town. He took a few tracks, noted vantage points, angles, and spots where he could see the town without being seen. And found the spot he needed.

A long day. But all part of the plan.

Once all that was done, feeling exhausted, he drove home.

"Annie, I've just followed this guy to Holyhead in north bloody Wales. He's hired a storage unit under a false name. I didn't get the personal details he used, but I got the unit number, and I hired a unit too. I watched him on the CCTV unit in their reception and watched him move a load of boxes inside."

"Great job, Simmo. I'll let Tom know."

Chapter Twenty Two

Friday 26th March 2010

Tom got picked up by Sharon at the usual time, and they drove into the office. On the way, Tom called Jamie.

"Morning, guv. You in the office for a bit?"

"I am."

"Good. I've had an update from the source, so we'll come in, update you, and do the contact sheet." He hung up.

Tom turned to Sharon and said, "Another fifty keys coming in."

"Excellent stuff. You are excelling yourself with this one, matey."

"We are. It's not just me."

"Thanks. But, to be fair, you always knew he'd be good."

"I've thought it for years."

"How's your head now, Tom?" She was watching him rub his temple.

"Better, maybe. Still getting headaches though, and my memory's shot to pieces. I have to keep writing everything down."

"That's not a good sign, is it?"

Tom gave a half-smile and said, "It depends on who you ask. My GP says to rest, but I say just crack on and don't push it too hard. I've got a job to do."

She didn't reply straightaway. The silence stretched.

"You're not invincible, you know."

"I know."

She reached over and touched his arm.

"Still. I worry."

"I'll get it checked again. After this is done. I'm due another brain scan anyway."

She didn't like that answer, but she let it go. For now.

After a brief pause, she joked, "That's because they couldn't find one the first time."

They turned to each other, and both smiled.

She tapped the steering wheel, remembering something.

"You remember that job in Caterham?"

Tom snorted. "You mean when I walked into a lamppost while looking down at the map on my phone?"

"Exactly. You've always been terrible at admitting you're hurt."

He didn't argue.

The car turned in towards the office, tyres crunching over loose gravel. Tom straightened in his seat, the smile gone. Time to go to work.

"Morning, guv."

"Morning. What've you got?"

"Another fifty keys of charlie. From Dublin to the mainland."

"Whoa. The Irish let him off the first lot?"

"Not as such. He's still got to pay for it, and they assumed it was the only way to get their money back for the first lot."

"So, what's the plan?" said Jamie, leaning back in his chair and clasping his hands behind his head.

"The Irish are going to put the loaded vehicle in Holyhead. As there was a leak last time, they've stated only Falstead may take possession of it, and he will only be told the location on the day of the handover. They also insisted that the source will be the only person allowed to drop off Falstead at the vehicle. That keeps everything as tight as possible and puts Falstead with, and responsible for, the gear."

"OK. Participating informant?"

"Agreed. But if our man didn't drive him, he'd get someone else to do it, so it's essential for us to know, and it would still happen without it."

"Yes, it fits. We can get that authorised with no problems, and I'll do the paperwork on it. Leave that to me. So, what's the next step?"

Tom shrugged. "We wait for the next update."

"OK, Sharon, I need to talk to Tom about his health, so leave us for the moment, please."

"OK. I'll see you in a bit," said Sharon as she left the office, shutting the door behind her.

Jamie leaned forward.

"OK, what am I missing?"

"Pinky and Perky will also be cleared by the Irish to drive the vehicle from the handover in Holyhead. So, we have to nick them on the morning of it to get Falstead in the vehicle."

Jamie took this in for a good thirty seconds. Then said, "And what are we going to nick them for?"

"We execute a warrant at their HA."

"What if there's nothing there?"

"There will be."

Jamie closed his eyes.

"I didn't hear that."

OK, Jamie, time to show how far you're prepared to go now.

"Understood."

"And what if they aren't in when we execute the warrant and one of them ends up driving the vehicle?"

"That's the chance we take, but there is a contingency. Falstead doesn't trust Pinky or Perky and thinks they may bugger off with the gear. They will have guessed it's a parcel of a decent size, so the source is going to drive Falstead to view the handover from a distance and follow it back. He'll be able to let us know enough to target the vehicle on the way back. So, whilst we may not get Falstead driving it, we will get the gear."

"I assume you were going to tell me?" said Jamie, looking Tom straight in the eyes.

"Absolutely, guv," said Tom, staring right back at him.

Chapter Twenty Three

Sunday 28th March 2010

Pete and Martina had spent the Saturday night at Le Manoir aux Quat'Saisons, the two Michelin-star hotel and restaurant just outside Oxford. They had a beautiful meal, including some fine wines suggested by the sommelier.

The dining room had glowed with soft candlelight and the hush of reverence. Martina had worn a navy silk dress that caught the light like water. The sommelier, a wiry Frenchman with a memory like a Rolodex, had paired their venison with a 2005 Côte-Rôtie that tasted like velvet and old secrets. It was one of Martina's favourites here, and she smiled. Pete watched her with his cheeky grin.

Later, in their suite overlooking the herb garden, Martina had kicked off her heels and curled up on the chaise.

"You're still somewhere else in your head," she said, not unkindly.

Pete smiled, poured the last of the wine, and sat beside her.

"Force of habit," he said.

"I don't want to leave, Pete. I want to live here forever."

"Not long now. I am almost there. Soon, I'll be able to stop all the nonsense and do something legitimate."

Martina turned her head, studying him.

"You always say that. Nearly there. Almost done. Like it's a finish line you can see but never cross."

Pete didn't answer straightaway. He watched the steam rise from the teacup she'd left untouched, smelling chamomile mingling with rosemary from the garden below.

"This time it's real," he said. "One last job. Clean. No looking for tails. All done."

He was admiring her beauty when the burner vibrated.

"Bugger. I need to take that."

She never stopped him, never asked him to change. She was aware of where the money came from. He held nothing from her, and she accepted it as part of him, his makeup and just how he had to make a living.

"Hello."

"Hey big fella. Tuesday flight, 9:40. Same hotel and wait for instructions on this phone."

Pete just said, "All received," and hung up.

"Tuesday morning I'm back in Dublin. We can stay another night if you want to?"

"I'd love to," she said, slipping out of her little black dress.

An hour later, he messaged Falstead.

0102 2

“Evening John. Our presence is required on Tuesday. Assuming one of your guys can drive us to Southampton Airport, can you pick me up from Guildford Railway Station at 06:30?”

“Will do. Pinky and Perky have a minor job to do in Southampton that day. Someone owes me a lump of money, and I need it on the hurry-up.”

“I didn’t realise your tentacles stretched as far as the south coast, John?”

“They don’t, but may the way we’re going. I’ve just traced this fella, so he’s getting a visit.”

“Well, don’t involve me in any of that stuff. See you Tuesday morning.”

He looked at Martina stretched out on the bed in the stockings and suspenders she’d bought for the weekend.

“Now,” he said to Martina, hanging up the phone, “let’s just enjoy the rest of today.”

***

Monday 29th March 2010

Tom and Martina were home late afternoon. He turned on his main phone and sent a message to Tom.

Address?

About ten minutes later, his phone vibrated.

“Hi, Tom.”

“I won’t message the address, so write this down.”

Tom gave Pete the address for Pinky and Perky, which Pete wrote in his phone and hung up.

Next call? To Hannah.

"Hi Pete."

"Hi, Hannah. I've got a job for you. Can we meet?"

"Of course."

"You can come round to my gaff if you like. Martina's in, and she'd love to see you."

"No problem. Give me half an hour."

Hannah was a rare breed, a female burglar, but she was of the highest class. Pete, Martina, and Hannah had all gone to school together, and Martina had kept in touch with her. They weren't best buddies or anything like that, but they always got on well when they bumped into each other.

Martina was chopping peppers when Pete walked into the kitchen. She didn't look up.

"Hannah's coming round. I've got a job for her."

Martina paused, knife hovering mid-air.

"You trust her?"

Pete shrugged.

"Enough. And she owes me."

Martina nodded.

"She always had a soft spot for you."

Pete didn't answer. He opened the fridge, grabbed a beer, and leaned against the counter.

Half an hour later, Hannah knocked once and he let her in. She wore black jeans, boots, and a faded hoodie that had seen a few crawlspaces. She had pulled her hair back, without makeup and without fuss.

Martina greeted her with a hug and a smile that was half genuine, half wary.

"Still breaking into places?" she asked with a smile on her face.

"Only the ones worth it, sweetie," Hannah said, grinning.

Pete gestured towards the living room.

"You two can catch up in a minute. Come through, Hannah."

They sat. No small talk. Just business.

"I need a plant job," Pete said. "A flat in Guildford."

"What am I planting?"

"Nine ounces of charlie."

"Blimey. Someone's pissed you off, Pete."

"The reason stays with me, Hannah, but this is very important and I need it done."

Hannah nodded.

"Entry?"

"It's the top-floor flat in this block." He gave her a map with the address on it.

"OK."

"It has to be quiet, with no traces. Tape it to the underside of the cistern in the main bathroom and find somewhere to put the roll of tape so that can be found too. There might be only one bathroom. If there's an en suite, ignore it and just do the main bathroom. It has to be done tomorrow morning after seven. Wait for a message from me to tell you it's all clear. I'll just send you a thumbs-up. That will be just after six thirty."

She nodded.

"You still pay in cash?"

Pete smiled.

"Always. How much do you want?"

"Five grand?"

"Here's ten. As I said, it's important. Very important," said Pete, giving her an envelope while looking into her eyes.

"Go to the address you know in Tringham Close, Knaphill, and pick up the parcel and a roll of tape. They know you're coming."

She got up without a word, walked out of the sitting room, and went to see Martina.

It's all coming together.

Chapter Twenty Four

Tuesday 30th March 2010

They picked up Pete just before six thirty. For that hour, he didn't feel too bad. An early start, but he'd had worse. He knew they had a few stressful days ahead of them, so had slept as much as he could after the wonderful weekend away. With relief, he saw that both Pinky and Perky were in the vehicle's front.

Once settled in for the journey, he sent a thumbs-up to Hannah.

There was little chatting between them, and his mind turned to the last few days of bliss. His thoughts drifted back to Martina, her smile over the Côte-Rôtie, the way her dress shimmered like water, the way it caught the light, then slipped from her beautiful legs. The scent of chamomile and rosemary rising from the garden below.

I love that woman so much. I have no idea what I'd do without her.

Soon.

In the event of a tragedy, he had provided well for Martina. He'd arranged insurance policies, hidden bank account details, stashed gold bars and cold cash in a safe deposit box. Two solicitors held identical keys, each sworn to release them two months after his death. He estimated it would take that long for the police to give up the chase. The solicitors received good payment in advance for their services. They were unaware of each other's details, so it was unlikely both of them would cannot deliver. A single set of keys plus the bank's confidential code would set her free and be sufficient for Martina to access the box and retrieve what she needed.

A conversation in the front seats interrupted Pete's thoughts. He was lying back with his eyes closed, but he was listening.

Pinky said from the passenger seat, "Falstead's got no idea what it's like, doing this every week."

"He just points. We do the rest," said Perky. His tone was flat, but there was something behind it. He glanced in the mirror. Pete's head was back, eyes closed. He was asleep.

"Don't you ever think it's too much?" said Pinky. "I'm fed up with this life."

"Does it matter? We're paid. And paid well."

The car hummed along the A34, tyres whispering against the wet tarmac. Streetlights flicked past in silence.

"I've been looking at that courier job," Pinky said. "Decent hours. No one screams when you knock."

"You serious?"

"Yeah. Might be time. This stuff... it sticks."

Pete stayed quiet in the back. The front seats weren't as aggressive as he'd thought. Just tired men, running out of road.

***

Hannah walked along the opposite side of the road from the block of flats, checking out her target.

All clear.

She slipped on a pair of thin leather gloves and pulled her lock picks from her pocket. At the front door, she glanced left and right. Coast clear. She knelt.

Sliding the tension wrench into the base of the lock, she angled it just enough to feel resistance. Then came the rake, quick, practised scrubs across the pins. One click. Two. Three. The cylinder shifted.

Fifteen seconds. She was in.

Inside wasn't as nice as it had appeared from the outside. Food wrappers on the stairs. Quiet, though. She ascended, soft trainers making no sound. Same drill at the flat door.

Fifteen more seconds. She was in.

A quick sweep confirmed the flat was empty.

Good. Time to work.

She moved fast, bedroom with en-suite, second bedroom, bathroom, open-plan kitchen and sitting room. Enough space. Enough risk.

Then, just as she reached for her rucksack, a noise.

Shit.

A key in the lock. A voice. Female.

She bolted into the main bedroom, scanned the room, and spotted the built-in closet. No choice. She got in.

Jesus Christ. We didn't plan for this.

The voice came closer, off-key, belting out a power ballad. Through the closet door, there was a clattering sound.

Then.....

The whine of a vacuum cleaner.

A fucking cleaner.

The singing got worse, louder, riding the hum of the motor. Twenty minutes of it. Then the sound shifted, closer now, into the bedroom.

Hannah flinched as the vacuum nozzle thudded against the closet door. Once, and then again.

If that door opened, she was done. No cover story. No way out.

She checked her watch in the dark, 8:05. Glowing digits. No comfort.

The noise receded. She might've got away with it. In all the time she'd stolen things from enormous houses, hotel rooms, art galleries, this had never happened. And here she was, in a pokey flat belonging to a couple of goons. Not even taking something out, putting something in.

In the darkness, she shook her head.

The vacuum stopped. The singing didn't. She wasn't sure which was worse.

Another twenty minutes. Then silence. A door closed.

She waited fifteen more minutes. Then, she eased the closet door open and crept out, rucksack clutched tight.

Cleaner gone. Thank fuck.

OK, put that episode out of your head. Get cracking.

Bathroom. Plastic bag of charlie. Tape. Lid off the cistern, placed on the floor. Bag taped inside. Lid back on. Bathroom done.

Sitting room. Put the tape inside a drawer in the sideboard.

Job done. Let's go.

She cracked the flat door open and listened. Nothing. She slipped out, closing the door behind her. Quiet down the stairs and out of the front door.

"Jesus fucking Christ. I'm glad that's done," she muttered, and let out a long breath.

***

The flight was uneventful, but tension curled through him like smoke as they neared Dublin. The low hum of the engines lured him in and out of sleep, each rest interrupted by the same grim thought:

If this goes wrong, I'm dead.

When they landed, he turned on his phone. Ping. A thumbs-up. He smiled.

Another part of the plan completed.

They stepped into the lift side by side. The doors closed with a soft whoosh.

"Be ready to move fast, John. Don't be in the bath with your plastic ducks or anything. We need to be out within five minutes of the call."

"No problem. I hate the waiting, though."

"I'll remind you once more. Without this parcel, you were a dead man."

"Alright, mate. Stop the life-or-death pep talks. It gives me the willies."

The lift dinged. Pete pressed the button for the top floor.

"Get some room service, John," he said as the doors slid open. "We don't know when we'll eat again. When I knock on your door, we have to go. Understood?"

"Understood."

Pete was sure they were keeping them waiting on purpose. Some kind of psychological warm-up. Let the nerves build, let the imagination run wild. Classic tactic. Get them edgy, then hit them hard.

He couldn't settle. One minute he was pacing the length of the room; the next he was flat on the bed staring at the ceiling, counting cracks in the plaster. Then up again, checking his phone, checking the time, checking the silence.

Pete sat back down, rubbed his face, and muttered, "Come on, Patrick. Let's get this bloody thing moving."

Then the burner rang. In reality, it hadn't been that long, but it felt like an eternity.

At last.

"Sorry to keep yous two waiting so long, big fella, but we's been busy doing a few bits and bobs, so we have. Be at that pickup point in fifteen minutes and the boys'll pick yous both up."

"Will do," said Pete, and hung up.

He put his shoes on, turned off the lights, locked his door, and banged on Falstead's door.

As before, they picked them up, and both of them went to undress.

"No need of that this time, fellas. I think we're past that now."

What a result. My balls have been itching for hours with this package next to my package.

Both just nodded, sat back, and let the ride play out. Pete thought about their situation and where this whole thing could lead. He stared at the rear doors of the van, thinking things through. His biggest worry was: what would the Irish consider his involvement in the gear's seizing once it was all over? To avoid being implicated, he had to distance himself from the vehicle's drop-off and pickup, but knowing the vehicle details when Pinky and Perky were nicked, which meant dropping Falstead off at the exchange, could still put him in the frame. Mind you, the obvious choice would be Pinky or Perky, or both, as they were the ones in custody with a chunk of charlie in their flat.

And then they were at the barn. Same people, same cold, same smells.

"Well, here they are. Tweedledee and Tweedledum. All ready for action," said Shaun, more relaxed than he had been last time.

Sat in the middle of the barn was a Range Rover Autobiography, identical to Falstead's. It even had cloned reg plates.

"We t'ought," said Patrick, "it best if our transport was a replica of yous own vehicle. That way, if the polis do a check on yous or even stop yous, yous are in yous own vehicle. The only way they would catch on is if they checks the chassis or engine numbers, and they just don't do that."

"Why didn't I just get one of my guys to come across in mine then?"

"Two reasons. One, we've upgraded the suspension and done other modifications so that, with the gear in the back, it doesn't sag. And two, because we wants the feckin' t'ing back after, wee fella. When you've emptied your gear out, yous drops it where we've told yous to and drives it away."

"Why?" said Falstead.

"Don't ask feckin' questions. We're running the show and yous do as yous are feckin' told, so yous do."

Pete turned to Falstead and said, "For fuck's sake, John. Just do as you're told when you're told. This isn't a debating society, mate. We've got a job to do."

"Sorry. I'm not used to this."

"Now," said Shaun. "Patrick, and the boys is off somewhere else, so t'ree of us is loading dis t'ing up."

Pete offered, eager to participate and impress the group.

There was a pile of blocks of charlie on the floor in the barn's corner. Pete had seen decent-sized parcels of gear before, but this was a big lump. On the table, next to the bottle of Jameson, was a box of nitrile gloves.

Shaun pointed to them and said, "Put some gloves on, fellas." They all did.

"Right. Let's go."

"I need a piss first, Shaun."

"Outside, big fella."

Pete went outside and retrieved the tracker from his underpants and put it in his pocket. He was glad that was out of there, it had been uncomfortable for hours. He gave everything a good scratch and went back into the barn.

With the three of them working, they got it done in short order. They packed the bricks tight into the space where the spare tyre should've been.

Halfway through the loading, he whipped out the small tracker and hid it under the pile of bricks of cocaine.

"Yous OK there, big fella?" said Shaun. "Yous are looking sweaty and red-faced there."

"I'm fine, Shaun. Just not used to doing the heavy lifting."

Christ. That was close.

Pete knew that one kilo of charlie, vacuum-sealed, took up a litre of volume. The Irish had done this before. It only just fitted, with no room to spare and no margin for error. They placed a circular wooden lid on top.

When it was done, they took off their gloves and threw them in the bin next to the table. Pete noted which ones belonged to which person and, as they both walked away from him, he picked up the pair Falstead had been wearing, using one of his own, careful not to leave a trace. Just in time, before either of the others turned round, and put them into a small bag he had been carrying in his pocket.

Phew, managed that just in time. That's the next part of the plan completed.

They sat at the table and, in silence, drank a glass of Jameson.

Shaun's phone vibrated on the table. He picked it up, and as he answered it, walked to the door of the barn.

Pete wandered over, catching fragments through the barn door as Shaun stepped outside.

"It's not just the charlie."

".....bigger fish to fry."

"Some reckon we shouldn't even be doing it."

"..... it's priced that way."

"....no clue, Shamus."

"Right. I'll see yous later, boss."

What was that all about? Shaun came back in. Pete sat down.

"There's an Aer Lingus flight to Southampton at twelve ten tomorrow, fellas. Be on that one and we'll be in touch."

Neither of them replied. There were no arguments or discussions. It was an order from someone used to giving orders, who didn't need to explain himself.

Outside, the crunch of gravel signalled the van's return. One man, who had been wearing a balaclava, poked his head through the barn door and gave Shaun a thumbs-up.

"Off yous go then, fellas."

No goodbyes. No, see-you-soons. No, stay safe.

And off they went. All the way back to Blighty. Back to whatever waited for them there.

Chapter Twenty Five

Wednesday 31st March 2010

Today was brain-scan day.

Tom let Sue stay in bed this morning. He took her up a cup of tea and went to sort out the girls. They'd got used to his presence when he was at home after the accident, but it was always nice to see him in the mornings.

The Falstead incident was being pushed to the back of their minds as each day passed. Every now and again, something would trigger a memory, and their eyes would dart around, looking for a threat, but their minds were improving.

"Come on then, girls. I won't put up with the grief you give your mother in the mornings. I want the beds made, your rooms tidy, and you all out the door on time."

All three just looked at each other with silly grins on their faces and laughed.

“What was that for?” said Tom, but he was already grinning too.

“Yes, sir!” said Evie, snapping a salute.

“Cheeky sod,” muttered Tom, but he was smiling.

As the girls ran upstairs to clean their teeth, he stood by the sink, mug in hand, watching the steam curl. The scan was scheduled for eleven. Still time to pretend it was just another Wednesday.

Tom wasn’t a worrier, but he was worried about this. True, his headaches had not been as severe as a couple of weeks ago, but he still had them. He was pretty sure his memory was not up to scratch too, which was a genuine worry. Suppose a defence brief found that out and challenged some of his evidence? That would be a nightmare.

Best just keep that under my hat. No pun intended.

He rinsed the mug and set it down, careful not to clatter. Upstairs, the girls were still giggling; someone had stolen someone’s toothpaste again. He smiled, but it didn’t reach far.

He’d briefed big operations many times with less tension than this. The scan wasn’t supposed to mean anything. Just a precaution. Just Sue being thorough, as always. He, like most blokes, would just ignore it all and hope it went away. But the word neurological had been used, and once that was out there, it was hard to reel it back in.

He checked the time. 08:17.

Still a couple of hours to play normal.

His phone vibrated. A WhatsApp from Pete:

Just a quick message. The job is still on. Believe the product is stashed in the vehicle ready to go. Awaiting final details. Cannot guess at timescales.

Tom replied with a thumbs-up.

Good. The job is still on.

An avalanche descended the stairs as the girls rushed to the front door. They were walking to school on their own now and had been for a few days, as Falstead was diverted to other things.

"Bye, Dad!" they chorused. "Have you made your beds and tidied your rooms?" "Yes, Dad!" came the replies, already halfway out the door.

He watched them go, knowing full well they hadn't. The door slammed so hard the glass rattled. A tremor ran through the frame, then silence. Just the hum of the fridge and the distant tick of the hallway clock. Tom stood still, mug in hand. The house felt hollow, as if something had left with them.

Sue pattered down the stairs. The difference between that soft tread and the previous stampede stuck in his mind.

"Are you ready to go?" she said.

Her mood had hardly changed for days, and he was still deep in the shit

"Just about, but it's a bit early, isn't it?" he said in as pleasant a tone as he could muster.

"OK. Plan to leave at ten."

"I can go on my own, Sue."

"OK. You do that."

She looked at him with what appeared, contempt and walked back upstairs.

St Peter's Hospital at Chertsey wasn't that far away, but both of them were sticklers for timekeeping.

The hospital visit was uneventful, though it stirred unpleasant memories of waking up after the crash.

Chapter Twenty Six

Sunday 4th April 2010

Pete sat reading the *Sunday Telegraph*, sipping rich black coffee. The house was silent, no hum of appliances, no footsteps. Martina had gone to her parents for morning coffee. He stayed behind, waiting for the call from the Irish.

The past few days had been quiet. He'd gone dark, letting the noise settle. Just sleep, food, and the paper. A necessary stillness. The paper lay folded, cryptic crossword half-done, headlines skimmed but not absorbed. His mind wasn't on politics or markets. It was on the kit in the boot. On the tracker. On the silence.

He checked his phone. Still nothing.

Another sip. Let the bitterness linger. Outside, the sky hung low and grey, the kind that promised drizzle but never delivered. He liked days like this. They kept people indoors.

Then the phone buzzed. One quick vibration. Unknown number.

"Morning, big fella," said the voice. Irish. Calm. "The vehicle's moving today, so it is. Await further instructions for the handover."

"All received. When is the handover?"

"This coming week sometime, but yous'll be told when and where." Click. Gone.

And we're off. No need for Falstead to know yet. Or Tom.

He called Martina. "I have to go out about five and won't be back until tomorrow morning."

"OK," she said. "Why don't you come over here for Sunday lunch, and we'll come back after that. You can have a quick nap before you go."

"OK. I'll get a cab over."

She was absolutely amazing. Not a single question. Just quiet acceptance that what he was doing mattered.

Pete left home at five. Lunch had been lovely; it always was. He'd napped too. Hugged Martina tight.

"Nearly there," he said and walked to his car.

He switched back to the Merc. Transferred the kit with care, tracker rig, antenna, booster, burner laptop, lithium packs. Everything in its place. Checked. Double-checked. He also packed flat cardboard boxes and rolls of parcel tape. Nitrile gloves.

The drive to Holyhead was long, but he didn't rush. He did some dry cleaning en route, habit now. Pull into services, note plates, watch for tails. Not paranoia. Protocol.

The sky stayed low and grey, blurring edges. He liked that. It gave him cover.

This was a big day. The Irish had confirmed the vehicle was coming. The charlie was in the boot with the tracker, buried deep. Midnight was the moment. One encrypted burst. One red dot. If it landed, everything moved forward. If it didn't? He was a dead man.

Shaun's giving him the fob for the Range Rover was a double-edged sword. He needed access to the transport vehicle. The fob saved him from having to find a way in, but left him exposed with the Irish. Nothing to be done about that now.

He passed Bangor just after eight. The Merc hummed beneath him, steady, quiet. He checked the kit again at a lay-by. Just in case. Missing something now would be a disaster.

By nine, he was heading towards Holyhead Mountain, promenade to his right. He'd already picked his initial holding point, Breakwater Country Park. Big enough to find a quiet corner. At 11:30, he'd drive northwest along a track to the spot he'd marked on his last visit. Elevation, line of sight, low interference. He prayed it would be enough.

He parked. Settled in. It was going to be a long night. But Pete was ready. This was when it all came together.

Eleven thirty.

Pete started the Merc, drove out of the car park, up the track towards his chosen vantage point. Shit. A car was parked there.

He drove past, checked the clock. Eleven thirty-five. He had to cross the mountain to the old quarry buildings at the northwestern point. Time was tight. He turned back. Eleven forty. Thank God. They'd gone. Thought I was a peeping tom, I expect.

He swung back into the car park to turn around again. Needed the car pointing uphill, boot towards the town. He pulled off the road at his spot and gave a deep sigh of relief.

Eleven forty-five.

Don't panic. Take a deep breath and do it.

Pete killed the engine. The Merc settled into silence. Just the faint tick of cooling metal and the low whine of the booster pack warming in the boot.

He stepped out, opened the boot, and began the setup.

Tracker rig first, laid flat on the rubber mat, antenna coiled beside it. Booster pack next, wired in, lithium cells snug in their foam cradle. Burner laptop powered up, screen dimmed to minimum on the passenger seat. How's the battery? Low, so plug it into the lighter socket. No logos or prompts on the laptop screen, just the SDR interface waiting.

He fixed the antenna to the boot lid, ran the cable through the seal, locking it down with a rubber wedge. He checked the angle to ensure he had line of sight to the town. Good.

Quick diagnostic, Andy's instructions. All good.

Eleven fifty.

He sat in the driver's seat, turned to his left, and watched the laptop glowing. The Merc's nose tucked into scrub, and its rear faced the town. Streetlights glowed below, blurred by mist. No movement. No headlights. He breathed. Slow and controlled. Let the silence settle.

Eleven fifty-five.

He tapped the screen. SDR ready. Listening. Now, just wait.

Eleven fifty-nine.

Slow breath. Eyes locked on the screen.

Midnight.

Come on. Please.

Ping. A dot appeared.

"Yes. You beauty. You absolute beauty," he muttered to himself.

He zoomed in to street level. The car parked near Caer Gybi Roman Fortress, tucked between Roman walls and a row of flats. Not unusual. Not memorable. Just another vehicle in a town that had stopped noticing things. A good spot, and one the Irish had no doubt used before.

He packed up the gear into the passenger footwell. He lowered the rear seats and, wearing gloves, taped the thirteen flat-packed boxes, ready for later.

A three-point turn. Then back towards town.

He didn't drive straight in. Better to recce the area first to see if anyone was watching. They might watch until the handover, but with everything at stake, he had to take the risk.

Pete parked the Merc a hundred yards from the Range Rover and got out. He froze. Listened.

The air hung silent, broken only by distant gull cries. Voices? Late-night revellers drifting home from a club. Laughter and scraps of conversation carried far.

He breathed again.

He sauntered towards the Roman Fortress. There was no point in playing drunk, no point in being sneaky. If they were watching, he was already done.

He entered the car park and slipped behind a parked car. He had a pee and needed one anyway. That gave him a chance to scan for eyes. Nothing obvious moved out of the shadows.

There it was. The vehicle's driver had backed it into the space, placing its boot tight against the wall. That was far from ideal, and he'd have to move it forward. That meant starting the engine. At least there was a space next to it he could reverse the Merc into. Maybe he could let off the handbrake and push?

Still, he would need to move it back afterwards and, if engine noise raised suspicions, he'd be long gone before any police showed up.

OK. This was it.

He took the fob from his pocket. Paused. Ready to run for his life if it came to that. Pressed it. Lights flashed. Sharp bleep.

He stood still. Breathing through his open mouth. Waiting. Nothing.

Time to move.

He hurried back to the Merc, drove into the car park with the engine purring as low as he could manage. He pulled up and reversed into the space beside the Range Rover.

Nitrile gloves on.

He opened the driver's door of the Range Rover and released the handbrake. Moving to the rear, he squeezed behind it, pressed his hand flat against the bricks, and strained. Come on, you bugger. Move. Jesus, these things are heavy...

It shifted just enough to get the tailgate up. He rushed back and reapplied the handbrake.

OK, now we move fast.

He opened the Merc's boot, then the Range Rover's tailgate. He looked inside and held his breath. All appeared normal, so he pushed the carpet aside and lifted off the wooden top cover of the spare tyre well.

There it is. Our future.

He packed four bricks of charlie into each box. Reached the last one. Hesitated. Bugger it. I'll take two extra. When they find forty-eight keys, they'll think the Irish shortchanged Falstead.

He didn't tape the boxes. That would wait for the storage place.

Just one more thing. He took the plastic bag from his pocket, removed the nitrile gloves, and tucked them beneath the top layer of bricks. That's you sorted, you bastard.

He replaced everything as it had been before. Tailgate down. Merc boot shut. He started the Range Rover engine and reversed back in. Vehicle locked. Key fob in pocket. Into the Merc. And away.

If he got a tug now from local police, he'd still be a dead man. Just locked up until the Irish paid someone to get rid of him.

OK, back to the storage facility.

Still wearing gloves, he taped up the boxes and used a flatbed handcart to get everything into the unit, including all the tech gear. After securing the roller door, he drove away in the Merc.

The North Wales Expressway took him from Holyhead, and he stopped at the A5 junction to catch his breath. He'd done it. So far, anyway.

He'd been running on adrenaline for hours and hadn't eaten since lunchtime yesterday. It was all catching up with him now. Leaning back against the headrest, he closed his eyes. Too risky for sleep, so best to crack on and get home.

He glanced at his watch. It was 01:30 in the morning. He'd be home for breakfast.

Chapter Twenty Seven

Monday 5th April 2010

"Morning, Tom."

"Morning, Andy. Have you got something?"

"Yeah. I've been logging your bloke moving on a map. Last night he drove to Holyhead and sat on top of Holyhead Mountain just before midnight. He received the ping from the tracker at one minute past, and then drove into town and parked up. The vehicle remained static for a while, then moved to a car park by the Roman Fort. After a while, he drove to the storage unit. The signal has shown the laptop there since then, so. I'm guessing he's just left it there."

"That's dynamite, Annie. Keep your phone handy whilst I give this some thought. I'll call you back in a short while."

It looks like Pete's nicked the gear from the vehicle, or at least some of it. OK.

"Annie. This is the next phase of this. Have you got a bit of kit that can open these units through the keypad?"

"Of course. Standard bit of kit, mate. Piece of cake."

"In which case, I want Simmo to drive down to Holyhead and, out of business hours so there's no one around, get into Pete's unit and move everything in it to yours. If your kit is in there, bring it back with you, and it's yours again. Got that?"

"No problem."

***

Pete didn't wake until 14:00. Martina had brought him a coffee and was sitting on the edge of the bed when he awoke. He examined her through bleary eyes and wondered at her beauty.

He knew he wasn't a bad-looking man, but what she found attractive in him, and had done since school, amazed him.

She was still in her jeans and a soft jumper, hair tied back, face calm. No questions. No tension. Just presence. He reached for the coffee, fingers brushing hers.

"Thanks," he said, voice rough with sleep.

She smiled. "It's a treble espresso. You looked like you needed it."

He did. The caffeine hit like a signal flare, but it was her quiet steadiness that grounded him. She didn't ask where he'd been. Didn't ask what he'd done. She just sat there, letting the silence stretch.

He thought about the charlie. The drive. The risk. Martina. The reason he still had a future worth protecting.

He looked into her eyes. "Nearly there," he said, and smiled back at her.

"I have to meet Tom today if he's available. I'll drop him a message now."

Can we meet today? One on one?

Tom was sitting in the office on his own when his phone vibrated. He viewed the message and sat back.

"I'm not feeling too bright today, Sharon. I think I need to call it a day. We're just about up to date with stuff, anyway."

"OK. Take four-eight and I'll see you back here tomorrow, if you like?"

"Good idea. I'll just clear it with Jamie."

He went into Jamie's office. "Got a minute, guv?"

"Of course. Sit down."

Tom went in and sat down.

"The source wants a one-on-one today. Just letting you know, as I've told Sharon I'm not feeling too bright, so I'm off home."

"Do you know what he wants?"

"No. Just a one-line message."

"OK. Go for it, and put the info on the contact sheet as a phone call. And just be careful," said Jamie.

"Will do. And I always am, guv. I'll take four-eight if it's not being used at the moment."

"No problem," said Jamie, and threw him the keys. Just quiet trust. Tom caught them mid-air.

Tom sat in the vehicle and searched on Google for a different pub in Horsham. They'd done The Black Swan twice now. Familiarity bred pattern, and pattern bred risk. The Black Jug on North Street appeared to be OK. Time to message Pete.

We've done The Black Swan twice now, so change of venue to The Black Jug on North Street. Same rules apply. You get there at 16:00. Me, 16:10.

The immediate reply was a thumbs-up.

He placed his wallet, phone, and anything else that could identify him in the Faraday bag in the boot and tucked it under the spare tyre. Then, straight to Horsham, arriving about 15:15, having checked he was clean. He parked in town and walked to the new venue. Edwardian brickwork. Warm light. Mid-afternoon lull. Just right. Then outside again to walk around and wait.

It was bang on 16:10 as he walked into the venue. He glanced around, surveying the room. Pete had a small glass of orange juice. He went to the bar, ordered a small drink for himself, and then sat down. Pete joined him.

"What's my name?" said Tom. "Tom Kirkland," said Pete.

"Well done," said Tom, and smiled.

Two men entered and took positions at the bar. One of them glanced over, locking eyes with Tom. Brief, but enough to raise the hairs on his neck.

"Don't look round, but I think we may have a problem. Two blokes just walked in, and I'm not sure I like the look of them. Just carry on as normal, but remember, I'm a potential client. I'm carrying nothing. No phone. No wallet."

"OK," said Pete. "I'll try to act normal."

"What have you got for me then?"

"I think the vehicle is on the mainland now. I don't know where, and I can't yet confirm make, reg, or anything. If it is here, then I can't see it being left with a parcel that size in it for very long."

"OK. We're on standby and can jump on it at a moment's notice. There's another bloke just walked in, Pete, and he's staring straight at you. Did you dry-clean yourself?"

"I thought I did," said Pete, but Tom could sense some doubt in his voice.

Then the voice. Thick, familiar, and unwelcome.

"Well, I never! What a coincidence seeing yous here, big fella," said Shaun.

Pete turned, and the blood drained from his face.

"What the fuck, Shaun. What are you doing here?"

"Are yous not pleased to see me, big fella? Who's your man here?"

He indicated Tom with a nod.

"I'm just surprised to see you, Shaun. That's all. This is not Dublin, mate. This is Horsham. Tom here is a mate. Someone I do a bit of business with from time to time," said Pete.

"I tell yous what, Tommy, me old son. You pops yourself over to my two buddies over there for a minute whilst I chats with the big fella."

Shaun nodded towards the two guys at the bar, the ones who'd grabbed Tom's attention.

Pete looked over and clocked them. The kidnap crew. No mistaking it.

"Sure," said Tom, and got up and walked over to them. Hands in pockets.

"We'll be going for a piss now. Yous follow me," said the shorter of the two.

Tom went, knowing he had nothing on him, but he was worried this might not end well.

In the gents, they searched him thoroughly.

"What's yous name, and why are yous clean as a whistle?" said the shorter one again.

"Tom Kirkland. And I carry nothing to a meeting. You could've been the old bill. I don't think you are, but you could've been."

They both stared at him for what seemed an age, but was only fifteen seconds. Then their heads swivelled in unison and they turned to each other.

"OK."

They both indicated with their heads that he should leave and go back to the bar. Tom led, and they followed. He was preparing for a kicking but hoped it didn't happen.

Just not the head, lads. I don't think my brain's got much left to spare.

Tom was relieved when they just went back into the bar area.

"Yous wait here," the shorter one said.

Tom did as he was told.

He looked over to see Shaun and Pete leaning in towards each other, elbows on knees, in deep conversation. They'd just have to brazen this out.

As quickly as it kicked off, it ended. Shaun got up, turned around, nodded at his two buddies, ignored Tom, and they all walked out.

Tom went back to sit with Pete. His hands were shaking. He had been seriously affected by all that had just happened.

"What the actual fuck, Pete. You could not have cleaned yourself. They must have been behind you."

"No, Tom. They've got a tracker on my phone. It didn't occur to me they would, or even could, do that.

They took my phone when I was in Dublin. That's when they must have done it."

"Bloody hell. I didn't even think of that."

Pete put his head in his hands. He'd left that phone at home when he went to Holyhead. Thank Christ for that, or he'd be dead now. The thought hit hard. He was shaking. Legs like jelly. No way he could stand.

"I need a proper drink, Tom, but I can't stand up. I'm not being funny, but not some blended crap. Get me a large single malt, please. Not oaked."

Tom did as he was asked. He wanted to be on top of his game now, so got nothing for himself.

Pete took a large sip and put the glass on the table.

"The best bit about this, Tom, is they've given me a clean bill of health. The vehicle is a ringer of Falstead's Range Rover and on the same cloned plates. It's parked in Holyhead, and they expect a handover on Friday afternoon. If this were still on script, then Pinky or Perky would get the key fob from Falstead in Holyhead and drive it back. That means you have to take those two out Friday morning.

"The obvious thing is that Falstead will then call me and ask me to drive the vehicle back because he doesn't want to. I'll tell him to bugger off, and he'll have to do it. I'll volunteer to drive him down there though and run interference on the way back. Then you'll have the full details of the vehicle confirmed and, as I'm following it back, you'll know where it is at all times. You take it out in Surrey. How is up to you."

Tom thought for a moment.

"I think," said Tom, "regardless of what happened this afternoon with the confrontation, this is going according to plan. We will tell no one what happened today. Sharon doesn't know we're meeting, but my guvnor does. I'm not telling either, though. And no meetings until this is all over."

They both sat back in their seats, heads raised to the ceiling, and sighed.

"OK, I'm off. You wait ten minutes and then leave. I've got a shedload of dry cleaning to do on foot before I get back to my car."

"What if they see you dry cleaning? Won't they think that odd?"

"No. In the Gents, I said I had nothing on me because I never do at meets. That shows I know what I'm doing and won't create suspicion."

Tom left and spent the next hour walking around Horsham. Up and down escalators. In the front of a shop and out the back. Up the stairwells of multi-storey car parks and down the ramps. It was so important for him to be clean before he got back to his car.

He was happy. As soon as he was in the driver's seat, he put on a baseball cap and a pair of glasses with clear lenses. Just in case any of the Irish were looking for him driving back.

"Guvnor, it's Tom. Are you still in the office?"

"No, I'm home, eating my supper with a delicate glass of red on the go."

"Ah, well. Sorry to spoil your evening, but can I pop by your gaff on the way home from Horsham? I've got a major update, and you need to hear it."

"OK. No problem. You've got the address?"

"I have," said Tom, and hung up.

Tom arrived at Jamie's address in Epsom having thought it through. Easy meet with the source. No dramas. And then here.

"You've met my wife before, Tom, haven't you?"

"I have, guv. Hi Penny, how are you?"

"I'm fine, Tom, thank you. Jamie told me about the altercation with that chap the other week. That must have been terrifying for Sue and the children?"

"I must admit, it wasn't much fun. The girls got over it in no time. You know what they're like at that age. It all just washes over them as long as they've got a phone in their hands."

"I do. And Sue?"

"She's OK. In a funny way, even though it's rare for such a thing to happen, it's shown how important this job is."

"Well, if she needs someone to talk to about it, she's more than welcome to call or meet up for a coffee sometime. Just let me know."

"That's very kind, Penny. She misses the camaraderie of the wives that she had in the army, and I think she would appreciate that very much."

"OK, enough of that. Let's go into the dining room and talk about where we are," said Jamie.

As they were walking in, Penny said, "Anyone want coffee?" They both declined. They needed to crack on.

Jamie nodded. "Right. Off you go."

"The handover's planned for Friday afternoon in Holyhead. The vehicle is a ringed Range Rover, the same as Falstead's, and on false plates with his reg. It's in the Holyhead area, but we won't know the details of where until the handover has taken place. We need a warrant executed early doors on Pinky and Perky by the locals. A search team will be required. There's gear on the premises, but the search needs to be thorough."

Tom stared at Jamie with a questioning gaze. “I get the point,” said Jamie, understanding where Tom was coming from without it having to be expressed.

“Once they’re in custody, driving the vehicle back to Surrey will be the job of Falstead. The source can drive him to the handover but refuses to drive it himself.”

“Good,” said Jamie. “I’ve done most of the paperwork for the participation and just need the last details. I’ve got verbal authorisation in principle, subject to a signature, but that won’t be a problem.”

“Excellent. Can you set up Guildford CID to do the warrant?”

“I’ve already spoken to their DI, Kevin Dean. They’ve got a little drugs unit running from there, a DS called John Thomson, a couple of DCs, and a couple of uniforms in plain clothes. I think they’d love to do it. Leave all that with me and you concentrate on the source.”

“I know Thomo,” said Tom. “A good guy. Ex-RCS and knows his stuff. The help of a search team would be a good idea.”

“I get the point, Tom. I know what you’re saying.”

There was a pause.

“Right. One question I’ll be asked is, why are we not searching Holyhead from top to bottom and taking this out there, along with some members of the INLA and Falstead?”

“Well, blowing the source is one reason, because we’d have to nick him, and if we nick him, we’d have to charge him. If we didn’t, they’d know he was the source.

“Second, we do not know where the vehicle is. It could be right in the middle of a public area, or it could be in a barn somewhere nearby, ready to be moved for the handover. Any search activity could blow the job wide open. We'd have to use the local firearms units and, without solid information, we'd be putting the public in danger."

"That's good enough for me. I can work with that."

"The source, once the handover has taken place, will be following the target vehicle, that's what I'm calling it now, back to Surrey. We'll know the location at all times. Where we strike is up to you. We could take it anywhere you like, or even follow it to its end point. We've got the equivalent of someone in the vehicle telling us where it's at all the time. That's what makes this job so different from the one at Ally Pally."

"I'm erring on the side of taking it all the way back to the end point," said Jamie. "It could go to a lock-up the source does not know of."

"Agreed. It could. But I think we should take it out as soon as we can when it hits our ground."

"OK. So, where do we pick up the surveillance? If we've got the source giving us the exact location at all times, there's no point in having the team behind it in case they show out."

"We could have a team plotted up at Junction 11 of the M25 and pick it up as it goes by. It's the obvious route, and if it's different, we'll get plenty of notice."

"That's one option, but I think I'd like us behind it further back in case he doesn't get to the A3."

"I'll check the route and figure something out," said Tom.

"OK. Have you spoken with Sharon yet?"

"No, I'll call her when I'm home. I'll just say I've had a call with an update and called you first."

"OK. See you in the office tomorrow morning."

"I've got an appointment with the neurologist tomorrow morning. Can we say tomorrow afternoon?"

"Of course. Tomorrow afternoon it is then. Write the contact sheet up as a call to you. On the contact sheet, you need to add in the information on Pinky and Perky holding gear in their flat. The source will say he'll be able to confirm the belief they're holding on Thursday. That way I can set up the DI at Guildford for the Friday morning. They can then get the warrant sorted during the day and a search team booked. Once we give them the nod that gear is in the flat Thursday evening, they can set up executing the warrant for Friday morning."

"Will do. See you tomorrow."

As he walked out of Jamie's house, he called, "Bye, Penny." "Bye, Tom. See you soon."

As soon as he was home, he called Sharon to update her on the 'call' from the source.

Chapter Twenty Eight

Tuesday 6th April 2010 – morning

"Come on, girls, I need to get you to the Breakfast Club this morning. Dad's got a hospital appointment at 08:00, and we can't be late. We're leaving here at seven, so up you get." "Oh, Mum. It's early," said Evie. "Come on. All of you. You don't want Dad to miss his appointment, do you?" said Sue, trying to make them all feel guilty.

She went downstairs to get the breakfast things out for them and to make a cup of tea. As the kettle boiled, she thought about how little she was looking forward to today. However, inside, she understood how important it was to have the truth. Once he had it, she knew he would deal with it head-on, so to speak.

The truth was, she couldn't take it anymore but, if she walked out on Tom now, she would feel incredibly guilty.

The girls came downstairs squabbling like squirrels fighting over the last acorn. "Girls, girls. Please. Just calm down, for goodness' sake. Please understand how important a day it is today. You're old enough now to understand that when I ask you to work with me on something, I mean it."

All three turned to their mum in total silence with blank expressions. And the penny dropped. They turned and sorted out their breakfast, saying nothing. "Thank you," said Sue, and took a mug of tea upstairs. As she walked up the stairs, she was aware of them all giggling, and smiled.

"Come on. Wakey, wakey," she said. "We've got half an hour before we have to leave."

"OK," Tom said, sitting up in bed.

Tom got out of bed and went into the shower room. He stood for a while, looking in the mirror and leaning on the sink. I'm not looking forward to this. "I'm not looking forward to this, Sue," he said in a raised voice so Sue could hear him.

"Neither am I."

He didn't reply but just got into the shower. He stood there for a couple of minutes with the showerhead cascading warm water straight down on his head and wondered how the day might play out.

The normal chaos ensued, but they dropped the girls off at the Breakfast Club and drove off to St Peter's Hospital.

"What is it with you bloody men? You just bury your heads in the sand and hope something will go away," Sue said, in the frustrated tone most women are born with and use when berating their husbands in situations like this.

Tom was silent. Sue stared at him and said, "Don't just sit there. Give me an answer."

Tom glanced over at her and said, "I thought it was rhetorical."

"Well, it wasn't."

"I don't know what to say. I'm not looking forward to this. And who would?"

"You are so frustrating. You deal with your work so differently from your home life."

"I wasn't aware of that."

Sue turned to him again.

"I think you bloody well were."

"Can we put this to one side for now? Please?"

"OK," said Sue. "We'll discuss it when we're driving back."

"I'm not coming back. Sharon's picking me up from the hospital at about nine," said Tom.

"Oh, great. No time to discuss the results then," said Sue in utter amazement.

"We can. We can go to the coffee shop and talk about it before I go. I'll stay as long as is necessary. Sharon won't mind waiting."

Sue said nothing and just thought that the entire episode summed up his work-life balance.

They walked through the hospital's main corridor, past vending machines humming and posters about stroke awareness curling at the edges. The air smelled of disinfectant and coffee. At the reception, Tom gave his name. The woman behind the desk nodded without looking up and gestured towards the waiting area.

They sat in silence. A child cried somewhere down the corridor. A porter pushed a wheelchair past, its rubber wheels squeaking on the linoleum. Sue glanced at the clock. Tom stared at the floor.

"Mr Kessler?" called a voice.

They stood and followed the nurse through a short corridor, past closed doors and muted conversations. The neurologist's office was small, clinical, and too cold. A desk, two chairs, a monitor showing a scan paused mid-frame.

"Morning, Mr Kessler. Mrs Kessler. Please sit down.

"Now, as you know, you were unconscious for around four hours. That is a considerable time and, under normal circumstances, if there is such a thing with a potential brain injury, we would expect that to leave some damage. The brain doesn't always reveal its injuries straight away. Swelling, microscopic damage, or delayed bleeding can take time to show up, which is why follow-up scans are so important.

"With your second scan, we're looking for several things: bruising of brain tissue, microscopic tearing of nerve fibres, tiny bleeds that weren't visible at first, and swelling or oedema, which can develop.

On this scan, there's evidence of mild diffuse axonal injury. These are tiny shears in the brain's connective fibres. They don't show up on a CT scan but are visible on an MRI. It's not catastrophic, but it may affect processing speed or emotional regulation for a while.

Now, the question I'm always asked, and I'm sure you'd wish to know, is, can the brain repair itself? The answer is yes, and remarkably so. The brain has neuroplasticity, which means it can rewire and adapt. Recovery depends on the severity and location of the damage, the age and general health of the patient, and rehabilitation efforts, which can include cognitive therapy, rest, nutrition, etc.

"Most functions return fully. Different parts of the brain will compensate for others. For example, if there are mild memory issues, the patient might develop new strategies or habits that bypass the damaged pathways."

"In your case, we're not seeing anything catastrophic, but there's a shadow here we didn't catch last time. It's subtle, but it's there. The thing that explains why you've been feeling off. This kind of injury doesn't always show up straight away. The brain's a slow revealer.

"I know this is all a lot to take in, and it's quite possible you'll both walk out of here and remember nothing of what I've said. The important thing to remember is that the brain can repair itself. But you have to take this seriously and understand it will take time. It could be eighteen months before we consider you back to normal. My understanding is you're a fit and healthy man, and there is no reason you shouldn't, in time, recover from this.

"However, one important thing to understand is, you must not have a repeat of this trauma. That could be, and would be, well, catastrophic."

"So, what next? How does Tom progress from here?" said Sue.

Looking at Tom, the neurologist said, "My understanding, Mr Kessler, is you are a member of the Drug Squad in Surrey Police?"

"Yes," said Sue and Tom in unison.

"I'll cover this," Tom said to Sue.

"I understand how traumatic this is for both of you," said the neurologist.

"The truth is," said Tom, "the job I do can be stressful and dangerous. I can't sugarcoat it, that's just the way it is. But I can't give it up. It's just what I do."

"Your notes clarify you were on active service in the Army, and you were in 2 Para, based in Aldershot," said the neurologist, looking at Tom. "I'm sure you're aware of plenty of injuries sustained by your colleagues during that time, and will know many of them, though not all, I'm sure, have recovered. The ones who recovered are the ones who accepted that it can be a long recovery and followed the advice of the therapists. I've worked with many servicemen and ex-servicemen and have extensive experience in this area. Your injuries, though received differently, could be similar, but not as severe.

"During the recovery process, your mind, in layman's terms, may not be as sharp as you'd like it to be. But if you accept this without allowing it to upset or stress you, that will aid your recovery. The job you now do, organising, planning, using visual checklists, having structured routines, will aid your recovery. You do not need to change careers, but you will need the support of your colleagues while you go through this process.

"You will forget things. But if you accept that will happen, without getting frustrated, that will help your brain make the new connections it needs for the future. In time, you'll notice your memory improve. It might be something trivial, a number plate, a phone extension, the name of a street you've driven a hundred times. Things that used to stick without effort. As you recover, you'll need to write that number down instead of relying on memory. You'll realise that part of your memory has improved, and you'll remember things you'd have forgotten just weeks or months before. Once you recognise that improvement, you'll come to believe that, one day, you'll be back to one hundred percent. That belief system is essential."

"So, what happens next?" asked Tom.

"I'd like you to have another scan in three months. That may seem a long time to you as we sit here, but we need that time for the brain to settle, and to give us something to compare this latest scan with. Whilst I'd advise you to rest as much as you can, I think I've worked out that may not be at the top of your list. I assume you don't play any contact sports?"

"No, those days are long gone," said Tom, with a little smile.

"Good. Because those would have had to stop."

The neurologist glanced down at Tom's notes one last time, then looked up with a softer expression. "Well, I think that covers everything for today. You've got a good foundation to work from, and a strong support system, by the look of it."

He stood, signalling the consultation was over. "Thank you both, and see you soon," he said.

Both Sue and Tom were silent as they left the consultant's office and followed the signs to the café. The corridor was long, sterile, and echoed with footsteps and distant voices. Neither spoke.

As they turned the last corner, the corridor gave way to the low hum of the café: clatter of cups, hiss of steam, the soft murmur of people trying not to talk too loudly. It was warmer here, more human.

Sue sat alone in the corner while Tom queued for coffee. She scanned the café, faces lined with age, accents drifting across tables, a quiet mosaic of lives. Most were elderly, some frail, all here for the same reason. She felt a flicker of gratitude to the NHS. Imperfect, yes. But without it? They would be in trouble. Private care wasn't even a conversation.

Tom sat down with the coffees and just looked at Sue. The cups steamed between them. Somewhere behind, a spoon clinked against porcelain. A chair scraped.

“I don’t know what to say,” Tom said. “I’m useless at dealing with stuff like this. If you want an operation planned to kick a door in, then I’m your man. But this stuff just seems to defeat me.”

Sue was quiet for a few seconds, as if searching for the right words. Then said, “It’s because you’ve always, army or police, been looking after other people first. Not yourself. Look at how this happened. You thought this bloke was going to get away, so you drove into the side of him. And look where we are now.”

A sudden crash. A cup hit the floor near the counter. Porcelain shattered.

Sue jumped out of her skin with shock.

A gasp, a muttered apology, the shuffle of feet. Heads turned. The barista froze mid-pour. Then the café resumed its rhythm, the hum returning like a tide. The moment broke, but only briefly.

Sue recovered, and her gaze fixed on Tom.

“You and the team would’ve caught him anyway. But maybe you wanted to be the hero. I know it was a split-second decision, but in that moment, you were only thinking about the job. Not about yourself. Not about me. Not about the girls.”

Tom didn’t interrupt. He just listened.

“For at least until you’re better,” she continued, “you have to change your mentality. Think of yourself first. Then, me and the girls.”

“I’m not sure I can do that,” he said. “I am what I am. I’m a man, and that’s just what we do.”

“Yes, I understand that. But just for a while, change the way you look at things.”

She paused again, then added, “You have to push the job down your list of priorities.”

"OK, I'll do that."

They both knew he didn't mean it, and this was all a waste of time.

Tom's phone vibrated. He glanced down. "It's Sharon. I'll tell her to wait."

Sue shook her head. "No. It's OK. I think we're done. There's no point in going on about it now."

She got up, turned, and said, "What are you going to tell the job?"

Tom was still sitting down. He folded his arms and his eyes turned skyward, as if the ceiling tiles might offer a solution. He was thinking this very thing. Then he turned to her and said, "I've just got to tell them everything's fine. If I don't, they'll kick me off the squad."

Sue didn't blink. "Maybe that would be a good thing."

"Trust me. It wouldn't," said Tom a bit too fast. And he meant it.

Sue said nothing. Just stared at him for a few seconds, long enough for him to feel the weight of it, then turned and walked away.

Tom sighed, still sitting in the chair. The café noise returned in fragments. Steam hisses, chairs scrape, someone laughs too loudly at the wrong moment. He stared at the coffee cooling in front of him and realised, with a slow, sinking clarity, that it had been exactly the wrong thing to say.

Chapter Twenty Nine

Tuesday 6th April 2010 - late morning

He found Sharon at the front of the hospital and got in the passenger seat.

Sharon turned to him and said, “And?”

“And what?”

Sharon tutted. “You know what. Don’t be a moron. How did it go?”

“Oh, fine. All good.”

Sharon glanced at him for a few seconds, but he just stared straight out the windscreen, avoiding her gaze.

“Mmm, ’course it is,” she mumbled, and drove off.

“Where are we going?” said Tom, changing the subject.

“Esher. Jamie called me. He’s had a call from John Saunders there. Know him?”

“I think so. Uniform skipper?”

"That's him. One of his PCs has nicked a girl for shoplifting. She's got loads of form and is on a suspended. She's got a child, doesn't want to go inside again, and has propped up info on a drugs importer. Jamie wants us to go over and assess it. We take her on if we think it's real and not just bollocks to get off."

"OK," said Tom, as he settled back in his seat, closed his eyes, and thought about the morning.

They arrived in Esher. Tom wasn't that familiar with the town but always thought it had the feeling of an upmarket village. Tree-lined streets, Georgian facades, and the soft hum of a town that moved at its own pace. It wasn't sleepy. Just content.

"Morning, skip. Tom Kessler and Sharon Girton, from the drug squad. I understand one of your PCs may have come across someone who has some info that could be useful? Our DI has asked us to come and have a chat with her. What's your opinion?"

"Thanks for coming. On the face of it, it seems genuine, but I'll let you be the judge of that when you speak with her. Claire Tripper, one of my probationers, has the info. She's just over a year in and shows real promise. Don't tell her I said that, though," he said, smiling.

He turned around and waved over a female PC.

"Claire, this is Tom Kessler and Sharon Girton from the drug squad."

"Morning, sir. Morning, ma'am."

Tom and Sharon both laughed out loud.

"Claire, trust me, we are not 'sir and ma'am'. We're the same rank as you, so, first names all round. Let's sit down so you can tell us what this is all about."

"OK, what have we got?" said Tom.

Claire was still red from calling them 'sir and ma'am'.

She paused, needing to get her words right, then said, "Her name is Samantha Gold. She's twenty-five and lives on that council estate at the bottom of Cobham and has loads of form, even armed robbery when she was sixteen. A real gun too."

"Blimey," said Sharon.

"There's a little boy, about two years old, and is frightened he'll be taken into care if she gets sent to prison again and she won't get him back. She's on a one-year suspended for a previous shoplifting conviction and is panicking. She says she knows a bloke in Staines who's importing drugs and she wants to give us, the police, the information if we can get her off this."

"OK. And what do you think of her?"

"I don't know, which is why I spoke with my sergeant, and he called you. I just hope I haven't wasted your time."

Sharon said, "Don't worry about that, Claire. You've done the right thing, no matter how it turns out. But you are the one who nicked her and has been talking to her. You've got some rapport with her or she wouldn't have told you what she has. You've done well."

Claire smiled at the compliment and glowed inside.

Sharon turned to Tom and said, "Tom, why don't you and Claire talk to her, and I'll sit this bit out. Three's a bit mob-handed."

"No probs," said Tom, getting up and adding, "Come on then," nodding at Claire to show they were doing this together.

“You want me to go in there with you?” she asked, eyebrows raised. “Of course,” said Tom. “She’s your source at this stage.”

Claire lit up. She’d never even considered informants before, let alone handled one. This was new ground.

“You lead the way,” said Tom, waving her ahead.

“Come on. Show confidence. Just introduce me as Tom from the drug squad. Keep it informal. Like I’m one of your mates and we’re just having a chat about stuff.”

“OK,” she said, voice steady but her eyes wide. She stepped forward.

The corridor was quiet now, just the distant hum of vending machines that dished out disgusting coffee and the faint buzz of fluorescent lights overhead. The interview room door loomed in front of them. Plain, grey, institutional. Claire reached for the handle and opened the door.

Tom stepped in behind her. The room was small, windowless, and heavy with the smell of stale coffee and disinfectant. A single strip light flickered. And then she stood up.

Jesus Christ.

Six foot two. Slim. Blonde. Her clothes weren’t designer, but they hung on her as if they’d been tailored in Milan. She moved with a grace that made you forget where you were. Tom froze. He’d rarely seen such a beautiful woman. She was the spitting image of Lady Diana.

He didn’t speak. He couldn’t and just stood there, stripped of his usual composure.

Armed robbery at sixteen? Surely not.

Tom pulled himself together but wasn't sure whether his expression, when he walked in, had shown his amazement. It had.

"Sam, this is Tom from the drug squad," said Claire. "He's come across so we can talk about what you told me."

"Hi," said Sam, holding out her hand for Tom to shake, looking into his eyes.

He shook her hand, and they all sat down. Her eyes are mesmerising. Pull yourself together, man.

He smiled at her and said, "Good to meet you, Sam. Before we go into that stuff, tell me a bit about yourself. How you've got yourself into this pickle."

"Claire arrested me for shoplifting, and I think I can help you with something about a guy I know who brings drugs into the country."

She even speaks well. What's going on here?

"I know that bit, but tell me about you. Where are you from?"

She hesitated, then said, "I'm from Kingston, but at age eleven I went into care in Epsom."

"OK. And why was that?"

No relatives were willing to take me in after my mum and dad were killed in a car crash.

"My God, that must have been awful." Tom wasn't playing a game here trying to build rapport. He genuinely thought it was awful, and it showed on his face.

"Yes, it was. And I went off the rails. From a grade A student to an armed robber in five years."

Tom couldn't stop himself shaking his head, then said, "Tell me about that."

"Well, a friend and I were doing loads of puff an older group of boys gave us in the town. We'd run away from the home weekly and just get stoned. I hated that place, and the only pleasure I had was smoking dope. I could never grieve the loss of my parents and took it out on the system."

"What about the armed robbery?"

"My friend and I stole a motor scooter. We'd been taught how to do it by a boy in the home. We drove it into town and borrowed a gun, including ammunition, from an older guy known to the boys we hung around with. He knew we were going to rob post offices and, in return, we agreed to give him a cut for lending it to us.

"We did three before we were caught. We knew that was inevitable, of course, but just didn't care. It was in the papers as the 'Lady Diana Robbers' because they thought I looked like her."

"You do," said Tom before he could stop himself.

Stop. Now. Pull yourself together.

"What did you get for that?"

"Six years. In 2001. Out 2004."

"OK. And the suspended sentence?"

"I got caught shoplifting about six months ago, and I got a year suspended last month."

"And why are you shoplifting? You come across as an intelligent woman. Can't you get a job?"

"With my record? They just laugh at me."

"So your little boy is two. What's his name? And are you married, or do you live with the father?"

"My little boy's name is Samuel, and I live with the father in Cobham. But he's a heroin addict. He takes my benefit book every week and spends the money on gear. I have nothing left to feed my baby, which is why I have to steal. He keeps a large knife above the front door, jammed in the door frame, which he holds every time he answers the door."

Tom was a tough guy, but on a human level, this story was heartbreaking.

"Can you not get into a shelter? Into a hostel of some kind?"

"I wish it were that easy. I've tried, but it's finding a place. Also, Patrick would find me and kill me."

"What's his last name?"

"Morestead."

"OK. What about this bloke you know then, the one bringing gear in?"

"Jonathan Morestead, Patrick's brother. He flies out to Gibraltar, gets a boat across to Morocco and back, having bought a load of gear, and flies back. He tapes the nine bars to his body and just wears loose clothing."

"That's novel. And he's from Staines?"

"Yes. I gave the address to Claire."

"Would you ever be likely to find out when he's going?"

"I would think so. I wouldn't know for sure every time, but I think he goes, maybe, once a month."

"OK. If you got a WhatsApp message from someone called Sharon, who's my partner, by the way, while you were with Patrick, would he be suspicious?"

"He would ask who Sharon was, he's always checking my phone, but I could say it was someone I met at the church playgroup thing I take Samuel to."

"OK. When do you do that?"

"On Monday and Wednesday mornings. Nine thirty until twelve."

"If we met you there, or just pitched up at, say, just after nine thirty, would that look suspicious?"

"If it were Sharon and you, it might do. It would be better if it were just her. Patrick doesn't get up early, but you never know."

"OK. I can get your phone number and all I need from Claire here. We'll leave it at that for now, Sam, and, subject to Claire speaking with her sergeant, I'm sure this can now all go away."

"Thank you."

Tom and Claire left the room and headed back to the crew room to see Sharon.

The corridor appeared colder now. Tom walked in silence, the echo of Sam's story trailing behind him like smoke. He'd come for intel. What he got was a woman with a past that didn't fit the image. Grace and grit, trauma and poise, all wrapped in a voice that still lingered in his ears.

He glanced at Claire. She didn't speak either.

The kettle in the crew room was still warm. They obviously didn't use the vending machine.

Tom said, "Jesus bloody Christ."

"What?"

"I'll go now, shall I?" said Claire.

"No, not at all. You're part of this. Sit down," said Sharon.

"Now, don't you two say I'm being all blokey and sexist here," said Tom.

Sharon looked at him with a quizzical expression and said, "What on earth are you talking about?"

"I have just seen one of the most beautiful women I have ever set eyes on in my life."

"What, even prettier than me?"

"Only just, Sharon, but yes," said Tom. "I know it's unprofessional, but it took my breath away, and I think she knew it too. It's such a sad story, Sharon. It's heartbreaking."

"Would it have been so heartbreaking if she'd been ugly?"

That brought a smile to Claire's face.

"Ouch. That hurt. And yes, it would."

Tom ran through Sam's story.

"OK. That's tough. Where do we go from here then?"

"We'll run it past Jamie and see what he says."

He turned to Claire and continued, "He's our DI."

"You've done well with this, Claire. Thank you," said Sharon.

It was good coming from her to a female PC.

"No problem," said Claire, buzzing inside.

"Where do you see yourself going in this job, Claire? What are your aspirations?"

"I just want to get through my probation first."

"Of course, but you must have some thoughts on where you want to go in the job?" said Tom.

"We're not encouraged to think that far ahead, I'm afraid."

"Well, I'll tell you a story. On my first day on division, after my first shift, a late turn at Woking, I was upstairs in the bar..."

"You had a bar in a police station?" said Claire with wide-open eyes and an open-mouthed stare.

"We did. Most nicks had a bar. And they never closed on time either. Anyway, I was in the bar and the barman, Alec was his name, asked me that question I've just asked you. I said that I was going to be on the drug squad. He said, 'Oh, you're *going to be* on the drug squad, are you?'

I had said it in such a manner that it wasn't just a desire, it was going to happen, and I meant it too. I had complete belief, and here I am. I've never been interested in promotion. What I'm doing now is all I ever want to do.

"So, I'll ask you again. Where do you see yourself going in the job?"

"I would like to specialise at some stage. Perhaps the drug squad, but I don't know what you do."

"Well, the clue's in the name, but it has many elements to it." He paused, thought for a second, stood up and added, "Give me five minutes."

Tom walked out of the crew room and returned a short while later.

"What are you doing for the next week?" He said to Claire.

"I start a week of lates tomorrow," she said.

"Not anymore. If you want to, you can have a week's attachment to the squad. It's a normal start tomorrow as we are planning for a tremendous job on Friday. Do you fancy it?"

"I would love to, but I can't see my sergeant going for it."

"I've already squared it with him."

"Have you? That's amazing," she said, grinning from ear to ear.

“What about your DI? Won’t he mind?”

“Not at all. He’d encourage it. He doesn’t need to be asked.”

They exchanged phone numbers, and Sharon arranged to message later with a pickup time for the morning.

“What shall I wear?”

“You can see what we’re wearing, so anything casual. It’s unlikely you’ll get out of the car much, but nothing to identify who you are. Have your warrant card with you though, and bring a coat. We may not get very close to the target until he’s nicked, assuming he is, of course, as he knows me very well.”

“Ain’t that the truth,” said Sharon.

The temperature in the room had gone up with Claire’s excitement, and you could almost feel the electricity in the air. The squad needed people like Claire coming through the system, and people like her needed support from the system with their aspirations.

They left Esher to see Jamie.

On the journey, Tom called Pete. “Hi, Tom. How are you?”

“I’m fine, mate. You?”

“Yeah, not bad. Good timing. I was about to call you. I’m told Pinky and Perky are going to be holding a lump of gear at their gaff in Guildford.”

“OK. Would it cause you a problem if we kicked the door in?”

“No, not at all. But don’t do it yet. I’ll find out for definite tomorrow late afternoon or evening that they are holding and, possibly, how much they’ve got.”

“OK. Any more for now or is that it?”

"Nothing else. The handover is still Friday afternoon."

"Good. Speak later."

"That's convenient," said Sharon after Tom hung up. "I don't know what you mean," said Tom.

"Yes, you bloody do, Tom Kessler."

The temperature in the car dropped a couple of degrees, and they drove the rest of the way in silence.

"Guvnor, got a minute?" said Tom through the office door.

"Of course," said Jamie. "Come in, both of you. Sit down."

"First," said Tom, "the handover is still Friday."

"Good," said Jamie. "He also said he believes Pinky and Perky are going to be holding. Tomorrow late afternoon, he'll be able to confirm they are and how much. He won't know where it is, though."

"Well, that works out. I've already got the DI at Guildford on board, ready to get a warrant sorted when I give him the nod. They get nicked on Friday morning. The source, who will be authorised properly, can drive Falstead to the handover. We're off and running with full knowledge of where the target vehicle is at all times.

"All we have to do now is work out where we start the surveillance, and do we let it run to a potential safe house which could have more gear in it, or do we hit it as soon as we've got it under control, or somewhere else?

"What's your view, Sharon?" said Jamie, trying to get Sharon involved in the decision-making. Not to involve her in any sort of conspiracy, but to get her to feel part of the entire process.

“I think it’s all bloody convenient if you’re asking me. The gear at Pinky and Perky’s. They get nicked. The source has to drop off Falstead. We end up with Falstead in the vehicle.”

Jamie leaned forward on his desk. Looking Sharon square in the eyes, he said, “Sometimes, Sharon, you just have to run with things, whether it sounds convenient or otherwise.”

“It sounds to me like this is something you two have cooked up between you.”

Fuck me, Sharon. Are you sure?

“If you dare speak to me like that again, DC Girton, you will no longer be on this squad. Do I make myself clear?”

“Yes, sir,” said Sharon. She immediately regretted the tone of her voice and the accusation.

After staring at Sharon for a good ten seconds, Jamie turned back to Tom.

“Confirm for me again what route they are likely to take so we can talk this through?”

“The obvious route is round Birmingham, M40 to M25 and down the A3. If we’re going to use a traffic car, then we can’t do it on a motorway. They just don’t do stops on motorways, it’s too dangerous. The A3 is just as bad, so we’d have to wait until it comes off onto normal roads.

“I think I’m in favour of hitting it with a full-on hard strike at that point. Not trying to be too clever and taking it to a potential lock-up when we’ve had no sign from the source that there is one.”

“If at any stage the source tells us they’re going to a lock-up, we can review that decision and have a change of plan. Or he may get told the location of a safe house, and we execute a warrant on it in slow time when Falstead is nicked and it's all under control.

"We have to plan for a late change, as he may not be coming back here. But having the source running with the target vehicle is absolute gold. I think we meet in the office at midday, or sooner if you wish, brief, and if there are no updates indicating he's going anywhere other than Guildford, we plot up at somewhere like Stokenchurch on the M40, that's junction 5, and pick him up on the way past.

"This also means we are behind him in plenty of time if there is a change of venue for the drop-off, which I suggest wouldn't be that far from Guildford, anyway. I've just thought of something else, too. The Irish want the vehicle back and will, at the handover, tell Falstead where to drop it off. They will have presumed he's taking it to the Guildford area, so the drop-off point is likely to be somewhere near. That just helps us with our assumptions. However, we still need to be ready for all eventualities.

"The handover's not happening until the afternoon, and it's a tad under four hours to Stokenchurch from Holyhead. It's reasonable to believe he will drive past that junction at about 20:00. Sunset is at 19:42, so it will be dark. We need to be plotted up there for 18:30 to allow a contingency, which means leaving the office at about 17:00. Nothing will change before we are in the office. If it does, we react."

Jamie turned to Sharon. "Any views?"

"I'm with Tom," she said, sullen. Her arms were folded across her chest.

Jamie paused. "You can always head to the canteen for a cup of tea if you've nothing to add to the debate."

"I want to be part of this."

“Then understand the day-to-day realities of handling a top-class informant and don’t get shitty about it.”

Tom had never seen the DI like this. Sharon had got under his skin.

Jamie leaned back, hands clasped behind his head in his usual thinking pose. Then, dropping forward, he said, “I think we’ve covered enough for now. Tom Banton’s got a job over at Caterham tomorrow. You two can bail if you wish. They’ve got enough cars. Your call.”

Tom said, “We’ve got a female probationer PC from Esher joining us for the week, guv. We knew you wouldn’t mind. She’s the one who spoke with that potential source.”

“Of course. I forgot about that. How did it go?”

“Very well. She could be very good. I won’t bore you with the details as it’s a slow burn. The female PC could be good too. Only a year in, but she seems to have her head screwed on. She’s here now, but you’ll meet her on Friday.”

“OK, I’ll leave that with you two. I’m off to see Blake.”

“What time’s the briefing tomorrow?” said Tom.

“06:00 at Caterham nick. Call Karen and say you’ll be there if you want to be.” “OK. Will do.”

They walked out of the office.

“Sharon. Have you got a death wish?” Tom said once they were out of earshot.

“Sorry, Tom, but it’s so bloody obvious.”

“Maybe to you. But how else do you think this job’s going to get jobbed?

"As I've said before, if you don't like the answer a snout might give, don't ask the question. With sources like Pete, you have to be flexible. We're not breaking the law. We're being smart. So is he. He knows what's needed to get the job done. We just have to be smart enough not to compromise ourselves by asking the wrong questions."

"OK," Sharon said. "I understand."

"You take the car. You're picking up Claire in the morning. Pick me up at 05:00?"

"Will do."

Chapter Thirty

Wednesday 7th April 2010 – morning

Sharon had picked up Claire and Tom as arranged. No one spoke much. You're always tired at this time of day, and you never get used to the early starts. The roads were still half-asleep too, headlights carving through mist that clung to the hedgerows.

It was all just part of the game they played. Work hard, long hours during the week, and hope the weekends stayed sacred. Then, it's time to patch up the damage created by the absence, to re-enter the domestic orbit without crashing it.

While Tom and Sharon had been progressing the Falstead operation, the rest of the team had been grinding through long hours on Dick Banton's target. They'd get some stick for that before the briefing, especially if the job came off today. Have an easy few days and then pitch up for the strike.

The car hummed along, tyres whispering over the damp tarmac. Claire watched the sky shift from black to bruised grey, wondering if this was what proper police work was like. Quiet, cold, and full of things unsaid.

They walked into the briefing room at Caterham at 05:45, bracing for the expected ribbing about where they'd been the past few days. Every police station in the world seemed to have a room like this. Damp, musty with old chair fabric, and still haunted by tobacco, even though no one had smoked in it for years.

Dick started it off. "Morning. Are you the new members of the team we've been expecting? My name's Dick Banton. Welcome to the Drug Squad."

He crossed the room with an outstretched hand, which Tom shook, grinning wide.

The rest of the team were already dropping comments left, right and centre. "You'll all be grateful tomorrow, guys, if this job comes off," said Tom.

The atmosphere was jovial, but there was always an undercurrent. Maybe some of them thought Tom and Sharon were the chosen ones.

Claire stood watching it all with mild amusement, before Tom, using her to change the subject, said, "Guys, this is Claire from Esher. She's with us for the week, so treat her gently. She turned a very good informant, so she's earned a look at how the real world works."

There were various comments of "Welcome" and "Enjoy" from the team, all happy to see someone outside the squad take an interest in their work.

Claire was thrilled. Not just in the welcome, but in the praise from someone who'd lived it. She scanned the group, struck by how ordinary they seemed. She hadn't known what to expect, but these were just regular people. In time, she would learn that that was what they were. She'd also learn they were sharp, committed, and good at what they did.

Dick began the briefing at exactly 06:00.

"Morning all. Same target as yesterday, but I'll go through the details for the benefit of the new members of the squad."

That raised a few titters.

"The target is James McDonald, date of birth the twelfth of December 1970. He is a white male, five foot eleven inches tall. He is of medium build with dark, short hair and has no facial hair.

"The target address is 12 Croyden Street, Caterham, and the target vehicle is a dark blue Toyota Celica, index number ZZ12 KTR. Every time we've seen him this week, he's been wearing blue jeans and a blue denim jacket.

"McDonald is a known heroin supplier propped up by the local CID for us. They have a couple of sources into him and believe he's due to go to East Croydon at some stage to pick up a kilo of the brown stuff.

"At no stage this week has he carried out any anti-surveillance, but of course, be aware, he could always start doing some.

"Sharon, I'll WhatsApp you a photo of him." Sharon gave him a thumbs-up.

"OK. Questions? No? OK, crews and plotting then.

"Four-zero, Lisa and Mo.
Four-one, Jack and Samantha.
Four-two, Jamie Carmichael.
Four-three, Charlotte and Karen.
Four-four, Sharon, Tom and Claire.

"Claire, what's your last name? For the log."

"Tripper," said Claire.

"Good name for a potential drug squad member.

"Four-five, Dick and Craig.
Four-six, Alex and Joe.

Four-zero, you're still in the OP and coming out.

Four-four, if you can give direction onto the main road from Croyden Street.

Four-three, cover the nearside onto the main road, and us in four-five will cover the offside.

Four-two and four-six, plot where you like, and four-six, do the log please.

If there are no questions, on plot for 07:00."

There followed the familiar scrapes of chairs and the low hubbub of the team getting their kit together. Zips, Velcro, the clink of thermos lids. The murmur of voices drifted through the room, half operational, half gossip, as they picked over the previous day's surveillance. Someone mentioned the van that lingered too long on Penrhos Road. Another flagged a face from the railway station. No one said it outright, but the mood had shifted. They were now concentrating on the day ahead rather than dealing with team banter.

"You drive, Sharon," said Tom, not looking at her on the walk to the car.

"It's your turn," she said, looking sideways at him.

"It's OK, you do it."

"OK. No problem."

Once in the car, Tom briefed Claire.

"Right, Claire. You can ask us anything you like this week, and we'll do our best to answer. However, if we're following someone, be aware that you may have to be quiet because we're concentrating on what's being said over the radio. It's not always clear what's said, which is why we have a glossary."

“What’s a glossary?”

“Basically, certain words are used only at certain times. For example, the word ‘stop’ is only used when describing something being done by the target or the target vehicle. There’s no such thing as a bus stop; it’s always a bus stand. And you say certain words three times to emphasise what’s being said and to allow for someone who may be on the edge of radio reception. Radios are much better nowadays, but the range some years ago was pretty awful. In about 2010 we got a new system called Airwave, which increased the range of the foot men’s radios. Nevertheless, we still relay the foot men, as reception can still be patchy, and it’s better to be safe than sorry, considering the time it takes to relay.

“You’ll hear loads of those keywords today. The first one being ‘standby’. As soon as the OP sees the target, you’ll hear ‘standby, standby, standby’ and then a description of what the target is doing, what they’re wearing, etc. That always gets the adrenaline going a bit and makes you sit up and wake up instantly. If there’s no movement today or it takes a while before he moves, then we’re all bound to fall asleep at some stage. Don’t worry if you do.

“Our commitment on this plot is to give a direction of the target vehicle, or the target if he’s on foot, at the junction of Croyden Street, the road he lives on, and the main road. We need to be parked as covertly as possible and for me to get out of the vehicle and give that direction. I’ve already spotted a bus stand close to the junction, which I’ll use if necessary. In an ideal world, I’ll still be walking towards the junction when the vehicle, or him on foot, appears, and I’m just a bloke walking down the street.”

“And don’t forget to turn your radio on,” said Sharon with a smile.

“Ouch. Thanks for that, Sharon,” said Tom with a pained expression. “A story for another day, Claire.

“Whichever way he goes determines which vehicle, or vehicle’s foot man, then takes up the surveillance. It’ll all become clear as we go through the day.”

“Fascinating. I knew nothing like this existed,” said Claire, her excitement obvious. “This isn’t working for a living. This is going out every day and having fun.”

“That’s the nub of the matter, Claire. It is more exciting being at work than it is being at home dealing with all the day-to-day crap that comes with domestic life. And be aware, if you ever decide you want your career to go in this direction, the domestic fallout can be severe, as many squad members know,” said Sharon, in a tone that showed she knew what she was talking about.

“You may not get out of the car all week, Claire, but you’ll learn loads just by observing what goes on. If possible, perhaps later in the week, I’ll see if I can get you out so you can act as a prop for me. Instead of me walking along on my own, there’s you beside me, which projects a different image.”

Whilst Tom had been talking, Sharon had discovered the perfect spot for them to park up. They were beside a row of garages that appeared to be derelict and unused. A few with rusted, broken doors and snapped padlocks.

“I’m going to do a bit of a recce on foot,” said Tom, getting out of the vehicle. “See you soon.”

Once he had gone, Claire said, “Tom seems a nice guy?”

“Tom is one of the good guys. He sees us all as equals. By that I mean you, me, him, and everyone else on the team. Just because you’ve got a year in and we’ve got loads more, in his eyes, doesn’t make us any better than you. It’s his army service that did that to him. He hates senior officers with a passion and thinks they could remove levels of management in the police to put more resources on the street. He refuses to call them superior officers, even if the actual definition of that is someone of a higher rank. The word superior will never leave his mouth."

"How long does it take to get onto the squad?" Claire asked.

Sharon glanced in the rear-view mirror, then out the passenger window. Tom was nowhere to be seen, but she lowered her voice.

"Well. First, you get onto CID. That's your entry point. You become a detective. It takes three or four years before they'll even look at you for a learner post. Tom did it in two, of course. Fast-tracked. Golden boy."

She shifted in her seat, eyes still scanning the street.

"Then you do your CID course. That's mandatory. After that, you need a couple of years handling proper cases, the murders, rapes, fraud, etc., before you're anywhere near ready to apply for the squad. So, five to seven years. Unless you're exceptional. Or lucky."

Claire nodded. "And now they're letting uniform PCs in?"

Sharon gave a tight smile. "They're talking about it. Not because it's a good idea, but because they're desperate. No one wants to be a detective anymore. When Tom and I were in uniform, the waiting list for learners was ridiculous. Now, PCs are being transferred into CID against their will. Just to fill the gaps."

She paused, voice dropping further.

"Anti-terror units came in and hoovered up the best people. Then the cuts hit. They retired a load of senior detectives early on a full pension. No handover, and they took decades of experience with them. What's left is a skeleton crew trying to train rookies while juggling caseloads that used to be shared across a team."

Sharon turned back to Claire, her expression unreadable. "And they wonder why detection rates are in the gutter."

Tom returned and got into the vehicle. "That's easy enough," he said. "What have you two been gassing about? What girly talk have I missed?"

"'Girly talk', cheeky bugger," said Sharon, with a smile. "I've been telling Claire about your love of the word superior."

"Don't start me on that," said Tom, looking around the inside of the vehicle. "What have you done with the *Telegraph*?"

Then the waiting began. That pause in your life when everything slows, and you learn to switch off the parts that aren't useful. You read every article in the paper, even the ones you'd skip. Property prices in Hull; a council dispute in Barnsley. Just because it takes time. The world outside keeps turning, but in here, you're suspended. Alert, idle, but ready at the drop of a hat.

[Comms]: "Standby, standby, standby."

"Here we go," said Sharon, as Tom threw the paper on the back seat and exited the vehicle.

[Comms]: "The target is from the premises. Wearing blue denim jeans, a blue denim jean jacket and white trainers. He is carrying a red briefcase. And he is left, left, left, on foot towards the main road. Four-four?"

[Comms]: "Four-four, yes, yes. Four-four foot is out," said Sharon.

[Comms]: "And loss of eyeball by the OP."

Sharon was relaying Tom.

[Comms]: "Four-four foot has eyeball on the junction. Contact, contact, contact, on the target as he approaches the junction on the offside pavement. And right, right, right, towards the town centre. Four-five?"

[Comms]: "Four-five, yes, yes. Four-five foot is out."

[Comms]: "Four-five can take it, four-four."

[Comms]: "Yes, yes, four-five, over to you."

[Comms]: "Four-five foot from four-five, permission?"

[Comms]: "Yes, yes."

[Comms]: "Four-three, can you deploy your foot man at the appropriate time to make up the three foot men?"

[Comms]: "Four-three, yes, yes."

[Comms]: "Back to you, eyeball."

Sharon explained to Claire what had gone on. "The OP saw the target from the HA. He went left towards the main road, then they lost sight of him. Tom was walking along and picked him up as he approached the main road, and then he went right towards the town. Tom would have been walking towards him on the other side of the road and in the opposite direction. I guarantee you the target wouldn't have even noticed him.

"Four-five, whose commitment was the offside, deployed the foot man to take it from Tom. Tom will turn round when it's safe to do so, and four-three foot will deploy their foot man when the target is past their location. They will not be in sight of the target. Then there will be three foot men out to take him wherever he goes. We use a special A, B, C system for that, which I'll explain later."

It was said in a professional tone Claire picked up on immediately.

"Can I say something?"

"Yes."

"So few words said and everyone knows what's going on."

"Exactly. You keep the air free as much as possible. The control is always with the eyeball, and you never just come up on the air without asking permission of the eyeball to do so. Many times you ask for permission and get told, no, no. That means the eyeball thinks something is about to happen and needs the air clear. If what you have to say is urgent, then you ask for urgent permission. You can still get turned down though," said Sharon, turning and smiling at Claire.

"We will all now shadow this in the vehicles in case he's picked up by someone. If he is, and we're the ones in a position to take it mobile, we do. Tom would then get picked up by another vehicle and reunited with us at some stage when possible. Can you read a map?"

"I think so."

"Well, we're about to see. Grab this A to Z." Sharon didn't look back but held the map book one-handed above her left shoulder, inviting Claire to take it.

"Whilst we've got SatNav in here, both Tom and I prefer to use a physical map. Your job now is to make sure you know where the target is and where we are at all times. Got it?"

"I'll do my best," said Claire.

The commentary from two of the foot men continued whilst Tom caught up with them.

[Comms]: "Stafford Close to the nearside."

[Comms]: "Eyeball. Four-four foot is with you now."

[Comms]: "Four-four, yes, yes."

Sharon said, "They now have three foot men in play. You have them on the map?"

"Yes."

"We can sit here for now and see how this develops. He's heading south, but if he gets picked up by a vehicle going north, we could take it," said Sharon. "As he gets closer to the town, we'll move south too."

[Comms]: "Relaying. Approaching the junction with Station Avenue."

"That's a good example of why we relay the foot men. We got that from the relay and didn't get the original from the foot man."

[Comms]: "Left, left, left. Station Approach towards the railway station."

[Comms]: "Approaching the ticket office. Four-four foot, can you close in and get behind him in the queue?"

[Comms]: "Relaying. Two clicks. Yes, yes, from four-four foot."

"Tom will now listen to what the target buys and buy three tickets for the same journey. All three foot men then get on the same train."

"Three singles to the same place as that previous bloke, please, mate," said Tom to the man in the ticket office. When he was handed the three tickets, he added, "Does it stop anywhere before we get to East Croydon?"

"Only Kenley, sir."

"And the journey time?"

"Twenty-four minutes, sir."

Tom nodded and walked away.

[Comms]: "Relaying. East Croydon, East Croydon. One intermediate stop at Kenley. One intermediate stop at Kenley. Twenty-four, two-four, minute journey. Twenty-four, two-four, minute journey."

[Comms]: "Four-five, permission?"

[Comms]: "Relaying. Two clicks, yes, yes."

[Comms]: "From four-five. Four-one and four-two to Kenley."

[Comms]: "Four-one, yes, yes."

[Comms]: "Four-two, yes, yes."

[Comms]: "All other units to East Croydon as soon as the train moves. Back to you, eyeball."

Sharon said, "Can you work out what's happening? Tom has bought the three tickets the foot men need. As soon as he'd done that, he asked the ticket bloke if there were any stops between here and the end destination and the length of the journey. One car and the bike are on their way to Kenley, as that's the only stop between here and East Croydon. East Croydon may be a ploy, and he gets off at Kenley. As soon as the train moves, we go hell for leather to East Croydon and pray we get there before the train.

"The eyeball on the train will call it as soon as they are past Kenley, so the car and the bike that went there can then go on to East Croydon. If he gets off at Kenley, we'll have a foot man available, which is why he sent four-one there, because they still had a foot man in the vehicle. If the target gets in a vehicle there, we'll have a bike and one car that should be able to survive until reinforcements arrive.

"When the target gets on the train, Tom will maintain the eyeball and sit somewhere behind the target in the same carriage. The other two will deploy, one in the carriage in front and the other behind, just in case he changes carriages mid-journey."

"This is just incredible. I had no idea it would be so intense. It went from nothing to full-on in a split second, and every single person knows where they should be and what they should do at all times."

"Imagine how you feel if you have to do this for twelve solid hours. That's why we go down the pub a lot after we've debriefed."

"What was the log they mentioned at the briefing?"

"The log is a contemporaneous record of everything that goes on today. It's the same as your pocket book, but just written by one team instead of us all individually, which would be impossible, of course. Four-six have the log and, you may or may not have noticed, have been left alone to do it. No commitment at the HA, no foot men out, and no instruction to go to Kenley. In reality, it's a ball ache of a job. You scribble like buggery and hope it's legible at the end. When we debrief at the end of this, we go through the log line by line. If there's a mistake, we correct it. If something needs to be added, we add it. Then, after everyone's happy with it, we all sign it. If we have a job off, we use the log to write our statements, once again, in the way you would with your pocket book."

"Makes total sense."

[Comms]: "Relaying. The train is pulling into the station, four-five?"

[Comms]: "Four-five, yes, yes."

"The reason I asked four-five to respond there was because I wanted to make sure, with the shortest amount of air time, that they are receiving this. Dick is the OC and needs to know everything."

[Comms]: "Four-five, permission?"

[Comms]: "Relaying. Two clicks, yes, yes, four-five."

[Comms]: "Four-one and four-two are now at Kenley. Back to you, eyeball."

[Comms]: "Relaying. Two clicks, yes, yes."

[Comms]: "Rapid series of clicks. Standby, standby, standby. It's an off, off, off. The train is away. All units to East Croydon and wait for news of the train when it's held at Kenley."

Chapter Thirty One

Wednesday 7th April 2010 – late morning

"Get in the front seat, Claire, and make sure you've got your seat belt on. This could get hairy. We have to beat the train. As we're driving, Dick will be looking at a map of the station in East Croydon and working out who goes where if we all get there in time. But my guess is, if these train scenarios go like they usually do, it'll be a bit fly-by-the-seat-of-our-pants and we'll get there in dribs and drabs. Craig will be driving like a bloody maniac as he always does, that's for sure."

"Like you, you mean?" said Claire, hanging on for dear life.

"Don't look out of the window, Claire. Get your head down in the map book and get it on the right page for East Croydon Station. You need to be ahead of the game now."

"I'm not used to reading whilst we're going along. Especially with you driving like this."

"Well, fucking get used to it," said Sharon, with no sympathy in her voice whatsoever.

Sharon was driving in a line of traffic towards a Pelican Crossing. There were about eight cars in front of her. As the traffic slowed, she didn't stop. She drove on the wrong side of the road, knowing no cars could come toward her since the crossing held them.

"Jesus fucking Christ, Sharon!" said Claire, hanging on to her seat even tighter.

As Sharon got to the crossing on the wrong side of the road, it cleared of pedestrians and she drove through, back to the correct side of the road. All of that traffic cleared in one go.

"What's your problem? My favourite move for making ground, that is."

"You could have warned me."

"No time. Got us on the map?"

"I don't know," said Claire.

"Tough, isn't it? Find us on the map or you are no use to me," said Sharon, with a little glance sideways and a smile on her face.

[Comms]: "From four-five, the train is past Kenley. The target remains on the train."

"Well, that's good news," said Sharon.

"I've got us on the map now. We're about five minutes out, at a guess. But so is the train."

"OK, good. Well done. You've got your big-girl pants back on. Don't forget, we should have four-one and four-two ahead of us as they were at Kenley. They would have picked up the radios of the foot men on the train and been away from there well before we had that message from four-five. And Jamie on the bike is just amazing. Guaranteed, he'll be first there."

"It's a big station, though," said Claire, getting into the groove.

[Comms]: "Four-two relaying four-three foot. Four-three foot has the eyeball as they exit the station towards George Street. Any other units on plot?"

[Comms]: "Four-five is less than five minutes away."

"He didn't ask permission," said Claire.

"No, he didn't," said Sharon. "But there are times you just make a call and run with it. Dick knows the foot men have got it and the target is just walking along at the moment, so he took the risk. Good you spotted it though."

"He's heading east out of the station, and we are on Park Hill Road heading north towards them. Stay on here until you get to the T-junction and turn left," said Claire.

Sharon glanced at Claire, bent down over the map with her left finger where the target was and her right where they were. She can do this.

[Comms]: "Relaying. Now approaching Addiscombe Road on the nearside pavement and left, left, left onto Addiscombe Road."

"Bear round to the left, sorry, nearside here," said Claire. "And join this road going south. Addiscombe Road is now on our right, so keep straight on as that's where the target is."

Good girl.

They took the nearside into a dead end just after Addiscombe Road, and Sharon stopped.

"Right. I'm getting out here to replace Tom. I'll find him and send him here."

Sharon jumped out and walked at normal speed to where she believed Tom would be. At the end of the cul-de-sac, she turned right.

[Comms]: "Relaying. At the T-junction, it's left, left, left. On the nearside pavement heading towards Cherry Orchard Road. He's now on the phone. No deviation."

[Comms]: "Four-four, Sharon, permission."

[Comms]: "Relaying. Yes, yes, four-four, Sharon."

[Comms]: "Four-four, Sharon is out to replace four-four foot. I can see you, four-four foot. Walk past me and the vehicle is next nearside. Back to you, eyeball."

"Four-five is on plot and can take the relay, four-two."

[Comms]: "Yes, yes. Relay with you, four-five."

Tom got back to the vehicle and jumped in. "That was fun."

"Does she always drive that fast?" said Claire. "I nearly shit myself."

"She would have been in total control at all times, I can assure you," said Tom as he strapped in and started the engine. "Did she do her Pelican Crossing manoeuvre?"

"Yes. And scared me to death."

"Excellent. I knew you'd enjoy it."

[Comms]: "Relaying. We are now on Cherry Orchard Road, heading north. Crossing the road to the offside pavement."

"You've got us and the target on the map then?" said Tom, looking over at Claire.

"I have."

[Comms]: "Relaying. Passing Cedar Road to the offside. No deviation. Offside pavement."

Tom said, "We have the target under total control here. I just wonder what he's doing. That briefcase may be a clue, of course."

[Comms]: "Relaying. Oval Road to the offside. The target is settled and still carrying the red briefcase."

[Comms]: "Four-five, permission."

[Comms]: "Relaying. Yes, yes, four-five."

[Comms]: "All units now on plot. Back to you, eyeball."

[Comms]: "Relaying. Two clicks. Yes, yes."

[Comms]: "Relaying. He is now on the phone again. No deviation."

[Comms]: "Relaying. It's a stop, stop, stop. At a bus stand for buses heading south. Confirming, four-three foot has the eyeball. Four-six foot, can you get to the bus stand and get on a bus with him should he do so?"

[Comms]: "Relaying. Four-six foot, yes, yes."

[Comms]: "Relaying. Four-three foot can hold this from a car park opposite. Four-four Sharon, hold back."

[Comms]: "Relaying. Two clicks from four-four Sharon."

Tom had parked up on Oval Road, short of the bus stand where the target was held.

"Why are they calling her 'four-four Sharon'?" Tom asked Claire.

"So, when signing up the log, she's not confused with four-four foot, which was you?" she said, a little unsure.

"Very good. Have confidence in your answers. You're doing great."

[Comms]: "Relaying. There is a bus approaching. The bus is held. Temporary loss of eyeball. The bus is away and eyeball regained as the target remains at the bus stand. And four-three foot is on the bus. Four-four Sharon, can you now go to the bus stand?"

"Four-six foot had to get on the bus or the job could have been blown," said Tom.

"I hope the target gets the next one or we're getting tight for foot men on the ground. Others will realise that though, and without being asked, they'll get themselves close by in case Sharon has to get on the bus too. I'm not burned by any means, but best to stay out of it for a while."

[Comms]: "Relaying. Four-four Sharon is now at the bus stand. The eyeball remains with four-two foot."

[Comms]: "Relaying. A bus is approaching."

[Comms]: "Relaying. The bus is held. Temporary loss of eyeball. Rapid series of clicks. This will be four-four Sharon. The target is on, on, on the bus and the bus is away. Eyeball with you, four-four Sharon."

Then it went quiet. Then, it all happened.

[Comms]: "Relaying. Rapid series of clicks. Standby, standby, standby."

[Comms]: "Relaying. The target is preparing to leave the bus. Bus slowing. The target is alighting the bus with the briefcase. All units. This is not the same briefcase, I say again, not the same briefcase. The target is from the bus. There has been an exchange on the bus, and he now has a black briefcase."

"I think we've got him," said Tom.

[Comms]: "Relaying. We can't identify the person with whom he exchanged the case, and we just run with the target. Four-five?"

[Comms]: "Four-five, yes, yes. Just stay with the target for now. We're in total control."

"Shame we can't identify the other bloke, but maybe we can turn this chap if he's now holding," said Tom.

"How can you all be so calm?" said Claire.

"Professionalism and experience. We can't cock it up from here or we'll all be sacked."

[Comms]: "From four-five. Call all units in and hit it, eyeball."

[Comms]: "Relaying. Units move in."

"OK, let's go. Nice and easy to see if we can all get there together."

Tom moved out of Oval Road towards the target. He could see other vehicles approaching. And then she called it.

[Comms]: **"Strike, strike, strike."**

For a heartbeat, everything held. Then, the street erupted.

"Sorry, Claire. You stay here," said Tom, yanking the handbrake. The car skidded to a halt, and he was out in a flash, sprinting towards the chaos, even while the vehicle was still moving.

No one was listening as Claire muttered, "How the hell do they do this every day? And get paid for it?" She shook her head, adrenaline still fizzing. She wasn't sure if she was terrified or thrilled. Maybe both. But she knew one thing; she'd never look at a map the same way again.

Claire stared out of the windscreen. The target was face down on the ground, arms pinned behind his back. Tom turned to her and waved, indicating she should come over. She got out, walked over. The briefcase was open on the ground with a plastic bag inside, about the size of a kilo of sugar. I suppose it would be about that size, she thought.

"You're a lucky charm, Claire. We've had people attached to the squad loads of times, and I can't remember any of them having a successful strike on their first day. You wait until tomorrow," said Tom.

"I just don't know what to say. This has just been amazing."

"The best of it is, we run this back to the local CID and they deal with it all. We debrief, I expect at Caterham, but that's Dick's call, do our statements, and bugger off down the pub."

Claire could manage only a silent shake of her head. She shouldn't have been thinking about her career path, but forget that. Her aspiration was to be another Sharon.

Dick took control of everything. A couple of uniformed cars had pitched up after someone dialled 999, thinking there was a fight or a road rage incident, which helped clear the substantial crowd that had formed.

"Best we get this wrapped up and back to Caterham," said Dick, loud enough to get everyone moving.

They put the target in the back of Dick's vehicle. In cuffs, of course. The briefcase went in the boot. That was it. Back to the factory, do what they needed to do, and then went down the pub.

On the way, Claire said, "Is Dick a DS?"

Sharon said, "No. Why?"

"Because he was running it all."

"Everyone runs their own operations. They're the Operational Commander for that op, and the DSs don't butt in. Karen, the blonde with short hair from four-three with Charlotte, is a DS. Every DC on this unit, however, has enough experience to assemble target packages, execute operations, and make crucial tactical decisions on the hoof, day after day. They wouldn't be here if they couldn't. That's why we're all experienced detectives.

"Think of the split-second decisions Dick had to make today. As soon as the target was getting on a train, he had to send units ahead. He has to be aware at all times who's on foot, which leaves those units single-crewed, so he sends the right vehicles to the right place. All that information is in his head, so he can make an instant decision. This isn't just a surveillance team. If Karen thought someone was making a decision that could put someone in danger, she would step in."

Tom added, "You could put any senior officer out here and they wouldn't have a clue what they were doing. They'd balls it up and then blame somebody else."

"Here we go again," said Sharon, looking back at Claire with a smile. "Don't go off on one, Tom. We want a pleasant drink tonight without you being in a bad mood."

"OK, I'll shut up," said Tom, in his grumpy voice.

They drove the rest of the way in silence, the adrenaline draining from their bodies.

The debrief went well, albeit with a bit of friction between the foot men who'd been on the train about something. The rest of the team let the three of them fight it out for a while before Dick said he'd had enough and called time. Everyone signed the log, including, to her delight, Claire.

"You were there," said Tom. "You're a witness. So, we'll do our statements now and then go for a pint. Sharon will help you with yours."

Tom, Sharon, and Claire were in the bar of one of the local pubs used by CID when Karen came over to them.

"Hi Claire, I'm Karen. How was your first day?" she said.

Tom and Sharon smiled and gave each other a knowing look. They knew how this was going to go.

"I can't believe you get paid to do this. It was beyond any doubt the best day I've spent in the job," Claire said with tremendous enthusiasm.

"Excellent. I'm so pleased. It's rare to get a strike on your first day, for sure."

"Tom said it doesn't happen often."

"So, you fancy doing this one day?"

"I can't wait. We're not encouraged to think this far in the future, which is a real shame, because this has given me something to work towards. I always know I've got Sharon and Tom to call on for advice without feeling like I'm being a nuisance. And if you ever need something checked over in Esher, you know you can call on me. I'll keep my mouth shut about it too."

Sharon smiled. "Good for you. In one day, you've learned more about this side of the job than many people bother to learn in their entire careers."

"Especially the bosses."

"For Christ's sake, Tom, not again."

But he was smiling and winding them up.

"You're an absolute inspiration, Sharon. I look up to you and want to be like you one day," said Claire, with huge affection in her eyes.

"Oh, be quiet. You're embarrassing me now," said Sharon, but she was pleased inside.

"For goodness' sake," said Tom. "Get a room, you two."

Sharon said nothing more, but the warmth in her eyes lingered long after Claire turned away.

Tom's phone vibrated.

"Tom, it's Pete. Confirmed, Pinky and Perky will be holding Friday morning. You need to hit them at six in the morning to ensure you take them out."

"All received, Pete. We're on it. Guaranteed." He hung up.

Tom turned to Sharon. "Pinky and Perky will be holding Friday morning," he said. "I'll call Jamie."

"Guvnor, it's Tom. Pinky and Perky will have gear on Friday morning. They need to be hit at 06:00."

"OK. Thanks, Tom. Leave that all to me. I'll call the DI at Guildford. They have it all planned and will be ready to go."

Well, it's been a good day. Let's hope the next couple of days are too.

Chapter Thirty Two

Friday 9th April 2010 – early morning

The stairwell stank of damp concrete and stale takeaway. A flickering strip light buzzed overhead, casting shadows that twitched across the peeling paint. Outside, the search team waited out of sight in silence, boots scuffing against the tarmac, radios muted. Inside, the air was tight. No chatter, no bravado. Just the quiet hum of adrenaline.

DS John 'Thomo' Thompson leaned in close. "Are you ready, Taff?" he whispered to PC Steve 'Taff' Thomas, who was holding the "key," and giving him a thumbs-up.

Taff nodded and whispered in his broad Welsh accent, "Ready when you are, Thomo."

They'd already used a real front door key, lifted by Thomo from the block's management company. He'd spun them some bullshit about parcel thefts to justify the early morning visit to flat 43.

They were ready with a search team outside prepared to do what was needed after entry.

"Go," whispered Thomo, and Taff whacked the single lock. It gave; he moved to one side, and the troops stormed in.

It wasn't a big flat: entrance hall, two bedrooms, one with an en-suite, a separate bathroom, and an open-plan sitting room and kitchen.

Thomo and Maureen 'Moors' Howard went into one bedroom. Charlie 'Gordo' Gordon and Richard 'Barts' Barton went into the other. They were all expecting a bit of a scrap with these two, but it didn't materialise.

Pinky had an astonished expression on his face as he sat up in bed. "What the fuck?" said Pinky. "Morning. Nice pyjamas, mate," said Thomo, smiling at the big lump sat up in bed in Peppa Pig pyjamas. "We're Guildford CID and we have a search warrant to search these premises for drugs."

He blinked, still half-asleep. "Drugs? You're having a giraffe, mate."

"No," said Thomo.

"We believe you've got drugs on the premises, and we're going to get a search team in to do the necessary. If you've got nothing here, then you've got nothing to worry about. Get dressed, Pinky. You're not going down the nick dressed as Peppa Pig."

In the other bedroom, Taff and Barts had Perky sitting on the edge of his bed. "Come on, matey, put some clothes on."

"What the fuck is this all about? I didn't get to bed until 16:00," said Perky.

Gordo said, "We're executing a search warrant on the premises, matey."

"There's nothing here, pal, for fuck's sake. What do you think we are?" said Perky, getting annoyed.

“Don’t kick off, mate. It’s too early in the morning for a scrap, there’s too many of us here, and you’ll only end up getting hurt. If there’s nothing here, then you’ve nothing to worry about.”

This was often the moment they kicked off. The initial drowsiness had worn off. They became angry about the intrusion as the adrenaline kicked in. Taff could feel the tension in the air.

“Just let us do our job, matey. If there’s nothing here, we’ll get the front door fixed and you can sleep for the rest of the day. OK?” said Taff.

“OK,” said Perky. “Let me get dressed.”

“Good man.”

Once dressed, someone led them into the sitting room and told them to sit on the sofa and be quiet.

They stared at each other with blank expressions.

“They took the piss out of my pyjamas,” said Pinky.

“I’m not surprised,” said Perky, jaw tight.

“Right. You lot, except Moors, who’ll be exhibits officer, go outside and send the search team in,” said Thomo. “There’s not enough room in here for all of us.”

Thomo and Moors remained while the rest of the team went outside.

The search team comprised four trained, uniformed PCs. The number always depended on the size of the premises, and this place was tiny compared to some. Working in pairs, they searched every nook and cranny, examined every drawer and removed every light socket. They searched every cereal packet, emptying and replacing the contents. It was all done respectfully, with nothing damaged, everything returned.

They found nothing that would show dealing on the premises. But that didn't mean they weren't hiding something.

"Sarge!" said one of the team in a loud voice. "Come here."

"What've you got?" said Thomo, hurrying to the bathroom.

One of the search team was holding the lid of the cistern upside down. A bag of white powder was taped inside.

"Outstanding," said Thomo. "Bring it through. Leave it as is. We'll take the whole thing, cistern lid as well."

As the officer entered the sitting room to bag up the seized lid and register it with Moors, Perky stood up. "What the fuck is that?"

"You know full well what it is, fella. Now sit down and be quiet."

Perky didn't sit down. He went to grab the cistern lid.

Thomo said, "Don't let him touch that under any circumstances. And you sit down, now."

"Fuck off," said Perky. "You bastards have planted that."

"I said, sit down or we'll make you. Understand?"

Thomo pushed Perky back down onto the sofa, nicked the pair of them, and recited the caution, eyes flitting between the two.

Pinky said nothing. Perky said, "Go fuck yourself."

The officer handcuffed both.

One of the search team walked over to inspect the cistern lid while it was being bagged up. He paused, scanning the room. His eyes landed on the sideboard. "Hang on a minute..."

He walked over and pulled out a drawer. "I thought so," he said, lifting out a roll of brown parcel tape. "This looks like the same tape."

"Excellent spot, mate. That's why we got you guys in here. Let me look at it."

Thomo examined the end of the roll and the tape used to secure the bag. "The end of the tape there, where it's been snapped, looks the same shape as the end of this roll. The lab will match that. Well done again, matey."

"As you said, that's why you get us in here."

The rest of the search was completed, and Pinky and Perky were led away.

Thomo watched the two lads being led out, cuffed and silent. Another job ticked off. But the look Pinky gave him, half defiance, half disbelief, stuck for a moment longer than it should have.

"Taff," said Thomo. "You stay here and sort out getting the door secured. You broke it. You fix it."

Taff muttered something in Welsh that sounded suspiciously like a complaint, then added, "Yes, Thomo."

Outside, the stairwell still stank. The takeaway wrappers hadn't moved. But something else had; these two were cuffed and heading for the van.

When Thomo got back to the nick in Guildford, he went straight to the DI's office. He stuck his head through the door. "Morning, guv." DI Kevin Dean had been at Guildford for as long as anyone could remember.

"Morning, Thomo," said the DI, looking up. "Any good?"

"About nine ounces of what looks like charlie."

"Excellent. Well done. I'll let the drug squad know."

Thomo left the DI to do that and went down to the custody suite to deal with the prisoners.

"Morning Jamie, Deano here. About nine ounces of what looks like charlie with two in custody. Thanks for the tip-off."

"Excellent news, Deano, and no problem. I'll let the troops know. We're very happy for them to have a solicitor as soon as they like. It affects nothing our end."

"OK. I'll let Thomo know," said Deano, and put the phone down.

Phase one completed, thought Jamie.

"Tom, it's Jamie. Two in custody with about nine ounces of what looks like charlie."

"Brilliant," said Tom.

"Phase one complete then?"

"My thoughts exactly. See you in the office about 11:00."

"That would be great. See you later," said Tom, and hung up.

Outstanding.

***

Friday 9th April 2010 – mid-morning

Pete sat at home waiting. He wasn't the nervous type, but he was now.

"You OK, Pete?" said Martina. "You look jittery today. Not yourself."

"I'm just waiting for a call, that's all. Depending on the result, I may have to go out and not be back until very late."

"Do you want me to make you an early lunch, just in case you have to rush out?" said Martina, ever the dutiful housewife.

"That would be lovely, thank you," said Pete, smiling.

She is my calming influence, he thought. In my world built on violence, tension and threat, she's the one thing that makes sense.

He was halfway through his lunch when his phone vibrated.

"Morning, Tom. I've been hoping you'd call."

"Pinky and Perky have been nicked and are at Guildford, so that's a good start to the day."

"OK," said Pete. "That's great news. I should get a call soon then. As soon as I do, I'll let you know." He hung up.

Only about fifteen minutes later, his phone vibrated again. It was Falstead.

"Morning, John."

"They've only gone and got themselves fucking nicked with a chunk of charlie, haven't they?"

"Who?" said Pete.

"Pinky and bloody Perky."

"What are you going to do now then?"

"Well, you're going to have to drive it back," said Falstead.

"No, I am not," said Pete. "I told you early doors I was not touching any gear, and that still stands. You drive."

"I can't," he said.

"Why?"

"Because I might get stopped."

"The vehicle is registered to you, for Christ's sake. If you get stopped, as long as they don't check the chassis or engine number, and they never do that, you'll be fine."

"I can't get there."

"Get the bloody train then," said Pete, trying to sound frustrated.

"I'll never get there in time. It's fucking miles away. You'll have to drive me."

"For Christ's sake, John. I'm a busy man. I've got stuff to do."

"Well, do your stuff tomorrow. We're going to let the dust settle for a few days before we start boshing this gear, anyway."

Pete left a pause in the air, as if weighing his options.

After a pause, he said, "OK, I'll drive you down there."

"Great. And you can run interference on the way back too, if it looks like I'm getting a tug."

"OK. What time do you want to leave?"

"Now, come and pick me up from my gaff."

"No, I'm not going near your gaff. I'll pick you up at the back of the club. I'll call you when I'm there," said Pete, and put the phone down before there could be any argument.

As he walked out to his car, he messaged Tom:

On my way to pick up Falstead. We're on.

Chapter Thirty Three

Friday 9th April 2010 – still mid-morning

Tom, Sharon and Claire were on their way to the office when Tom received the WhatsApp.

On my way to pick up Falstead. We're on.

Tom checked it. "We're on," he said. "The source is on his way to pick up the target."

Sharon turned towards Tom. She caught his eye and didn't have to say anything. She knew he and Jamie had engineered this. And the worst part? She believed it was the right call.

Tom turned to Claire. "Today is a big day, Claire. You will see the biggest parcel of gear you're ever likely to see outside of the movies. Everything has to stay locked in your head, and you should not say much to your colleagues when you get back. Say you were there. Say you were involved. But no names. And never, I repeat, never, say the words 'source,' 'informant,' or 'snout.' Is that clear?"

"Clear," said Claire.

"OK. Let me tell you what we're doing then. We're on our way into the office now, where we'll brief at midday or maybe a bit later. There's a vehicle being driven up from Holyhead by the target. The target is a man named John Falstead, who's local to Guildford. We've already seized fifty kilos of charlie that we understand belonged to him, but we didn't have the evidence to tie him to it."

"Crikey," said Claire, eyes wide. "That's... a lot."

"We now have info that he's collecting another parcel of charlie from Holyhead this afternoon and driving it back to Guildford. I can't go into details of how we know this bit, but we'll have constant updates on the vehicle's location, which means we don't have to be behind it all the way. The obvious route is round Birmingham, M40, M25, A3.

"Just in case he diverts away from the Guildford area, we're going to plot up in Stokenchurch, which is junction 5 on the M40, and wait for it to go by. We'll then pick it up. Once we get off the A3 onto normal side roads, we'll hit it with a hard strike."

"My God," said Claire. "I didn't sleep last night after that amazing day yesterday. How on earth am I going to sleep tonight if this comes off?"

"When, not if," said Sharon.

Tom glanced across at Sharon and smiled. She wasn't sure when she'd stopped resisting. But she had.

Tom watched her for a beat longer. I think she's on board. Fortunately, she doesn't know the full extent of how this was done.

Tom messaged Jamie.

Source is on his way to pick up Falstead. He's driving him to Holyhead for the handover and will be running interference on the way back.

He got an almost instant reply.

Fabulous. I'll have the paperwork all signed by the time you get to the office.

Tom sat back and contemplated how it was going so far. Let's hope it's straightforward from here on in.

They walked in the back door of the office just as Jamie walked in the front. He was carrying a sheaf of papers. He gave Tom a thumbs-up. Tom nodded. No words needed to be exchanged.

All legal. Good.

The team drifted into the office in dribs and drabs. Inserting body set batteries into chargers. Swapping out the charged ones. Grabbing coffee. Checking kit. No one rushing. No one slacking. Just the quiet choreography of people who knew what they were doing.

Tom sat back and watched.

He didn't need to speak. Didn't need to direct. The rhythm was already there. The muscle memory, shared history, the trust you don't build overnight.

"What time are we briefing, Tom?" said Charlotte.

"It should be midday, but it could slip. We're awaiting an update," he said, voice dry.

"Alright," she said.

He winked and smiled.

This was his happy place.

Not because it was calm. It wasn't, not really. But because it was what he was part of. The team; the tempo; the quiet competence. The way people moved and just got on with things with no need to be told. He didn't need to be the loudest voice in the room. He just needed to be in it.

There was a kind of peace. Not the soft kind. Not the kind you get from sleep or silence. But the kind that comes from knowing your place in the machine, and knowing the competence of the other parts of that machine. From watching it turn, knowing you helped build it.

He'd been in rooms like this before in other parts of his life. Unfamiliar faces. Different ops. But the same feeling. That edge-of-something energy. That sense that today might be the day everything works. He didn't romanticise it. He knew what it cost. The missed birthdays and missed socials. The weight of decisions made on the hoof. But he also knew this: when it worked, when the timing was right, the intel solid, the team sharp, there was nothing like it.

Across the room, someone laughed. Someone swore at a dodgy charger. Someone dropped a pen and didn't bother picking it up. Tom sat back and let it all happen around him. He felt calm, knowing he belonged there.

This definitely was his happy place.

Jamie called from his office and broke the spell. "Tom, Sharon."

They went into Jamie's office, closed the door, and sat down. Jamie was leaning forward with his forearms on the desk.

"Right," he said. "We are off and running. The paperwork's all done. Blake has insisted I come on the plot today, but I'll not get in your way, and I was going to anyway. I don't want to miss the fun of this one. It's just to cover the participation element and stop any defence objections at any subsequent trial."

"That's great because Dick is over at Caterham clearing up any loose ends on yesterday's job. You can crew with Craig."

"OK. Great," said Jamie. "I'll hang around here for a bit and be at the briefing then."

Tom said, "We were due to brief at midday, but I think we'll wait for confirmation the handover's been done."

They left the office, sat down, and waited for the update. Once they knew what was happening, they'd rally the troops and get on with it.

***

Pete had picked up Falstead from behind the club as arranged. He could see Falstead was nervous and tried to calm him down.

"The old bill has stopped how many times in your motor?" asked Pete.

"Never," said Falstead.

"Then what are you worried about? There's no reason to think you might be stopped today, is there?"

It was a statement, not a question. The last thing Pete needed now was for Falstead to pull out.

"And remember, if you pull out of this, you are as good as dead," said Pete, emphasising the predicament Falstead found himself in.

"Don't keep bloody reminding me," said Falstead, his expression tight with worry.

"Anyway," said Pete. "What happened to Pinky and Perky?"

"I don't know," said Falstead. "They must have been doing a bit of dealing on the side. The old bill called my brief, of course, so I know what's going on. It was about nine ounces of Colombian marching powder taped under the cistern lid, for Christ's sake. They're insisting the old bill planted it, but they don't plant that much, ever. A bit of personal, maybe, but not nine ounces. They just can't keep that back from a bust for use later. They've nowhere to keep that sort of weight."

"I agree," said Pete. "Pinky and Perky are more worried about what you're going to say than being caught with it. One of their customers must have bubbled them up."

"That's all it can be."

"Are you going to tell Shaun they've been nicked?"

"Not a chance," said Falstead. "I'll deny all knowledge if asked and say it was always my intention to do it myself."

***

Friday 9th April 2010 – afternoon

They continued in silence for about an hour until Pete's phone vibrated.

He answered. Shaun said, "How are yous, big fella?"

"I'm fine," said Pete.

"You're still tracking me then."

"What makes yous say that then?"

"Well, you know we're on the way."

Falstead stared at Pete with a quizzical expression. Pete put a finger to his lips, the soft hiss of tyres on tarmac masking his whisper.

"Shush," he said.

"I do, big fella. I know yous got your man in the car wit' yous. He driving dis t'ing back?"

"He is. Where are we meeting up with you?"

"I'll send yous a message with a location when yous are nearer. We'll know when yous two are near. Just sit there and wait for us." He hung up.

"How the fuck does he know where we are, and how does he know I'm with you?" said Falstead, amazed.

"They've been tracking my phone. And I guess yours too. When I found out, I didn't take it off in case they thought I was trying to get away with something."

"Jesus Christ. I wondered why my battery was going down so fast. It never occurred to me they could do that."

"No, me neither. They must have done it when they took our stuff at the barn. Nowadays, you don't even need a passcode. They just changed the battery. The new battery has all the kit embedded in it. It's a bit more powerful, but still drains quicker than the original."

"Why didn't you tell me it was in there?" said Falstead, indignant.

"Because if I had, you'd have stopped taking the phone with you, and they would've known you knew. That would've pissed them off. And I'm not in the habit of pissing them off."

"Fair enough," said Falstead. "They are a bloody scary bunch, that's for sure."

They fell into a comfortable silence again, each lost in their own thoughts.

Pete's phone buzzed with a message.

You are coming in on the A55. Take the turning off onto the A5153. Turn first left on Lon Trefignath. Drive 100 yards and stop. Then, wait for further instructions.

He handed the phone to Falstead to read. "I wonder what that's all about," said Falstead.

"They're checking for a tail," said Pete.

"I bet someone turns up with a bit of kit that checks if there's a tracker on this."

And after twenty minutes, that's what happened.

Another message came through.

Stay in the car.

A Toyota pickup pulled up in front of them, two up. Both occupants wore black balaclavas, their eyes unreadable behind tinted lenses. The passenger got out and, using a square box-shaped device, swept around the vehicle. His boots crunched on gravel as he moved around the wheel arches. He then checked the same areas using a mirror. Appearing satisfied, he got back into the pickup. It reversed, turned around, and drove off the way it had come.

Then another message.

Now drive to the T-junction. Turn left. Drive to the end and stop.

Pete followed the instructions. The pickup faced toward them. One of the balaclava wearers got out, walked to their car, and climbed into the rear seat behind Pete.

"Yous follow my instructions to the letter..." He leaned forward, voice low. "...or I'll put a bullet in yous spine."

"Of course," said Pete. "Whatever you say, matey." The accent wasn't as broad as Shaun's, but this guy was Irish.

Someone directed Pete in toward the town. He could guess where they were going, but he couldn't give the impression that he knew where they parked the Range Rover, assuming it was there at all.

"Stop here," said the new passenger.

It was clear this was all part of an anti-surveillance routine. They weren't worried about trackers anymore. This was about eyes, spotters posted at key points, watching for tails. Pete had learned plenty from Tom and knew the drill. They sat for a full ten minutes.

"OK, drive again."

They were satisfied. They were now heading to where Pete believed the vehicle to be. About fifty yards from it, the passenger said again, "Stop."

"Yous have the key fob?" he asked Falstead. Falstead nodded. "Then yous follow me."

The man and Falstead got out of the vehicle and walked toward the car park of the Roman Fort, disappearing from view.

Pete glanced at his watch. What do I do now? It's 16:00, and we're behind schedule.

He waited. Five minutes later, he saw the Range Rover driving toward him, with only Falstead inside. Pete spun his vehicle around and dropped in behind it. His phone vibrated.

"What happened, John?" said Pete.

"He didn't say a word. Gave me a piece of paper with an address on it, where they want me to put the Range Rover after we've emptied it. Just pointed, turned, and fucked off. Like it was nothing."

"OK, that's it. Let's just get back. Where are we going then?" said Pete, hoping to get a sign of where a lock-up might be. He didn't want to ask. He would wait if Falstead didn't offer the location.

"I've got a lock-up. Just follow me."

Pete followed the Range Rover out of Holyhead. As he did, he messaged Tom.

Range Rover picked up. Stolen vehicle. Identical to Falstead. Cloned plates. Just leaving Holyhead. Behind schedule, I guess. Five hours from Guildford. Falstead says we are going to his lock-up. No location given but assume near Guildford.

Chapter Thirty Four

Friday 9th April 2010 – late afternoon

Tom had delayed the briefing until he had an update from Pete. Then the message came in on a number Tom didn't recognise.

Must be a burner.

Range Rover picked up. Stolen vehicle. Identical to Falstead. Cloned plates. Just leaving Holyhead. Behind schedule, I guess. Probably five hours from Guildford. Falstead says we are going to his lockup. No location given but assume near Guildford.

Tom stood up and said, "OK, guys. We're on. Briefing as soon as everyone's here, please."

He showed his phone to Sharon and then took it into Jamie's office to show him. Jamie read it and handed the phone back.

"No sign Falstead has examined the gear in the boot to make sure it's there?" said Jamie.

"No, but we have no choice but to run with what we've got and hope the Irish haven't done a dirty on him," said Tom. "Briefing in a few minutes."

Jamie gave him a thumbs-up.

"Everyone here?" said Tom. "Then we'll kick this off.

"Apologies for the delay. I know we don't discuss these things, but we've been waiting for an update from a source. That was late, as the target is running behind schedule.

"The target is John Falstead. All the HA details, description, target vehicle details, etc., are on the briefing notes and you've all got copies.

We suspect that the fifty kilos of charlie we seized at Ally Pally belonged to the target. Having lost that parcel, he was in deep trouble. The only way he could get out of that was to keep supplying to repay the debt over time. It's suspected that the same group that supplied him the first time round has agreed to work with him to square this all up.

"He is driving a ringed Range Rover Autobiography, the same as his own vehicle, even with cloned plates. The presumption being, if he's stopped in a vehicle matching the plates, no traffic officer would bother to do anything other than a PNC check and find it registered to him.

"The reason the vehicle is a ringer is that secreted inside is another fifty kilos of charlie. The supplier in secret carried packing that in the vehicle out, prior to the handover of the vehicle to Falstead this afternoon."

"Is this linked to the two nicked by Guildford this morning?" asked Mo.

“Not specifically, but the two that were nicked work for Falstead,” said Tom, without going into any more detail than necessary.

Mo nodded. He and the team understood they should take that no further.

“At around 16:00 today, the vehicle left Holyhead, North Wales, en route to a lock-up in the Guildford area. You don’t need to know how, but we have constant eyes on the vehicle.

“Even though we believe it’s heading here, we’re aware it could divert somewhere nearby. With this in mind, we’re going to plot up next to junction 5 of the M40 at Stokenchurch and pick up the vehicle on the way past. We expect the target vehicle to pass that junction at about 20:00. I reiterate, we don’t need eyes on the vehicle. We will know when it’s passing the junction.

“It’s about 40 miles to Stokenchurch from here, so allow an hour. I want to be plotted up no later than 19:00.

“Questions so far?”

“Broken taillight?” said Karen.

“No access or time, Karen, I’m afraid.”

“We’ll be hitting this vehicle on our manor. If he travels the expected route of the M40, M25, A3, we have no option but to hit after it exits the A3. As usual, the eyeball will call it, but if possible, consider putting the bike in front to hold the traffic at an r/a or somewhere Jamie considers suitable to back up traffic. We then box it in as best we can. Don’t ask me for clearance to hit it. When you say we go, we go.

“OK, crews:

Four-zero: Lisa and Mo
Four-one: Jack and Samantha
Four-two: Jamie Carmichael

Four-three: Charlotte and Karen
Four-four: Sharon, me, and Claire
Four-five: Craig and the DI
Four-six: Alex and Joe

"If we plot up in Lewes Close, which is off the A40, we can do the nearside onto the A40, then just join the motorway as normal.

"As we'll be getting the live location, four-four will be the first vehicle onto the motorway. Follow in convoy order after that. That means four-zero, you'll be the back-up.

"We've never done this before, and I can't remember doing it on my surveillance course, so it's a new one for us all. We've got plenty of time though, so it shouldn't be that difficult. It's about five miles to the next junction, so we've got plenty of time.

"I think we're done."

The usual scrapping of chairs, rustling of papers, and murmurs of those discussing the job. A few phones buzzed on the table, screens lighting up with last-minute messages. Someone coughed. Someone else muttered about the traffic on the M40. Sharon leaned back, arms folded, scanning faces. Karen tapped her pen against her notepad, already half-doodled with route diagrams and question marks. She appeared pensive, working something through, and Tom could guess what.

The air was thick with anticipation. Not nerves. Not yet. But the focused tension that came before a live one.

Tom stood at the front, waiting for the room to settle. He didn't raise his voice. He didn't need to.

"See you at the strike, guys."

No one replied, but a few faces smiled at him. They scraped back chairs, folded papers, and pocketed phones. The room emptied with the efficiency of muscle memory. Crews moving in pairs, each knowing their role, their timing.

Sharon lingered a moment, eyes on Tom. He gave her a nod, nothing more. She turned and followed the others, Claire trailing in her wake like a puppy. Tom smiled at that. Claire would be another Sharon one day. He could sense it. It's funny; you could always spot the good ones early.

As Tom expected, Karen walked up to him with her DS's hat on. "How are you getting the live location, Tom? A participating informant?"

"Yep, Jamie's done all the paperwork. It's all authorised."

"OK. Great. Well done, mate," she said. She smiled, patted him twice on the arm, and walked out to her vehicle.

As they walked to their car, Claire said, "What did Karen mean about the rear light?"

Sharon paused, turned to Claire, and said, "This is one you keep in your bin. If we're doing surveillance at night, we try to get someone close to the vehicle while it's unoccupied, with a very thin electrical screwdriver. If you put it in the centre of the plastic cover and give it a whack, you make a tiny hole that's very difficult to see. Then, using the screwdriver, you break the rear light bulb. It makes it easier to follow in the dark. But you didn't hear that from me."

Claire didn't reply straight away. She glanced at Sharon, then down at the pavement as they walked. "Doesn't that cross a line?" she said.

Sharon shrugged. "Depends on which line you mean."

They reached the car. Sharon unlocked it with a click, the indicator lights blinking once. "Sometimes you just need a little help," she added, opening the passenger door and climbing in.

"Ingenious," said Claire, settling into the rear seat and buckling her seat belt.

Timing the journey to junction 5 of the M40 could have been better, it took them an hour and a half to get there. 18:40. But there was still plenty of time. Dusk was at 19:47. It would be dark when they picked up the target vehicle.

Tom called Pete on his burner.

"Hi mate. How's it going?" Tom didn't want to use Pete's name in front of Claire.

"Hi Tom. Fine. Pretty undramatic so far. He's travelling just over the speed limit, so all looks good. Still on the same timescales, I think we should be with you around eight."

"When you're about five miles away, call me and talk me through the junction. You should be able to give me the one-mile and half-mile markers with no problem, but I could do with a bit more notice than that just to get people on their toes. We're all here waiting, so all ready to go."

"You should know something else, Tom. Falstead's phone also has a tracker in it. So as soon as you hit it, I suggest you get hold of his phone, turn it off, remove the SIM card, and put it in a Faraday pouch."

"OK. All received, mate. Catch you later."

Tom turned to Sharon. "Did you catch that?"

"No," she said, shaking her head.

"The target's phone has a tracker in it. We need to get hold of it as soon as possible after the strike, turn it off, remove the SIM, and get it in a Faraday pouch."

"OK, I'll take that on. Leave it to me," she said, then glanced at Claire. "You didn't hear that."

"Hear what?" said Claire.

Tom gave a faint smile in response to Claire's response. Good girl. Sharp, but still green. He liked that. Sharon turned back to her window, scanning the verge as they sat stationary in Lewes Close. The light was fading now, the sky bruising into evening.

19:10.

"What do I do if I need a wee?" said Claire.

"I'll leave that one to you, Sharon," said Tom.

"You go in the bushes over there," said Sharon, pointing out the passenger window. "But I'd go now if I were you."

"OK," said Claire, getting out and running into the bushes, feeling embarrassed.

Tom had his head back on the headrest, swivelled it left and said, "Can you remember when you had just a year in?"

"I can," said Sharon, sighing. "But I can't say I enjoyed that time as a probationer. I just wanted it over with so I could get on with stuff without that hanging over me."

"Yeah, me too," said Tom. "I had this tutor called Andy Bristol. He was bloody useless. Smoked a pipe and stunk the car out. He never wanted to take any jobs, and I used to love it when he had a day off and I was working, I could go out on my own.

"We had a uniform skipper called Frank Beard. Old school. Woe betide anyone who called him Skip, Skipper, or Sarge. Frank made us take our paperwork out with us, and we weren't permitted to return to the station unless we were on a meal break. We had to do our paperwork in a phone box. Absolutely bonkers."

"Did you wash your hands?" said Tom as Claire got back in the car.

"I can't...... "

"I'm pulling your leg, silly," said Tom with a giggle.

Claire buckled in, cheeks flushed but smiling. The embarrassment was fading, replaced by something steadier. Belonging, maybe? Sharon glanced at her in the rear-view mirror: "Don't worry. We've all done worse."

Claire nodded, grateful but unsure what to say.

Tom checked his watch. 19:14.

"Right," he said. "Let's settle in. We've got forty-five minutes, maybe more." He reached into the glove box, pulled out a half-squashed protein bar, and offered it to Sharon.

She waved it away. "I'm good. That's festered in your pocket for a week."

He shrugged and took a bite, chewing slowly, eyes on the fading light.

The car was quiet now. Outside, the wind stirred the hedgerow. They could hear the motorway in the distance. Claire leaned her head against the window, watching the sky turn from bruised purple to ink. She didn't know what would happen next. But she knew she wanted to be part of it as soon as it was possible.

Tom's phone vibrated.

Must still be an hour away.

Tom replied with a thumbs-up.

"From four-four. For information, the target is still about one hour away. Four-five?"

"Four-five, yes, yes."

Sharon turned to Claire. "Why did Tom ask for a confirmation receipt from four-five?"

"Because the DI's in that car with Craig?" said Claire, her voice rising at the end.

Sharon turned to Tom, smiling.

"We've got a future Sharon on our hands, I think," said Tom.

Claire was exploding with pride inside.

Tom finished his energy bar, settled down in his seat, and closed his eyes.

Forty winks before the fun starts.

Chapter Thirty Five

Friday 9th April 2010 – evening

Tom woke with a start. His phone was vibrating. It was the burner.

"Tom, we're about five miles out from the junction, mate. All normal this end."

"OK. Stay on the line now until we have him under control."

Tom put the phone on speaker and handed it to Sharon.

[Comms]: "From four-four, the target is about five miles out. Four-three?"

[Comms]: "Four-three, yes, yes."

[Comms]: "Convoy check."

All the cars replied in order to confirm their radios were working.

"We're about four miles out, Tom."

"What speed are you doing?"

"About seventy-five."

"OK, seventy-five. How many cars between you and him?"

"None."

"OK, try to drop back, get some cars between you. What lane are you in?"

"Three miles out, Tom. Same speed. One car between us now. Middle lane."

[Comms]: "From four-four, three miles out. Speed seven-five. Lane two of three."

"Two miles from you now, Tom. Same speed. Two cars between us. Middle lane."

[Comms]: "From four-four, two miles out. Speed seven-five. Lane two of three."

"One mile marker. Same speed. Three cars between us now."

[Comms]: "From four-four, one mile marker. Speed seven-five. Lane two of three."

"Half mile marker. Same speed."

[Comms]: "From four-four, half-mile marker. Speed seven-five. Lane two of three."

"We're at the junction now, Tom, and he's staying on the motorway."

[Comms]: "From four-four, he's now past the junction. Speed seven-five. Lane two of three."

Tom gunned the engine and did the nearside onto the A40, followed by the slip road onto the M40.

"I'm just coming onto the motorway, mate. What lane are you in?"

"The middle one. He's three ahead of me. Same speed. He must be on cruise control, I think."

"OK, I'm coming up the outside lane but don't want to draw attention to myself. OK, I think I can see you. And I can see him. OK. You just keep going and we'll speak later, but drop back so I can slot in front of you. We've got it now."

Yes, got you, you bastard.

[Comms]: "Contact, contact, contact from four-four. Lane two of three. Two for cover. Speed seven-five. Convoy check."

[Comms]: "Four-zero is your backup."

[Comms]: "Four-one in three."

[Comms]: "Four-three in four."

[Comms]: "Four-five in five."

[Comms]: "Four-six in six."

[Comms]: "Four-two is in the convoy."

[Comms]: "Convoy is complete. No deviation. Lane two of three. Two for cover. Speed seven-five."

[Comms]: "Now approaching junction 4. Convoy close up. Four-zero?"

[Comms]: "Four-zero, yes, yes."

[Comms]: "Lane two of three. Two for cover. Speed seven-five."

[Comms]: "No deviation. Remaining on the M40."

The M40 rolled out beneath them like a conveyor belt, grey, predictable, and forgettable.

Pete sat back, elbow resting on the window ledge, watching the same sequence of vehicles drift past like background actors in a play they'd rehearsed a hundred times.

No deviation. Just the hum of tyres on tarmac, the occasional flicker of brake lights, and the steady tick of the eyeball's updates over comms. Sharon scribbled notes without looking up. Tom checked the rearview, not because he needed to, but because habit demanded it.

Surveillance like this was bread and butter. Eyes on. Minds half elsewhere.

Claire shifted in her seat, trying not to yawn. “This is it?” she asked.

“This is it,” said Tom. “If it’s exciting, we’ve done something wrong.”

And on they travelled. From the M40, down the M25 towards the A3, changing the eyeball at regular intervals.

The convoy held its shape. Nothing out of the ordinary. Then Tom’s phone vibrated.

Update coming in.

“Tom,” said Pete, “he’s just called me. He’s going to take the gear to his club. I said that’s risky, and he said no one knows he owns it yet, so it’s safe as houses.”

“OK. Which way do you think he’ll drive to get there?”

“The obvious way is to come off at Burpham and go past the Sainsbury's roundabout.”

“OK, mate, thanks,” said Tom, and he hung up.

“Right, Sharon,” said Tom, switching into planning mode. “He’s taking the gear to his club. The source thinks he’ll come off the A3 at Burpham and go past the Sainsbury's r/a. We’ll just do a hard stop after the Sainsbury's r/a.”

Sharon nodded her assent.

“You’ll enjoy this, Claire,” said Tom, turning to look at her. “The eyeball will get to a position where they’ve got no cover as they enter the slip road. Backup will move behind the eyeball, and everyone will close up tight. As we approach the Sainsbury's roundabout, the backup takes over the commentary, and the eyeball and the bike overtake the target vehicle. The eyeball, now in front of the target, jams his anchors on, and so does the target. The bike does its best to hold up the traffic coming the other direction. The target will do his nut and stop behind what was the eyeball. Now behind the target vehicle, the backup goes right up its arse end, and the car in front will reverse back to the front of the target. With me so far?"

"Yep," said Claire.

"The next car goes alongside the offside, which should be clear because of what four-two has done, and the next one down the nearside, which will be on the pavement.

"In theory, it's now boxed in and there's nowhere to go."

"Wow," said Claire.

"But it never works out like that. Something always goes wrong," said Tom with a smile. "You can get out of the car this time if you like, but only after we've secured it."

"Brill," she said. "Do you want me to do anything specific?"

"Just stick with your hero," said Tom, and laughed.

Sharon then put the plan out over the air.

[Comms]: "Four-four, permission?"

[Comms]: "Yes, yes, four-four."

[Comms]: "All units, information in that the target is going to go to his club, the details of which you have. The obvious route being off at Burpham. With this in mind, we are looking at a hard stop before the Sainsbury's roundabout. We close up on the A3 as we

leave the M25 and follow our normal procedures as we approach the Sainsbury's r/a. Back to you, eyeball."

[Comms]: "Yes, yes."

And here we go.

[Comms]: "Four-three has the eyeball as we enter the A3. Nearside lane of two. Speed six-zero. Convoy close up."

The convoy closed in as tight as possible without showing out. The tension was rising now, because they'd all done this many times before, and it never went well.

[Comms]: "Passing the one-mile marker. Nearside lane of two. Speed six-zero."

[Comms]: "Passing the half-mile marker. Nearside lane of two. Speed five-five."

[Comms]: "Approaching the Burpham turnoff. Nearside lane of two. Speed five-zero. Nearside indicator. Left, left, left, onto the slip road, four-four."

[Comms]: "Four-four, yes, yes."

[Comms]: "Back-up identify."

[Comms]: "Four-one is your back-up in position."

[Comms]: "Four-one, yes, yes. Commentary to you."

[Comms]: "At the approach to the r/a and slowing."

Karen was driving four-three and Jamie was behind her on the bike.

[Comms]: "At the r/a. Held at pole. On the r/a. Not one, not one. Taken the second, taken the second."

And Karen and Jamie made their move. It was tight for the bike with traffic coming the other way, but he just got there.

This is going too well.

[Comms]: "Strike, strike, strike."

And then it all kicked off. Karen braked hard. The target reacted as predicted, slamming his brakes and nearly rear-ending her. Jack braked hard too and got as close to the target vehicle as possible. Dick in four-five surged up the offside, tight to the target vehicle, as Jamie held the traffic at bay. But Alex in four-six was baulked, boxed in by a van that hadn't cleared the way in front of him.

Falstead by now, even though it was only a matter of seconds, understood what was going on and did what they all do, even though it's fruitless. He jumped out of the passenger side and ran like fuck.

"He's running!" shouted someone.

Over the first thirty metres, they can run faster than Usain Bolt as the adrenaline pumps through them.

"He's in the gardens!" someone called, voice sharp with urgency.

This is not good. Lose sight of him, and it can all go wrong.

There was a crashing sound as Falstead smashed right through a wooden fence, leaving nothing but splinters behind him. Claire had got out of four-four a bit early, but she was in hot pursuit, full of adrenaline too. She didn't think. She just ran. Not for the arrest, not for the glory, just to prove she belonged.

It's funny what goes through people's heads at times like this, but she wanted to repay the kindness shown to her by Tom and Sharon over these two days, and just kept running. Through bushes, through more fences, and then she had him. He was climbing over a wire fence, which had slowed him down, when she got a hold of his leg.

"Come here, you bastard!" she yelled, grabbing at his leg.

All he did was kick her in the face and fend her off. But she'd slowed him down, and it appeared he was running out of steam.

Sharon knew this area well and ran back the way they'd come, down Orchard Road and into Belmont Place. She was puffing like an old steam train when Falstead burst through a garden and straight into her arms. Claire was right behind him, Dick and Alex not far off. And he gave up. He had nothing left. He knew it was over.

Sharon turned to Claire and gestured, "Claire... nick him."

And she did. And she cuffed him. And she took his phone, turned it off, removed the SIM card, and put the lot in the Faraday pouch Sharon had handed her.

Sharon keyed her radio. "One in custody at Belmont Place."

Tom had arrived in four-four and said to Claire, "Did you have sight of him all the time after he left the vehicle?"

"Yeah," said Claire. "I just kept my eyes on him and kept running."

"Good for you. Did you see him ditch anything?"

"No, but I can't say he didn't."

"That's OK. We'll get a dog unit here to check the route, anyway. Is your face OK? You look like you've taken a whack?"

"I'm fine," she said. "I'm red from running after this tosser."

"What time was he nicked?"

"21:25 by Claire," said Sharon.

"Well done, you," said Tom, looking at Claire with a broad smile.

"Right," said Tom, "let's get some uniforms, a SOCO and a dog unit down here as soon as possible. No one touches the vehicle. We need it put on a trailer, taken to Guildford nick."

"There are two uniform cars here already, Tom," said Karen, who had joined them on foot.

"OK. Can you three get him into Guildford and booked in? I'll stay with the vehicle and sort that out. I guess we reconvene in the canteen later."

Once Falstead was on his way, Tom went back to the scene of the stop. It had quietened down now, and the processes kicked in.

They needed peace now. The vehicle sat quietly, waiting for the trailer. People drifted off. Neighbours who'd watched from in front of their houses at the carnage stepped back into their lives. The street breathed again.

Once the car was on the trailer and taken to Guildford nick, the scene dissolved. Lights flickered in living rooms. A dog barked somewhere down the road. And just like that, you wouldn't know anything had happened. If you had driven down that road five minutes after it had cleared, you wouldn't even have known of the chaos that had ensued only a few minutes before.

Tom met Jamie in the car park, and they walked together through the quiet corridors of Guildford nick. The background hum of voices in distant offices and the clatter of uniform boots on tiles marked the 22:00 shift change.

Tom already knew what was coming. Jamie had kept him briefed on the drive in. But first, they reached Kevin Dean's office, the door half open, light spilling out across the floor.

"Evening, chaps," said Deano, looking up from his desk. "What have you got for us then?"

Jamie stepped forward. "Well," he said, "with a bit of luck we'll find fifty kilos of charlie in the boot of that Range Rover that's now sitting in your garage."

Deano blinked. "Blimey. That is a serious chunk of gear."

"John Falstead's been nicked and is booked in," Jamie continued. "He'll be in a cell by now, so we're in slow time. But we haven't seen the gear yet, so I suggest we get the vehicle searched sharpish. Have you nominated a couple of your guys to deal with it?"

"I have," said Deano. "The drugs unit is buzzing after your tip yesterday, so they can have it. Thomo and Taffy Thomas will do the search. Richard Barton's your exhibits officer. Moors did the exhibits this morning, so no need to mix the two up. And I think Falstead should be present at the vehicle search. You can't plant fifty kilos of charlie, but these buggers'll say anything."

"Agreed," said Tom. "And he's a difficult bloke to deal with. Slippery and arrogant. I know we've handed this job to you now, guvnor, but I'd like him there when it's found. I want him to see it. And I want to see him see it."

The debrief wrapped up, and Tom, Sharon, and Claire made their way to the garage. The Range Rover sat under harsh strip lighting, its paintwork dulled by the artificial glare.

Inside the rest of the team were writing up statements. But Tom, Sharon, and Claire stayed. They wanted to see Falstead's face when they opened the boot and found the gear, when his lies ended.

Thomo brought Falstead out to the garage. He was cuffed and wearing a white paper suit, his clothes seized and bagged. He appeared smaller now. Hollow. Thomo instructed him to sit on a bench next to the side wall of the garage so he could watch the proceedings.

The concrete floor was cold. The air smelled of oil and damp metal.

As Thomo, Taff, and a photographer moved towards the vehicle to begin the search, Tom sidled towards Falstead, leaned in close, and whispered, "I told you. You ever fuck with my family, you piece of shit."

Falstead didn't speak. Just stared at him with sunken eyes, eyes that had once held swagger, now hollowed out by fear. He knew. He was a walking dead man.

His fingers twitched in the cuffs, a nervous tic he couldn't suppress. The paper suit rustled with each movement, sterile and humiliating. A shadow of the man he used to be. A transition that had taken but a few hours. Stripped of his clothes, his lies, and whatever power he thought he had.

"OK," said Thomo. "Boot first."

Taff opened the boot. Empty, or so it seemed. He took out the carpet. There was a circular wooden cover over the area that held the spare tire. He lifted it and said, "Fuck me."

Tom, Sharon, and Claire turned to each other and smiled. Nothing needed to be said. Claire exhaled, her shoulders dropping. Sharon gave a single nod, eyes locked on Falstead.

Taff stood there for a good twenty seconds, frozen, staring at bricks of white powder stuffed into the space. Even Thomo, as a DS who'd seen decent chunks of gear before, was impressed by the amount. He waved to the photographer to take photos.

The flash lit up the garage like fireworks, brief, brutal bursts of light in celebration of the find. Falstead flinched at the first one. Tom didn't move. He just watched Falstead, eyes cold.

As the bricks of charlie were lifted from the boot and stacked into two plastic crates, Richard Barton scribbled in his exhibits book, logging everything with quiet efficiency.

"Interesting," said Taff, holding up a pair of nitrile gloves.

"Barty," said Thomo. "Got a small bag for those, mate."

Barty nodded, bagged them and tagged them without a word.

"I make that forty-eight bricks of white powder," he said, sealing the crates with security tags and noting the numbers in his log.

Tom glanced at Sharon. "Looks like he got ripped off for a couple of kilos. Just to add insult to injury."

Thomo and Taff kept searching. Nothing more in the boot. Seats out, nothing. Then Taff paused, hand deep inside the rear offside door panel.

"What's this? More gear?" he said.

Tom moved around the vehicle, leaned over Taff's shoulder, and froze. "Jesus Christ," he said. "That's Semtex."

"Semtex?" Thomo was already moving, circling the car. "Fucking hell, it is too."

"I know what Semtex looks like, Thomo. The clue's in the name. It's written on the packages. Semtex-H."

Thomo stared at it, then, turning to Tom, said, "What do we do now?"

"We evacuate. This could be a bloody bomb, mate." Tom slammed the fire alarm button on the side wall.

The shrill ringing tore through the building. Chaos followed.

Thomo shouted over the noise: "Taffy, get him back into custody. Tell the sergeant to shift any prisoners to other nicks. Grab the keys to the transit van and give him a hand.

"You," he pointed at Sharon, "go find Deano. Let him know this is the real deal.

"You," pointing at Claire, "spread the word. Tell the control room we need every uniform car in Surrey here to set up a cordon. Start with five hundred metres. Anyone evacuating, get them knocking on doors of the nearby residents. Tell people to get out. And get the bomb squad on the line."

He turned, voice raised to reach anyone within earshot: "No mobile phones!"

Then, to Tom: "What have I missed?"

Tom didn't blink. "Shit loads, I expect. But let's just do the best we can. Once control knows, they'll have a procedure. They always do."

Thomo nodded, breath short. "Right. So what now?"

Tom cracked a grim smile. "Let's get the fuck out of Dodge."

Chapter Thirty Six

Saturday 10th April 2010 – morning

Once outside the cordon, Jamie had rallied the troops to meet at the Spectrum Leisure Centre car park, leaving Guildford personnel and anyone else drafted in from neighbouring divisions to get on with it. Having parked their vehicles, they drifted in one by one on foot to the gathered group, boots scuffing tarmac, eyes dulled by fatigue.

Jamie scanned the room and took in his team. Every one of them was exhausted. Some had been on shift for over twenty-four hours, and there was no sign of anyone clocking off soon.

The gym inside the leisure centre had opened for the day, and members of the public were trickling in, oblivious to the chaos that had unfolded overnight, but the car park was quiet. The sky hung low and pale, the kind that threatened drizzle but delivered silence. Engines idled. Radios crackled. No one spoke unless they had to.

Jamie checked his phone, then raised his voice just enough to carry.

"Right. In from Deano. The Bomb Squad's gone. Semtex's gone. Cordon's lifted. We're clear to head back to the nick. We'll reconvene in the canteen."

What Jamie didn't say was that he, Tom, and Sharon were to go to the conference room. That showed a potential blame exercise being planned. Shit flows downhill, as they say.

As he walked to his car, he motioned to Tom and Sharon.

"We're all called to the conference room. I think we know what's coming. And Tom, we're all tired, but that doesn't give you licence to go off on one. Let me do the talking."

Tom turned to Sharon, then back at Jamie, and just nodded in resignation. They'd been here before.

No one cheered, and no one groaned. They just moved tired bodies towards their vehicles, engines starting like yawns. One by one, they rolled out, leaving the leisure centre behind.

The conference room smelled of old carpet and tension. The blinds were half-drawn, as if shielding the room from accountability. Jamie didn't mind taking heat, but he hated the way it always came from people who'd never made an actual decision in their lives.

As the three of them walked in, Deano and Superintendent Blake sat at the conference table.

"Please. Sit down," said Blake. "Now tell me from start to finish how this shit show happened."

Jamie ran through the operation from start to finish, leaving out any details he thought might be smelly. He clarified that at no time had there ever been any sign the vehicle was transporting explosives and drugs.

"If the INLA were involved in this," said Blake, "did you not consider informing Special Branch?"

"We thought about it, but since the INLA is now regarded as a criminal organisation rather than a terrorist one, I ruled it out."

"Well, that went well, Inspector."

"Actually, sir, I rather think it did. Thanks to the professionalism of my team, we've not only seized a large quantity of cocaine but also a large quantity of explosives that, we can only assume at this stage, was meant to create some sort of major incident on the mainland."

Well done, Jamie. You go on the offensive, fucking tell him.

"And what's your view, DC Kessler?"

"I concur with DI Capstick, sir. We did not know any explosives were involved, only drugs. We are a drug squad, and our last three seizures have been fifty kilos of cocaine, a kilo of heroin, and now forty-eight kilos of cocaine. For a county drug squad, I would say that's outstanding, and we should be congratulated... sir."

"Do you now."

It was a statement, not a question.

"Well, I've asked Professional Standards to review this from start to finish so we can make sure nothing untoward occurred with this operation."

The door had opened. It being behind them, neither Jamie, Tom, nor Sharon were aware of the rubber heel squad walking in. By name, by nature.

"With that in mind, I've asked Superintendent Litt here to carry out a review."

Blake was looking over them towards the door and, when all three of them turned, the man they all knew as 'Litt the Shit' stood there with a stupid grin on his face. Five foot six of poison with small-man syndrome. On steroids.

Jamie didn't need to look at Tom or Sharon to know they were bristling. Litt's grin was the kind that came before a slow dissection. And Blake? Well, Blake was already halfway out of the blast radius.

"Morning, everyone," he said.

No one replied. In reality, even Blake didn't like him. But he served a purpose. He was likely to find something behind which Blake could hide, and shift any blame elsewhere. Job done.

Tom muttered something under his breath. Not loud enough to be heard, but loud enough to be felt.

"Here we go," he whispered, just for Jamie. "The Witchfinder General's arrived."

Jamie didn't smile. He didn't dare.

Sharon's silence wasn't just discomfort; it was strategy. She was already thinking two steps ahead, mentally reviewing every report, every call, every loose thread. She knew the other two had crossed a line somewhere along this operation and would need to distance herself from any decision-making. In reality, that shouldn't be too hard, but she was loyal to these two and would have to tread carefully.

Sharon leaned back in her chair, mentally and physically distancing herself.

She'd seen it before. Outstanding officers undone by bad timing and worse optics. Sharon would not be one of them, not if she could help it. She didn't need Litt to tell her where the cracks were. She had been aware of them forming days ago. Now she just had to make sure she didn't fall through one.

"Can I point out, sir," said Jamie, "my team have been on duty for over twenty-four hours and are in no fit state to be interviewed by anyone. There's nothing here that cannot wait. Inspector Dean has all the information he needs to forward this investigation, and I will liaise with him to make sure there are no gaps in his knowledge.

"We all know Detective Sergeant Thomson is an excellent detective, is an ex-member of 6 RCS, and is more than capable of dealing with an enquiry of this nature. We also know there was an authorised participating informant involved with the intelligence regarding this operation, which is sensitive. I have already spoken to Inspector Dean about this, and he agrees with me. We need to bring in the Complex Casework Unit at the CPS at an early stage.

"I suggest my team go home, get some rest, and reconvene here on Monday morning where they can all complete their statements. I will be available for the rest of the weekend on the phone if the DI needs me and should be considered his first point of contact for anything to do with my team's involvement."

Blake just stared at him. You could see his mind working: Is there anything else I need to get in place now to cover myself from any future shit hitting the fan? He decided there wasn't.

"OK, Inspector. Reconvene here or in your office Monday morning as you see appropriate," he said, as if it was his idea.

He got up and walked out of the room. As he passed Litt the Shit, he said, without looking at him, "Follow me."

Jamie turned his head, surveying the room. Solid to a fault, he hoped.

To Deano he said, "Anything you need over the weekend, Deano, just call. This is all your job now, of course, but I suggest Falstead is unlikely to know anything about the explosives in the vehicle. If he had, I can't imagine he would have driven it back here. It also explains why the Irish wanted the vehicle back, of course. I imagine all you're going to get is a 'no comment' interview with a prepared statement, but with all the potential complications we could have in the future, that is likely to be a good thing in the short term. He's bang to rights, anyway.

"Don't you think it's amazing?" Jamie said. "We've worked our nuts off for over twenty-four hours, pull forty-eight kilos of cocaine off the streets, bound for Surrey, I might add, and stopped a terrorist incident. We've saved countless lives, and we're sitting here wondering if we'll have a job next week.

"Deano, I need to have a quick word with these two before we all bugger off. I'll pop by your office on my way out."

"OK, mate. I feel for you," said Deano, and left them sitting there. It was silent for a little while as they caught their breath.

"Before we all disappear for the weekend, I want to be clear about one thing, Sharon," Jamie said, his voice steady. "No one in this room has done anything wrong. Least of all, you. If there's noise around this later, and there might be, you need to remember that. You weren't brought into anything because there was nothing to bring you into. Tom and I made sure of that."

He paused just long enough for it to land. "You did your job. You asked the right questions. That's all anyone can ask." He glanced at the two of them. "OK. Let's all get some shut-eye."

They stood, the fatigue settling into their bones. Sharon led the way, Jamie close behind, Tom trailing. As soon as Sharon was out of sight, Jamie turned, caught Tom's eye, and made the gesture, thumb and little finger extended, thumb to his ear. He tapped his chest, then pointed at Tom. I'll call you. Tom nodded once. No words needed.

It's like Bosnia all over again. Different war. Same rules.

On the drive, Tom said only one thing to Sharon before she dropped him off. "See what I mean about not asking a question of the source if you think you might not like the answer?"

She didn't reply. It was rhetorical anyway. She turned to him for a second or two, and just nodded.

They just needed to get some sleep.

Chapter Thirty Seven

Saturday 10th April 2010 - late morning

"My goodness, Tom. You look exhausted," said Sue, as he walked through the door. "That was a long shift."

Although he wasn't top of her Christmas card list at the moment, she couldn't help but feel for him.

"Agreed. That was a tough one. Did you see the commotion in Guildford on the news?"

"I did. Was that you?"

"Well, not me personally. But it was our squad. We got what we wanted, a big parcel of charlie, but we also got an unwanted parcel of Semtex. At a guess, about a hundred and fifty kilos of it."

"Wow."

"It was total bloody chaos. With the nick being where it is, we had to evacuate residents and put a five-hundred-metre exclusion zone in place. It was like being back in the army again."

"But you got the result you wanted?"

"Well, Falstead, if he survives inside, will not be coming out for a very long time. This is a fifteen to twenty-year stretch, if the Irish let him live that long."

"Did you tell him?"

"Tell him what?"

"You know what, Tom Kessler."

"I might have had a brief word in his shell-like at one stage," said Tom, with a smile on his face. "I'm going for a shower and will try to get some sleep."

As he walked up the stairs, Sue whispered to herself, "Don't fuck with Tom Kessler."

Before my shower, I have a couple more jobs to do.

"Pete, how are you doing?"

"Morning, Tom. Did you get what you wanted?" said Pete.

"We did. Nice touch with the gloves, by the way. I didn't see that coming."

"Well, if the busts didn't go as planned and Pinky-and-or-Perky ended up driving, I wanted Falstead's DNA to be with the gear."

"Smart thinking. Do you know what else was in the vehicle?"

"No."

"About 150 kilos of high-grade explosives."

"Fuck me. Are you kidding? Was that the cause of all that palaver in Guildford last night?"

"No, mate, I'm not kidding, and yes, it was what caused all the commotion in Guildford last night," said Tom. "Where will this leave you with the Irish?"

"I don't have a clue. I've not even had a call from Shaun, and I can't even speculate what that means.

That amazed me, because they've been tracking both of our phones and must know by now what's happened. Thinking about the explosives, that's why they wanted the vehicle back."

"It must be. We stopped a terrorist attack on mainland UK. Not that you'd think that from the reaction of the higher-ups, the way they've done a fucking bomb burst in all directions.

"By the way, as soon as he was nicked, one of our guys took his phone, turned it off, removed the SIM card and put it in a Faraday pouch, just as you said they should, so the Irish would have lost him at that point. But you, I assume, just left yours on and drove home at normal speed?"

"I did. And have been awaiting the call from them ever since. Maybe they'll just pitch up here?"

"It's possible, but I don't think so, Pete. I think they'll stay well away from the mainland for a while. You should get a call soon, though. What are you going to say?"

"I'm just going to say he got busted. There was nothing I could do, so I drove off."

"And what if they blame you?"

"They can't. I didn't know where the vehicle was. They checked my vehicle for electronic trackers, and the road behind for normal surveillance before we went anywhere near the handover, so they know I wasn't followed. When I called you, I was using a burner. If they get an itemised billing of my phone, they'll see the only call I made was to Martina."

"Smart move, matey. OK, well, I've been up all night and am going to get some sleep. The phone will be off, so just message me if Shaun calls and I'll call you back when I turn the phone on."

"Before you go, taking a backward step, Tom, I wonder if the bosses in the Irish firm have blamed Patrick and Shaun for all this, and they've paid the ultimate price?"

"Blimey. That makes sense, Pete. Perhaps only time will tell. It's possible we'll never find out, of course."

"OK, mate. Sweet dreams."

Tom could feel the smile on Pete's face.

One to go.

"Hi Jamie, it's Tom."

"Hi, Tom. Have you spoken to the source?"

"Yes, I've just put the phone down after talking to him. He's yet to have a call from the Irish, which has surprised him."

"That's interesting. I wonder why that is?"

"I can only assume they're keeping their heads down and waiting for the dust to settle, but he thinks these two that he knows may have paid the ultimate price."

"Wow. I guess that's possible, but we'll just wait and see, I suppose. Anyway, I just want to check something now that Litt the Shit's involved. Can you assure me that every phone contact, from you to him or from him to you, is logged on a contact sheet?"

"One hundred percent I can. Up here for thinking, down here for dancing, as they say. They will do an itemised billing of my and his phone, looking for shit to spread around and to catch me out. I was prepared for that, and everything is bang on. You and I know there have been a couple of 'off the books' meets, but they are safe. Each time, my phone has been off and locked in the car's boot in a Faraday bag, so no cell site tracking going on there.

"Jamie... I can assure you. Everything is 100 percent covered."

"Good," said Jamie, then added, "What about Sharon? Is she solid?"

"I don't think there's anything she needs to be solid about, to be honest. We've said nothing in front of her; she could tell anyone. She may suspect we engineered a bit of this, but she can't prove it or even point anyone in the right direction."

"And what about the source?"

"He's solid. He knows that when the dust settles, he's in for a huge payday for this one. Especially now that the Semtex has been found. That could be a fifty-grand payout. That one should come out of central government funds too, as it must be classed as national terrorism and can't come out of our informant budget."

"Yes, Tom. You're right there. When we get through this further, I'll start putting that request together. As for now, we keep our heads down and survive the rubber heel squad crawling all over us."

"OK, guv," said Tom, adding in a final mark of respect for his boss. "I'm going to get some kip now. See you on Monday, or speak before if you need to call me. The phone will be off for a while, though."

"Well done, Tom. You're a top man. Bye."

"Jamie?"

"Yep,"

"Before you go, do you think Litt the Shit will want to speak to the source?"

"I'm pretty sure he'll want to."

"Well. He's only going to get told to fuck off."

"Good." And they hung up.

One great bust of Charlie. A hundred and fifty kilos of chaos. Time to wash off the night and sleep like the dead.

And he did.

***

Tom woke with a start.

For a moment, he couldn't place himself. Bleary-eyed and bone-tired, he sat up in bed, disoriented. He shook his head, then rubbed his face with both hands, trying to scrub away the fog.

He stood, shuffled towards the en-suite, and twisted his neck from side to side, vertebrae clicking. It always took days to shake off these long shifts. Unless you've done it, you've got no idea.

He gripped the sink with both hands and leaned forward, staring into the porcelain like it might offer answers. He splashed his face with cold water and wondered what time it was.

16:00.

I won't be able to sleep tonight now.

He pulled on a pair of old tracksuit bottoms and his faded England rugby shirt. The fabric hung loose, as if it had given up trying to fit him. He staggered downstairs, legs still heavy.

The girls were in front of the TV, but none of them were watching it. Eyes locked on their phones, thumbs scrolling, faces lit by screens. They didn't even glance up.

"Hi girls."

"Hi, pops," they said in unison, heads down, voices flat.

For a moment, he stood there. He'd been gone for days, and they hadn't even been aware. Shaking his head, he went to the kitchen.

"Hey, you," said Sue. "How are you feeling?"

"Knackered. I'm getting too old for this, Sue."

"You're only thirty-six, Tom. What are you going to be like when you're forty-six?"

"I won't be doing this in ten years. I might have to bite the bullet and try for a promotion. If Jamie can do it, maybe I can."

"I've never heard you talk like that before, Tom. Are you serious?"

"Do you know, I think I am," he said, looking up at her. "I think I realise that, as much as I love what I'm doing, I can't do it forever and have to accept that. Have you ever heard of 'The Peter Principle'?"

"No."

"A bloke called Laurence J. Peter coined it in a book called The Peter Principle. The fundamental claim is, 'Each worker in a hierarchy advances to their level of inability.' As we see in most of the senior officers I've ever come across, everyone ends up in a job they're shit at. Just because you're a great PC doesn't mean you'll make a great sergeant, and so on.

"It happened little in the army. But in this outfit? It's like they've built their own bloody castle. Thick walls, narrow gates, and only their kind get in. Clones of themselves. If someone's decent at the job, they get promoted. Then promoted again. And again. Until they hit the ceiling, the point where they're crap at what they do. That's where they stop. They know they're out of their depth, so they retreat. No decisions. No risks. Just keeping their heads down, hoping no one notices.

"Anyway, I've been working with Jamie Capstick. He's a great bloke and a fantastic DI. He's practical, caring, and knows his stuff. He knows how to play politics with the fuckwits above him.

"You know, shit runs downhill, and Jamie's got a bucket to catch it in to stop it hitting us. He never mentions it, and it's not until you work with him on stuff that you realise what he does day to day to protect you from the idiots, and that allows you to get on with your job.

"I could do that, or, perhaps more accurately, I could learn to do that. As I get older, I think I can learn to deal with the politics without going off on one like a schoolkid. I don't mean kowtowing to them, but being able to play them at their own game. I saw it today in Guildford. Even after being on shift for over twenty-four hours, Jamie took what he had to take and then gave it back in such a clever way. Respectfully, but saying to Blake: don't fuck with me, because I know what I'm doing, and, perhaps more importantly, I know what you're doing.

"I want my own bucket."

"Blimey. Have you been on some of that gear you're seizing?" said Sue.

Tom walked upstairs feeling as though he'd reached a crossroads in his life. He'd never been like this before, but maybe, just maybe, this was the challenge he needed to move on.

There was a problem, though.

How did this new Tom, the one who wanted promotion, who wanted to lead, reconcile with the old Tom? The one who'd crossed to the dark side. The one who'd bent rules, blurred lines, and made choices that didn't always sit clean.

Could he do both?

He wasn’t sure. And he wasn’t sure there was a way back into the light.

He wondered if he'd crossed the Rubicon.

Chapter Thirty Eight

Monday 12th April 2010

The team drifted into the office over the course of the morning, still bleary-eyed and slow-moving. A few had stopped by their local nicks on the way in, showing their faces, catching up on gossip, pretending everything was normal.

Sharon told Claire to take the day off and keep her head down until she called with the arrangements for Tuesday.

But it would not be a normal day.

They all knew what was coming. Professional Standards would pull each of them in for an interview over the next few days. Specifically, with Litt the Shit. The nickname had stuck for a reason. Twisted words, baited responses, and made good coppers feel like suspects.

Most of the team couldn't say much, because they knew little. The only ones with any real detail were Tom, Sharon, and Jamie. Claire had been in the back of the car during the operation, trying to take it all in.

She remembered the final strike, that she'd never forget, but the rest was a blur. She could recall phone calls between Tom and someone, but not enough to be useful.

Tom had logged every call on a contact sheet. Bulletproof. He'd made sure of it.

He and Sharon had kept quiet around Claire about the possibility of an interview. No coaching, no prepping. They couldn't twist anything into "influencing a witness." But Tom wasn't about to leave her exposed.

He'd called Barry Siviter, the Police Federation rep, and laid it all out. When interviewed by Professional Standards, officers had the right to a Fed Rep. And they always took that right.

Barry said he'd call Claire to explain the way it worked and to make sure she was ready.

No one wanted Litt the Shit to get her alone in an interview room, play his dirty tricks, and put words in her mouth. Claire was sharp, but she was young, and Litt was a master at making people doubt their own memories. Tom would not let that happen.

Having sorted that out, he popped into Jamie's office.

"Got a minute, guv?"

"Morning, Tom. Of course, mate, come in."

Tom sat down.

"Anything from Deano?"

"Only that it went as expected. Falstead had his brief, no-comment interview and a prepared statement. The gear and the gloves, nice touch, by the way, have gone off to the lab, and the army is dealing with the Semtex. The vehicle's been proved to be a ringer and has gone off to the pound. That's about it. Job jobbed, and we move on."

"Brilliant. Just Professional Standards to deal with then. Any idea when they'll want to interview us?"

"I'd imagine they'll want to do an initial interview today, so you and Sharon swan around here all day and wait for that."

"OK. I've spoken to Barry Siviter, and he's aware. He's also going to get hold of Claire and brief her on her rights. He promises he won't let anyone get to her. We gave her the day off and told her to keep her head down for now."

"Perfect. Well done, Tom. In the meantime, I guess we move on to the next job then?"

"Just between you and me, Jamie, I've had a few more headaches over the last couple of days. That long shift took it out of me, so I need to just have a few peaceful days."

"Do you want to go off sick?"

"No, no way. That would alert the powers that be that something's wrong, and I couldn't bear the scrutiny. Litt would have a field day too. Please just keep this to ourselves for now, and if I need a bit of a break, I'll let you know. Just an odd day here and there will sort it.

"The funny thing is, the consultant said the sort of work I do will assist in my long-term recovery."

"I bet he wouldn't say that if he were following you round from 17:00 Friday morning until Saturday lunchtime."

"Well, that doesn't happen too often, but it's set me back a bit."

"Alright, Tom. I'll keep that to myself. You and Sharon, and the rest of the team, to be fair, have a peaceful day in the office. If I'm asked, I'll say you're all catching up on paperwork, getting vehicles sorted, that sort of thing."

And that's what they did until Tom got the call from Barry.

Litt wanted to speak to Tom, Sharon, and Claire, in that order. Barry arranged for Claire to come in from her home in Byfleet so Litt couldn't catch her unawares at Esher one day when she wasn't expecting it. He'd seen that trick before, Litt turning up unannounced, all smiles and faux concern, then twisting a casual chat into a formal statement.

Barry had arranged for the interviews to be carried out at the Federation Office, in its interview room. Neutral ground. No surprises.

Litt tried his usual tricks, twisting timelines, planting doubt, leaning in with that oily tone that made you want to scrub your ears. But he came away empty-handed.

Tom was too sharp. He answered in a clipped, precise manner, delivering the answers calmly enough to make Litt twitch. Sharon was too seasoned. She treated him like a junior clerk who'd misfiled a report, polite, firm, and unimpressed. And Claire, young but well-prepped, held her nerve. Barry had walked her through every scenario, and she stuck to what she knew. No embellishments, no speculation. Just the facts. Another tick in the box on her journey.

Litt pushed. He prodded. He even tried the old "friendly chat" routine with Claire, soft voice, gentle questions, the kind that made you lower your guard. She didn't fall for any of it. She kept her answers short and her eyes steady. By the end, Litt looked like he'd bitten into a lemon. Sour, frustrated, and very much outplayed.

Claire had learned more in just a few days with Sharon and Tom than anyone could imagine.

Barry debriefed them all afterwards. “He’s not happy,” he said, grinning. “Tried to get clever with Sharon, and she gave him that look. You know the one. Like he’d just farted in church.”

Tom smiled. “Good. Let him stew.”

“Tom. A word of warning, mate,” said Barry. “Be aware, Litt is gunning for you. For the foreseeable future, just keep your nose clean. OK?”

Tom said nothing. Just nodded and gave him a thumbs-up.

He knew the game wasn’t over. Litt had missed the mark, but he’d be back. And next time, Tom thought, Litt might not come alone.

And he was right.

***

As Tom opened his front door, he could sense something was wrong. It was silent. He glanced into the sitting room. It was empty.

He went to the kitchen and came to a sudden halt. There was a letter on the work surface. No name on it, but he knew what it was. He opened it with shaking hands.

Dear Tom

This is a letter I never thought I’d write.

As much as I love you, I can’t live like this anymore. The constant worry is making me ill, and the girls have noticed. They don’t know what to do, and I don’t know how to help them.

What happened with that man, that line you said would never be crossed, changed everything. I can’t find a way back from it. For their safety, and mine, I have to leave.

I asked you more than once to try something else. It's clear now you won't. Maybe you can't.

I could keep writing, but you need to understand it's over. There's no coming back.

We are all safe and well. Just not with you anymore.

Sue

Tom was heartbroken. He leaned back against the wall, slid down, put his head in his hands and cried like he'd never done before.

Chapter Thirty Nine

Tuesday 13th April 2010

Pete and Martina were drinking coffee in their sitting room when he jumped up.

"How do you fancy a trip to North Wales?"

"North Wales? What on earth for? I thought that was where people came from, not went to."

"I want to show you our future. Our retirement plan. We don't have to go there and back in one day. I know it's North Wales, but there are bound to be some pleasant hotels there."

"OK, let's go. I'll pack us a bag for the night."

She paused at the doorway. "Pete... this isn't just about retirement, is it?"

He smiled too. "Of course it is."

But she caught the flicker in his eyes. And she didn't press.

Pete had ditched his old phone and bought a new iPhone 4, same number, but a clean phone. He didn't want Shaun to track him anymore. The more he thought about it, the more convinced he became that Shaun and Patrick had 'been retired'. Whether he'd ever get a visit from anyone, he wasn't sure.

He glanced at the screen. Blank. No messages. No missed calls. Just silence.

The kind that made him nervous.

All he could do for now was keep plugging away, one step at a time. One lie at a time. Until the truth caught up, or didn't.

In the BMW this time, and a steady, uneventful drive. Spring was in the air, and life was good. They both loved 80's music and sang along as they travelled towards Holyhead. Pete kept one hand on the wheel, the other tapping to the beat of Duran Duran. Martina laughed when he tried to hit the high notes. For a moment, it was like the recent past, stressing Pete out, was behind them. The road ahead was smooth for now.

"Her name is Rio and she dances on the sand..." he sang, off-key but enthusiastic.

Martina laughed. "You're no Simon Le Bon, Pete."

"Good thing I'm not trying to be," he said, eyes on the road, heart somewhere else. "I'm better looking than him though."

"Oh, I'm not sure about that."

They arrived at the storage place.

"What's this?" said Martina.

"You'll see," Pete replied, smiling.

They walked through to Pete's unit. He punched in the number, lifted the roller door, and switched on the light.

And froze.

The unit was empty.

He stared, speechless. His eyes flicked up to the number above the door. It was the correct one.

Where the fuck had it gone?

Martina stepped closer, sensing the shift. "What's wrong, Pete?"

He was struggling to speak. "Someone's stolen everything. There was over four million quids' worth of gear in here... and it's gone."

His legs buckled. He reached for the wall to steady himself. The colour had drained from his face.

Martina said nothing. She didn't need to. The silence said it all.

Pete sat on the concrete floor and buried his face in his hands. He was dizzy with despair.

"Who could do this, Pete?" said Martina, panicked. She'd never seen him like this before.

After a few seconds, he stared up at her. "There's only one person it could be... Tom."

"What? No way. How?"

"I don't know. But I have to find out."

Pete struggled to his feet, shut the roller door, and they strolled back to the car. He was deep in thought and had to play this carefully.

He drove up to the OP he'd used only a few days ago to track the Range Rover. Staring out of the windscreen, he sat in silence, thinking how to play it. Martina said nothing. Didn't even move. This wasn't her world, and she knew she had to let Pete deal with it in his own way.

He checked his watch. 18:00.

He picked up his phone.

"Tom, it's Pete."

"Hi Pete. How are you?"

"Well, if I said I'm in Holyhead, you know how I am."

"In that case, yes, I do."

"You fucking bastard. What have you done with it all?"

"First, suffice to say, it's safe. Second, I take you back to the conversation we had on the 21st of March in Horsham. You made me a promise. Quote: 'It's not even a zero-sum game. It has to work for your end more than mine. I promise you I will not use this as an opportunity to raise my stakes and will treat it for what it is.' Unquote. Remember?"

Pete paused, then said, "Yes."

"You made the mistake of taking me for a mug, and I warned you that wouldn't be a good idea. The sad thing is, Pete, I like you. You're very smart. But you underestimated me and tried to be too clever.

"Now, that gear is locked away. It hasn't gone up in smoke, but it is our pathway to the future. And who knows, when we've had enough of locking bad people away, there may be some left."

"I fucking hope so, because that was my retirement fund."

"Oh, we can't have you retiring yet, Pete," said Tom, with an element of sarcasm. "We've got work to do. Why don't you take Martina away on holiday for a couple of weeks? I'll be in touch."

And Tom hung up.

Martina couldn't look at him.

"Don't you dare say, 'Nearly there.'"

Chapter Forty

Friday 9th July 2010

Detective Constable Tom Kessler sat in the back of Courtroom 3, arms folded tight across his chest, jaw clenched in anticipation. The air was thick with the scent of old varnish and institutional fatigue. A fly buzzed near the strip lights overhead, tracing lazy loops above the judge's bench, and then landed. A low murmur rippled through the room as the tension built.

The jury had returned after only three hours of deliberation. Tom couldn't decide whether that was a good or bad omen. He scanned their faces, trying to read their expressions. Nothing. Not a glance in his direction. That was never a good sign. You often got a clue if a juror caught your eye and gave you a smile.

And then he got it. The woman in the middle looked straight at him and smiled. He couldn't stop himself from smiling back.

"Court rise," said the clerk.

Everyone stood as the judge waltzed in, full of self-importance.

"Here we go," muttered Tom.

"Have you reached a verdict with which you all agree?" the clerk asked the foreman.

"We have," he replied.

"And do you find the defendant guilty or not guilty?"

"Guilty."

"Mr Falstead, the jury has found you guilty of serious offences involving the trafficking of substantial quantities of Class A drugs and a large quantity of explosives. The evidence presented was clear and compelling.

"These offences are grave. They cause untold harm to individuals, families, and communities. You played a central role in a sophisticated operation, and greed motivated your actions, with no regard for the consequences.

"In determining the sentence, I have considered the scale of the operation, your level of involvement, and the need to deter others from engaging in similar criminal activity.

"The court sentences you to twenty-five years' imprisonment."

John Falstead looked over at Tom. He was a shadow of the man who had stood in that same dock just last January.

Tom winked at him and mouthed, "Better luck next time, John."

Dedications

To SB, HH, & PT in no particular order.

You know who you are and I could not have done this without you.

If You Enjoyed This Book...

I'd be incredibly grateful if you'd help others discover it too.

In the world of self-publishing, reviews are like gold dust, they make all the difference. They help new readers take a chance on my work, and they keep the stories alive.

If you could take a moment to leave a review, it would mean the world to me.

Thank you for reading, and for being part of the journey.

Get the Free MI5 File on Tom Kessler

An exclusive for readers of the Tom Kessler series

Building a relationship with my readers is paramount. I want you to feel part of the world I've created, and part of the team.

When you sign up to my mailing list, you'll receive:

1) A copy of the highly classified MI5 file on Tom Kessler

2) Insider updates on upcoming releases in the Tom Kessler series

3) Early access to bonus content, behind-the-scenes intel, and exclusive giveaways

This isn't just a newsletter, it's your clearance badge to the darker corners of Kessler's world.

Should you choose, you can also gain access to my Advanced Reader Copy (ARC) Group, where you'll be among the first to read and review new releases before anyone else. Share your thoughts, shape the story, I listen to my group and make changes accordingly.

Join the list. Get the file. Stay in the loop. 👉 Get your freebies here and unlock the secrets.

About the Author

I write crime fiction with a procedural edge and authentic detail, the kind that comes from having been there and done it. Before joining the police, and eventually, the Surrey Drug Squad, I served in the Royal Air Force, where discipline, precision, and a sharp eye for detail weren't just ideals, they were survival tools. That foundation shaped how I see the world, and how I write it.

My stories draw on real experience, shaped by years in the field and the people who moved through it. The characters I write are complex, the operations grounded in reality, and the tension is never just for show. Whether it's a quiet surveillance job or a high-stakes bust, I aim to capture the grit and nuance of the work, and the lives behind it. Many of the stories in my books are based on true events. It's up to you to decide which ones.

When I'm not writing, you'll find me walking the countryside, fly fishing, or watching rugby with a pint in hand. It's a slower pace than the one I used to live, but the stories haven't stopped.

If you'd like to stay connected, get exclusive content, or be part of my ARC Group, you can sign up to my mailing list. I'd love to have you along for the ride.

First published in the United Kingdom in 2025.

Made in the USA
Monee, IL
15 January 2026

41619386R00207